Town House

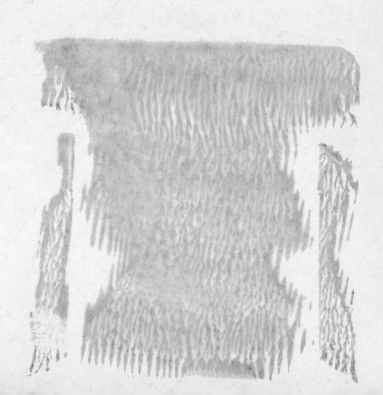

Town House

A Novel

Tish Cohen

HARPER PERENNIAL

NEW YORK • LONDON • TORONTO • SYDNEY

HARPER ● PERENNIAL

P.S.™ is a trademark of HarperCollins Publishers.

TOWN HOUSE. Copyright © 2007 by Tish Cohen. All rights reserved. Printed in the United States of America. No part of this book may be used or reproduced in any manner whatsoever without written permission except in the case of brief quotations embodied in critical articles and reviews. For information address HarperCollins Publishers, 10 East 53rd Street, New York, NY 10022.

HarperCollins books may be purchased for educational, business, or sales promotional use. For information please write: Special Markets Department, HarperCollins Publishers, 10 East 53rd Street, New York, NY 10022.

FIRST EDITION

Designed by Joseph Rutt

Library of Congress Cataloging-in-Publication Data
Cohen, Tish.
Town house : a novel / by Tish Cohen.— 1st. Harper Perennial ed.
p. cm.
ISBN: 978-0-06-113131-8
ISBN-10: 0-06-113131-8
Agoraphobia—Fiction. 2. Inheritance and succession—Fiction. I. Title.
PS3603.O384T69   2007
813'.6—dc22   2006043638

07 08 09 10 11 ID/RRD 10 9 8 7 6 5 4 3 2 1

To my boys,
Steve, Max, and Lucas

Town House

In Which Baz Finally Gives a Flick

The pills clung to the bottom of Baz's dry tongue like barnacles. He held his breath, waiting for the nurse's tyrannical bosom to swing away and lead her downstairs, toward the street where her teenage son was waiting, or honking rather, in his shiny new '78 Pinto.

"*Swallow,*" said the nurse, narrowing her eyes.

He opened his mouth to show his empty tongue. "Were you always this bossy?" One of the pills struck the underside of his tongue stud.

"Only with the sneaky ones."

The Pinto beeped again.

"Go ahead, Louisa." Baz's words hung, wafer-thin and dusty, in the stale air of his bedroom. He closed his eyes and swallowed, sending trickles of pain across his temples and down his neck. "I'm going to sleep until Francine comes up with my dinner."

"How that fine woman ever birthed a wretch like you, I'll never know." She gathered his mane into a loose ponytail and stuffed it down his T-shirt. "Your hair smells nice today."

Baz cracked one eye open as she lifted the leather jacket from his shoulders and replaced it with a soft quilt. Having assured himself she wasn't mocking him, he glanced up to admire the giant Bazmanics logo on the back of the battered jacket as she hung it on a chair—right next to his Fender Stratocaster electric guitar and three framed gold records. The logo, cracked and peeling from years of abuse, was a gray outline of Baz's profile—his mouth open wide enough in midscream to bite the head off a half-grown cat (an onstage stunt he might have considered, had he any hope of recovery); his hair streaming down to his waist; his long, barbed, craggy nose giving the whole image a witchy feel.

She flicked off his bedside lamp and nodded toward the infamous emblem. "We'll turn this off so the sight of Your Highness doesn't keep you from sleeping." Moving toward the door in the dark, she added, "One look at that nose of yours before closin' *my* eyes'd give me the night scares for weeks." Her son honked again from the street. "See you in the morning, then."

He said nothing. Just listened to her footsteps clunk down the old wooden staircase and her keys scatter across the foyer floor. Then a few clicks and grunts, and the heavy door slammed shut.

He spat out the pills.

Laying a jaundiced claw on the bedside table, Baz heaved his body upright until his feet touched the icy floorboards. He swayed a moment while the walls rose and fell around him, grew bigger, closer.

Jack, he thought, steadying himself. Do it for Jack.

His nine-year-old son. A timid boy, far too small for his age. So small that, with his pillow and stuffed dog, he watched every one of his father's concerts from inside a wooden Coke crate backstage.

A boy whose mother—once a Bazmanics groupie, then, later, a Rolling Stones groupie, whom Baz last saw boarding a bus with her arms wrapped around the neck of one of Mick's longtime roadies—died making freebase cocaine in a bathtub, the ether triggering a spontaneous explosion that caused one of Los Angeles's most notorious and costly hotel fires.

A boy whose father, tormented by his obsessive-compulsive disorder, had been far too busy fretting over the freshness of his trademark mane, lining up the windows on the tour bus for spirit-soothing symmetry and, on the less neurotic days, banging his own groupies on scratchy hotel bedspreads to give a flick whether his boy might need a better life.

And soon, after the creditors swooped in and plucked out anything of worth, there wouldn't be much of a home left for the boy, either. The busted-up plaster walls would remain, along with the four fireplaces, the leaded-glass windows (cracked panes and all), the impossibly dark fourth-floor stage, the creaky dumbwaiter that young Jack had claimed as his playhouse; but not much else. The Boston town house was fully paid for and, thanks to a rare moment of lucidity, in which Baz actually followed his lawyer's advice, in his mother Francine's name. But his best guitar would go, along with his beloved leather jacket and any bits of furniture that had escaped Baz's drunken fits of destruction.

Sliding his bony feet into boots, he tried to stand. A cacophony of firecrackers exploded inside his head. Standing was clearly too ambitious. Crouching over, he managed to shuffle to his dresser and yank open the top drawer. He fumbled around toward the back until he felt a thin plastic bag covering something large and bumpy and hard. Pulling it out from behind the socks, Baz smiled.

It wasn't just any turtle shell. It was all that remained of a bad-tempered snapper. All that remained of the agent of his all-too-imminent death.

Reaching for a felt pen, he turned the shell over. The underbelly was surprisingly small. Before scrawling his name across it, Baz touched the green felt tip to his tongue. One, two, three times. Three was his magic number. Touching a thing to your tongue three times could ward off any sort of evil. Protect you. Or, in this case, protect someone else. He reached for a piece of paper. At the top, he wrote, *Jack*.

When he was finished, he tucked the note neatly inside the shell and stumbled into the drafty, darkened corridor. He maneuvered himself toward Jack's dumbwaiter. The boy was staying overnight at the neighbor's house, but, with his sleeping bag rolled into a tight ball and his stuffed dog under his arm, Jack would ride the tiny elevator up to the third floor when he returned in the morning.

It was important that no one else find the shell.

He stepped closer. The hallway began to whirl. So much so that it was hard to know which way was up. His legs buckling, Baz staggered toward the elevator button and clung to the gaping dumbwaiter doorway for support as he pounded at the button with his fist. The ancient gears squeaked and groaned in protest as the car rose through the shaft from the cellar.

Baz closed his eyes and clutched the shell tighter. Just a few more seconds. The elevator car was in sight now, climbing closer.

All he had to do was stay on his feet.

He touched the shell to his tongue for fortitude.

One.

Two.

Three.

A thunderous roar sawed through Baz's head, and he felt his legs crumple beneath him. As he fought to hang on to the ledge, his knee whacked against something hard.

The floor.

Chapter 1

He Bangs

Jack Madigan squeezed his eyes shut. Hard. He wasn't going to cry over this. There were exactly three events in his thirty-six-year-old memory that had brought him to tears, typically life-splintering events: such as his father dying on him while he was away at a sleepover; his son, Harlan, bursting—squalling and bawling—out of the womb and into his heart; and his ex-wife sashaying out the front door of the old Boston town house and wishing Jack a good life.

She'd forgotten the tweezers.

Sucking back a fortifying breath, Jack trapped another hair between the pincers and yanked. *Shit!* Tears streamed down his cheeks. He wiped his face with his palm and peered into the mirror. His brows looked worse than before he started. The left brow ended way too early and the right one bulged in the middle like a python digesting a mole. The photo in the magazine sure didn't look like this. Checking the instructions again, he ripped away at the right brow until the gastric-wrapped mole looked more like a supine mouse.

Leaning on the huge porcelain bathroom sink, he pushed his face closer to the mirror. Eyebrow hairs probably grew back slowly. It would be his luck. If they grew back at all. He tugged at his dark hair until wet bangs carpeted his forehead, masking what was left of his brows. Looked a bit strange, but it would have to do. Eyebrows stinging, stomach grumbling, he reached down to tighten the towel tied around his narrow hips before hurling the tweezers and the magazine at the metal trash can.

He hadn't set out to pluck his brows this particular Wednesday evening in November. It was all Harlan's fault.

Teenage hormones being what they were, Harlan's eyes were fool-
ishly affixed to a blonde on a passing bus when they should have been
doing what eyes were designed for—scanning oncoming terrain for haz-
ards, like uncovered manholes and wolves. And while it wasn't a man-
hole or a wolf that got him, the puddle was, apparently, sufficiently deep
and murky as to necessitate a thorough cleanup once Harlan finally
found his way home.

And teenage hormones being what they were, Harlan's shower went
on far too long. So long that his friends—Stevie, Kirk, and three girls with
wholly forgettable names, having stopped by to pick him up for a night of
unintelligible conversation and untold attempts to sneak into local bars—
were forced to choose between polite chat with Jack in the living room
and a *Glamour* magazine fortuitously pulled from someone's purse.

The magazine won.

Jack never would have dreamed of flipping through it after Courtney
or Brittany or whoever left it behind. For one thing, it was nearly seven
thirty, and he hadn't yet had dinner. For another, a guy his age trolling
through *Glamour* was just plain creepy. But it was just lying there on his
favorite chair, folded open to an article titled "Five Surefire Signs He'll
Suck in Bed."

How could he not check . . . just to be sure?

And there it was. Surefire sign number four. "Scraggle Brows. A guy
who doesn't clean *his* house upstairs won't be keen on polishing *your*
silver downstairs, so to speak."

If there was one thing Jack wasn't going to be accused of, it was
having a complete and utter disregard for tending to the silver.

PEERING INTO THE old Frigidaire, head bopping to the Clash's
"London Calling" thundering from the living room, Jack smiled. One
heaping helping of Monday's tuna casserole had somehow escaped Harlan's wolfish eye.

The sun had all but set, leaving blackened, cut-out profiles of
nineteenth-century Beacon Hill town homes nestled up to office
towers against a sky muddy with navy, purple, and red. Jack spun
away from the fridge, chipped plate in hand, and kicked the door
shut with his foot. Harlan would be out for hours. And by the time

he returned, he'd have murdered a pizza or several, and would have no interest in digging up two-day-old leftovers.

By the time the sky had completely inked over, candlelight danced on the refrigerator door, Pinot breathed in a chipped scotch glass, Elvis Costello crooned from the front room, and Jack's perfectly heated leftovers begged to be devoured. He sampled the first bite and closed his eyes. Impossible. The casserole got more delectable by the day.

When he opened his eyes, another set of eyes stared back at him. Well, one eye, anyway. Mrs. Brady, Harlan's childhood pet—a morose, one-eared, one-eyed beast of a tomcat acquired during Harlan's fifth year—sat on the opposite chair.

Like Jack's date.

The animal stared at Jack's forehead. Sadly aware he was primping for a cat, Jack smoothed his bangs. "What are you looking at?"

Mrs. Brady blinked back what appeared to be a smirk.

"Like you're so much better? Get down, phsst," Jack hissed and tried to wave the cat away. Was it too much to want to eat a meal in peace? Mrs. Brady didn't budge. Instead, a low, guttural moan emanated from somewhere between his throat and his feet.

"Go on now. You've been fed." Jack had reminded Harlan six or seven times before he'd left.

The cat blinked again and glanced down at the tuna.

"You heard me."

Mrs. Brady licked his lips and groaned.

The animal hadn't paid this much attention to Jack since he'd had his stitches removed after the great snowplow incident of '99. And even then, only to rake apart Jack's flesh as he held the beast still for the vet. Jack let out a long breath. Clearly, the cat hadn't been fed. Pushing back his chair, Jack crossed the room and opened the cupboard, hunting for a can of Pretty Kitty cat food.

Nothing.

He checked the fridge. No cat food and, worse, no reasonable substitutions. The cat wasn't going to appreciate limp broccoli, expired hummus, or strawberry-flavored applesauce with no artificial sweeteners. Jack closed the door and paused. Harlan. He could pick up some cat food from the variety store. It wouldn't be Pretty Kitty, but Mrs. Brady would just have to deal.

He dialed Harlan's cell phone number and waited. After what must have been twenty or thirty rings, a robotic voice informed Jack that Harlan's message box was full. Terrific. No cat food. No hope of cat food. And by now, his tuna must be cold.

Mrs. Brady cocked his head and batted his eye. "Mew." Damn thing was so hungry he was trying coquettish persuasion now.

"All right," Jack crossed the room, picked up his plate, and scraped half his dinner into the stainless steel cat dish before setting it down beside the back door. The cat bolted from the chair and perched himself over the bowl as Jack returned to his seat and picked up his wineglass, tipping it toward the cat's twitching tail. "*Salut*, old man."

He lifted a forkful of casserole to his mouth. It was cold. Ravenous as he was, he couldn't stomach cold, fishy noodles. Sighing, Jack placed his dinner back into the oven. At least it would reheat quickly. There wasn't much left.

Casserole finally reheated, he sat himself down again at the table—a turquoise-and-silver-speckled Formica with wide chrome trim and matching vinyl chairs. The music had turned itself off in the other room, but Jack wasn't willing to leave his dinner one more time.

After one bite, the back door flew open, and Harlan stumbled into the kitchen.

"It's freezing outside." He folded his six-foot frame down to tickle Mrs. Brady under the chin, before standing up and tossing his coat onto an iron hook. His burgundy flares didn't come close to covering his white vinyl loafers, though they matched the puffed daisy on his knitted vest perfectly. Obsessed with the '70s, Harlan spent much of his spare time rooting through thrift stores for clothing too uncool to be called vintage. Which was Harlan's statement. Uncool is the new cool. He prided himself on his extra-long skateboard, his extra-long sideburns, and his cereal-bowl haircut.

The kids at school called him "Haustin Powers" and begged to see his room, rumored to have lilac shag carpeting on the ceiling—which it did, only Harlan rarely brought anyone upstairs to show it off.

"Whoa." Harlan picked up the cat and nodded toward Jack's forehead. He laughed. "What's with the fancy fringe?"

Jack swallowed irritation. He happened to know bangs were back in style. He'd just read it in *Glamour*. "How was your evening?"

Harlan shrugged. "Dull. Depressing. You shoulda come."

"Apparently."

"You could have scored with Ginnie's cousin from Seattle. She's, like, ancient. Twenty-nine. She talked about you all night. Said you look like that guy from *High Fidelity*."

Dear God. "Not Jack Black?"

"No. The main guy. The one that keeps being dumped by hot girls."

"Cusack?"

"Yeah. That's the one. Though I'm not sure he decorates his forehead quite the same as you."

Jack leaned sideways to peer at himself in the reflection of the darkened window. John Cusack? He turned his head to the left. To the right. Rubbed his jaw between his finger and his thumb and narrowed his dark eyes. Maybe if he kept his eyebrows covered. "Will this Ginnie's cousin be coming around again?"

Harlan slumped into a chair and adjusted his enormous brown glasses. He ignored Jack's question. "We waited for, like, an hour at a Chinese place and figured we could get something at Burger Bay quicker, but when we got there, they had a CLOSED sign on the door and stacks of wood and tools and shit inside on the floor. I thought I was gonna hurl from hunger. So then we went to Oliver's for pasta 'cause the bartender was supposed to score us a good table. But Mark's ex was lurching around in the doorway, she's their new hostess, and by that time Ginnie's cousin had to catch a train—"

"Train? She's not from around here?"

"New Jersey."

Didn't that just figure?

Harlan continued. "By then I realized I had no money anyway, so I came back home. I'm starving. I think I'm gonna die if I don't eat soon." He shot a hungry look at Jack's plate.

Jack took hold of his dish with his free hand. "I think there's some applesauce. Strawberry, I think. And crackers in the cupboard."

"I'm going through a hu-uge growth spurt."

"Mm. Again?"

"Yeah. I can feel my bones stretching. Hurts like hell." Harlan rubbed his legs.

In the interest of steering the conversation firmly away from his dinner plate, Jack wiped his mouth with his napkin and said, "You know, when I was your age, we were sneaking into bars, not Italian bistros. Not that I condone that sort of thing."

"You? Sneaking into bars?"

"It's so hard to imagine?"

Harlan laughed and dropped Mrs. Brady to the floor. Cat hair covered his pants, and he set about picking it off, hair by hair. "Well, kinda. Considering."

"FYI, I used to do all sorts of crazy things."

"Like go to the store?"

Resting his fork on the edge of his plate, Jack stared into his noodles. "Yes," he said, his head suddenly feeling heavy. "Like go to the store."

Harlan chewed on his cheek while he processed this information. "Cool." He picked up Jack's wineglass and sniffed it. "Are you going to eat all that tuna?"

With a silent sigh, Jack slid his plate across the table and got up to get himself some applesauce.

Chapter 2

The Groper

Jack peered past the curtain. There it lay. All thick and rolled up tight in a blue rubber band. It looked wet, too. No real surprise on a drizzly Thursday morning, not when the newspaper boy had thrown it onto the steps again, *miles* away from the front door. Well, miles away to Jack, who needed a fistful of tranquilizers and the company of his griping son to leave the house with any sense of ease.

Of course, he should just trot the hell out there and scoop it up. Wasn't that what he'd promised his therapist? Just once this month, he'd skip across the threshold and perform some perfunctory domestic duty. Remove a fallen leaf, wipe at the window, retrieve a newspaper gone astray. Anything, so long as it was outside and scared the living shit out of him.

Shrewd agoraphobic therapy to the doctor. Certain death to Jack.

His house was his only true safe zone. The only permanent place he'd ever lived, having been raised in the back of a tour bus. His childhood bedroom, before Baz bought the town house, was the last seat on the left side of the bus.

He turned away from the grayness of the city outside and paced the floor. The massive living room dwarfed him. Barely five foot nine and nearly two decades too old to hope for a last-ditch growth spurt, Baz Madigan's boy could just about step inside the massive mahogany fireplace, the house's primary source of heat ever since the furnace sputtered out. Two stuffed armchairs faced the fire, huddled close enough for their occupants, usually Jack and Harlan, to build up a nice sweat, but not so close as to attract any flying sparks.

The only other objects in the cavernous room were a few ragged books on the mantel, a ladder for changing lightbulbs at ceiling height and displaying a couple of very necessary ratty plaid throws (folding your blankets over wooden ladders was considered ultrachic, he had read in his ex-wife's decorating magazines), and a television topped by a framed picture of Jack sitting on Baz's knee, his father's arms wrapped around him like a real dad's.

He couldn't remember posing for the photo any more than he could remember any instance Baz had done *anything* like a real dad.

The only thing Jack felt the room was lacking was a cat scratching post for Mrs. Brady, who'd slashed the living-room curtains so badly that closing them to cut out drafts had become, well, embarrassing. Peeling paint on the façade of the grand downtown home was bad enough, but imagine the good people of Boston strolling along the historical Beacon Hill Street and seeing shredded strips of beige velvet stretched across the enormous window.

No. Being broke was one thing. After all, it wasn't simple for a man who detested leaving the house to bring in an income outside of his neurotic father's dwindling royalties. And working as a paint-color consultant would certainly be more lucrative if he was emotionally capable of actually visiting his clients' sites.

He could handle the lack of funds. But being pitied by passersby was unacceptable. As much as he could, Jack Madigan tried to present himself as normal.

Somewhat normal.

HE PEEKED OUT the window again. The blasted paper was lying on the second-to-last step, so his broom handle wouldn't help at all. No. He needed a hook. A long hook. That way he could snag the rubber band and reel the paper through the doorway and into the darkened asylum of the foyer.

After a quick search through the cellar, he came back up the servants' staircase with a coat hanger, electrical tape, and a hockey stick. Of course, Jack's life being what it was, this wasn't just any hockey stick. It was Phil Esposito's favorite stick, given to Baz, his biggest and, likely, most debauched fan, nearly thirty years ago . . . the very year Baz died.

It was the perfect solution.

He settled himself on the black-and-white checkered tiles in the butler's pantry, a room he had very little use for, never having had a butler. He remembered having a cleaning lady when he was young. She found Baz's lifeless body lying beside the dumbwaiter in the second-floor hallway and had been hysterical. Inconsolable.

Mrs. Scaub's English was splintered at best. And the nosy questions fired at her by the press—who, for the longest time, seemed to forget all news unrelated to rock stars dying from snapping turtles who bite back when being devoured onstage—terrified her.

Most people assumed what killed Baz was an overdose of salmonella from biting off "the soft bits" of the infamous snapper onstage and swallowing them whole. But that alone wouldn't have done him in. Jack had gone over and over it in his head many times.

Baz's mistake was not biting the head off first.

Jack had been watching from backstage. The whole thing happened in syrupy-slow motion: the turtle, freed from its zippered duffel bag by Baz's manager, made its thumpity-bumpity way across stage. It drove the crowd into delirium. They knew Baz's weakness for onstage hyperbole. They knew what was next.

So did young Jack.

From inside his Coke crate, he watched Baz reach for the reptile and thrust it high above his head, basking in the crowd's roar. It was then that Jack began to call to his father. And it wasn't that he was thinking about the turtle . . . it was that he knew his father's habits too well.

As Baz brought the snapper closer to his face, the daggered feet swatted uselessly in the air. Jack called out again, but it was too late.

Baz had launched into his ritual.

Instead of chomping hard and fast, Baz stuck out his tongue and licked the turtle's right foot once.

The crowd went wild.

He licked it twice.

The band members roared.

The third lick never happened.

Snappers are fast. They have powerful jaws and long necks, and not only that—they've got attitude to burn. They don't give a shit if you're trying to save them from being flattened under the wheel of the next UPS truck. You lean too close, they'll spin around and take your face off.

Not that Jack had ever tried this. Being on a country road in the first place would require too much advance planning. The car would have to be in good working order, Harlan would have to be willing to get off his bony posterior, and Jack would need not only a fistful of pills but a good half-bottle of backup meds for the journey.

What happened was, while Baz was in midlick, the turtle's head lunged at his mouth, slashing his lower lip. The cut was easily stitched, but salmonella raced through his bloodstream. *That* was what killed him. Underestimating the surly nature and lightning-quick reflexes of a snapper. Snapping turtles allow very little time for laborious, obsessive, three-part compulsions.

The infamous turtle shell was never found. One moment, the bumpy turtle was hanging from Baz's face. The next moment, Baz was down on the gritty stage floor, surrounded by people. By the time he was helped offstage, the shell was gone.

It drove the press crazy. It drove his fans crazy. If Baz died, the shell would be worth millions, they speculated. Where was it?

The other mystery was, why was he lying beside the dumbwaiter—dead? What was Baz Madigan, who'd been flirting with death for *weeks*, doing out of bed?

They all wanted to know. Jack, too, wanted to know.

Everything Baz loved was in that bedroom with him, his guitar, his jacket, even his drugs—the ones the doctor didn't know about but that Baz had taught young Jack to hide for him beneath the floorboards. And his nurse said he was too sick to get up.

So, why was he out wandering the hall?

What Jack wanted to believe was that Baz was heading for his room; that, in his delirious state, he had forgotten his son was sleeping away that night. He was maybe coming to watch his boy play soldiers or sing him a song with that famous croaking voice. Maybe sit Jack on his knee and wrap his long tattooed arms around him, like in the mysterious picture above the TV.

Was it so hard to imagine?

● ● ●

Sighing, Jack opened a drawer in the butler's pantry, pulled out the scissors, and set himself to work. He twisted the hanger around the hockey stick—the puck-shooting end—and, tape in teeth, bound the wire wings tightly around the stick with the hanger's hook poking out at the end.

Smiling, he twirled his new instrument in his hands. Amazing, really, that no one had thought of such a tool before. The hook was pure genius. It needed a name, he thought. The Scooper, maybe.

No. Too canine.

The Grasper.

Too desperate. Anything that rhymes with *gasp* sounded desperate.

The Groper.

Yes. Perfect.

With the Groper, Jack would not be the paperboy's victim one more day. Whistling, he heaved the front door open and slid a foot onto the threshold. He held the stick behind him, pretending to watch the darkening sky as he planned his move. If he held the door frame and stretched way out, the Groper would ju-ust reach. This tool, he realized, could benefit more than just agoraphobes looking to dodge their therapist's just-step-the-hell-outside advice. Anyone with a weak-wristed paperboy could use it to collect their paper on a rainy day.

"Hey there, Mr. Madigan," a trio of underdressed teenage girls called from the street. A big-boned redhead pulled a smaller girl, a brunette wearing an unzipped sweatshirt over a T-shirt about three sizes too small, out from behind and called, "Dini here wants to know if you can come out to play." Dini giggled and hid her face.

Jack smiled and nodded toward the churning sky. "Tell Dini she'd better take cover." That unseasonal attire of hers wasn't going to afford much protection once the clouds emptied their loads on the streets of Boston.

Looking over their shoulders and giggling, the girls made it to the corner and disappeared with a wave back at Jack.

The street was empty. This was good. Lowering the Groper down toward the paper, he slid it over the next two stairs and tried to wiggle the hook under the rubber band. No. The blasted band was too tight. He needed to approach it from the other side, the side where the pages met with the folded newsprint spine.

Down on his knees, he held the Groper way out to the right and approached the paper from an angle. But just as the hook slipped beneath the rubber, the clouds burst. Crushing rain almost knocked the Groper out of Jack's hand, but, swearing, he lunged and jabbed at the paper again. Finally, he felt a comforting tug, a sure sign that he'd secured it, and reeled it safely inside.

There. Homework complete.

Sort of.

Jack breathed a huge sigh of relief and shook the sodden paper over the doormat. Death successfully cheated once again.

Savoring his moment of triumph, he watched a mist rise from the force of rain hitting the now empty sidewalk. The fog grew so thick it was as if a cloud, overburdened by heavy rain, had dropped from the sky and settled on the street. Jack peered down the road. If he squinted, everything disappeared into the murkiness except for flickering gaslights and darkened trees encased in fancy wrought-iron grilles. He looked the other way. Same thing, only an SUV parked on the street ruined the image. Then, through the soupy haze over the sidewalk, something moved.

At first, all he could see through the mist was a flash of legs: long, brown-trousered, and none too sturdy. Jack knew those rickety stilts. In a few more strides, the entire tweed-suited gent would be visible, in all his liver-spotted glory.

Dr. Snowden wore shirts so heavily starched, the collars threatened to slice into his windpipe; could trace your every anxiety back to your mother's regrettable decision to bottle-feed; and, most important, still made house calls. But then, how else would a psychiatrist counsel a diehard agoraphobe?

"Mr. Madigan," Dr. Snowden called out from deep inside an enormous black umbrella. For a wisp of a man growing more brittle by the year, his voice had somehow maintained the same rich, deep resonance that lulled Jack into something resembling complacency the first time they met. "It's nice to see you outside. Almost."

Jack slid his tool behind the front door. The good doctor would definitely not perceive the Groper as a psychosocial victory. He held up his soggy paper, his prize. "Just following orders."

"Mm. Do I detect a passive-aggressive undertone?" The old doctor grasped the handrail and tottered up the front steps.

"Could be," Jack said with a smile.

Dr. Snowden paused. He eyed Jack and stepped past him into the foyer. "Good. Wouldn't want you to become too compliant. The shock of it might very well kill me."

DR. MYRON SNOWDEN'S bony knees jutted out from the chair closest to the fire, a little too close for Jack's comfort. While a break in his therapy sounded tempting, Jack preferred to keep the old man intact.

Snowden was a good name for a man whose skin was so pale with age you could see blue veins underneath, tangled all over his bones and sinew—pretty much all that was left of him. Not only that, but what few hairs remained on his person were as white as December snow. In his countless hours "on the couch," Jack had run through many possible names for Dr. Snowden's particular shade of pale. The one he'd ultimately settled on was Headstone White.

The doctor cracked his knuckles. "So you say you marched straight outside—into the torrential rain—and picked up your paper?"

"Pretty much," Jack lied.

"Astonishing you managed to stay so dry."

"I was quick."

"Hm. And you say that, in the last two weeks, this has been the one and only opportunity to step outside for this simple task?"

Jack stretched his arms high above his head and yawned. "Paper's been lying right there on the mat, day after day. Within easy reach."

Snowden nodded his head, his scanty eyebrows shooting skyward. "Your paperboy's skill level is clearly without equal. I can't remember a single day when I haven't had to rummage through my neighbor's rhododendrons for my morning news."

"That's a shame. Care for a coffee?"

"Perhaps you should move to an area with less dependable delivery. This paperboy is clearly blocking your progress."

Jack laughed. "Yeah. Moving wouldn't kill me. Not much."

"Consistent desensitization requires that you take baby steps, Jack. If your newspaper happens to land at the foot of your bed, you still need to find a reason to step out that front door. Knock a caterpillar from your stoop, pick up a candy-bar wrapper, anything that can be done quickly and without raising your anxiety beyond a level three out of ten."

Snowden's theory of desensitization involved exposing yourself to your own very special anxiety-provoking stimuli in bite-sized doses, preferably with a dependable friend or, lacking this, your lanky son. The theory was that if you performed your miniature miracle without wetting yourself, vomiting on your dependable friend, or losing consciousness, you'd achieved a cool level three on the freak-out scale and were all set to try it again with full confidence and clean trousers.

"Tomorrow. I'll try it tomorrow."

"Forgive me if I don't hold my breath." The doctor tilted his head upward and sniffed at the air, shooting Jack a suspicious look. "Speaking of suffocation, have you been painting the kitchen again?"

Jack sighed. "I am a painter."

"I don't like it. Not when it's the same room over and over again. In the very same color."

"That's where you're wrong. It's a different color every time." Jack stood up. "Come, I'll show you."

The doctor shuffled down the long hallway and into the kitchen, brown leather notepad firmly in hand. Jack smiled from the middle of the room. He'd repainted the kitchen that very morning. White, but not just any dull, lifeless white. A carefully concocted shade he'd been tinkering with all week. "I think I've finally found the perfect white," Jack said.

Without disguising his concern, Dr. Snowden asked: "So this is the one you've been chasing for how many years? Three? Five?"

"Absolutely. The problem with the last white was that I added too much black. It gave the whole room a chill. Remember?"

"Not particularly."

"I call it Heirloom White."

Dr. Snowden scribbled something in his notepad.

"See, Penelope's textbooks from design school didn't go into color very deeply. Skimmed right over the surface, really. When I read them, I thought you could slap up a nice off-white and call the job complete. It wasn't until I really looked into the color that I realized how many hues make up a good, complex white." Jack looked over at Snowden. "In this case, an impartial, respectful white with highly historical undertones. See it?"

The doctor rocked back on his heels. "I see a budding obsessive delusional with highly *compulsive* undertones."

Jack studied Snowden's face. "Is that supposed to be psychiatric humor?"

"If I may flatter myself."

"Nicely done." Jack reached out to push down on the lid of a paint can. "Anyway, you'll try it next week after the paint's had time to cure. It'll look completely different once it's cured. You'll see the difference."

Dr. Snowden turned and shuffled toward the hall. "There is one thing I did notice."

"Yeah?" Jack grinned, following Snowden closely. Warm and cozy, historic yet fresh—that was what Jack was looking for.

"You've got so many layers on the walls that the room's getting smaller." The doctor chuckled to himself and stomped back to the warmth of the fire.

Jack sighed. It was exactly what his ex-wife, Penelope, had said. And she was an interior designer. She, of all people, should understand the subtle nuances of a color as understated as white.

Jack's proficiency with whites had launched his career (if you could call one or two clients each season a career) as a high-end color consultant to the interior-design trade. Designers and tradesmen alike called on his expertise for anything from custom-matching caulking to exterior window trim to developing a white to convey a client's memory of a particular flower in her late grandmother's garden. Jack thought of himself as a troubleshooter. Only not enough trouble had come his way over the last couple of years. And if it had, it required a house call.

Of course, no client had ever been as demanding as he was on himself. A nice, clean white wasn't good enough. It had to be perfect. As far as Jack was concerned, there was only one white for his kitchen, and he was willing to go to any length to find it. His kitchen had become something of a test laboratory or artist's canvas, depending on how you chose to look at it. And he saw nothing wrong with repainting again and again.

So long as the color was white.

SNOWDEN SMOOTHED OUT his stiff trousers. "You missed our appointment last week. I nearly froze to death standing on your front

stoop. Were you out on the town?" One corner of his mouth twitched.
"Dancing perhaps?"

That was the trouble with the psychiatrist coming to the agoraphobe.
Very few rational excuses worked on days when one just couldn't face
another inquisition. Penelope had mistakenly believed that, aside from
the highly needed psychiatric counsel, Snowden's visits would be comforting to Jack. That this paid friendship might help stave off loneliness.

She was wrong. What kind of friend left you with homework that
would probably kill you, guilt over not having died attempting the previous week's assignment, and then charged you a hundred bucks for the
pleasure of his own murderous company?

"Might have been upstairs napping. Sorry about that."

"You realize I'll have to bill you."

"I do."

"Your neighbors' dog nearly scared me to death."

"What dog?"

Dr. Snowden gestured toward the brick wall on the west side of the
house. "Sounded to me to be a Rottweiler or a Doberman pinscher. I
may have seen it once. Big and black, I think."

Jack swallowed another yawn. The old guy was hearing things now.
"Samantha and Rick would never harbor a dangerous animal; they've
got a couple of kids."

"Must have been recycling day," Snowden continued. "It was nearly
dinnertime, but your receptacles were still outside."

"Blue boxes are Harlan's job."

"I think for your assignment this week, you might think about re-
trieving the bins yourself."

Jack busied himself with poking at the dying fire. "They're pretty
cumbersome."

"I wouldn't have brought it up," said Dr. Snowden. "But when the
men with the cameras showed up, I thought perhaps you'd been called
in for having a slovenly exterior. Crumbled plaster, paint chips, abandoned recycling bins. All typical of agoraphobic lodgings, but try to get
anyone to understand. Particularly in a neighborhood such as this." He
shook his head. "Society can be very cruel to the mentally unstable."

Jack looked up sharply.

"Just a figure of speech, Jack."

"They took pictures?"

Snowden nodded, making a church steeple with his hands. "Photographed the house, took notes, measured the frontage."

"Measured my house?" A thought occurred to Jack. Measuring a thing generally required touching it. And living twenty-seven years in a historic mansion set on a busy street had made Jack highly territorial. Just because the sidewalk ran right up to the bricks didn't mean the house was public property and available for use, or abuse, from every drunken louse who needed a place to vomit, or every adulterous couple who thought they couldn't be seen necking on his steps in the dark. "They didn't touch the house, did they? Did you see them actually touching my house?"

"Simmer down, Jack. It's just bricks and mortar, not your wife."

Jack folded his arms and said nothing. Frankly, in some ways, he'd rather Penelope be manhandled than his beloved home.

"Jack," Snowden continued. "These intimacy issues are preventing any sort of breakthrough. My other agoraphobes are all out buying their own shoelaces and ant traps on anxiety level *two*. They've broken the level three barrier! Just look at yourself. You're even hiding behind your hair now."

Jack reached up and rubbed his face with both hands. His head was starting to pound. He exhaled slowly. "I suppose we should be thankful I don't have conformity issues."

Snowden sighed. "Not yet, you don't. No, the root of your problem lies in your lack of a stable childhood home. Lack of parenting. Lack of a solid family life. Your father was an obsessive-compulsive with olfactory issues who left you to sleep in a Coca-Cola crate."

"No, I didn't *sleep* in the crate," Jack explained for the umpteenth time, but the doctor was already struggling to his feet. Jack beat him to the front door and held it wide open.

Passing the hidden Groper, Dr. Snowden stepped onto the porch and popped open his umbrella before climbing down the stairs. Without looking back, he called out, "By the way, you know I don't like my patients rigging up ridiculous contraptions aimed at enabling phobic behavior. It's bad for business."

Chapter 3

The Most Terrible Inconvenience of All

Shit!"

Just as the doorbell rang, Jack sliced into his finger with a dull knife. It might have been wiser to have sliced into what was left of the slightly moldy cheddar rather than his right index finger, but, Jack's life being what it was, not everything was under his control. He held his hand under cold water to wash off the blood and called, "Harlan!"

No answer. "Harlan! I need you to get the door. Then go out and pick up Band-Aids!"

It was no use. The boy couldn't hear anything from his second-floor bedroom. Reaching for paper towel to wrap up his finger, Jack found the roll empty. Nothing but useless shreds dangling from one end.

"And paper towels," he added to no one but himself.

The doorbell rang again.

Wrapping his finger in a tea towel, Jack trotted to the front door to find an expressionless blond girl of about seven or eight standing on his stoop. She wore a green ski jacket over her school uniform and was holding a large box. What sounded like cello music wafted from headphones hanging around her neck. Bach, maybe.

"Good evening, sir. Would you be interested in purchasing any one of our varied selection of candy bars to support Hilltop Progressive School's Nontraditional Gymnastics Program?" The moment she stopped speaking, she craned her neck to look past him and into the house. "Two dollars each."

Jack peered into the box and caught sight of a sales script taped to the inside flap. Her cheeks glowed red when she caught him spying, and she slammed the flap shut.

"What's nontraditional gymnastics?" he asked.

Her transparent eyebrows inched together in irritation, and she peeked at her script before answering robotically. "Nontraditional gymnastics stresses diversity, creativity, and setting your own standards free from the critical expectations of the traditional gymnastic community." She sucked in a deep breath and leaned her face down to scratch her cheek on the side of the box.

"In other words, a cartwheel is a cartwheel, even if you do it lying on your back? Is that what they're teaching kids these days?"

"Children learn basic gymnastics concepts and select the level of skill they wish to achieve. Mister, are you going to buy some chocolate?"

"I might."

"We have plain chocolate, dark chocolate, white chocolate, rum raisin—"

"I'll take chocolate almonds. Two boxes."

"We don't sell chocolate almonds anymore. Because of society's growing trend toward childhood food-hypersensitivities."

"Any peanut?"

She shook her head gravely. "Again, because of society's trend."

"But rum is okay?"

She shrugged, looking past him into the foyer again. "Don't you have any furniture in there?"

"I really only like the chocolate almonds." He stepped sideways to block her view.

"Okay." She flipped open the box flap and read: "Hilltop Progressive School thanks you for your time and we hope you have a good day." Blowing hair off her forehead, she leaned down to set the box on the ground before readjusting her headphones. "I hope I sell something soon. The box is heavy."

"You know, I think I'll take two rum raisin bars after all," he said, counting out four dollar-bills and dropping them in the box.

With a happy squeak, she placed two candy bars in his hand, replaced her headphones, picked up her box, and trotted down the steps. Before she reached the sidewalk, he realized she'd given him caramel candy bars. Caramel! He could barely afford the chocolate bars; he certainly couldn't afford a dental bill right now.

"Excuse me," he called. "Excuse me, miss! You gave me the wrong chocolate bars!" But she couldn't hear him over her music. Halfway between his stoop and his neighbor's, she stopped, placed her box on the sidewalk, and squatted down to tie her shoe.

This was his chance. She was only, what . . . ? Fifteen feet away? He could run the fifteen feet, ask to swap the bars, and hightail it back into the house, couldn't he? Snowden would be all for it. Definitely. He'd say that if a little wisp of a girl with a head full of cello music could walk fifteen feet with a giant box, Jack probably could, too. Jack placed one foot on the porch, then the other, and held his breath, waiting for the worst to happen. Death, disaster, locusts. But none came. He simply stood outside the house, as if it was the most normal thing in the world.

Fully aware his breathing was growing too quick and too shallow, Jack realized the girl was just about finished fussing with her shoe. He bolted down the staircase and across the sidewalk. By the time he caught up with her, dropped his caramel bars into the box, and bent himself over to get a proper breath, she was standing again.

She looked into the box and squinted up at him, confused.

He needed to speak quickly, blurt out what he wanted, and get the hell back inside. Just say, "I asked for rum raisin." Breath came in sharp gulps, and the world began to spin. *Just say it!* He stepped from one bare foot to the other on the ice-cold concrete. *Say it!* But, somehow, there wasn't enough breath to get the words out. It was too late.

"No returns, mister. All sales are final."

"No!" he managed to say. "Not . . . returning . . ." Then the spinning hit him like a ten-foot wave. He staggered sideways, and suddenly all thoughts of chocolate bars vanished. All that mattered now was getting up those steps and back inside.

"You want another flavor?"

Jack shook his head, aimed his body toward his front door, and propelled himself to safety.

He wasn't ready to play outside like the other little girls, not yet.

• • •

A HALF HOUR later, having decided that doorbells that ring unexpectedly should, henceforth, never be answered, Jack followed the soft-rock beat of some flowery band from the '70s up to Harlan's room. Like most of the music that drifted out from under Harlan's door, this sent imaginary cartoon daisies, peace signs, and butterflies floating down the hall.

Still clutching the tea towel around his wounded finger, Jack rapped on Harlan's door.

"Yeah?"

Popping his head inside the psychedelic "Den of Cheese," as Harlan called it, Jack held up his toweled finger. "I need some Band-Aids from the store. Paper towels, too."

Harlan turned away from his desk and slid his thick, brown, goggle-like glasses farther up his nose. "Okay, big guy. I'll watch the house till you're back." Spinning his chair around, he returned to his homework.

"Not funny. Your dad's bleeding to death here. You can buy yourself a bag of chips or a soda." Jack caught sight of a pair of recently acquired crepey suede lace-ups strewn beside his son's chair. "Or some prune juice to go with your old-man Wallabies."

Harlan sat back in his chair again and spun to face Jack. He narrowed his eyes. "For your information, the footwear you so callously besmirch just so happens to have unparalleled abilities to not only bewitch but attract the most desirable females at Boston High. Try 'em out at the Band-Aid store if you want."

"Generous offer, but I'll pass."

"S'okay." Harlan sniffed, looked down at his chest, and smoothed out his shrunken cowboy shirt. "Few men possess the verve."

"It might be nice if you head out before I lose consciousness."

"What are we gonna do with you?"

"The drugstore closes in about half an hour."

"Please try to go out there, Dad. Just go to the smoke shop; it's only a block away. One block! You promised this year you'd do it, remember? On New Year's Day, you woke up and said, 'Harlan, this is the year I am gonna groove.'" Harlan stood up, wearing striped flood pants so short they could almost be mistaken for gauchos. He kicked his lady-killer shoes to a safer spot under his desk and blinked at his father. "Remember?"

Jack reached out to affix the corner of a HANG IN THERE kitty poster that had come loose from the wall. "I'm not sure I've ever used the word 'groove,' but yes, I did say something to that effect."

"Well?"

"Well what? The year's not over yet, is it?" Jack smiled and held out a ten. "Hurry. If I pass out on your rug, we may never get the bloodstains out."

"How about I go with you. But no pills."

"How about *you* go. But no pills and no Jack."

Harlan sighed and shook his head. "Dad. You'll never get any better if you don't take any risks."

"Yes. A shame, isn't it?"

"Anyway, I'd like to help, but Stevie and Kirk will be walking down the street any second now on their way to a movie. And if they see me, they'll want me to come. So, sadly, I cannot help you."

"Go to the movie and pick up the Band-Aids after. I'll just keep my finger in the towel until you get home." It was a terrible inconvenience, of course, but Jack was used to terrible inconveniences. It had been cumbersome to wake up from a warm sleep in the back seat of the bus and drag your splintered Coke box behind a group of stumbling rockers, all the time worried that if you fell asleep, they might forget to load you back on the bus after the show.

Jack's first full-on dizzying panic attack didn't happen until he was twenty-two and married to Penelope, his longtime girlfriend. Harlan was a toddler, at home with a sitter. Penelope sifted through a stack of tapes at an overheated music store near Faneuil Hall, while Jack waited in a long line of post-Christmas returns.

The couple in front of him in line were fighting. The girl thought her boyfriend was checking out Penelope in her tight sweater, and he denied it, though Jack had seen him looking back at her every time his girlfriend turned away.

"I know who she is," the girl said with a sneer.

The guy made all innocent. "Who are you talking about?"

"Lover girl over there. The one you can't take your eyes off of." Jack couldn't blame the girl there. Penelope's long, dark hair and big smile were difficult to ignore.

The guy turned to look, as if seeing Penelope for the first time. "Yeah, right," he scoffed. "As if."

"She's that chick from over on Battersea Road. Lives in Baz Madigan's old place."

Jack coughed in her direction. His scarf prickled and itched his neck, which was getting sweaty. People behind him began pushing, crowding him, in an effort to get closer to the returns desk.

"Who cares?" the guy said, making a face. "You're *way* prettier."

She wasn't, but Jack thought he'd better keep quiet. The guy was almost twice his size.

"Probably Baz's daughter." She stood on her toes to get a better look at Penelope.

"What? Baz hated kids. I read it in *Rolling Stone* once." The guy laughed, picking up a Tears for Fears tape. "Baz Madigan did *not* have kids."

"Did so, asshole," mumbled Jack. He pulled his hat off and rubbed his forehead, which was throbbing. The crowd pushed again, and three men blocked his view of Penelope.

"What did you say?" she asked her boyfriend. "Did you just call me an asshole?"

"No!"

"Look at her now." The girl laughed at Penelope. "She's looking in a mirror."

In between the men, Jack saw his wife wave at him.

The girl's jaw dropped. She glared at her boyfriend. "That slut! She waved at you."

"Hey!" Jack shouted. The girl spun around to face him, and Jack saw, for the first time, the faded kitten on her shirt. He started to say, "That's my wife you're talking about," but stopped. A sickening wave of dizziness washed over him, and he had to bend over.

The dizzies were terrifying this time. Worse than he could ever remember. For the first time, he thought, they just might kill him. By the time Penelope reached him, he could barely breathe. He was dying. This was what dying felt like. It was heat, claustrophobia, dizziness, and terror all mixed together; wrapping itself around you until you were mummified, and then you imploded.

He could never remember clearly what happened next. He remembered leaning against a sale table until Penelope led him out, but other than that, the only thing he knew for sure was that he had been about to die.

Dying, Jack thought as he waited for Harlan's answer, was the most terrible inconvenience of all. Anything less, he could handle.

So, no. Holding his sliced finger in a tea towel for three or four hours was nothing Jack couldn't deal with.

"I'm *not* going to the movie with Stevie and Kirk," said Harlan. "That's the whole point. If they see me, they'll want me to come with them, and that idiot Carl Larston is going. The guy's too pathetic for words. Thinks longboards are for hippies." Harlan shook his head. "Doesn't get that the only real cool is *un*cool."

"So what? Ignore him."

"Nah. I'd rather stay home and rot with you than spend one second with that new-school wannabe."

Jack sucked in a deep breath and turned to leave. "Well. While this is all very flattering, I think I'm going to go sit by the fire, which is definitely uncool." Before opening the door, he paused. "Why don't you invite your friends over here tonight? Not"—he cleared his throat—"the new-school wannabe, of course. Just the other two."

Harlan laughed. "Into this house? With all the bashed-up walls and the rooms without real furniture? Are you serious?"

"You had friends here last night!"

"No. They swooped in when I was too soapy to stop them. I don't need my friends becoming overly familiar with one of Jack Madigan's Magnificent Odysseys into, you know, Panicville. Episodes like those tend to reflect somewhat miserably on the innocent offspring."

"Oh, come on. You're exaggerating."

Grinning, Harlan hoisted himself up onto his desk. "You want examples? In list form perhaps?"

Dropping down onto the bed, Jack shrugged. "Sure. Won't be much of a list. You won't even make it to five."

"Number one is the time my hamster rolled out into the road in his hamster ball. I was seven or eight and had to dodge rush-hour commuters to save it, while you tried to direct traffic from the front door."

"Please. You were fourteen and there wasn't a car in sight."

Harlan raised his eyebrows. "Perhaps your memory will improve upon hearing number two. The time the Jehovah's Witness dudes came to the door in their suits and the tall one handed you his Bible. Then he left without it and when Mom told you to chase after him, you pretended you wanted to read it. You fake-studied it all day!"

Jack waved this one away. "I did *not* fake-study. It was fascinating. I found out that nowhere in the Bible are egg-laying rabbits or velvet-suited elves mentioned."

"Okay. Number three. This one's killer." Harlan began laughing so hard, he slumped back against his bulletin board. "The summer the neighbor asked you to pick up her mail while she went in for surgery and you said you were allergic to sun exposure and she should ask again closer to winter solstice. Number four was when she did!" Harlan wiped tears from his face, giggling like a little girl. "You said you were under house arrest. For mail fraud!"

"That was pure genius," Jack opened up the tea towel to inspect his finger. "She never spoke to me again."

"Neither did the mailman."

Jack slapped his thighs and stood up. "Well, it's been a real hoot, but I've got to get downstairs and finish bleeding."

"Wait, Dad! Number five—"

"Nah. I'll stick at four." Jack adjusted his tea towel and dropped a few bills onto Harlan's bed. "Pick me up a chocolate almond bar as well," he said as he started to close the door. "I've had a craving."

DOWNSTAIRS, JACK BUILT up the fire as best he could without newspaper and settled back in his old armchair, the one facing away from what was left of the curtains and toward the photo above the television, and reached for the bundle of mail he'd retrieved from the mailbox after Snowden left.

The usual pizza flyers and home improvement ads were on the top of the stack, along with a free temporary membership to a local gym, which Jack tossed immediately into the fire. He flipped through a brochure for a new menswear store just around the block, admiring the fine lines of suits he couldn't afford. A navy blue one caught his eye. How exciting it would be to try on this suit. Stroll into the store as if it was the most natural accomplishment in the world and slip into the suit. Preen in the mirror. He stared, unseeing, at the corbels supporting the heavy fireplace mantel, imagining how the blue wool would enhance his eyes.

He knew he would never do it.

After the music store attack, his "near-death" experience, Jack began finding excuses to avoid shopping areas. It wasn't difficult at first; no one questions a man who claims to dislike shopping. Even Penelope didn't realize what was happening. Eventually, the dizzy spells happened in other places—parks, cafés, cars. But Jack kept the ferocity of the attacks very private. He never admitted to anyone, not even Penelope, that he wasn't just dizzy—that he believed, for certain, that he was truly going to die each and every time.

It wasn't until Harlan was four and Jack was driving him to pre-school that Jack knew he had to get help. Out of nowhere, while he was driving along Beacon Street, it hit him again. He couldn't breathe from the spinning, and his hands went completely numb.

I'm going to drop dead and crash, he thought as he looked back at Harlan, who was singing sweetly in the back seat. Harlan's innocence only amplified the panic, and Jack pulled to the side of the road, collapsed on the passenger seat, and sucked in air from his cupped fists. All the while, Harlan called, "Daddy? You sleeping, Daddy?"

The next morning he was in Dr. Snowden's office being prescribed his first container of Nervy Durvies, as Harlan later called them.

Yawning, Jack picked up a real estate flyer. Some blond agent in a red jacket. Doreen Allsop was her name. Pretty girl. Her smile was a bit keen, though. Below her photo was a slogan:

BUYING OR SELLING? SHOW ME YOUR DWELLING.

Sounded like housing-market porn. *I'll show you my dwelling if you show me yours.* Jack tossed the flyer into the fire and watched the edges curl up and burn, then the slogan, the phone number, and, lastly, the annoying smile.

Next in the mail stack was a letter from David Strom, his bank manager. It wasn't the usual sort of Boston National envelope, the kind the mortgage bill came in. This was a thicker envelope, without the cellophane window.

Jack stuck his good index finger into one corner of it and tore it open very slowly.

Chapter 4

A Goddamned Lobotomy

B oston National."

"Yeah, David Strom, please. Tell him it's Jack Madigan."

The silence on the other end was thunderous. Then Jack heard whispering, and a hand muffled the receiver before the voice returned. "One moment, Mr. Madigan."

Gentle music poured into his ear, the tail end of some Pat Boone song Harlan could probably sing in his sleep. Then the radio announcer said he had a real oldie for everyone. One of the few slow tunes from a wild band. Jack recognized the tune on the second note. It was Baz singing one of his first hits, titled "The First Time."

"Jack, Dave here. How are you doing?" From his enthusiasm, you'd think he'd just bumped into Jack on the tenth hole at the golf club.

"How the hell *am* I?" Jack said, trying to keep his voice steady. "How the hell would you be if you'd just found out the bank was taking *your* home?"

"Okay now. Let's be reasonable . . ."

"Imagine my surprise when I opened the envelope, half-expecting an early Christmas card from my bank manager, to find he's foreclosing on me? And that a fucking real estate agent is coming over to view my house for sale? My home!"

Jack could hear papers being shuffled and the whack of a stapler. "Now, now. This wasn't exactly a total surprise now, was it, Jack? I sent you a letter of warning a couple of weeks ago. You've had two weeks to rectify the situation. You knew that your mortgage payments were getting seriously behind . . . again."

"I never saw a warning. There most certainly was not any warning—"

"I have a copy of it right here in front of me. It's dated October 30, 200—"

"I know the fucking year, Dave!"

"Yes. At any rate, it begins, 'Dear Mr. Madigan . . .'" he read on. Jack hadn't seen any such letter. And he knew precisely why. Harlan had collected the mail from the mailbox a few times recently. He had an annoying tendency to pitch the entire stack into the fire when confronted with too many flyers and junk-mail brochures.

". . . before November 15 to reestablish your regular payment schedule. If you do not do so, Boston National Bank assumes the right to foreclose on your property and . . ."

"This is insane. It's just a big waste of paper, Dave. I'm expecting a royalty payment any day now. It's, it's . . ."

"The royalty payments are getting lower and lower," Dave said. "And less and less frequent. They can't pay for that house. Heat alone must cost a fortune."

"Paying for heat isn't a problem." Jack stared at a deep gouge in the living-room wall, where Baz had smashed up a guitar after a string broke in the middle of practicing a solo. The gash was in the shape of a bird in flight. Sort of like a seagull with its wings stretched out almost flat as it sailed, not a worry in the world other than where he might swoop down to snap up a French fry or crap in a convertible. Of all Baz's leftover splinters and bruises and holes in the house, this one was Jack's favorite.

Penelope had always ragged on him to patch the holes up. She'd never understood that to Jack, they sparked and crackled with life, with Baz. They made him, an orphaned child, feel like his dad wasn't gone forever, but had just stepped out the front door to pick up a new bike for his son's birthday. If he'd remembered his son's birthday.

But Dave was right. The royalty check, if there was a royalty check this month, wouldn't come close to making the missing mortgage payments. And no one in the entire city seemed to be interested in achieving white perfection on their walls. "I know for a fact there'll be a royalty check next month. Just while I was on hold I heard a Bazmanics song . . ."

"I'm sorry, Jack. But this may not be a bad thing. You'll walk away with a nice sum of cash, more than enough to buy yourself a little apartment somewhere around town. Maybe buy yourself a boat and settle out on the Cape. Look at this as a good thing. You'll finally be able to stop struggling and start enjoying life."

Hm. Start enjoying life. On a boat. On the Cape. He couldn't walk to the fucking variety store! He was going to pitch himself out onto the waves with only his long-limbed, arborescent son, half-headed cat, and the Groper to keep him safe? He wouldn't need pills for that. He'd need a goddamned lobotomy.

The thing was, it was his own fault. Baz had left the house, fully paid for, to Granny Fran in trust. She then raised Jack and turned it over to him when he was twenty. It was Jack's foolish idea to start up his own band and try to follow his dad's still-steaming trail. He'd borrowed against the house to finance The Rotted Core's Great North American Tour. There were instruments to buy, facilities to book, and, most important, there was a tour bus to lease.

Jack, lead guitarist and singer, always sounded terrific at home on the fourth floor, which consisted of a huge stage and seating area and not much else. The acoustics were supreme up there, where he and his bandmates, three friends from high school, had been jamming for the previous few years.

He hadn't counted on the crowds. The noise. Most of all, the increasingly terrifying distance from his front door.

The Rotted Core's Great North American Tour hadn't hit three small towns before Jack called the whole thing off, going home to an unsympathetic wife and a whopping mortgage.

Dave Strom coughed. "Of course, you'll have until any potential sale closes to redeem your mortgage. That remains your right . . . should you be able to pay it off in full between now and then." He sounded doubtful. "But as you're probably aware, a house that size on Battersea Road won't sit on the market very long.

"Jack?

"Jack?"

Jack dropped the phone into its cradle and shut his eyes. Very slightly, so slightly that he wouldn't have noticed it if he didn't know the feeling so well, his head began to spin.

•   •   •

HE LOOKED AT the alarm clock. Almost two a.m. There'd been a sound. A bump or a bang. Holding a pillow in front of his chest for protection, he sat up in bed, looking for Mrs. Brady, making sure he wasn't preparing another bloody attack on Jack's feet through the covers. One more time, and, Jack swore, he'd smother the monster.

There it was again. Too big to be a cat, even a half-blind cat, it sounded like it was on the first floor. Near the front of the house. Maybe in front of the house.

Outside.

Throwing back the sheets, he sprung from the bed and to the window in one movement. Heart racing, he pressed his face to the glass and narrowed his eyes.

Two college-age boys faced his house, one with his foot against the brick wall, and were unzipping their pants. "Drunken bastards," Jack swore as he fumbled with the window lock. He managed to turn it and tugged the old window up. He got it open a few inches and leaned down to push the frame upward with his shoulder, swearing under his breath. Heaving it up all the way, he stuck his head and shoulders out into the night air and shouted, "Hey!"

One was in midstream, the other was just getting things started. They both looked up, swaying, smiling when they saw Jack's bed head peering down at them. "It's the Piss Patrol," one said, stumbling backward as he looked up. "The Piss Police." He fell backward, laughing, onto the concrete. "Isn't that a song? Cheap Trick, remember?" He started singing, "The Piss Police, they live inside of my head . . ."

The other one laughed and took aim at Jack's front steps.

"Cut that out!" Jack squealed. "That's private property."

The first urinator flipped Jack the bird and turned around to flick up his coat and flash his flaccid, white ass. "Take that, Hermit Boy!"

"What?" Jack looked around the room, desperate for something to throw. He grabbed hold of his pillow, all the while knowing he'd regret it. "Get away from my house!" he called, throwing the pillow down toward the second urinator, who was still leaking all over his steps.

The pillow landed between them with a puffy thud, infuriating Jack more. The second urinator turned and finished the job on top of Jack's pillow. "Why . . ." Jack raced barefooted out of the room and down the stairs. He slipped on the second landing, crashing his foot against the newel post and hobbled down the next flight, swearing and panting.

Nothing spun Jack Madigan into a rage like the heedless, bawdy mistreatment of his home's shabbily elegant façade. Especially today. And a ripping fury superseded all emotions, worries, or anxieties.

Even agoraphobia.

He flung open the massive front door and tore after the urinators, who ran down the street trying to zip up, one of them still leaking. "It is still . . . my . . . house!" Jack called after them, his feet slapping against the cold sidewalk. He chased them down to the next block, where they leaped into a cab and sped down Charles Street.

"Dirty, filthy . . . public urinators," Jack spat, leaning over to catch his breath. A middle-aged couple in long coats strolled by with their dachshund, also jacketed up to the chin. With raised eyebrows, they took in Jack, bare-footed in baby-blue pajamas, bent over and gasping for air. He looked up as they passed. Straightening, he adjusted his PJs, muttered, "Good evening," and stomped back down Battersea Road, too damned outraged to think about how far he was from his own front door.

In a silky Hugh Hefner robe and cravat, Harlan slumped on the Formica table, staring into his orange juice as he chewed his toast the next morning. Hair flopped into his face, covering the top half of his glasses and making them look like gigantic bifocals. He blinked at Jack. "Jesus, Dad. You look like shit."

Jack wiggled his still-stinging bare feet and drained his coffee cup. "Long night."

Harlan winked. "Long night with *the ladies*?"

"Just eat up, Hef," Jack said, standing up. "You've got to be out of the house in exactly thirty-five minutes or your mother'll blame me." He crossed the checkered kitchen floor and filled up both chipped Harvard mugs with fresh coffee. After finding there was only enough milk for Harlan's cup, he opened the fridge and eyed a half-empty container of plain yogurt and checked the due date. Five days left. He peeled back the lid and sniffed.

It all came from the same place, didn't it?

Reaching for a spoon, Jack scooped up two teaspoonfuls of lumpy yogurt and dropped it into his coffee. As he stirred, the yogurt swirled around in thickish white stripes, finally dispersed into something half-way between melted Häagen-Dazs and clotted paint that had been left out in the unheated garage all winter.

He sipped. Tasted lousy, but anything was better than drinking it black.

Glancing at his son, Jack decided it was a good thing it was Harlan's weekend with his mother. He needed some time to think. Plan.

"Can't I stay here with you?"

"Afraid not. It's your mother's weekend."

"Come on. I got you your Band-Aids. And your paper towels. We can play Monopoly. I'll let you buy Boardwalk and Park Place."

Jack shook his head.

"Okay, *you* get to be the top hat; *I'll* be the old shoe this time."

"Sorry. Court-ordered rules are rules. Besides, your mother has special plans for you this weekend."

"Oh yeah." Harlan groaned. "The Busted Families' Cultural Enrichment Weekend." He sat back in his chair and pushed his hair off his face. Now it stood straight out sideways on one side. With a mouthful of eggs, he held his hands up like a sign. "A two-day whirlwind tour of Boston's famed science museum and art gallery, full of divorced parents desperate to impress upon their offspring that life after divorce is shinier than ever before."

Jack pursed his lips and nodded his sympathy.

Harlan shoveled a half piece of toast into his mouth and stared at Jack, chewing. "And Mom's bringing Yale."

Jack said nothing, but busied himself with cutting the fat off his bacon. Once he was certain all that remained was the smoky, nitrate-soaked pork, he pierced the delicate tendril and popped it into his mouth. It was so small he could barely chew it.

Penelope had been dating Yale Strasser for the better part of a year now. In Jack's opinion, she'd launched herself into the whole dating thing way too soon. She hadn't been gone from the house three months before she headed out, probably laughing and flirting, to every party in town. Tossing her long, dark hair around and crinkling her nose every time she told a story. Wearing sexy clothes, too, no doubt. She'd always had a smashing figure and didn't mind showing it off. Minis and boots to every party. It had always been minis and boots.

Minis to show off her thighs, boots to hide her calves.

Penelope thought of her puny calves as a deformity. It was a dominant gene in her family, on her mother's side. Her father's family had well-developed legs—thighs *and* calves—and it killed her that neither she nor any of her siblings inherited the trait.

Underdeveloped calves must be like brown eyes, Jack always told her. Clearly, they kicked the shit out of the bulging-calf genes, little powerhouses of puniness that they were. Even when paired with the genes responsible for Jack's robust calves, really, the only robust part of his physique, the scrawny-calf genes had won out in Harlan. Penelope and Jack had made a pact never to mention the inherited flaw to their son, who hadn't yet noticed and seemed to be managing perfectly well in his ignorance.

"I *said*," Harlan repeated, "she's bringing Yale." In his present, victimized state, Harlan made a quick attempt to gain an ally. "Cool Yale."

The ultimate insult from Harlan. Inside, Jack smiled. "That'll be nice."

Harlan pulled his chin into his neck and furrowed his brow in attempt to mimic Yale. "'Harlan, I hope you've started on those B supplements I recommended. Take those with vitamin C and you'll never get a cold. Ever.'"

Jack looked up. "Never? How much B do you need to take?"

Harlan continued as if Jack hadn't spoken. "'Harlan, are those M&M's you're eating? Do you know what the dye in just one of those things will do to your liver?'"

"And your mother—is she into all this healthy living?"

Harlan stood up and dropped his plate into the porcelain sink with a clatter. "I don't know. She's working all the time now. Even on weekends. Then I have to hang with dynamic Yale, who wants me to go 'sink a few at the schoolyard' or 'sail the trails' on mountain bikes. Can you really picture me rocketing along the edge of a muddy trail on a dirty bike?"

Looking at Harlan, in his Playboy-mansion paisley robe and pillowy white ascot, with his long, underdeveloped calves and brown, shiny, old-man slippers, pushing his hideous-on-purpose glasses up his nose, Jack couldn't see it, either.

THERE HAD ALWAYS been a competition between Jack and Penelope when it came to Harlan. Initiated by Penelope, of course. Who could make him stop crying? Penelope, but only because she had been willing to use anything at her disposal as bribery. Her breasts being Harlan's item of choice. She'd always been *so* competitive, as a matter of fact, that Jack had secretly wondered if Penelope's whole insistence upon nursing the child well into his second year had less to do with any real conviction that her breast milk was actually better for him (Jack had seen her, on more than one occasion, staring longingly at babies sucking from plastic bottles) and more to do with needing to be better than Jack in satisfying their son's most basic need.

Naturally, she'd wanted Harlan to live with her after the split. "What kind of life will he have living with you?" Penelope asked, when she announced her big plan to leave. "He needs the kind of stimulation I can offer him, living in an exciting condo by the water, with a full gym and indoor/outdoor pool."

Luckily for Jack, Harlan refused to leave his cat, his best friends Stevie and Kirk, and his school, in that order. (Jack could only assume that he himself was too obvious to mention.) The exciting condo by the water, apparently, didn't allow pets. Though, Jack living alone with Mrs. Brady might just have been the jolt he needed to make the house more frightening than the world outside.

Penelope consented. Harlan only had one year remaining in high school, and she had a burgeoning business to build. Living with Jack in the decaying grandeur of 117 Battersea Road had given her an appreciation for architecture, historical features, and living with less. So, after she graduated from interior design school, with Harlan finally in school full-time, she began gathering a growing list of clients who loved her signature style, a style she'd spent years perfecting at home, rooms that reeked of rock-star money once had, now lost. In a good way, of course.

The magazines called Penelope Madigan's style "the Million-dollar Pauper" look. Where rich paneled walls were bashed up further in the way only a costly electric guitar like Baz's and a nice angry swing (also like Baz's) could. Furniture was draped in velvet, which was then tattered and shredded at the bottom. Luxurious Aubusson rugs were beaten with a shovel until they tore, then left out in the sun to fade away to near nothingness.

And once the shell of the room had been created and then destroyed, that was when the real treasures came in. The Jackson Pollocks, the Amedeo Modiglianis, the Vincent van Goghs.

In Baz's honor, Penelope favored painters with a tendency to self-destruct.

The whole look was one of controlled wreckage, though Jack didn't remember Baz's demolition being one bit controlled, or adorned with lavish furnishings and spectacular art.

GLANCING UP AT Harlan again, Jack pushed his chair away from the table. "You've been awfully quiet about the house being put up for sale."

Harlan said nothing, just leaned against the counter and thumped the back of his legs against the lower cabinets.

It was important for kids to talk about their feelings, and not bottle everything up until one day they start sneaking out of the house wearing your trench coat to go shopping for ammo. Jack wanted to keep an open dialogue with Harlan throughout this whole miserable ordeal. No one ever spoke to Jack about his problems when he was a child. Certainly not Baz, who would have been too loaded or, if he was sober, too riddled with his own anxieties to notice anything was wrong. And not Granny Fran, who did her best to pretend her son was the most attentive father ever.

"If I were you, I might wonder *why* all of this was happening to me," Jack said.

With an impressive snort, Harlan straightened his ascot.

"I might even feel some anger."

The cabinet-thumping grew louder.

"Confusion?"

Harlan grunted.

"Fear of the unknown?"

"I'm not the one who's afraid, Dad."

Not great dialogue, but at least they were discussing openly. "This is good. You're expressing yourself. Very good. I might also wonder, if I was your age, where I might be going to live . . . should this sale ever take place."

"I thought you said the house wasn't going to sell."

"Yes, yes. I did. But I want you to feel comfortable with every eventuality. That way, you'll have peace of mind."

"Peace of mind, but no bedroom."

"Now, now—you'll always have a home with me. And, of course, the likelihood is that we won't be moving at all. But should the unthinkable happen, I want you to know that *we will be fine*."

"Fine? I've spent years getting my room exactly the way I want it. Do you know how long I saved up for that ceiling shag?"

"I promise you if we move, and that's a big 'if,' I will spring for the new ceiling shag."

Kicking at the floor, Harlan grunted. "Won't matter. They discontinued the lilac two years ago. I'd end up with something disgusting, like beige or taupe." He mashed a piece of paper towel into a ball, tossing it across the room toward an open garbage bag. They watched the little wad hit the wall and bounce into the cat's water bowl. Still staring at the cat dish, Harlan mumbled. "I don't want to move. I was *born* here."

"I know, son." Jack gestured toward the front of the house. "Right there in the living room. With a midwife holding your head as you crowned, ready to swaddle you in a blanket, and a father holding the phone, ready to call 911."

"When I was little, you said I'd never have to move. You said I'd never have to go through a life like—"

Jack rubbed the back of his neck. "I did say that. I know. And I plan to keep my word. I just don't want you to feel stressed while I'm working things out. I want us to communicate."

Harlan was quiet for a moment, then laughed. "Remember the year I painted the inside of my closet?"

Jack laughed. "Black. So you could pretend it was a bat cave."

"And I painted right over that big, honking spider?"

Nodding, Jack said, "Is it still there?"

Harlan grinned and held his hands up like craggy spider legs immortalized in hardened oil emulsion. "And I busted my front tooth on the dumbwaiter ledge. Remember?"

"Your tooth chip is probably sitting there still . . . right down at the bottom of the shaft."

"Nah. Mrs. Brady ate it. Remember he puked it up on the front sidewalk?"

Jack shook his head, smiling. "I don't believe I actually saw it . . ."

"Right." Harlan nodded, his face growing serious. He thumped his legs against the cabinets again. "It was pretty far from the door."

Silence.

"Anyway, how I feel doesn't matter," Harlan said, his tone softer. "How are *you* going to manage to leave this place? Seriously. That's what I'm stressing about. It's not like you're going to walk out of here, jump on a bus heading across town, and start scrubbing floors in the new house, right? You'd probably be dead before the bus turned off Battersea Road."

Jack sniffed. "While your confidence in my demise is poignant, we're discussing you and your feelings. That is what matters today."

"Not really. What matters is that we're then left with a dead dad on the aisle of a bus and an orphaned son, who has nothing left but a kick-ass wardrobe and a pockmarked cat, and *that* stresses me. Big-time." He stared at his slippers a moment, then stood up straight and motioned toward the clock. "I better go get ready for Mom."

Well, Jack thought as he played with the crust of his toast. Shows what he knows. He wouldn't be an orphan at all. After identifying the body being dragged off the Battersea bus as her ex-husband's, Penelope, drunk with full custody, would snatch up her son without so much as a backward glance.

Chapter 5

Half a Head Like That

The door buzzer rang downstairs. Pushing the blankets off his head, Jack squinted at the alarm clock. 7:55. The real estate agent wasn't due till nine. Must be someone at the wrong house. He closed his eyes and tried not to think about the size of the rat droppings he'd found in the cellar the day before. At least as big as the leavings in Mrs. Brady's litter box. Maybe bigger.

It buzzed again, this time in quick, staccato beats.

"All right," he called, jumping up and pushing his legs into rumpled pants from the floor.

The buzzing beat changed now, to three long, three short, three long. Like SOS. Swearing silently, Jack hopped in place, trying to push a foot through the stubborn right leg hole, and crashed against his dresser. "I'm coming!"

He tore down the last staircase and across the black-and-white floor to the door, angry words already forming on his tongue. He yanked the door open.

There, on the stoop, was a tiny woman in a huge red blazer.

Barely acknowledging Jack, she marched inside. "I know just what you're going to say—I'm way on the worm's side of early! It's just that I was *so* excited to meet you and see the house for myself, I just couldn't sit home one more second waiting until the clock crept closer to nine." Deep inside the foyer now, she turned to face him and sucked in a breath. "Oh!" Coloring, laughing, she pushed a strand of bent hair behind her ear only to have it fall back again. "Dave didn't mention . . ."

Jack waited. "Yes?"

"Nothing. Look how rude I am." She held out her hand, which barely poked out of the long sleeve of her red jacket. "Doreen Allsop. But everyone calls me Dorrie."

Allsop? Jack knew that name. She was the one with the terrible real estate flyer. What was it? *Whatever you're selling, I'll show you my dwelling?*

"Jack Madigan," he said, shaking her narrow hand. She couldn't be much more than thirty, with flyaway blond hair half in, half out of a muddled ponytail, a Heritage Estates blazer with inventory tag still attached to the sleeve, and a smear of lipstick across one of her teeth. He wanted his hand back.

Eventually, she released it. She shifted uneasily, her gaze resting on Jack's face, dropping down to the floor, then back up to Jack's face, where it seemed to want to stay. Then she blurted out, "I tried bangs once." She blinked her eyes and smiled. "But it felt like flies were in my eyes."

Jack attempted a sympathetic smile.

"I guess Dave told you all about me." She looked so hopeful that Jack had to nod. "Good. When Uncle Dave heard I'd just joined Heritage Estates, he told my mother, that's his baby sister, that he'd give me my first house to sell." She paused to breathe. "Dave's a real sweetie."

Jack nodded again, though *sweetie* wasn't quite the word he'd come up with to describe Dave Strom.

He watched as she bent over to remove her brown ankle-boots. She pulled a pair of big red pumps from her bag, dropped one to the ground, and slid a small foot into it. Then she stuffed a folded-up wad of tissue down behind her heel and repeated the procedure for the other foot. The pumps were at least two sizes too big, maybe three.

She stared down at the shoes. "I got them on sale at the thrift shop near my apartment. Secondhand Rose it's called. Ever heard of it?" When Jack shook his head, she continued. "My friend who owns the place hand-painted giant cabbage roses all over the front of the store. I told Rose, that's her name, she should maybe become an artist and if she did, that I'd certainly buy a painting. Once I make a sale, that is. Anyway, the color was so close to the H.E. red, I just had to have them. Only three dollars and fifty cents." She tapped her toes together and waited for Jack to admire the shoes.

"Nice," Jack managed with a smile.

"I never, ever wear street shoes into my clients' houses. It's not going to help any sale to have street dirt collecting in the front hall. I'm sure Uncle Dave told you that the house has already been appraised. Glen and Gram Greene were here, oh, sometime last week and came up with a value based on the location, size, historical aesthetic, and other sales in the area. You're sitting on a very valuable piece of real estate, Mr. Madigan."

"Yes, well." Jack looked around stupidly. "I suppose you'd like a tour?"

"Love it." She took a step toward the living room, then glanced back at him with a bright look on her face. "Will your wife be joining us?"

"My wife?" Jack laughed. "Ah, no. She's . . . well, she's not my wife anymore."

"Oh. Sorry."

"'S okay."

"I'm forever doing that. Asking personal questions that get people upset . . ." She shook her head and followed him into the living room.

"Who's upset?"

"See? I did it again. It's not so bad to do it in your personal life, but in a business situation, it's very important—whoa." She stopped as Mrs. Brady crept into the room from the hall. "That's some cat."

The cat settled himself on the bottom step of the staircase and began scrubbing his missing eye with a moistened paw as if by some miracle, if he rubbed it just right, he could bring it back.

"That's my son's cat, Mrs. Brady. Not the handsomest of felines, but, uh . . ." He struggled to think of something nice to say about Mrs. Brady. "Well, Harlan loves him."

"It's a male cat?"

"Yes. We didn't know it when we brought him home from the pound."

She couldn't even look at Mrs. Brady. Turning to face the wall and stroking the plaster, she said, "Does it have to stay here during the period of sale? I mean can we move it to a neighbor's house or can we put it outside or anything? One of the surest ways to turn off a potential buyer is to have the smell of kitty litter hanging in the air."

Hel-lo kitty. Jack smiled without moving his lips. "The cat stays."

"And then there's the problem with allergic house hunters. I've heard some people won't even step inside a home with a cat inside. A cat, especially *that* cat, could seriously impair my ability to sell this house."

"There's really no place for him to go."

"Small children could develop night terrors from seeing him. With his, his," she risked a very quick peek, "his head like that."

"I'm sorry. I can't budge on this. Mrs. Brady has to stay."

Dorrie pursed her lips and scribbled something on her clipboard. With an upside-down smile and now flushed cheeks, she said, "All right then. I guess if I'm going to make it to the Golden Jacket Club next year, I'll have to learn to overcome a few obstacles."

Just a few. Jack smiled. "Shall we start in the cellar?"

She darted back up the cellar steps in her enormous shoes. "Don't worry, Dave will call in the exterminators right away. I've never seen a rat so big." Her chest heaved up and down inside her jacket as she tried to catch her breath. "It's a wonder your cat hasn't killed it."

"It's a wonder *it* hasn't killed the *cat*." Beaming, Jack followed her up and shut the door. He couldn't have dreamed up a more perfect introduction to the house. Just as Dorrie stepped behind the oil furnace with her clipboard to check the last time the furnace had been serviced, a rat swollen to the size of a raccoon shot across their feet. He could still feel the cool, naked flesh of the tail as it snaked across his bare toes. And even though he'd shrieked louder than she, the timing tickled him. If things kept going this way, Jack would be home free. He shook his head in grave concern. "We can only hope rat-borne diseases aren't transmitted by air."

Dorrie's pointed chin dropped. "Let's just keep this cellar door locked, all right?"

"Will do." Jack grinned. He could afford to be generous now. The place was crawling with killer rats. Plague-infested rats. "Can I offer you a cold drink?"

She chewed on her lower lip, her eyes drifting toward the ceiling. Jack could practically see her thoughts swirling in the air. She was mentally scanning some real estate code of ethics for regulations on accepting beverages from clients. Handsome clients.

It never hurt to give oneself an edge.

"Yes," she eventually said. "I'd love a drink."

Peering into the fridge, Jack immediately regretted his princeliness. "We've got, uh . . ." He scratched his head. "A bottle of unsweetened and expired cranberry juice that may or may not be pasteurized, a half bottle of Dr Pepper or a can of Coors Light. The Coors is unopened."

As if she'd just been offered a bottle of 1995 Krug champagne, unopened, she smiled her thanks. "I'll take the Dr Pepper."

A brave choice, when fully considered.

Jack twisted off the cap with a sheet of paper towel and made a grand, waiterly gesture of handing it over. She tucked her clipboard under one arm and sipped from the bottle.

"Let's head upstairs now," Jack said. "I'd like to show you Harlan's room while he's in the shower."

Ah, what pleasures await.

"Feel free to stop me if I talk too much," Dorrie said as they tramped up the stairs. "I tend to ramble on a bit when I'm nervous. I always told myself I'd warn every single client I ever meet. Tell them to just come right out and say, 'Zip it, Dorrie.'"

"No. I don't mind." She's going to scare off every single house hunter in Boston, Jack thought, nearly hugging himself. I've hit the lousy real estate agent jackpot!

She slowed to run her hand along a deep gash on one wall. It was a gash Jack particularly hated. It happened after a long night at a local concert. Jack hadn't been feeling well and, in spite of his efforts to keep himself awake, fell asleep in his Coke crate backstage before Baz croaked his way through the first song. He supposed he should be thankful that Baz and the boys didn't leave him there to raise himself among the snaking cables and dirty scaffolding and cigarette butts. But whoever carried Jack and his crate back to the car (the tour bus was only used for long distances)—and it was never clear *who* carried Jack—whoever it was had dropped his stuffed Snoopy. This Snoopy had been to every concert with Jack since before he could remember. It meant more to him than anything but his own dad, and he started wailing in the car on the way home. "Take me back," he cried. "We have to go back!"

At two in the morning, there was no going back, so, the car took Baz and Jack to Battersea Road, where Jack bawled himself to sleep. When he woke the next morning, the wall had been freshly wounded. He never knew for sure whether his father's rage was caused by his incessant howling or Baz's fury that he'd let it happen.

"Quite a few holes in the walls," Dorrie said with a cluck of her tongue. She glanced back at Jack. "Holes in walls don't really call to mind that solid, homey feel potential house buyers want to see in their future residence. We did a whole day on it in class. You want to create an atmosphere of serenity and peace. Serenity and peace. We should probably get the whole place patched up and painted before—"

"NO."

Dorrie spun around, shocked.

"I'm sorry," Jack said. "I didn't mean to shout. It's just that it's still my house. And no one is patching up *anything* in my house. Every hole stays exactly as it is and the only room that gets painted, ever, is the kitchen."

With a dour look, Dorrie set her Dr Pepper down on the steps and scribbled another note, presumably about Jack's being difficult, but maybe about his willingness to paint the kitchen, before picking up her bottle, clumping up to the landing, and stopping in front of Harlan's room. She stared at the door and let out what sounded like a small whimper. Jack knew exactly what she was staring at. The macaroni sign on Harlan's door spelled out WELCOME TO THE DEN OF CHEESE.

Taking the stairs two at a time, Jack could barely contain his delight as he rushed to open Harlan's bedroom door and turn on the mirror ball.

BY THE TIME Dorrie, followed into every room by the startling countenance of Mrs. Brady, had seen the whole house, she appeared to be near tears and had launched into an unending rationale, mostly designed to convince herself that *every* Golden Jacket Club member had likely endured much, much worse over the course of her or his career serving the real estate needs of the greater Boston area.

"After all," she said, "it's still an enormous property on Battersea Road. A fine address. More than a fine address. A desirable address. Four stories plus a . . . a cellar. Good strong structure and extraordinary architectural detail. It's not well preserved, but it's nothing a good contractor can't fix once new owners take possession. I might have to work a little harder than I'd originally thought, but that doesn't scare me." She sniffed. She sounded scared. "I think even Mrs. Brady won't hurt things quite as much as I originally feared."

Settling himself on the bottom step of the staircase, Jack yawned and stretched his arms above his head. "Oh yeah. It's going to go great."

She reached up to pull a wide ribbon from her hair, which tumbled down around her shoulders in a mess of limp strands and snarls. "And I think if the cat is going to insist on walking around with half a head like that, we'll just have to take the emphasis off its face. Give the eye some-place else to focus, just like I'll do with the rooms." She bent down and, without looking Mrs. Brady in the eyehole, arranged the red ribbon with a big bow under the missing parts of his face. Standing up and placing her hands on her hips, she smiled, her eyes shining with either pride or tears. Probably tears. "There." Her voice cracked. "That looks better al-ready."

BY THE TIME Dorrie pulled on her short brown boots, Jack was feel-ing just fine; almost guilty with pleasure. After all, she was a sweet girl. He was almost certain that someday she'd succeed. Someday when she'd become too old and too tired to talk so much, when she'd grown into her clothes and shoes and bought herself a strong light for her makeup table. The determination was there, certainly. If it hadn't been for the whole being-turned-out-of-his-childhood-home thing, he might have actually wanted things to go well for her.

"That's it, now, Jack. I'm all done. Whew, ten o'clock already. I'd better check in at the office. My phone's probably jangling off the desk." Jack somehow doubted her phone was doing much, if any, jangling. "If you could just help me get the FOR SALE sign from my trunk out front, I'll be all set." She stood looking at him, her huge red pumps in her hands.

Jack froze. "Excuse me?" She'd stopped talking and started waiting for him to go outside. What could he do? Say no and hurt her feelings? Make her wrench her tiny back? His palms began to sweat. He certainly wasn't going to say, "No. I'm thirty-six years old and afraid to cross the sidewalk."

"Right out there, see?" She pointed to a small black car parked out front.

"Yes." Jack sucked in a breath. Couldn't get a good one. Already his fingers tingled. He looked at the car again and noticed a woman sitting in the passenger seat. Nodding toward the car, Jack asked, "Friend of yours?"

Dorrie grinned and waved to the closely shorn redhead, who stuck a heavily braceleted arm out the window and waved back. "That's Rose. You know"—she held up her big shoes—"of Secondhand Rose fame. She's wonderful." She held up an index finger to Rose, indicating she'd just be a minute, before turning to Jack. "You'll find the sign right there in the trunk."

"Yes. I don't suppose Rose could . . . ?"

"Oh no. Recent gall bladder surgery. It's why I brought her along for the ride. We're stopping off at her doctor's in about an hour. For her post-op exam. It's near my office. So if you don't mind . . ."

"Hm?"

"The sign?"

There was no way out of this. He had to go. He bent over and reached for a shoe, busying himself with untying the laces.

"I wouldn't rush you, except her appointment's at eleven. And I need to stop off to check—"

"Yes," Jack said. "Your jangling phone."

She laughed. "Let's hope it's jangling."

With no laces left to tie, he stood up and tried to smile. A wave of dizziness sloshed over him like a bucket of muddy water. His breath coming in gulps, he shuffled toward the door, praying he wouldn't drop dead from dizziness and pounding heartbeat. Another foot forward. He felt his head sway. If only she'd pee on his steps. He could get fuming mad and run out there, if she'd only squat on the porch and pee.

"Are you okay, Jack?"

His heart pounded so hard he was certain it would go into arrest. It couldn't be good for it to pound like this. He pushed another step forward.

"You look a little faded out. Pale." She came closer and put a hand on his arm. "Is it the sale?"

The sale. That was it. "Yes," he breathed. "I'm feeling faint, I think."

Putting his arm around her shoulders, she turned him away from the door and into the living room. "Okay now, let's get you down on the floor. That's it." She helped him lie down on the gritty, wooden floor. "There you go." She patted his shins and stood up again. "Shall we raise your legs?"

"No." He stared up at the chandelier directly above his head and tried to calm his nerves.

"It might help redirect the blood flow."

"No. Thanks."

"Dave told me all about your . . . situation."

Jack said nothing, just focused, really, on staying alive. Discussing his "situation" right now was only going to lead him toward the white light.

"These forced sales are never easy. Or so I hear. But it's my promise to you that I'll get top dollar for your house, so money will never be a problem, ever again."

Comforting. Maybe the padded walls of his cell in the asylum could be lined with his cash.

Harlan's high-heeled chunky boots echoed in the hallway.

"Hi," Dorrie said, holding her hand out to Harlan, who clumped into the room, wearing tight salmon-pink corduroys and a Bay City Rollers T-shirt over a way too girlish blouse.

He introduced himself to Dorrie and stood over his father. "Whoa. Need a hand?"

"Yes. No. Dorrie does. Be a sport and help her with her sign, will you?"

"Want a Nervy Durvy?"

Dorrie looked at Harlan. "A what?"

"Nothing," Jack snapped. "I'm fine, everyone. Harlan, please get the sign."

"Your father's really not himself," Dorrie said, her hair falling in front of her face. "He's come a bit undone with all the stress of moving, I think."

"You may be right," Harlan said before leaning down and whispering to Jack, "You want to try my new love shoes now? I can go get them for you." He winked. "This might be the *perfect* time for a test drive, if ya know what I mean."

"The *sign,* Elton John." Jack swatted at Harlan's platform boots.

"I'm going, I'm going."

Just then, Rose herself shuffled into the room with one hand held protectively over her abdomen. She wore a long navy dress and what appeared to be white Keds. Though from Jack's vantage point—flat on the floor and giddy from scanty oxygenation—he really couldn't be sure.

"What happened? I saw him pass out from the car," Rose said. A gold chain dangled from her eyeglasses and swung next to her cheek. Back and forth. Back and forth. Jack wished she'd stand still, just for a moment, until the chain came to a full stop.

"No, I didn't *pass out*," Jack said too fast as his son, his newbie real estate agent, and now her ailing secondhand–shoe vendor stared at him. It had to be an all-time low in terms of his public persona.

"He's having a spell. Stress, we think," Dorrie said in a loud whisper. "But you shouldn't have walked all the way in here after having major surgery."

"You worry too much," Rose said. "I'm fine."

She's fine. Probably stitched up from bow to stern and she's the one still upright.

"Have you tried raising his legs?" asked Rose.

Dorrie shushed her. "He didn't seem to like that."

"He's always been fairly blasé about blood flow, now that you mention it," Harlan added, eyes narrowed and arms crossed.

"Okay," Jack said. "That's enough. Show's over. Thank you Dorrie, I'll be fine. Nice to meet you Rose, and good luck with your recuperating. Harlan, after you haul out the sign, have a nice day at school!"

Chapter 6

The Hole Behind the Cabinet

Jack slammed the car door and jogged through the alley to the great iron gate leading into the frozen backyard and, more important, his kitchen door. The temperature had plummeted, and the clouds were weighted heavily with snow. And worse, Jack's little pills were wearing off fast.

He stepped between partially buried cat droppings and over an ancient bird-feeder the cat had managed to knock down in one of his fumbling one-eyed attempts on the lives of the neighborhood sparrows. When the tiny yard wasn't functioning as Mrs. Brady's arena of failed avian executions, it was the cat's outdoor litter box, not much bigger than the indoor litter box, actually.

"If you hadn't spent so long flirting with the cashier, the pills would've lasted until you were safe inside, cooking us up some nice big cheeseburgers," Harlan called from the ramshackle garage. "Maybe whipping up some milkshakes, too. I'm starved."

"I wasn't flirting. She got a haircut, that's all. It's impolite not to comment." Jack hurried up the back steps, set down the grocery bags, and fumbled with the keys. His hands were shaking with relief as he pushed the door wide open and pulled the bags through the doorway. Inside, he leaned against the chipped marble counter and breathed deeply.

"Jesus, it's cold in here." Harlan tramped through the kitchen with his arms full of paper sacks. "Make sure you load the burger up good with cheese, for *I am* . . ."

Steadied now, Jack picked up his bags and started to unpack. "I know, I know, the Cheese Boy."

"No. It's the *Man of Cheese,* now."

"Much more dignified." Jack piled dented cans of mushroom soup, which had been on sale—three for one—into the towering white cupboard and closed the glass door with unintended force. He stared at the wall just past the cupboard door and cocked his head. In this light, the paint was stinking of violet. It wasn't antique-looking at all. It was looking terribly, modishly violet.

"Do these walls have just the slightest cast of violet to you, Harlan?" He looked up to see Harlan's hand stuffed deep inside a package of chocolate chip cookies. The self-proclaimed Man of Cheese pointed toward his bulging cheeks with his free hand and choked on cookie bits for further effect.

The phone rang.

Rolling his eyes, Jack reached for the receiver. "Yes?"

"Hey, sweet cheeks." It was a girl's voice.

After a pause, Jack said, "Just a minute, I'll get him for you." Grinning, he tossed the receiver to Harlan. "It's for you, *sweet cheeks.*"

Harlan's face fell as he caught the phone and spun around to face the fridge. "Hey," he whispered after a mighty swallow.

"Yeah." He glanced back at Jack and rearranged his body around the phone to muffle the sound.

Pause. "No. Not here. Why not at your place?"

He covered his mouth now. "Well, I better study alone then."

"Okay. See you.

"Mm-hmm." Pause. Then, barely audibly, "You *know* I do." Quick pause. "I can't. I'll say it later." He spun around and hung up the phone, slipping out of the room.

"Hey, hey," Jack called, his hands inside the fridge. "Not so fast."

Harlan's face poked back into the room. "What? I need to study."

"Who was that?"

"Just a friend."

"Must be one hell of a friend to call you sweet cheeks." Jack pulled the old egg carton from the fridge, opened it up to sniff it, and tossed it into the garbage. He'd have to remember to put the bag out back later or the cat would climb inside to suck the rotten eggs and suffocate in the plastic sack. He needed that cat around, at least until the FOR SALE sign out front disappeared. "Maybe I *should* try those shoes of yours."

"Don't make a big stink out of it."

"No big stink. My son has a girlfriend and I'm a bit curious, that's all. What's her name?"

Harlan flopped his gangly body against the wall, bracing himself with his long legs. "Melissa. Can I go now?"

"Melissa and Harlan. I like it. Why don't you invite her over?"

"Some other time."

"Don't you think your father should meet her?"

"It's not like I'm getting married, Dad. Can I go now? I want to go upstairs and turn on my heater."

"Call her back and tell her I'm making cheeseburgers and milk-shakes."

"She can't come."

Jack looked at Harlan and looked away. He tore open a box of frozen hamburger patties and lit a burner. Reaching into a lower cupboard for the frying pan, he asked, "Has your mother met her?"

Harlan shifted his legs and said nothing.

"Well, has she?"

"Sorta."

"Melissa's been to your mother's?"

Harlan scowled, busying himself with pulling off his big boots.

"Harlan. Has Melissa been to your mother's?"

Harlan groaned. "She comes to Mom's for dinner sometimes on Tues-days."

Jack turned and set the pan on the glowing burner. He slid two frozen patties onto the blistered Teflon and returned the box to the freezer. Walking over to the sink, he turned on the water and lathered his hands under a feeble stream of water. "Does she like your mother?"

"I dunno. I guess."

Clenching his jaw, Jack toweled off his hands. "That's nice."

"You think so?"

"Yes," Jack lied.

Harlan thought about this for a moment. "Good, 'cause Mom's taking Melissa to some chick flick next week."

A pain shot through Jack's jaw and he dropped his chin down toward his neck to stretch out the tension. "A chick flick? Great. Are you going?"

Harlan laughed. "No chance."

"So it'll just be Penelope and Melissa? Bonding over licorice and buttered popcorn?"

"Unbuttered. Neither one of them eats animal products. Can I go study now?"

"And they've been to the movies together before?"

"Once."

"With probably quite a few Tuesday night visits."

"Not so many. Six. Seven, maybe."

Jack grunted. "Six or seven? That many?"

"I have a test tomorrow."

"But she can't make it here, even once?"

"She lives closer to Mom's. Sorta." Harlan looked back and forth from Jack to the hallway, clearly dying to be set free from the interrogation. "My test is first period."

Jack pulled two plates from the cupboard next to the sink. "Off you go then." He walked the plates to the turquoise table and set two paper napkins beside each. Silently, he crossed the tile floor again and reached for the glasses while Harlan started to leave the room. "Just tell me one thing," Jack asked, turning to face his son. "And I want to know the truth. Is it me or the house you're more ashamed of?"

MAYBE IT WAS the chill that had settled in the vast, paneled rooms, or maybe it was Harlan's having left to study at Melissa's, but that night the house seemed emptier than usual. Jack called the dumbwaiter to the third floor to load up his book, dirty laundry, and collection of water glasses from his bedroom, and send it all downstairs, where he planned to build a big fire and spend the evening with a little Dickens and more than a little wine.

With gears griping and screeching in protest, the dumbwaiter chugged ever so slowly toward the third-floor landing. It usually took a minute or two to arrive, so Jack poked his head into the third-floor study where his computer sat atop an old wooden desk. Time to see if there was any action on Baz's oldest guitar. An old Gibson Les Paul, bashed up as all Baz's guitars were. A keepsake like that could bring in up to seventy thou, Jack figured. Just enough to smooth things over with the bank for a while and make the real estate agent disappear. The home page of VintageNotes.com popped up on screen, and Jack typed in his account number.

YOU HAVE 0 OFFERS read a banner above his name.

Zero offers? On one of the first electric guitars of a musical legend? That was insane. Sitting in his squeaky chair, he tapped off a note to Brian Coleson, the Webmaster, asking if he was having any technical problems on the site, then headed off to fill the dumbwaiter, which sounded as if it had arrived.

After loading it up and sending it back down to the first floor, Jack started down the stairs, rubbing his hands together for warmth, then stopped. The dumbwaiter gears were making an unusual *clunk-scritch* noise. In all the years, he'd never heard it utter a sound like this one.

He trotted down the rest of the steps to the main level and pressed his ear against the wall. Yes. Definitely a *clunk*, followed by a very high-pitched *scritch*. Sliding the wooden door upward, he took the dirty laundry out first (the dumbwaiter door down in the cellar had been stuck tight for years) and set it on the floor to carry to the cellar the next time he was feeling brave—and wearing hip waders—and reached for the rest of his load.

After dumping the dirty glasses in the sink and shuddering at the garish violet walls, he padded into the butler's pantry. It had always seemed to Jack to be just the right place to keep a few bottles of wine. Certainly, if he had a butler, the butler would insist on keeping all enter-tainment-related items in his pantry, within an easy stroll of the dining table. The tiny room—a large closet with white cupboards, a small sink, and marble counters as in the kitchen—separated the kitchen from the dining room to give the poor manservant a place to hide from either the hostess or the guests. Or, most likely, both.

He reached up and over the sink to the top shelf and pulled down a bottle of merlot, wiping off a thick film of dust. It had been a while since he indulged—not since Penelope last came by with a trunkload of new clothes for Harlan—regular clothes that Harlan wouldn't be caught dead in, like Nike running shoes, Gap jeans, and Ralph Lauren tops. Harlan had taken one look at the embroidered equestrians on the sweat-ers and just about passed out laughing, and Jack, quite frankly, had been offended by Penelope's implications. As if he couldn't be counted on to provide his son with a winter wardrobe. Of course, he could. He'd chew off his left foot before he'd allow Harlan to do without. That Harlan's penchant for fashion's underachievers dictated a wardrobe that probably cost less than one of Penelope's pastel Polo shirts was a damned lucky break, though.

With the grimy bottle, a corkscrew, and a wineglass in hand, he headed through the dining room to build his fire and get started on his evening. Halfway across the room, he slowed and looked around, eyes narrowed. Something was different.

It *looked* the same as always. Dark red peeling wallpaper ran all the way up to the ceiling from above wainscoting near black with age. An empty metal card table stood in the center, looking a little self-conscious in the high-priced surroundings. His grandmother's china cabinet stood at attention along the far side—the exposed brick wall that connected his house with the Ballards' next door. The cabinet looked as fussy as ever. So what was bugging him? He moved in a circle, thinking.

It was too warm in the room.

Confused, Jack walked back toward the center and stopped beside the table. A warm draft tumbled and swirled all around him, tickling his skin and luring him farther into the room. Strange he'd never noticed it before. With bottle and props still in his hand, he walked over to the wall that connected his house to the big house next door. The bricks were impossibly toasty.

He pressed his back against it and smiled. It was like a mother's hug. Or a father's maybe. How was he to know? He'd never experienced much of either. He ran his hand along the craggy bricks and felt a wave of heat coming from behind the china cabinet. Poking around behind it with his hands, he felt the bricks stop and something soft begin.

The source of the delightful draft.

He leaned against the old cabinet and slid it easily along the floor until he could see behind it. Down below knee level was evidence of another Baz attack. A nasty one. It was a big hole in the bricks, about the size and shape of an oblong platter one might use to serve Thanksgiving dinner, with the turkey still on it. Yes. Jack smiled. He'd forgotten all about this hole.

He'd first discovered it before Baz died. Never having spent much time in the dining room, he couldn't think of quite when it happened, but when he first found it, he remembered seeing right through to the house next door. His grandmother had stuffed it full of old rags and pushed her china cabinet in front of it.

He knelt down and touched the brownish rags. They were so toasty he wanted to push his face into them. Tugging on a twisted cloth in the corner, right about where the turkey's lobbed-off foot would have been, he peered into the hole and found himself staring into a piece of wood with a faded and stained label on it. The back of some sort of cabinet on the Ballards' side of the wall. From what he could see of it, the label appeared to be square, and read THE DOMBROWSKY BROTHERS, PHILADELPHIA, 1888. Above that, it said THE CABINETMAKERS WHO— The rest was hidden behind the bricks.

He pulled out a few more crumpled rags. The Ballards' cabinet appeared to be supported by thick, turned legs, which held it about a foot and a half off the ground. When he pushed the next rag lower, he could see pale blue carpeting stretched clear across the room. Unless the Ballards were lying on the floor, they'd have no idea of the hole's existence.

Sweet, hot air, air from the other side, fluttered against Jack's eyelashes. He tugged at a few more rags until so much heat poured through that he could close his eyes and imagine a hot Caribbean sun tanning his whole face. Crossing his legs under him, he reached for his bottle, all thoughts of a roaring fire fading. Why go to all the trouble when he could sit here and toast the Dombrowsky Brothers, the cabinetmakers who . . . cared?

Several glasses later, Jack was drunk. Leaning against the brick wall, his arms wrapped around his knees, he stared at what little remained in his glass. Harlan hadn't answered him. It had been a fairly straightforward question.

"Is it me or the house you're more ashamed of?"

Swaying, he topped up his glass, then rested his head back against the wall and sipped. Harlan couldn't answer. He was a good kid. The best. Didn't want to hurt his dear old, fucked-up dad. He held his glass in the air. "To the Dombrowsky Brothers, the cabinetmakers who . . . hole themselves up inside their cabinets. One free Dombrowsky with every order," he slurred.

Harlan would be much better off with his mother, Jack thought. Hell, he'd be better off with this Yale guy, who takes all the vitamins. Only the most selfish of fathers wouldn't see this. Closing his eyes, he set the glass down and stretched out his legs. He'd never been so tired.

"To the Dombrowsky Brothers, the cabinetmakers who shame their offspring, then stash them away in the drawers. Lock 'em up. One Dombrowsky and Son with every order."

Chapter 7

Hair of the Cat

Staring up at the bathroom ceiling the next morning, Jack waited for the eyedrop to fall. This was one of life's terrible moments: holding your eyelid open and forcing oneself, against every natural instinct, to squeeze the tiny bottle and let a speeding droplet land smack onto the center of one's most delicate body part. He pumped the bottle with his fingers. Nothing happened. He squeezed again, too hard this time, and what felt like half the bottle splattered into his eye and poured down his face and neck.

"Ah, shit." With eyes clamped shut, he fumbled for a tissue and sopped up the useless liquid. No way was he going to entertain his ex-wife with eyes still bloodied up from his night in with the Dombrowsky Bros. He blinked stupidly and stared into the mirror. Already the redness had faded some. Not completely, but some.

He'd spent the entire night snuggled against the dining-room wall. And when he woke up, after working the cramps out of his neck and shoulders, he replaced a few of the rags he'd pulled out of the hole, but left a nice, apple-sized opening hidden behind the well-placed Ballard family hutch. Not so big as to blast the Ballards with a sudden icy draft, which they would surely investigate and seal over; just big enough to function as a sorely needed heating vent.

He dressed carefully; khaki pants and his good black turtleneck, the one he got after a radio station out in Dallas held a weeklong Bazmanics tribute—Bazmania, they called it—earning Jack an unusually plump royalty check and raising his hopes that other cities would pick up on the trend.

Sadly, they didn't.

Stuffing his feet into an old pair of black slip-ons from the back of his closet, he looked in the mirror and smiled. Not bad for an old recluse with a hangover.

Downstairs, he scooped up last night's empty bottle to purge the house of any and all evidence of life having gone downhill since Penelope's departure. True as it may be, he didn't need her silently crowing about it. As he warmed his hands at the brick wall, he heard crashing noises coming from the front stoop. Undoubtedly, Penelope, pulling a paint scraper and a bottle of turpentine out of her bag and using it to rid his front door of years' worth of old paint and city grime. Grime Jack could never be counted on to scrape away for himself.

Hoping to catch Penelope in the act of thinking him useless, he flung open the door. Sitting on his stoop was the chocolate-bar kid. Bundled up in two coats, jeans, and a pair of furry mukluks, she sat cross-legged, surrounded by miniature plastic horses, jumps, and flowerpots. The jumps were arranged into some sort of cross-country course and, back at what appeared to be the stable, where horses were lined up along a series of water troughs, there were tiny bales of hay, horse blankets, and curry combs scattered everywhere.

"What's going on here?" Jack asked, incredulous.

She pointed at a snorting stallion with flared nostrils, a wild mane, and no back legs. "It wasn't me. It was HIM. He got pawsy with Buttercup again and she let him have it. I told him it would happen. I said it a hundred times."

Jack looked down to find a fresh gash at the base of his front door, with two broken horse legs lying beneath. "You bashed up my door?"

"HE bashed up your door. He's a dirty kicker."

Glancing at the girl, with her wool hat pulled down over her eyes, he wondered what kind of parents sent their daughter off to play on the doorsteps of strangers. "This is private property, you know. Private means it belongs to someone else. Me!"

"Yeah." She looked at her herd. "They like your porch better. Ours has prickly brown matting and it makes my mares fall over." Her hand knocked against a can of Crush, tipping it and sending a grape river flowing down the steps.

"Do you live around here? Do your parents know where you are?"

Ignoring him, she pointed out the horses at the trough. "I name my horses after flowers. This is Daisy. That's Petunia. My stallion, he's not named after a flower, since he's a boy. He's called Spruce, like the tree. My sister keeps calling him Bruce. But that's because she knows nothing about horses." She pushed her hat back and blinked at Jack. "Nothing."

"You need to go home. Now."

Pulling herself up onto all fours, she started tossing fallen mares, fence rails, and severed fetlocks into a pink plastic bicycle basket. "It's okay. I live close." She stopped and looked up at him, her eyes resting on his hands. "You can go back to your rum bottle now. I won't leave any parts."

Quickly, he glanced down. Shit. He'd forgotten the empty bottle in his fist. Not yet nine a.m., and he'd already branded himself an alcoholic. "It's not rum. It's wine. Was wine, rather."

"Whatever. It's your liver." She sniffed. "Can you shut the door now? I don't like people watching me pack up."

PENELOPE, LATE AS usual, blew in like a puff of exhaust. She flicked her long hair and stepped past Jack into the foyer. After slipping a black cape from her shoulders, she held it up uselessly, as if she hadn't lived in the house for some eighteen years and didn't know that when a guest arrived, they were expected to toss their coats over the banister. Themselves.

When Jack walked straight past her and into the living room, she managed to figure it out.

"You're looking well," Jack said, taking in the glittering diamond studs, the fitted charcoal dress, and, naturally, knee-high boots. "Care to take your boots off?"

Penelope ignored the taunt and settled herself on Jack's favorite chair. "What's with the sign out front, Jack? You're selling the house?" She crossed her long legs and wiped a little cat fur from the padded arm of the chair.

Joining her in front of the fire, which was at the height of its roaring and crackling, just as he had planned, Jack leaned against the mantel. "Just checking out the market," he lied. "See what the old shack is worth." He noticed his shoe was covered in dust, and rubbed the toe against the back of his other pant-leg.

She grunted, pulling her hair over to one side. "You don't need a real estate agent to tell you it's worth a small fortune. I hope this Doreen Allsop person has priced it properly."

"She seems to know what she's doing." Actually, he was fairly certain she'd priced it too high. Four and a half million sounded like an outrageous price for an old house, any house, let alone a house with a shuddering dumbwaiter and forty-year-old roof tiles. But then, who was he to interfere with his house not selling?

"You'd better hope that big dog next door doesn't swallow your house hunters whole. Sounds like a savage. What breed is it?"

"Never seen it myself."

Penelope studied Jack's face. "You're looking tired. Aren't you sleeping?"

He sat down and stared into the fire. "Maybe your boyfriend could recommend some supplements . . . ?"

"You'll never change," she said with a laugh. "Always critical of those more successful than you."

"Only the ones who are sleeping with my wife."

"Ex-wife."

"Yes. Thank you for clarifying."

Unfolding her lean body, she walked across the room and began to pull the blankets off the antique ladder leaning against the wall, and to rearrange them, one by one. She'd always needed to control his environment. Ever since they married. It drove her mad that he fought every change as if his life were at stake. Not that the changes were all that significant. There'd never been enough money for her to make any permanent improvements. Not until she graduated from design school and was suddenly swarmed with clients. But by then, she was long gone.

Each blanket was rearranged to look as if it had been casually tossed on the ladder when the user had grown too toasty. Jack got up and followed behind her, refolding each blanket and placing it exactly the way it had been before Penelope and her expensive design skills had arrived.

"You'd like Yale, you know. He's terrific with Harlan. Wants to take him on a boys' weekend in January. Fly him up to Northern Quebec and teach him how to camp in the winter. Build snow caves. A real father and—" She stopped herself just in time. "A real survival experience."

Jack laughed. "Sounds perfect for Harlan. He can wear his silken orgy robe to breakfast. Tell Yale to go ahead and ask him." He'd love to be there when Harlan snorted, "As if," and clicked out of the room in his shiny boots.

She had to know Jack was undoing her every décor adjustment, but Penelope started next on the woodpile, rearranging it in a more artful fashion. "You're dressed sharp today, Jack. Someone special coming over? Or are you going out?"

"I might be going out."

She smirked in disbelief. "Really. You?"

"Never know." He nudged at the perfectly stacked pyramid of logs until it tumbled sideways and scattered into its usual jumbled disorder. Penelope said nothing.

"I walked straight down to Boylston Street the other night without a worry in the world."

"What, chasing another homeless drunk who vomited on your stoop?"

"Matter of fact, no. I just took a stroll, chatted with a lovely couple out walking their dog."

"Hm," she grunted. "I'll bet. You are still seeing Dr. Snowden, aren't you?"

"I'm seeing him, but he doesn't see all that much of me."

She suppressed a giggle. "Don't tell me! Is he still falling asleep in the middle of your sessions?"

Nodding, Jack sat down. "The last time he was here, I had to take his pulse. His head was right down on the kitchen table, his mouth gaped open, saliva pooling all over the Formica. I actually thought, for a moment, I'd finally bored him to death."

Penelope burst out laughing; her pretty, infectious laugh that made everyone around her laugh, too, even when they had no idea what had amused her in the first place. Once, in a movie theater, before they married, Jack had spilled his entire box of jujubes on the floor in the middle of *Good Morning, Vietnam*. Penelope was laughing hysterically because he'd made it very clear at the snack counter that he would not be sharing with her; he didn't want to catch the cold she'd been battling all week, and that she should get herself her own box if she was in a chewy-candy mood. And so, she had.

No one in the darkened theater could have known what had happened, but the whole place started laughing, simply from Penelope's contagion. Her laugh, not her virus. At a certain point, the crowd seemed to come to the collective conclusion that nothing amusing had actually happened, and stared straight ahead at the screen—which was showing a particularly gruesome scene—with mortified expressions on their faces.

This, of course, just killed Penelope and Jack, but not as much as the usher shining flashlights in their faces and escorting them, collapsing with giggles, from the theater.

"Oh Jack," she said when she'd composed herself. Mrs. Brady rubbed his head—the good half of his head—against her boot. Penelope always got the cat's good half. He apparently saved the pitted half for Jack. "I'm sorry." She paused, tickling the cat's ear. "I'm just so sorry."

"Don't be."

"I just couldn't do it anymore. I had too much living to do; I was only thirty-three, for God's sake. I couldn't spend one more day bolted up inside this house with you." She looked up, apologetic. "That came out wrong. You know what I mean."

He nodded. "I don't blame you. I never did."

"And then I walk in here all hostile and judgmental. It's not who I am, but somehow, when I'm back in here with you, I, I don't know. I feel like I'm being flattened or something. It just happens."

"What can I say?" With a shrug, Jack smiled. "It's a gift."

She smiled.

"Remember that time, back when we were still running the Bazmanics fan club, and you insisted we set up a real office?" Jack said. "So we went down to an office supply store . . ."

"The one down on Mason Street?"

"That's right."

"It was before you got dizzy," she added.

"Before I *admitted* to getting dizzy." He crossed his legs under himself and leaned toward her. "There's a big difference." Touching her knee, he continued, "Anyway, when we got there the sales guy refused to touch anything I'd touched first? Remember?"

Laughing, she nodded. "You kept trying to hand him that stupid plastic business-card holder and he pretended you weren't there! Just looked the other way and kept right on talking."

"See? What I do to people; it's a gift. And a curse, but mostly a gift."

She laughed again, wiping a tear from her eye and pausing for a moment before looking up. "Jack, I came here today to tell you something."

Still smiling, he pulled a cat hair from his tongue.

"Yale and I are getting married."

Chapter 8

Harlan Doesn't Want to Smell Like a Summer Day

Calm down, Jack," Dr. Snowden scolded into the phone. "You knew this day was coming."

"I did?"

"She's a successful, intelligent young woman. You didn't expect her to remain single forever, did you?"

"Hey, that's my wife you're coveting."

"Ex. And I've never coveted anyone but my own wife."

Jack grunted. "Your second or your third?"

"We're not discussing my life here. You're deflecting again."

"But how can Penelope be so sure? We've only been apart for a year and a half and here she goes, leaping into another committed relationship."

Dr. Snowden tsk-tsked. "Such latent anger. You never received confirmation of your father's love for you. You wanted it more than anything, but fate didn't allow it. Your father was cruelly torn away from you before achieving the maturity that age would certainly have bestowed upon him. Well, age and thrice-weekly therapy sessions to rid him of his obsession with clean hair."

Jack chuckled. "As it was, he relied on cologne. Lots of it."

"You remember this cologne, do you?"

"Remember it? I wore it after he died. For years."

Snowden's voice softened. "Ahh. You loved your father's smell."

Shrugging, Jack said, "It was nice cologne. Sort of musky." He stared into his water glass. Half-empty.

"It doesn't matter how it smelled. To you, it represented your father. When did you stop wearing it?"

"This isn't about Baz."

"Why do you call him Baz?"

"It's his name."

"Just say it. 'My father.'"

Jack said nothing.

Snowden covered his receiver and mumbled to someone in the background, before returning to Jack. "Don't you see your father was riddled with obsessions? He loved you, his only son, but his own demons kept all his energy focused inward. The sooner you see this, the sooner you'll be able to rid yourself of not only this chronic resentment but your own anxieties."

"There should be some kind of law. Otherwise, what's to prevent ex-wives from leaping into successive relationships with their heads so far up their backsides—?"

Snowden interrupted. "You know, with some of my more . . . progressive patients, I've seen great success with role play."

"What?"

"Role play."

"Playacting?"

"If you'd like, I could play the role of your father. Tell you what you needed to hear. You'd be young Jack. If you're open enough, if you let yourself feel it, it might prove beneficial to your progress."

"I don't think so."

"We could begin with a small hug."

Midsip, Jack coughed and sputtered, tepid water having trickled straight down his windpipe. The idea of Snowden wrapping his brittle limbs around him in a medically prescribed display of false affection was more than he could bear. When he'd finally cleared his throat, he croaked, "God, no."

Jack could practically hear the old doctor's face freeze as he scribbled in his notepad. Probably a reminder to refer Jack to a younger, more resilient colleague. When Snowden did finally speak, he sounded wooden, tired. As if he was running out of ideas, patience, and the ability to keep his eyes open. "Then next time you're feeling especially hostile, I strongly encourage you to release your fury in a healthy and appropriate manner. My more advanced patients report that throwing balled-up socks against the wall is tremendously therapeutic."

Jack said nothing. At this point, throwing himself against the wall would be tremendously therapeutic.

He'd always known Penelope was the truly marketable one in the relationship. That, should they ever split, he was the one that would sit on the shelf growing more tattered and outdated with each passing year, plastered with faded red sale stickers. But did it have to hurt so much?

"Jack?"

"Jack?"

"I've gotta go. Harlan's calling me." He dropped the phone into its cradle and stared at the chipped wall. He should have known Snowden would turn this ultimate rejection from Penelope into further evidence of a deep-rooted flaw on Jack's part. His gaze drifted down to his computer screen. Maybe his guitar had had some action. Saving his childhood home might go a long way toward erasing his ex-wife from his mind.

YOU HAVE 0 OFFERS, the screen read.

Still nothing. Except for an e-mail from Brian Coleson, assuring him that he shouldn't worry. It can take up to six months to sell a treasure like Jack's.

Six months. Very reassuring, indeed. This was shaping up to be one hell of a day. He leaned back in his chair and stared at nothing. This Dorrie had better fuck up big-time in front of her house hunters.

"Dad," Harlan called from down the hall. "I'm out of shampoo!"

Steam poured into the hall from under the bathroom door, which Jack yanked open. "Jesus, Harlan! You're going to scald yourself in water this hot." He reached under the sink for the bottle of ninety-nine-cent Summer Breeze shampoo for normal/oily hair, which he'd brought home from the store the other day, and passed it to Harlan behind the white bath curtain. "Do you know what it costs to fill this gigantic tub with boiling water?"

"This is ladies' shampoo!" Harlan croaked. "I don't want to smell like a summer day."

"Oh, stop it. No one'll notice the smell of your hair." Jack strained to crack open the tiny window.

"What'd you get this one for? It's all pink."

Jack pursed his lips as he watched steam tumble out into the frosty air. "When you're paying the bills around here, you can choose to have your hair smelling any way you'd like."

"Mom buys me men's shampoo. With NO flowers on the bottle."

"Harlan, please!" Jack snapped. A great, throbbing pain crashed around in his head. "I *cannot* talk about your mother right now."

"Mm. I guess she told you."

Staring at the closed white curtain, Jack sighed and rested his hands on his hips. "Yes. She told me."

Water sloshed around on the other side of the curtain. "It's no big deal, Dad. It's not like she was coming back here, anyway. I asked her and she said she couldn't. Not ever."

Jack smiled sadly. However misguidedly, the boy was trying to help. "You're right. It's not like she was ever coming back." Looking down at the iron claw feet of the old tub for a moment, Jack said, "Listen, I was thinking I'd like to make a nice dinner for you and Melissa tonight. Just the three of us. Okay? I'll make my famous spaghetti. And this time, I won't take no for an answer. Tell her cocktails will be at six, dinner at seven. Got that?"

"Cocktails?" Harlan sounded hopeful.

"Virgin cocktails."

"Awghh." A loud splash indicated a lanky limb striking out in protest.

"And Harlan?"

He didn't answer.

"Harlan?"

Jack pulled the bath curtain to see Harlan completely submerged in bubbles, only his great, bony knees poking up into the air. "We'll be eating in the dining room."

MELISSA SAT NEXT to Harlan, and directly across from Jack. Since she was the guest, she got to sit closest to the new dining-room heating vent, partially hidden by a lumpy chair, and Jack had seen her shiver only twice. Three times, if you counted the time she tasted Jack's raisin–lemon rind salad dressing. The recipe called for lemon juice, but Jack had always felt a real cook knows when to improvise. In this case, when the rind was all that was left of the lemon.

"So, Harlan tells me you've just moved here from Florida," Jack said, twirling spaghetti around his fork. "How do you like it so far?"

She smiled a crooked smile and shrugged. "Pretty nice, I guess."

"Is it cold enough for you?" Jack knew before he said it that Harlan would roll his eyes in embarrassment over the banality of such a comment. On cue, Harlan rolled, and with remarkable drama.

"I guess" was all she said.

The room fell silent again, except for the scratching of forks on plates.

"I think I just heard a dog sniffing over there," Melissa said, turning toward the brick wall.

"Might have been the cat," said Jack.

"Nope. Definitely a dog sniffing," she said. "And I know dogs. My mother breeds affenpinschers in our kitchen at home."

"Affenpinschers," Jack repeated. "Born right in your kitchen?"

She took a deep breath and began reciting, as she'd clearly done many times, "The affenpinscher is a loyal, affectionate, terrier-like dog with a square compact body and a monkey-like head. Originally bred in Germany, he was raised to hunt down rodents in kitchens, barns . . ."

"Rodents?" Jack interrupted.

Melissa nodded, while Harlan, manly man that he was, looked as if he might be sick.

"You know, any time you'd like to bring a couple of your mother's dogs over here for a romp . . ." Jack started to say.

But Melissa was no longer listening. She pointed at Harlan's paper napkin. "You should tuck it into your collar. So you don't spill sauce on your good shirt."

Jack continued, ". . . they could have the run of the cellar."

Harlan blushed and did just as he was told. It would have been, after all, a great shame to spill tomato sauce on his shiny, flowered man blouse. He flashed a little tulip-shaped smile, to which she responded by reaching over to pat his knee.

"Your hair smells pretty, Harlan," she said. Harlan immediately dropped his gaze into his pasta and rapped Jack with his foot under the table.

As they ate in silence, Melissa and Harlan alternated between staring into their pasta and grinning stupidly at each other. Though it couldn't have been easy for Melissa to see past her thick, lengthy bangs. She had to tilt her head back and look down her nose (through perfectly round plastic glasses—white ones; the kind one might find on a doll who speaks when you squeeze her left foot) to get a good look at anything. A more perfect girl for Harlan could likely not be found. Anywhere. Aside from the mod-Barbie glasses and long mousy hair with bangs that only came in extra long, she wore a go-go dress and lime green wrinkly boots with matching tights. It was no wonder she'd gotten the answer wrong when he'd asked her what color the walls in the kitchen were. Everything paler than neon must look utterly blanched to her.

Jack chewed on a breadstick, trying to decide whether Melissa could possibly have just shown up at Boston Central High already cheesed up, like Harlan, or if Harlan had found her one day, simply and sensibly dressed, and glimpsed in her a terrific canvas for fashion horrors from the ladies section of the local Goodwill.

"You must have spent a lot of time at Disney World," Jack said, thinking that dinner at Penelope and Yale's probably wasn't this quiet.

"*Dad.*" Harlan whispered. "She's not a child."

Melissa backed this up with, "I don't like rides. Or parades."

"Mm." Penelope probably laughed her sparkly laugh throughout dinner and had Melissa believing she was having an outrageously good time, whether she was or not. He wished he possessed such an enchanted weapon. All he had was the Groper, and it certainly wouldn't do to have the girl go home with tales of Harlan's father's Groper.

Wait a minute. He did have his guitar upstairs. And a beautiful wooden stage. That was it. He'd play some music for the kids. That might impress Melissa and make Harlan look as if he comes from a long line of rockers.

Jack topped up their glasses with Coke. More caffeine could only help liven up the party. "I was thinking, after dessert—my renowned no-bake chocolate cheesecake—I might give the two of you a concert upstairs. Melissa, did Harlan tell you about our little stage on the fourth floor?"

She scrunched up her nose until it hit her bangs. "I don't know. I have this earache . . ."

"That's okay, Dad. We'll just watch TV in my room."

"I have to put in special drops," she added. "Three times a day."

"We'll keep the volume way down low." Jack stood up.

"*Dad*," Harlan groaned, bugging his eyes in protest. "She has an ear-ache."

"The ear drops are freezing cold when they go in. They really hurt." She dug through her purse and produced a tiny squeeze bottle, holding it up for all to see. "But the drops don't hurt as much as loud noises. Loud noises pierce right through my brain like long, burning-hot needles."

Forcing a smile onto his face, Jack dropped his head, exhaled, and slowly began stacking the dinner dishes.

PUTTING THE LAST of the dinner dishes away in the cupboard, Jack peered into the hallway to see Melissa and Harlan holding hands and whispering at the front door. She was already jacketed and tightly wrapped in a long striped scarf, which, no doubt, would be wound around her delicate ears before she raced through the cold night air to her mother's car.

Feeling his father's glance, Harlan placed himself between Jack and Melissa, his back to the kitchen. Jack turned away. He didn't need to look to know what was going on. It was the wettest, sloppiest-sounding kiss he'd ever heard.

A horn sounded from out front and the hallway grew silent after the kids ran outside, Harlan in holey socks, no doubt. An icy wind shot through the already chilly house, and Jack rushed to close the front door. He couldn't afford to lose a trace of warmth.

As he pushed the door shut, he could see Melissa calling and waving to him from beside her mother's double-parked navy Saab hatchback. "Mr. Madigan, my mother wants to meet you."

Jack smiled and waved to the well-coiffed blond woman in the front seat. Four or five gray dogs barked and leaped around hysterically in the back. The passenger window lowered itself, and Melissa's mother motioned for him to come over to say hello. "I'm Gwendolyn Mathers."

He waved again. "Jack Madigan." Shivering, he backed inside.

"Come out here, Mr. Madigan. She wants to meet you," Melissa called.

Harlan's face paled as he danced from foot to stockinged foot on the sidewalk. "Aw, it's okay. It's too cold out here for him," he said.

"Just for a second," Gwendolyn called through the window.

"Please, Mr. Madigan," Melissa said, cupping her hands over her ears. "I'm freezing."

His mouth twisted into a tiny knot, Harlan tucked his bare hands under his armpits and jogged back toward the house and up the front steps. "Dad. Stay inside. Melissa can't find out about . . . you know."

Jack narrowed his eyes and looked from the car to the porch and back again. "Has your mother met this Gwendolyn?"

"Yeah, but forget it."

"More than once?"

"Maybe. But—"

"Then I'll do it." Jack flipped up his shirt collar and blew warm air into his clenched fists. "I'll just step out there and do it."

This was Jack's chance to outshine his ex-wife. The thought of Penelope's face—shocked upon hearing about the curbside introduction—combined with the chance to make his son proud was too tempting. The extra glass of wine Jack consumed at dinner didn't hurt, either. He stuffed his feet into shoes. "I'll just walk out there, say hello, and run back inside." Jack waved at Melissa's mother, held his breath, and stepped outside, doing his best to ignore the onrushing dizziness.

"Dad, please!" Harlan tugged on Jack's sleeve. "It's a bad idea. Don't do it."

"But you're always saying I should get out there. Take risks."

"Yeah, but not in front of my girlfriend. And her *mother*!"

"Don't worry. I'm going to make you proud."

"Dad, no. I'm already proud of you. Really. *Don't do this!* Not now!"

Poor kid's a terrible liar, Jack thought as he visually measured the distance between the house and the barking Saab. Thirty-five feet. Maybe forty. Just walk across the pavement, shake the dog lady's hand, and race back. That's all it would take.

He took a deep breath and grabbed Harlan's elbow, dragging him down the steps. Still smiling at the ladies, Jack whispered, "Just keep walking and don't stop until we reach the car."

"Oh God. This is so wrong," Harlan muttered as he hung on to his father all the way down the steps and onto the sidewalk. "*Please* hold it together."

His ears roaring, Jack clutched his son's arm tighter. The wind hit his face hard, nearly taking his breath away but not his resolve. They were nearly there. The barking grew louder as Harlan led him to the curb. Jack stopped and steadied his breath before stepping onto the road and allowing Harlan to guide him between two parked cars toward Melissa and her mother. He glanced back at the front door, wide open, with light from the foyer spilling out onto the porch, beckoning him back inside. The glow from the house was nearly orange with warmth, safety . . .

"Mr. Madigan," said Gwendolyn, shouting over the yapping dogs. "Nice to finally meet you."

He put a hand on the roof to steady himself. "Yes. You too."

"Melissa tells me you're something of an artist."

Too many tails were wagging, thumping against the windows, the seats, the doors. Jack looked away and tried to focus. "Not an artist." He sucked in a deep breath. "Color consultant."

One dog, an incessant barker, gnashed its little teeth against the window in a way that would surely have Snowden break into a run. Then that dog was gone, to be replaced by another—a jumper—though it could have been the very same dog; they looked identical. There were so many, twirling, jostling each other, yapping; it was nightmarish. Ratty gray dogs began throbbing and spinning before his eyes.

Gwendolyn followed his gaze into the back seat. "They really seem to like you."

Melissa opened the front door and slipped inside, nearly taking the head off a smaller dog trying to escape from behind the seat. The whole street was spinning now, and Jack was losing himself. Gwendolyn asked him something, but he'd already forgotten it.

Harlan was speaking. Something about his dad being unwell. It made Jack queasy. Reaching down, he propped his hands on his knees, trying to breathe. *Damn it!* The dizziness was winning. He stepped backward and stumbled against a parked car, Harlan catching him before he fell flat out onto the road.

"What's wrong with him?" Melissa's eyes were huge with worry.

Harlan hid his face. "He's got a bug. The flu, I think."

"He seemed perfectly well a moment ago," Gwendolyn said.

Jack looked up to say he was fine, though he was far from it, but Harlan was steering him away, supporting Jack's weight from under his arms.

"We're good," Harlan called back. "Just need to get him inside. Where it's warm."

Having jumped out of the car to follow them, Melissa whispered, "He looks like he's dying. You should call an ambulance."

Harlan stopped and, for a half-second, seemed to be considering dropping Jack onto the icy sidewalk for the paramedics to haul away, and returning to the car with his girlfriend. "It's okay, Missy. I'll explain later."

As he hauled Jack up the front steps, the yapping, howling Saab pulled away and sped along the darkened street.

By the time Jack fell through his front door, he could barely keep himself upright. He leaned against the wall and slid down onto the floor. If his heart would only slow, just a bit, he could explain. The dogs had all but finished him off. He might have managed the introduction, remained relatively steady, if not for the teeth gnashing against the window. The sound of tiny, razored fangs striking shatterproof glass echoed inside his head. He'd just explain it . . . Harlan was there; he'd witnessed the riot. He'd understand.

Harlan kicked the door shut. "Oh. My. God," he said, panting and white-faced. "Are you trying to trash my life?"

Jack dropped his head between his knees and concentrated on slowing his breathing. Slowing his racing heart.

Harlan bent down close enough for Jack to feel his breath. With his head still dropped, Jack raised a hand to indicate he was okay. Or, if not quite okay, at least not dead. Yet. "Melissa's mother seemed pleasant," wheezed Jack in effort to lighten the mood.

It was the wrong thing to say. "Pleasant? Pleasant?" Harlan asked. "She was trying to hide her horror that Melissa is dating the son of a drunk . . . or a lunatic!" He paced the floor, pulling his hands through his hair. "Jesus, Dad!"

"It might not have been a good idea, with all those dogs . . ."

"Yeah, they might have licked you to death. They were real fierce!"

"I needed more warning. If I'd known, I'd have taken my pills and . . . and mentally prepared myself to leave the house."

"*This house* has turned you into a prisoner. It being sold is, like, the best thing that could ever happen to you. And me! Let's get the hell out of this piece-of-crap asylum you think is so sacred. As for me, I'm sick of it!" He bounded up the stairs, two and three at a time, and slammed his bedroom door.

Dropping his head into his hands, Jack stared down at the floor.

ONE BY ONE, Jack ripped the rags from the hole between the houses and threw them down. Every last one of them. Fuck cold drafts on their side, he thought. He was sick of being cold. Sick of a lot of things. He plunked himself down on the floor and crossed his arms behind his head, feeling the warmth creep across his torso.

With a nod to the Dombrowsky Brothers, he closed his eyes.

It didn't seem like a dream. Too real. He could feel the wind, warm wind, from all around him. Up on the roof, there were no walls, after all. Only air, sweet and soft. Penelope looked up at him, her hair in a pony-tail high on top of her head, the way she wore it when she was pregnant with Harlan, but Harlan was there, too. Younger, still young enough to be playing with little plastic army men. "You be the general, Dad," he said to Jack. Penelope smiled. "Yes, Jack. Be the general."

So, he did. He was suddenly wearing army fatigues and bossing the soldiers, who had grown to the size of three-year-olds, to fall into line. They marched across the roof overlooking Battersea Road and ducked their heads down when they reached the edge. On command, they dropped to their green bellies—Harlan, too—and waited for Jack's next word. He was meant to say, "Fire," and had every intention of doing so, would have done so if Penelope hadn't sashayed across the rooftop with that sexy smile on her face.

She slid her hand inside his khaki shirt, pushing him down until he was lying on the gravelly rooftop on his back. Swinging her leg across his thighs, she propped herself on one elbow and looked down on him, her hair falling across his face. He was so relaxed. So content. He glanced at Harlan, who was surrounded by flowers and drinking a milkshake, flinging the army men, who had turned into hammer-wielding carpenters, hundreds of dwarflike Dombrowskys, off the roof to float above the street and laugh at Jack.

Penelope mouthed the word "Brave," but when she smiled again, she had lipstick across her teeth. He tried to wipe it away with his finger, but it wouldn't rub off. He scrubbed harder and harder. Only the harder he scrubbed, the darker the stain grew. She floated above him now, higher and higher, until he couldn't reach.

He woke with a start, rubbed his eyes, and pushed his sleeve up to check his watch. 12:39.

He stuffed enough rags into the hole to cover about three-quarters of it, and shuffled up to bed with a silent good-night to the Floating Dombrowskys.

JACK COULDN'T QUITE believe his eyes. He read the note again.

Mr. Madigan, Interested in your 1960 Gibson Les Paul, as noted on VintageNotes.com. Please call to discuss, Forrest Carmichael-Jones (212) 555-6210

Forrest Carmichael-Jones. Some uppity kind of name. With a 212 area code. Must be in New York City. Jack grinned. Baz would love the irony of a man of the manor, a swanker, buying the guitar of one of rock's most lawless lead singers of all time. He ran up to the fourth floor and pulled the old Gibson Les Paul Standard case from the closet.

It was a beauty. A Gibson Les Paul 1960 Flametop reissue still in its original case. Flipping the lid wide open, he ran his hand along the honey-colored wood, stopping to touch each ding and scratch. Baz's dings and scratches. Detesting the thought of parting with it, he carried it back down to the office, where he'd call this most intelligent gent who clearly had a solid appreciation for musical history.

Seventy thousand dollars. Once he had the check, he'd call up Dave Strom. Tell him to put a muzzle on that Dorrie character and remove the metal sign out front. The same sign that had been keeping him awake each night, crashing against the tree's iron grille every time the wind blew. With a wide smile, he imagined peering out his bedroom window as Dorrie dragged it back into the trunk of her little car and sped away to answer her jangling phone.

Picking up the phone, he dialed Carmichael-Jones's number in New York.

A male voice answered. "Carmichael-Jones, Falstaff and Lawson, how may I help you?"

"Forrest Carmichael-Jones, please."

"May I tell him who's—"

"Jack Madigan." He didn't have time for idle chat. Not where saving his house was concerned. "Tell him it's about the Baz Madigan guitar."

"Mmm." The voice sounded irate now. "I'll check if he's available."

Almost immediately, Carmichael-Jones picked up. "Madigan. What's your ground-floor price?"

"Excuse me?"

"For the Gibson Les Paul. Ground floor."

Jack glanced at the guitar. "Well, it was one of Baz's first electric guitars. And it's covered in evidence of many long nights of frustrated gigs. Though, in those early days, the gigs would have been much small—"

"Signed?"

"What?"

"Is it signed by Baz Madigan?"

Jack snorted. "No, but I'm his son. It's been in our family home for decades and it's still in its original case."

Carmichael-Jones let out a long sigh. "It isn't signed," he repeated stupidly. "I thought your ad said it was signed."

"If it was signed, I'd be asking double."

"All right. Give me your best price." The guy sounded exhausted. Like he'd traveled the world over, on foot, to discover his treasure was a fake.

"I'm only asking seventy. I could get more, but I'm in a hurry."

"Yeah, I'm not paying seventy. Saw one on an Australian site for just under *seven*. And that's Australian dollars."

Jack scrunched up his face. "This isn't just any old guitar. It was one of Baz Madigan's first. Still in its original case. Doesn't get any more authentic than this."

"Yeah, but it isn't even mint."

"If you know anything about Baz Madigan, you'll know that nothing he owned stayed mint for very long. This is a Baz Madigan Gibson Les Paul. With all his scratches and dents and scuffs—"

"Sounds like poor condition. I'll give you ten for it."

"Ten?" Jack had to steady his anger. "Forrest, I think you're missing the point . . ."

"No one calls me by my first name," Carmichael-Jones said.

"Sorry." Jack couldn't afford to lose his one and only lead. He softened his tone. "I was just explaining, Mr. Carmichael-Jones, that a guitar owned by a star as big as Baz, my father, has a much higher intrinsic value *because* of the physical evidence of its owner. I'm saying the flaws raise its value; they don't lower it." He ran his fingers along the metal strings. "There's a dent he made at Madison Square Garden one year, when a fan asked for an autograph. Another scratch was made when he tried to bring the guitar down on a bouncer who—"

"I'll give you eleven. But not a dollar more."

Jack's jaw dropped. "I can't sell it for eleven."

"All right, then." And Forrest Carmichael-Jones hung up.

Chapter 9

The Big Black Dog

The window was thick with ice. Jack peered outside to see his tree-lined street covered by a deep dusting of snow. Pure, unsullied white. Chaste, he'd call this particular white. People were tramping along sidewalks still thick with the fluffy stuff. He turned away, shivering, and pulled a thick sweater out of his dresser.

Eleven thousand. He'd been up half the night worrying. Eleven thousand would help, certainly. Wouldn't buy him a whole lot of time, but he could call up Dave and at least get things squared off for the winter months, then worry about what to do afterward in the warmth of the spring.

He shuffled into the office to call Carmichael-Jones back and accept his tawdry offer.

"I'll get him for you." The receptionist seemed to have cooled off from the day before.

"Madigan. What is it?"

"I've decided to accept your offer," Jack said, glancing at his father's guitar and closing the case. "I'll lower my price to eleven."

"Madigan, Madigan, you're a whole continent too late. Lulu and I have made a monumental decision. We're going Brit."

Going Brit? "You mean you're buying British memorabilia?"

"Exclusively. Lulu read yesterday that British instruments appreciate quicker than American. But then, you probably know that already, being Baz Madigan's son."

"But—"

"Oh and Madigan? Lulu thinks it's wonderful—you toiling to keep your father's memory alive like this." Click.

Jack swore under his breath, slamming the phone down. He dropped into his big chair and spun slowly from side to side. British instruments didn't appreciate any faster than American. They only rusted quicker from the dampness.

Speaking of dampness, Jack rubbed his icy hands together. His head felt a little woozy and his nose was tingling. On top of everything else, he had a stinking cold.

He went back to his room to gather up last night's dinner dishes—he'd eaten dried-out mandarin oranges and leftover spaghetti in bed—and his book, and loaded them into the dumbwaiter on the third floor. He then trotted back into the office to grab the Gibson Les Paul and prop it inside with everything else. Pulling the wooden door shut, he pressed the first-floor button, waiting until he heard the tired gears kick into motion and watching his dishes disappear, before heading downstairs himself.

Stopping on the stairs to sneeze too many times and swear at himself for not having taken Yale's roundabout advice about the vitamins, he heard a loud, grating sound before the elevator came to a halt somewhere around the second floor.

Shit. He raced down to see the bottom of the car stopped about two and a half feet below where it should stop if it was being sent to the second floor. Which it wasn't. Through the open doorway, he could see the top of the dumbwaiter, and—if he stuck his face in really close and peered through the four-inch gap—the dinner dishes, with about a fist-ful of meat sauce and noodles pushed to one side and a small tower of orange peels, and the lower half of the guitar case inside. His not-quite-emptied glass of milk and his book were hidden from view.

Pressing the button on the second floor did nothing but cause a whir-ring and grinding sound and then silence. This was not good. Baz's guitar was now stuck inside.

Not that the guitar was in any hurry to go anywhere now, he thought, fuming mad. He reached down inside the elevator car and wrapped his fingers around the neck of the guitar. Maybe he could slip it through the tiny gap between the car roof and the dumbwaiter ledge. Moving slowly, he managed to get the headstock and neck through the opening, but the instrument's curvy body was far too thick and wide to squeeze through.

He wasn't willing to risk damaging the guitar further. Baz's old onstage dents were one thing. Brand-new scrapes from the son of a rock star bashing it through a narrow crack might cut the value in half. Resting the guitar gently back inside the dumbwaiter, Jack strummed his fingers uselessly on the roof of the car. "Damn!" he muttered, leaning against the wall and staring at the floor.

He was standing on the very spot where Mrs. Scaub had found his father's body. "Right under the stupide-waiter," she'd said. The *New York Times* and the *Boston Globe* had both used her words as a headline above a photo of the upper hallway. Jack didn't set foot on the second floor for a long time after, even asked his grandmother to move his bed to a spare room one floor up.

He sneezed again and stood up straight, staring at the closed door to Baz's room. The one room in the house he rarely entered. Sighing, he turned and headed downstairs, hoping to have a chance to speak to Harlan. Apologize again. Things had been awfully quiet between them. Ever since . . . well, in the last couple of days.

Downstairs, he treated himself to taking the long way into the kitchen—through the much warmer dining room and into the butler's pantry, where any good butler would likely be found nipping from a brandy snifter on a frosty morning like this. Crossing the enormous kitchen, he stopped. Something was different, felt different. And it wasn't just the purplish walls. He spun around.

Sitting at the kitchen table, *his* kitchen table, was a small girl.

Too stunned to speak, he stared. Her feet didn't even touch the ground; they just swung back and forth under the table. A skinny little thing with chin-length blond hair and a pointy jawline, she looked up from her toast, which she held in wooly red mittens, and smiled. "Jack! Hi." One of her front teeth was shorter than the other.

He stared at her for a moment before he realized she was the girl from his front stoop. The one with the randy stallion and the aversion to selling almonds.

"Uh." He looked around for Harlan, who must have let her in.

"He's gone to school early. Melissa wanted to meet him in the caf before class, he said."

Shit. He'd left. Praying Melissa wasn't meeting Harlan to break up with him, Jack rubbed his head and exhaled hard. He looked at the child. "Who are you, anyway?"

"Lucie. From next door." She appeared to be wearing some kind of skater's skirt—a red, shiny one that flared at the bottom—and a patterned sweater. A red woolen hat matched the mitts.

"From the Ballard house?"

"Lucinda Ballard." She nodded, taking a delicate bite so as not to get wool in her teeth. "I always knew it was cold in here, but not this cold."

"Yes, we're, uh, having furnace troubles. Did Harlan let you in?"

She shook her head. "He was still sleeping. I came in real quiet." A handful of small, pale freckles were sprinkled across her nose. "I heard your phone call. You sure swear a lot."

"Was the door unlocked? Is that how you—?"

"The hole." She pointed with the thumb of her mitten toward the butler's pantry. "The hole behind our hutch in the dining room. I crawled right in."

His hole. Thankfully, he hadn't slept there last night, or he'd have woken to bony elbows and knees landing atop his face.

"Coffee's on," she said with a nod toward the counter, where a half-pot sat warming on its heating element. "And don't worry, I hardly take any milk in mine, so there's still lots for you."

He poured himself a cup, nearly overflowing, and skipped the milk altogether. He needed a jolt. A big one. He sat at the table, opposite Lucie, and rubbed his chin.

She clicked her tongue against the roof of her mouth and stared at him through colorless lashes, awaiting his response.

Jack gulped his scalding coffee. "Do your parents know where you are?"

"Mom's at Pilates. Dad's away. And you better watch out; Mom said she heard voices in the dining room the other day. She thinks the walls between our houses must be thin as Kleenex."

"What about school?"

"I called in sick. Listen." She sat up taller and jutted out her chin, deepening her voice. "Good morning, Mrs. Myers, my daughter Lucinda will not be at school today. She's got the chilblains."

"Chilblains? What are they?"

Lucinda shrugged. "I don't know. I read about them in an old book once. But Mrs. Myers sure didn't want me to come to school and give 'em to everyone. My mom'll never know. She's out for the whole day. Anyway"—she pulled a bit of red yarn from her coffee and sniffed—"if she says anything, she knows she'll just get bitten in the ankle."

Jack squinted. "So he does bite, then?"

"Who?"

"The big black dog. The one that tries to break through the front window to get at my . . . friend when he stops by. Sounds like quite a beast."

She giggled with crumbs in her teeth. "I know."

"Frankly, I'm surprised your parents would have such an animal in the house; you can't be more than seven years old."

"Nine and three quarters, and they have no choice about the big black dog."

"Why not?"

"I *am* the big black dog."

Jack looked up. "You mean all the barking and scrabbling? It's you?"

She shrugged her tiny shoulders. "I just have to be real careful to bite high up. Not near her toes. That's why I aim high."

Narrowing his eyes, Jack said, "Why bite your mother in the first place? She seems like a lovely woman."

Lucinda snorted and rolled her eyes. "You only think that because she's crazy for your dad. She plays his music in her car all the time." She pointed at the sugar bowl. "Can I have some sugar?"

Hm. Sadly, Samantha was one of the few remaining Baz fans on the planet. Sliding the blue bowl across the table, Jack said, "It seems to me that skipping school and biting ankles might not be much better than swearing. I hope you don't swear as well. Or smoke."

Stirring her coffee, she considered this. "Swearing's rude. And smoking kills. Biting can only kill me if I swallow a toenail." Her eyes widened. "Especially if it's all fungussy and gets into my stomach and latches on tight, rotting me from the inside out. Slowly eating away at my stomach lining and making everything turn all green and crusty and hard. But that won't happen. 'Cause I always—"

"I know. Aim high."

She nodded and licked her spoon. "My mother says you hide inside your house all day, every day. That's why I came in. To see if she's right."

"I am *not* hiding."

She looked at him doubtfully.

"I'm not *hiding*."

"Then why won't you get rid of the dead bird beside your steps?"

He laughed. "Because I've never seen a dead bird beside my steps."

"Why don't you go right now? Go and see the bird?"

"I might. After you crawl back through the hole in my wall and I finish my coffee."

"It's frozen solid, you know. Soon it'll be stuck to the sidewalk and buried under the snow and it's *exactly* where I want to build my skating rink. Right between our front stoops. If you leave it all winter, I'll never get to practice my skating. And then when spring comes, you'll have to worry about maggots. Once the snow melts, the dead bird will start to putrefy and stink until it's squirming and bubbling with maggots. Eventually. Did you ever think of that?" She stood up and started skating across the black-and-white tiled floor in her socks.

"You should probably skate at the park. There's a huge rink there. You won't have room for a rink between the houses."

She twirled in a circle on one leg. "My parents can't take me." She twirled faster.

"Stop that, that spinning." It was making Jack dizzy watching her. He stared into his coffee. "Why can't they take you to lessons? Lessons are only . . . what? Once or twice a week?"

"They have their jobs and classes and stuff."

This Samantha didn't have an hour to spare for a skating class?

Still spinning, Lucie asked, "What happened to your cat's face?"

"Mrs. Brady? Ran into a snowplow a few years back."

"Looks kinda gross. Like her head's turned inside out or something."

"Yes, well." Jack had no answer to this. It did rather look like his head was inside out.

"Are you a hit man?"

Jack spat a mouthful of coffee back into the cup and wiped his lips. "What?"

"A hit man. You don't have to answer out loud. Just tap your finger once for yes, twice for no. Just in case."

"In case of what?"

Glancing left, then right, she leaned closer and bugged her eyes. "The feds." She straightened and stared at his hands, waiting for her answer.

"I'm not a hit man!"

"Were you ever a hit man?"

"No!"

"Mm. You look like one I saw in a movie once. Only he was nicer than you."

Jack pushed his hands through his hair and closed his eyes. Maybe when he opened them, she'd be gone.

She wasn't. "Watch this." She jumped in the air and spun at the same time. "I call it a spinny-hop single. If I had more space, I could do a spinny-hop double."

"Don't you have *anyone* who can take you for proper lessons? On actual ice?"

She shook her head no, while holding one leg straight out behind her and spreading her arms out wide. "I call this a birdwalk tippy glider. Pretend I'm going really fast. Pretend my hair's really long and flying out behind me." Jack watched as she tilted her face up into the rushing wind. Then, presumably having slowed to a reasonable speed, she lowered her back leg and walked into the butler's pantry toward the dining room. "Thanks for the coffee. And don't forget about the maggots."

Sighing deeply, Jack swallowed the rest of his coffee. A nagging feeling had settled over him like a thick layer of grime. But what was it? Certainly, it was unexpected to find a queer little nine-year-old girl sitting at your kitchen table—wearing mittens, drinking your coffee, and nagging you about swearing—but that wasn't quite it. It was much more than that.

He crossed the room, tugged open a junk drawer, and dug out a few tools to use to fix the dumbwaiter. A Phillips screwdriver. A pair of rusty pliers and a miniature hammer, though what he'd do with them, he didn't really know.

As he was stomping toward the old elevator, tools in hand, it struck him: this peculiar child with the maggot obsession reminded him of someone.

But whom?

•   •   •

TWISTING THE SCREWDRIVER, he tightened the brass plate covering the elevator push buttons. He'd secured anything that seemed loose, but it wasn't helping. The problem lay in the gears and pulleys inside the shaft. Or maybe even, God forbid, the motor itself. And he definitely wasn't going to shimmy up from the fourth-floor doorway and start mucking around with something he knew nothing about. Especially when one wrong move might send him plummeting down to the cellar.

He needed a dumbwaiter repairman.

He needed some bucks.

Back downstairs in the kitchen, Mrs. Brady squatted on the kitchen table, licking the crumbs off Lucinda's plate. He looked up at Jack as he entered the room, and rolled his eye.

"Scat!" Jack stomped his foot and pulled the back door wide open, sending the cat tearing crookedly outside. Mrs. Brady's peripheral vision and depth perception seriously impaired by the loss of his eye, he tended to run in very much the same fashion as a grocery cart with broken back wheels that twirl all the way around—on a forty-five-degree angle, with his haunches swung far ahead on his good side.

The neighborhood birds were well acquainted with Mrs. Brady's right-sided limitations and found countless ways to ridicule him. Some days, they lined themselves up on the eaves of the old garage on the right side of the yard and mocked him silently. Other times, a young bird, one with particularly good reflexes, would walk along on the cat's right side, mimicking his every move. It drove Mrs. Brady crazy; he could smell the earthy tang of young feathers steeped in worms and puddle water, but no matter how many times he circled toward it, the delicious scent remained just out of reach.

Today, as the cat made his lopsided way across the snow, leaving two sets of tracks behind him, the birds took turns swooping down past his head, the broken side, and back up to the overhead wires, where they chattered and trembled with delight. They watched Mrs. Brady stop and look around, the end of his tail twitching with the instincts of a hunter.

Jack couldn't watch anymore. He turned away from the closed door and pulled a can out of the fridge, scooping an extra-large helping of

Pretty Kitty cat food, turkey-and-giblets flavor, into the metal bowl on the floor.

He was rinsing the meaty fork when the phone rang. Dropping the fork into the sink, he wiped his hands on the seat of his pants and hurried to the black wall-phone. Maybe it was Carmichael-Jones, changing his mind about the Brits.

"Yes?" he said with enthusiasm.

"Is that Jack?" It was a woman's voice. "Dorrie Allsop, from Heritage Estates? Remember we met—"

"I remember. Hello, Dorrie."

"I know just what you're thinking: this woman has flat-out abandoned me *and* my house. Though"—she laughed—"in your case, you probably breathed a huge sigh of relief."

She paused for air here, or for Jack's reassurance that he hadn't. Jack said, "I've been very busy, actually . . ."

"Good. There's very little worse than having nothing at all to do. That's why I went into real estate in the first place. There's always somebody moving. Always. People get transferred, or else they have twins and need to move into a three-bedroom, or they get divorced—those are the real sad ones."

"I'm actually in the middle of something here. Was there something you needed?"

"See? There I went again. I'm glad you stopped me. I'm bringing a couple around for our first showing. A couple of art dealers from Cambridge who want to live closer to their work. Now, his name is Milton Yaeger and she's, wait a minute . . . I know I have her name somewhere." Jack heard papers being ruffled. "Ah. Yes. She's called Alannah Yearwood. Both with Y names. What are the odds of that?" She paused, Jack thought, to give him time to calculate the numeric probability. "Anyway, I'll be coming at eleven tomorrow morning. Sound good?"

"Tomorrow?" Jack struggled to think up an excuse. What could he say—I'm going out? "Well, I was planning to do a little painting tomorrow." He'd been thinking very carefully about adding a splash of yellow into the white paint he'd last used for the kitchen walls. Or, he should say, the violet paint. Not enough to show as yellow, but just enough to warm the walls with the slightest blush of amber undertones. To give a splash of antiquity, while cutting the undercurrent of iciness that was teetering way too close to the edge of modern to give Jack any peace while he had his morning coffee.

"We'll be out of your hair in no time. Now, there are a couple of things I'd like you to do. To prepare for the Yaeger-Yearwoods. First off, can we slip the litter box into the backyard? It would help freshen the basement."

"No. Mrs. Brady might mess in the house."

"Oh." She sighed, sounding deflated. "Alrighty. What's next . . . ?" He pictured her at her desk, scanning some sort of checklist they'd given her in real estate school, every line on her jangling phone flashing like mad. "Ah. Did the exterminator arrive yesterday?"

"No." He could practically hear the tiny X being scrawled next to Exterminator with a No. 2 pencil.

"Did you get time to wash the windows?"

"No."

"Clear out the clutter in the office, below the window?"

"Ah, let me think . . . no."

"Fix the drip in the kitchen tap?"

"No. Sorry."

"Get some heat pumping through the house?"

"Now that I have done. Sort of." The dining room was damned near tropical. Loud checkmark.

She paused a moment. "Is . . . Mrs. Brady still wearing my bow?"

Jack glanced out the back window to see a bird pecking Mrs. Brady in the ribs with its sharp little beak. The bow drooped down flat against the cat's right side. "Dorrie? I've got to go. We'll see you tomorrow, okay?"

As he started to replace the receiver, he heard her call, "If you could pop some cookies in the oven, it might help create a homey—"

The phone clattered in its cradle as Jack yanked open the back door and called Mrs. Brady for breakfast.

DOMINICK PUSHED BACK his Citywide Elevators cap and sniffed. He'd been on the fourth floor, tinkering with the dumbwaiter mechanisms for a good half hour and seemed to be resenting the dumbwaiter's very existence. Lolling about on the floor beside Dominick was Harlan, rooting through the Citywide toolbox and exclaiming "Right on!" whenever some shiny tool caught his fancy.

"Dumbwaiters I repair are not usually this old," Dominick said, sniffling and kicking his toolbox out of Harlan's reach. A streak of grime slashed Dominick's face into two, and his nose was red and swollen from the monster-sized cold he was battling.

Jack made sure to stand a good two feet back. He'd managed to successfully fight off his own burgeoning virus from the other day and was not willing to entertain any further microbes quite yet. "Yes, well, it's an old house," Jack explained.

"Old as all hell," Harlan added.

"Most people nowadays, they replace 'em. You know, put in new guts."

"Right," Jack said. "As you can see, I still have the original 'guts.'"

Harlan snorted in disagreement. Jack supposed, after the debacle with Melissa's mother, it might not be a good time to be discussing "guts" of any kind.

"You've never upgraded your system?" Dominick asked.

"As you can see, no."

Dominick sniffed again and hoisted up his drooping pants. "Yeah, these parts are maybe ninety, maybe a hundred years old."

"Mm." The conversation appeared to be jammed tighter than the elevator. "I'd really just like to know if you can fix it." Jack waited until Dominick blew his nose into a rag and dropped it into his toolbox. "Do you think you can repair it?"

"I'm gonna be straight with you. This here machine's a dinosaur. To get this thing up and running, I'd have to locate *antique* parts—from I don't even know where. Maybe another country. Replacement parts alone are going to run you a fortune. And that doesn't include labor and installation." His face seized up, as if he was going to sneeze; he tilted his head back, aiming himself straight toward Jack—who stepped to one side—and then, slowly, relaxed. The sneeze had passed. For now.

"Nice save," said Harlan.

Jack moved closer again. "But isn't labor part of installation? I mean, aren't labor and installation the same thing?"

Without warning, a mighty, thundering sneeze showered Jack with a fine mist of teeming mucus so alive the germs could almost be heard chattering and bustling for position as they prepared for invasion. Dominick smiled. "Sorry there. That one kind of snuck up on me."

"Yes. Apparently so." Jack wiped his face with his sleeve. Harlan pulled a travel-sized bottle of hand sanitizer from the pocket of his cowboy shirt and rubbed antibacterial gel into his hands. "And what about the cost of simply moving the elevator car to the nearest floor, just pushing it far enough so I can retrieve my things? And in the meantime, I could think about whether it's better to repair or replace."

"Replace. Definitely replace." Dominick dropped his tools into the toolbox and snapped the lid shut. "And as for moving it, I'd have to repair it first. Gears have totally seized up. Which means ordering the antique parts from I don't—"

"Yes, yes," Jack interrupted. "From you don't know where. Thank you, Dominick. You've been most helpful."

With toolbox in one hand, Dominick wiped his runny nose with his free hand and held it out to Jack to shake. "Good-bye, then."

Jack stepped backward, holding his hand up straight in front of his chest. "You'd better not risk it," he said. "I've been fighting a cold."

Chapter 10

White Kitchens Sell Houses

Jack?"

Of course, Dorrie was early. Jack scrubbed the paint roller in the kitchen sink and glanced at the clock. Not even ten. Way on the worm side of early. He turned off the taps and shook the water from the fuzzy roller until its fur poked straight out like a waterlogged cat, and set it carefully on a square of paper towel under the sink.

"Jack? You in there? Jack?"

"In the kitchen." He took his time, knowing he had until she pulled her $3.50 pumps from her bag and stuffed the heels full of toilet paper before she'd come clomping back to the kitchen. He wiped the lip of the paint can, every last drop, before pressing down on the lid. Then, covering the can with a soft rag, he tapped all the way around the top to ensure that no air could seep in and prematurely clot his newest shade. Certain that he'd be reproducing this color for years to come, he reached for a black marker and printed FRENCH LINEN on the lid, along with the tinting formula. The most perfect white he'd ever created. Ever seen, actually. Fresh enough to feel lively and clean, while aged just enough to complement the seasoned patina of a 150-year-old house.

He could only hope that oxygenation was kind to the color and that it held its weight after the dreaded one-day curing process.

"The door was unlocked, so I figured I'd come . . ." Dorrie's tangled head poked through the doorway. "Oh, Jack. This isn't a good time to start painting." She hurried in with a small pot of flowers and set it on the kitchen table. The flowers were, of all things, African violets.

"I've finished. Just," he said, opening the cellar door and leaning the paint-roller rod against the cellar steps.

"White?"

"White." It was hard to hold back his smile, waiting for her reaction. Penelope had always hated the white kitchen. Called it soulless. Lifeless. Unimaginative. Dorrie shouldn't prove to be too different. Women, he grinned to himself, loved drama.

She pushed a tumble of hair from her face. Noticing she'd removed the tag from her jacket sleeve, Jack wondered how she came to eventually notice it was there. Had her boss cast a beady, sardonic stare as she reached for the jangling phone? Had she snagged it on her lip while reaching up to scratch her forehead? Or had it simply been torn off, without any fanfare at all, as she slid her bagful of cheap pumps up her arm and onto her shoulder?

"I'm so relieved it's white," she gushed. "You know what they say, white kitchens sell houses. They said that in my real estate course, anyway. White walls, white cabinets, and white counters give the potential buyer the sense of good hygiene. And this factor can be amplified when the toaster and electric blender are cleverly hidden away in the lower cabinetry. Very wise choice. Now"—she smiled up at Jack, pulling a fresh red ribbon out of her pocket—"where is that cat?"

ALANNAH YEARWOOD STEPPED out of her stacked-heel boots and onto the floor, wrapping her coat tightly around what appeared to be a thin, fragile body. Lank, black hair, really more like long fuzz, cupped the sides of her face. "If you'd been quicker, we'd have gotten the parking space *first*," she snapped at Milton Yaeger, who pulled rubber overshoes off his black loafers and shot back with, "You can't squeeze a Range Rover into a cluttered space like that! Not with all those mountains of snow."

She shifted her droopy eyes, ringed beneath with dark, smudgy half-circles, toward Dorrie and Jack, who both smiled uneasily. "Would one of you inform him that that's what SUVs are for? Or shall I?"

Jack saw his chance and took it. "Frankly, I'm surprised you found a spot at all. My guests generally have to park two blocks up, closer to the, um, asylum."

"Asylum?" asked Milton. "What kind of asylum?"

"I swear to God, Milton, you've got to come out of your little Louis Vuitton box and live a little," said Alannah. "If we're going to move to the city, we're going to be closer to the mentally unstable. Get over it." She smacked her gum and looked from Dorrie's Heritage Estates blazer up to her face. "So, is this the foyer or what?"

WHILE DORRIE POINTED out the rusty pipes under the bathroom sink, Jack checked his watch. Certainly, if the Yaeger-Yearwoods didn't murder each other, they'd soon drop dead from Dorrie's endless chatter. They'd been in the house for nearly half an hour and had seen the disco ball and Harlan's carpeted ceiling. They knew about the broken furnace and the jammed dumbwaiter with the rotting spaghetti sauce. When Dorrie admitted to the rodent habitat behind the slumbering furnace, Alannah nearly lost her lunch. And any moment, once they reached the fourth floor, they'd see evidence of the leaky roof in the half-filled buckets he'd left out from a particularly rainy period a few weeks prior.

All in all, a successful first showing.

Footsteps sounded in the hall once again.

"We'd have to hire a very talented plasterer to smooth over the damage on the walls," Milton commented. "I've never seen so much damage."

Pompous ass, thought Jack.

"No," Alannah said. "Rip out the plaster. It's too old. Probably filled with dampness and mold. We'd have to have it ripped to the bones and install drywall instead. Drywall is a much flatter surface to display paintings."

Dorrie asked, "Do you ever buy paintings of really big cabbage roses? Because I have a good friend—"

"We own the Yaeg-Wood Gallery on Newbury. We're strictly avant-garde." Milton Yaeger's voice. "No flowers."

"Oh." Dorrie sounded deflated.

"The high ceilings would be ideal," said Milton.

"Maybe you're even ready to make an offer?" Dorrie asked hopefully.

"I really don't like all these holes," Milton Yaeger said again.

"I could write up the offer in the freshly painted white kitchen."

"Some of the holes are *huge*," Alannah said with a whine.

"It's clearly never been cared for," Milton added. "Shameful if you ask me."

Jack stood up and stormed into the hall, nearly colliding with Alannah Yearwood and her shadowy eyes. Just as he opened his mouth to give the Yaeger-Yearwoods a lesson on respecting what has come before them, Dorrie stepped in front of him.

She squared her shoulders and glared at Milton. "These holes were made by the legendary Baz Madigan," she said. "Surely as a man of the arts, you can see that 'smoothing over' the markings of a genius would be like, like painting over a precious painting. Like spackling over the cracks in a priceless antique. There are certain things you just don't do."

"What's she talking about?" Alannah moaned, rubbing her feet.

Jack felt his face flush hot. "She's talking about my father and the house he left behind. She's talking about respecting history. Respecting what came before you and appreciating a valuable home like this for what it is. Resisting the *urge to purge*."

"Oh my God, move out of the way." Alannah Yearwood pushed past them and started toward the stairs. "He's going to be sick."

"I HOPE YOU didn't honk in *my* bathroom," said Harlan later, his mouth full of salad. Only recently had he deigned to communicate with his father in anything beyond grunts and shrugs. Words, however crass they may be, were vastly preferable to simian body language and virtual silence. Not that, under the circumstances, Jack could blame him.

As usual, Harlan treated dinner with great respect, changing his clothes to mark the occasion. Tonight he'd chosen a blue-and-red two-piece stretch jumpsuit worthy of any small-town trampoline competition. Mostly blue, the shirt had two jazzy racing stripes across each bicep, and the pants had the same stripes across one thigh, and on the other, a vertical stripe from hip to flared heel.

"I managed to contain myself, but your concern is touching." Jack plunked a dish of macaroni and cheese in the center of the table and admired it. After mixing in the milk, butter, and packet of orange powder, Jack had come up with a clever way to spiff up the overcooked noodles.

He reached for what was left of a bag of busted-up pretzels and sprinkled them over the top. Then he popped the whole thing under the broiler for few minutes.

It looked delicious.

Jack scooped several heaping spoonfuls onto Harlan's plate and headed back to the counter to slice the bruises off the last apple. What was left of the apple appeared somewhat meager, so he flipped the bruised parts upside down and arranged all the slices into a fan shape. Fancy macaroni deserved some sort of celebratory side dish.

"I don't want to move," Harlan said. "I've finally got my room the way I want it."

"As it turns out, your room being 'just the way you want it' is a major deterrent to any prospective buyer. However, one good thing did come of their visit. Before they left, Milton Yaeger came into the kitchen to inquire about the paint color. Loved my perfect white. His taste in wives and business partners may be disgraceful, but his eye for subtlety in hue is to be commended. Highly."

Harlan looked up at the white walls and shook his head in disbelief. "So, is she really terrible, this real estate agent?"

Jack sat back in his seat and took a deep breath. She had pointed out every flaw. Pointed out the very defect in the cat she'd worked so hard to disguise. It had been magic to watch, actually. She was a master of real estate don'ts.

But she stood up for the house. Stood up for Jack, even though she risked the sale. He took a bite of macaroni. "She's not so bad."

Harlan shook his head, stabbing a clump of noodles. "Bummer," he said. "Maybe you'll have to step in. Rattle some chains in the basement or stuff a few day-old fish sticks into all the curtain rods." He paused to hold the empty milk carton over his glass, waiting until the last drop splashed into the glass. "She does have pretty nice ankles; I was noticing the other day. The day she was trying to revive you."

"You're joking." Jack laughed. "She's got about as much sex appeal as that cat over there." Harlan turned to face Mrs. Brady, who had passed out on the windowsill, flat on his back, with only his bad side showing. His mouth, upside down and pointed toward the kitchen table, was hanging open just enough for his scratchy pink tongue to poke out a half inch or so.

Although, just after the Yaeger-Yearwoods finally got themselves out the door and the house fell silent, while Dorrie had been pulling on her little leather boots and prattling on about throwing a surprise party for Rose, she had looked up at Jack and laughed. Not a carefully constructed, ladylike laugh, as Penelope would have offered up. More of an accidental moment of pure excitement. Her eyes shone, her nose crinkled, and her hair fell in front of her face. She wanted so badly to please Rose, who, aside from her operation, appeared to have had a hard year, losing custody of her son to her husband and fighting with her landlord. Then she caught herself—possibly silently reprimanding herself for dropping her real estate hat—and slipped back into professional mode, promising Jack an open house in the coming weeks.

Her laugh rang in the empty foyer long after she'd gone.

Harlan snorted, turning away from Mrs. Brady. "That cat probably gets more action than you. *Definitely* gets more action than you. And is a hell of a lot less picky about potential mates."

Jack pushed his chair back to answer the ringing phone.

"I hope I'm not interrupting anything," said the voice on the other end. Penelope's voice.

"If, by anything, you mean a lovely pasta dinner with my son, then I'm afraid you are."

"Are you entertaining Melissa again?" Her voice sounded playful. She'd obviously heard about the smashing success of his evening with Melissa and Harlan.

"Harlan and I are dining man-to-man tonight. But thank you for asking. I'd invite you to join, but there's really just enough for the two of us."

"Sweet. Listen, I'd like to ask you a favor. We'd like Harlan to stay over two days this coming weekend. Friday and Saturday night. Yale's chiropractic office is having a holiday party on Friday and he'd like to bring Harlan along, show off his future stepson."

Jack was silent for a moment. Stepson. He'd never thought of Harlan's relationship with Yale offering up specific titles. Somehow, it stepped—no, stomped—all over Jack's place in his son's life. "Do you think that's such a good idea? I mean"—he glanced at Harlan, who was stuffing pretzel-crusted macaroni into his face and reading a magazine, not paying any attention to his father's phone call—"the *event* hasn't taken place yet. Any number of things could happen between now and then. That sort of introduction, once made, can be taken very seriously by this particular person. And very confusing if the entire event winds up in smoke."

"*My wedding* is not going to end up in smoke, Jack. And Harlan wants to go to the party. He's even bringing Melissa. Ask him."

Harlan laughed at something in the magazine and snorted a bit of milk through his nose, which he wiped on the tablecloth, before turning the page.

"No. It's irrelevant. Friday, he and I have plans. Immovable plans." He didn't, of course, have plans, immovable or not. But if she was willing to remarry and try to feed his son a second father on a Friday night—rather redundant in Jack's opinion; the boy had a perfectly good father already—he wasn't going to make things easy for her.

"We haven't heard back from you regarding the wedding."

"How so?"

"You haven't RSVP'd. Are you making some kind of postmarital statement?"

"No. We've had a bit of trouble with our mail, that's all. January fifth, hmm." Jack paused, checking his imaginary date book. "What time?"

"Funny. About the time you'd be piling your dinner dishes in the dumbwaiter to send them up to your room, where you can eat in solitude. Away from the crowds on the main floor."

"If you're talking about Mrs. Brady, he follows me up."

"Hm. Very social of you to dine with the cat. Are you coming?"

Jack scratched his eyebrows. Nothing sounded more distasteful to him than filling himself up with Nervy Durvies (a waste of three perfectly good pills) and getting all dressed up so he could sit in a roomful of Penelope's relatives and watch her publicly affirm that she was never coming back to him. She'd look beautiful, of course, and would be wearing knee-high lace boots under her gown, to hide her calves from the videographer later, when Yale peeled the garter off her thigh with his teeth. And Yale, Yale would probably be glowing with health and vigor, with the perma-tan Jack always pictured on him and big, gleaming white teeth. In Vitamin White.

And Penelope's sister would be there, shooting sorrowful glances at Jack, glances that said, Buck up, little soldier, it could happen for you, too. One day. Maybe. Her father, the judge, would ask him all sorts of questions about his comings and goings. And all Jack would have to discuss would be his stayings, really.

"It would be good for Harlan to see his mother and father in a positive coparenting relationship, don't you think?" Score two for Penelope in the "I care more about Harlan's state of mind than you do" contest.

"Yeah. Okay, I'll come."

"Terrific. And be sure to send back the reply card. It's already stamped, so you don't have to go to the store to buy stamps. Just stick it in a mailbox."

"I can get my own stamps, thank you." I can walk to the store if it kills me, he thought, and I can pay the fifty cents or whatever it costs for a goddamned stamp.

"I'm saying you don't need to. It's stamped already."

Jack thought he'd get his own damned stamps and stick them on top of Penelope's wedding stamps. Just for the hell of it.

"And what about the mailbox?" she asked, before he answered.

"What about the mailbox?"

"I mean, how will you get to it? Will Harlan take you? It's just that I'm not the one tallying the reply cards. It's one of Yale's sisters. So it's important that you send it in and mark whether you're going to be one or two."

"Two?"

"You're welcome to bring a date."

Date. Who on earth would he bring as a date? Dr. Snowden? The little kid with the lopsided teeth who barks like a Rottweiler and crawls through the wall? The real estate agent from hell? "I'll send the little card. Is there anything else? My dinner is getting cold."

"Just that the affair is black tie. You know, tuxedos and long gowns. Yale's family is very formal and insists on the affair being extremely elegant."

Jack wished she'd stop calling it an affair.

She continued, "So, if you don't have one—" She paused. She knew perfectly well he didn't have one. "Yale and I would like to rent one for you. It's not a problem; we're doing it for all the ushers—"

"No. I'll get my own." He slammed the phone into its cradle with a crash, causing Harlan to look up from his magazine for the first time.

"Telemarketers?" Harlan asked, orange cheese gathered at the corners of his mouth.

Jack said nothing, pushing his plate toward the center of the table. Presumptuous woman! Taking pity on him . . . assuming he needed handouts from her vigorous fiancé. He could just picture the two of them lying in bed, discussing The Problem of Jack. She'd be wearing nothing—she'd always slept in the nude—and Yale, God only knew what a guy named Yale wore to bed. Probably silky pajama bottoms and nothing else, so he could admire his pecs while watching reality TV.

"Jack's flat broke," she'd say. "He'll probably show up in some ratty suit from his high school graduation."

"It must be prevented," Yale would answer, gazing at his chest and flexing his bulging man breasts in the glow of the television. "My formal family would take it as an assault. Whatever is to be done . . . ?"

"I know," she'd say, popping out from the satin bed sheets Yale favored. "You're so wealthy and successful and tanned, Yale." He'd beam here—still flexing, a guy as wholesome as Yale can surely beam and flex simultaneously—teeth gleaming in the semidarkness, maybe casting off one dramatic sparkle that would hit Penelope in the eye, momentarily blinding her. Once she could see again, she'd continue, "Maybe *you* can pay for Jack's tux."

With an uncertain glance at his bulging wallet on the bedside table, Yale'd hesitate just long enough for the smile to fall off Penelope's admiring face, then grin. "All right. I'll do it. Anything to prevent your ex-husband from ruining our day." Of course, she'd throw her arms around him at this point, at least as far as she could reach around his gigantic, muscular torso. And he'd hug her back, mashing her face into his bulging chest.

ABOUT SIXTY SECONDS later, he slammed the front door behind him and trotted down the front steps, beside himself with fury—no, not just fury—humiliation and no small amount of disgust. For a moment, he'd considered charging up to the third-floor medicine cabinet for pills but changed his mind, knowing full well he'd never be able to get the child-proof lid off in his agitated state.

As he passed the first house, he heard his own front door swing open behind him and imagined Harlan's cheese-covered mouth gaping open as he watched his crazy old dad doing something so terribly normal for anyone else but utterly and completely outrageous for Jack.

"Dad," Harlan called, his voice laced with worry. "What are you doing?"

Jack shoved his hands into his pockets and trudged across the frozen sludge toward Beacon Hill's tony alternative to the corner store.

"Dad! Hang on! Wait for me."

Jack didn't answer. So long as he could maintain his anger, stay lost in the churning bubble of hate that was forming in his stomach, he'd be able to get his stamps and get home again. Maybe he'd even pick up a whole carton of eggs—for therapeutic purposes. Wouldn't that give Snowden a thrill? He should not need his son's help. He marched past two town houses very similar to his own but beautifully maintained, with black iron mailboxes and fancy new coach lamps on either side of the front doors, then a Thai restaurant and a small gallery, before passing a pumpkin-colored front door. He slowed momentarily, mostly to be repulsed at the combination of orange door with red bricks and wonder how such a garishly modern hue had escaped the beady eye of Beacon Hill's architectural commission.

Quickening his pace again, he focused on his blistering anger, rechanneling it toward his ex-wife, where it belonged. He couldn't afford to lose his focus.

His breath sputtered from his mouth in puffs of steam. Damn, it was cold. The snow under his boots crunched in the way that made you wonder if being outside was even safe. Inside his nose, icy shards of pain pierced his tender flesh. He flipped up the collar of his canvas jacket and tucked his chin beneath the zipper, which soon frosted up with his breath.

He was almost there. He'd almost done it. As he saw the antique brass sign of the Smoking Bostonian, his heart began to flutter and lurch. Keep going. March forward. Just keep marching forward, mad, mad, mad.

A group of girls stood outside the shop, smoking, most of them hatless and gloveless. Teenagers didn't feel the cold, he thought. Didn't really know much about fear yet, either. One of them shivered, with nothing more than a sweatshirt and the burning embers at the tip of her cigarette to keep her warm.

Footsteps slapped against the frozen sidewalk behind him as Harlan raced full-speed to catch up. Panting, he grabbed Jack by the coat. "What are you thinking? You know you can't do this." He stopped Jack and tried to turn him back toward the house.

"I'm okay," Jack said, knocking Harlan's hand away. "Go back home. I'm fine."

"That was no telemarketer. It was Mom, wasn't it? Is that what this is all about?"

Jack walked on, tripping on a chunk of ice and nearly landing face-first on the sidewalk. By the time he righted himself, his head was whirling so fast he nearly stumbled again. He slowed his step. Penelope, he thought. Don't let her win again. She doesn't have to win every time. A feeble burst of anger shot through him but was too frail and thin to convince his spinning head that anger was any longer his principal driving force. It was hard to be angry in the face of death. And if this spinning got any stronger, Jack was convinced that was exactly where it would lead him.

This was very bad. Fear was rising up taller and stronger than his anger.

Just then, one of the teenage girls called out. "Harlan? Is that you? Out here without a coat?"

Jogging beside his father, Harlan looked up and nodded, grabbing Jack's coat again. "Let's go back. Now," he whispered.

Jack's steps grew slower still until he came to a stop, leaning forward on his thighs to regain his balance. He shouted "No!" inside his head so violently he thought he might have screamed out loud. Don't stop now! You've almost done it. So close. Just get past the girls and into the store. Mumble, "One stamp, please," and throw all your change on the counter. Pick it up and run the whole way home. It'll take five minutes, tops. Do it, Jack. *Do it*.

"Harlan," the girl sang. "Come over here. Sandra's got something she wants to tell you." The girls laughed.

Another girl asked, "Is *he* your dad?"

"Dad. Turn around. These girls are from my school," Harlan hissed.

"We're going for coffee over at Brewzer's. Wanna come?" the first girl asked.

"He's got a girlfriend, Ginny," someone else said.

"Isn't that Hermit-Boy?" a horrified voice whispered.

"Is your dad okay? Maybe we should call 911."

Turning his back to the crowd, Harlan said, "Dad. Let's go. Now."

Jack thought of Penelope, haughty and mocking. Then he thought about the picture above the television, with Baz holding him. Baz would laugh at him, tell him not to be a weenie, just "get the fawk" into that store.

The girls seemed like a hazy mirage now, like the kind of fake steaming pond he used to see up ahead on the road from behind the huge windshield of the tour bus. Only much noisier and moving toward Harlan.

Too dizzy. His heart crashed around inside his jacket. He could no longer feel his hands. He could tell himself it was the cold, but it wasn't. Still bent over his legs, he turned away from the Smoking Bostonian sign. Suddenly a big girl appeared in front of him, talking at him, but he couldn't process her words. Harlan was waving her away. Almost shouting at her. She was saying something about calling for help.

"He's fine," Harlan said, looking as if he was going to be sick himself. "It's okay."

That was all Jack needed. A 911 call and being strapped to a board by guys in uniforms and stuffed into the bowels of an ambulance, red lights bouncing off the elegant buildings of Battersea Road. All in front of his son's friends. That oughta inspire some filial pride in Harlan.

He shook his head no, and straightened. Taking a shaky step, he stumbled a little and half-limped, half-ran back toward his house with Harlan stomping along beside him, his face tucked into his chest.

"Harlan, wait!" the giantess called. "The ambulance is on its way. Stay here."

Jack trotted faster, cupping his hands over his ears for warmth. If he could have made himself disappear at that moment, he'd have done anything to make it happen.

He passed the pumpkin-orange door, which only made his heart race faster. Orange was a color that stimulated the circulatory system, strengthened the heartbeat, something Jack certainly didn't need. Orange was not a color to be embraced by anyone suffering from *any* kind of anxiety.

Jack staggered up his front steps and into the house. He headed straight for the kitchen, where he sank into a chair, still winded and dizzy. When Harlan came in behind him, Jack tried to make light of the situation. "Those were friends of yours?"

Harlan took a Coke out of the fridge and kicked the door shut. "Friends? I wish. They're only the hottest girls in school. Not only that, but they're total gossips! Monday morning should be just buzzing with tales of Harlan and his daddy's Big Night Out!" He flipped open the can and guzzled, then slammed it onto the counter and stared out the window into the darkness.

"I'm sorry those girls had to be out there, Harlan. But I needed to prove to myself that I—"

Harlan spun around. "News flash, Dad! *People are out there!* If you plan on having these panic attacks on the outside, guess what? People are going to see you. And in this neighborhood, whether I like it or not, you're known as my father!" He snatched the car keys off the window-sill and opened the back door. "I'll be at Mom's."

Chapter 11

What the Gray Squirrel Saw

Jack woke the next day hung over from lack of sleep. Harlan's car hadn't coasted into the garage until long after one a.m., by which time, Jack had convinced himself the boy would only be staying long enough to pack up his Wallabies and scribble down some instructions about how to dismantle the disco ball in his room and safely ship it to Penelope's. It wasn't until nearly two that all sounds from Harlan's room ceased and Jack felt it was safe to finally fall asleep.

He needed to talk to someone. This was when having a friend would really come in handy. Wait a minute. Jack pushed the covers off his head, reached for the phone, and dialed Dr. Snowden's office line. At this point, even a hired friend would do. He listened while the phone rang two, three, four times, and then went to message: "You have reached the workplace of Dr. Myron Snowden . . ." Jack hung up. Of course, a friendship is much more satisfying if said friend shells out his home phone number.

His eyes drifted toward his wallet, lying next to him on the bedside table. Leaning on one elbow, he reached for it and pulled out a business card. There was someone he needed to speak to. Sort of.

She picked up right away. "Dorrie Allsop. Heritage Estates."

"Hey, Dorrie. It's Jack."

"Jack, hi. If you're calling to find out if the Yaeger-Yearwoods are making an offer, they aren't. I just got off the phone with Alannah."

No surprise to Jack, but welcome news, nonetheless. "Well, cheer up. What are the chances a person would sell their very first house on their very first try? It probably takes a fair bit of practice, this whole selling-four-and-a-half-million-dollar-property thing."

"Maybe. Is there something I can do for you? Because I'm bowled under with work, here."

"Bowled over," Jack said.

"Pardon me?"

"No, you just said you were bowled under. I'm pretty sure it's bowled over."

"Just a minute, Jack. I have to sign for something." She held her hand over the phone for a moment, then returned. "I'm sorry. Where were we?"

"I was just about to say that your FOR SALE sign seems to be banging against the iron railings around the tree out front. It keeps me up on windy nights. I wonder if there's another place you could put it?"

"Gee, I don't think so. All you've got is cement other than around the tree. There'd be nothing to stick the post into." She paused for a moment. "I've got an idea, why don't you pick up some of those Styrofoam ear plugs? They're terrific at blocking out noise. And they come in neon colors. Green, red, blue. Maybe even yellow. Or maybe it was orange? No, it was definitely yellow. But you've got to be very careful leaving them around if you have pets, which you do. My cousin's cat used to play with them and, one day, completely refused her meals. Well, after a couple of days they took her to the vet and . . ."

He supposed he'd asked for it. With the cordless phone wedged between his shoulder and his ear, he wiggled into his tattered bathrobe, yanked on a pair of yesterday's socks and offered up comments such as "mm-hmm" and "tragic," as he started down the stairs, knees still shaky from the previous night's particularly agonizing public failure.

Shuffling along the main-floor corridor, Jack heard a whole lot of clattering and thumping sounds coming from the kitchen. As Dorrie rattled on and on about the cost of the veterinarian's bill—$3,300—and the number of stitches the cat needed to be sewn up tight—seven—Jack prayed the noises coming from the kitchen weren't Harlan banging the toaster against his freshly painted, perfectly creamy white walls.

He stopped at the kitchen entrance. The little girl from next door was standing on a chair, spreading cream cheese on a badly sliced poppy-seed bagel.

"Excuse me, Dorrie?" he said, interrupting her recount of just how many ear plugs were found in the cat's stomach—three—and what color they were—two neon green, one neon red. "I'll have to call you back." He set the phone down on the table.

"I thought you'd never get up," Lucinda said, pointing toward Jack's coffee cup on the table. Filled with steaming hot coffee. It smelled too good to be true, and he slid into a chair with a yawn.

"How did you get past the big armchair?" he asked. "I can barely move it myself."

"Didn't need to move it. I crawled right under it." Wearing figure skates with blue plastic guards covering the blades, she crossed the room with two creamy bagels and set one in front of Jack. "You're almost out of coffee. I had to make a full pot. On Saturdays, I like to sip a few cups, don't you?"

"I don't eat breakfast."

"I fed your cat."

Jack looked at the cat bowls, where an appreciative Mrs. Brady hunched over his morning feast. He wore a blue *Little House on the Prairie* bonnet, tied neatly under his chin. Dorrie's red bow was nowhere to be seen.

"It's from my Holly Hobbie doll. It's perfect for her, 'cause it hides her missing chunk. Does she have any baby kittens?"

Pouring milk into his mug, Jack grunted. "She's a he."

Lucinda studied the cat again, leaning over to peer underneath his squatting haunches. She stood up and shrugged. "Oh well. He still likes the hat."

Squinting into the morning light, Jack admired his walls. He couldn't have hoped for a better curing. They'd dried into a neutral cream so rich he'd have liked to pour it into his coffee. Very calming. Peaceful. Perfect for a guy like me, he thought.

"You painted again," she said, her jaggedy teeth full of poppy seeds. "What's with all the white?"

"I like white."

"Hm." She tilted her tiny face up and examined the impossibly straight edge where the French Linen met the dark wooden windowsill. A beautifully executed line Jack was particularly proud of. "You should have done red."

Jesus. A red kitchen would send him into cardiac arrest each morning. He'd have to switch to decaffeinated coffee, most certainly. "I prefer the subtlety of white," he repeated.

"I'm starting the rink today. Between our porches. I'm going to shovel it out and pour some water on it, let it freeze. Want to help?"

Jack looked up. "No, no. You go right ahead."

"Whatever. I'm going to pour water on it every day until it gets thicker and thicker and thicker. Until I can skate on it without my blades cracking through and hitting the cement. 'Cause that would damage the metal. Do you skate?"

"No."

"Hm. My mom called you a hermit this week. Are you a real hermit?"

Jack snorted. "Absolutely not. A hermit chooses his seclusion."

She chewed thoughtfully for a moment. "You don't?"

He ignored her. "What grade did you say you were in?"

"Fourth."

"And your sister . . . ?"

She nodded. "Sixth." Sighing, she pulled her red hat farther down over her face and dropped her chin into her hands, which were mittenless this time. She must be adjusting to the cold, Jack thought.

"What do you do for fun over there on your side of the bricks?"

She made a bored face. "Take care of my pet rock, Willie, or read books about girls who skate."

"Does your sister play with you?"

"No. Mostly Rosalind's with my mother."

"And they're not with you?"

She shook her head no.

"Where are they?"

Shrugging, she said, "I don't know. Putting on makeup or watching soaps or something."

"All the time? Don't they hang out with you? Build snowmen or bake cookies?"

Lucinda didn't answer, dipping her nose into her coffee and trying to lick off the drips instead.

"Do they know where you are right now?"

"They're at Rosalind's dance recital. I didn't want to go."

Jack was incensed. How could they ignore this child? It sounded as if she was raising herself in a den of narcissistic wolves. The whole situation was smacking of a lonely childhood he was all too familiar with.

Aha! That was who she reminded him of. Himself. A lost child. "Tell me something, Lucinda . . . does your mother tuck you in at night? Read you bedtime stories? Kiss you good-night?"

Lucie shrugged. "She hugged me once. After IT happened."

"It?"

"They weren't with me. They were watching their soap again."

"Where were you? What happened?"

"I was in my room reading a book about a girl who had a window seat. That was where she sat to look at her pony. I *always* wanted a window seat so *I* could look out at *my* pony. My pretend pony. So I pushed my window up high and just jumped up." She grinned. "Worked pretty good for a minute, too. Until I blew my horse a kiss. I never should have done the kissing part."

The bonneted Mrs. Brady had finished his repast, and Lucie snapped her fingers below the table to coax him into a petting. "Here pretty kitty," she said.

"Why? What happened?"

Pulling the prairie cat onto her lap, she tickled him under his chin. Mrs. Brady almost seemed to enjoy it. She continued, "The screen broke out and I fell backward. The whole world looked upside down." She stuffed the last of her bagel into her mouth and sat back in her chair. "And my horse was gone."

"Dear God! You were just hanging out the front window? Didn't anybody see you? Didn't you scream?"

"A gray squirrel saw me. He was climbing the tree in front of your house; only to me he was crawling down." She paused to wash down the bagel with coffee. "That was when I screamed."

"This is terrible. Just terrible." Jack's hands had tugged his hair up into standing, as he saw reflected in the window. He pushed it back down again.

"No one heard me," she said. "So I lifted my head and tried to pull myself back up; only I lost my grip and then both hands were hanging and my body swung down again. The back of my head hit hard against the brick wall of the house. That part really hurt, if you want to know the truth."

"But you could've been killed," Jack roared. Was that purring he heard? Was it possible that the spiteful Mrs. Brady was purring?

"The squirrel just kept watching me. I thought she was maybe a mother squirrel and she was worried. Like she knew how bad it would be if it was her baby hanging upside down. Do you think she could have been wondering that? Do you think squirrels care about their children?"

"Forget the squirrel— What happened next?"

Her eyes narrowed. She obviously disliked being rushed. The cat was definitely purring now, stretching his head straight up, anything so the tickling wouldn't stop. "Well, I swung there a bit until *The Y & R* ended. I could sort of hear the stupid music. Ros thinks it's such a good song, but I hate it."

"And then?"

"Then, Ros came upstairs to spray herself with perfume. She screamed pretty loud when she saw my knees poking through the window. Then she tried to help." Lucinda checked her teeth for poppy seeds in the reflection of her coffee spoon. "Stopped to spray herself with her stinky perfume first, though."

"Didn't she pull you up?"

"She called for my mom. *She* came upstairs and pulled me back inside. Then she got me to my bed and lied down beside me. All wrapped around me, sort of. I was really scared."

Jack fell backward in his chair. Why was it that every time this child appeared, he desperately needed a cigarette?

She was raising her*self* over there, with a little misguided help from some irresponsible children's books that should come with warning labels. And having two parents with extremely limited attention spans clearly wasn't all that much better than one parent. The difference was, she seemed to throw herself headlong into life, whereas he preferred to, well, hide.

"I wish I'd heard your screams," Jack said after a while. "I'd have helped you."

She smiled, revealing only one tooth. "Maybe. If you weren't a hermit."

"To hell with that. I'd have helped you, believe me." He drained his cup and walked to the sink to let it soak in water before he started washing the dishes.

Lucie shook her red head. Her hat had slipped down so low he could barely see any eyes, only a little nose and a busily working mouth. "You wouldn't."

"I most definitely would have." Jack was sure, almost positive that he'd have been able to overcome his anxiety in the face of such a near catastrophe. Very nearly certain.

"Really?"

"Really."

"Then pretend it's happening right now," she said, pushing her hat up and out of her eyes. "Go out on your front porch and pretend to see me hanging there, just like the squirrel saw me. Go. Try to save me."

He turned away and busied himself with the dishes. Plugging up the sink, he turned the hot water on and dumped in a dollop of dish detergent. "Ridiculous. I'm not playing make-believe. I've got too much to do."

"Okay." She walked her plate over to the sink and plunked it into the scalding-hot water, then looked up at Jack solemnly with her hat tilted to one side. "You want to know something? When she hugged me? THAT was weirder than the window."

LEANING OVER TO pick up the paper, which had landed blissfully close to the door this time, Jack heard the loud thump of a car trunk being slammed shut. He looked up to see a black car.

"Glad to see you're up and about, Jack," Dorrie called as she trotted across the sidewalk in fuzzy brown boots. Her weekend boots, Jack guessed. She wore a puffy flared coat with a fuzzy collar and a black ski toque with a figure skater embroidered on the front. Lucinda would kill for that hat, Jack thought with a smile.

"Yes. Nice to—"

"Yoo-hoo, Jack!" called a voice from inside the car. Rose reached across a suitcase on her lap to wave to him. "Feeling any better?"

Oh God. The living-room-floor incident. "Yes, thank you, Rose. And you?"

She squinted, shrugging her shoulders and waggling one hand as if to say so-so.

Jack turned to Dorrie. "She's not recovering well from the surgery?"

"Oh no. She's fine from that," Dorrie assured him. "She's going in for another one." She rotated her shoulder. "Shoulder surgery."

"That's terrible."

"You're not kidding. You know how bad things come in threes? For Rose, they come in fives. And this next surgery is her fourth for the year."

"Fourth surgery?"

"Fourth bad thing."

"Well. That's just a superstition."

Dorrie and Jack smiled at Rose, who lit up a cigarette and waved again.

Dorrie sighed. "Anyway, don't worry; I'm not here for a showing. I wouldn't do that to you so early on a Saturday. Actually, I hardly ever show on Saturdays. That's the day I drop my blazer off at the dry cleaner's. It only takes one day, so I'll be all set for the open house tomorrow." She seemed to have run out of words and stared at Jack, smiling a few seconds while she reloaded.

She handed him a large package covered in tinfoil. It looked very much as if it might be a cooked turkey, and Jack began to wonder if it was to be placed in the oven to create a homey atmosphere and disguise the scent of orangutan habitat drifting up from the kitty box in the cellar.

"Flowers," she explained. "Just set them in the foyer on the table to create a warm and welcome feeling for anyone who might wander in. Unless you think that cat might get at them, in which case, keep them in the fridge overnight and we'll set them up in the morning."

Jack, who had already pulled back a small section of foil, was reading aloud from a card stuck on top of the bouquet: AQUINNAH AND DEX, DE-CEMBER 2006. He didn't know what shocked him more—that she had swiped the centerpiece from her friends' wedding or that she could possibly be acquainted with anyone named either Aquinnah or Dex.

"I was at my cousin's wedding last night. She's just finishing law school and he's a pediatrician. They're the stars of the family at the moment."

Jack couldn't help himself. "So, after their heartfelt speeches, you crammed their beautiful centerpiece into your purse and ran off into the night?" The corners of his mouth twitched. "I can only hope that the copious amounts of baby-pink taffeta slowed the bridesmaids and you were able to escape unscathed."

Her eyebrows shot up. "Shows what you know. The taffeta was baby-blue."

"But all the gowns were strapless," Jack said. "Despite the fact that poor cousin Betsy's body type is such that she hasn't fit into a strapless costume since well before her premature growth spurt in the fifth grade."

"Her name's Virginia and it was the sixth grade. But we all told her she looked smashing."

They nodded at each other as a young couple strolled by, arm in arm.

"I hate weddings," Jack said.

Dorrie stood up taller. "Of course, my own wedding will be different. No taffeta. No baby-blue. And all the bridesmaids will wear tuxedos. Black tuxedos."

"Mm. Yes. I suppose Virginia would appreciate the coverage."

Dorrie's nose crinkled up. "And the support."

They stared at each other too long. Jack glanced down, trying to think of something else to say as the pause grew uncomfortably long.

"I didn't steal it off the table." she said. "I asked every single solitary person if they minded. But they didn't. Or at least they said they didn't." Her face clouded over with worry. "They *said* they didn't mind."

Pushing the foil closed, Jack moved closer. "I was kidding. Besides, any self-respecting wedding guest should have been far too inebriated to focus on flowers. Relax."

She nodded her head, looking unconvinced, and pulled a slip of paper out of her pocket. Her coat fell open to reveal a thick black turtleneck topping faded jeans.

Somehow he'd never pictured Dorrie Allsop in jeans.

He looked away, staring into the foil-covered centerpiece instead.

"I should probably warn you," she said. "I've placed an ad in the *Globe*, advertising the open house, so we can expect a really good turn-out. It might be a good idea if you leave the house. I know it got a little difficult for you when the Yaeger-Yearwoods made noises about drywall. Maybe you should head off to the zoo or something."

Jack pursed his lips, trying to appear in deep thought. "I'll have to check my schedule . . ."

"And one other thing, there was a teensy, really very tiny typo in the newspaper ad. It wasn't anyone's fault, but the girl in the classified section should really just get her eyes checked, because I typed *very carefully,* and I've been known all my life to have schoolteacher's spell—"

"Can I see the ad?" Jack motioned toward the paper in her hand.

Battersea Beauty. 4 story historic town house with wrkg dumb-waiter and orig. woodwork. All-white kitchen, 5 poss. bdrms and sep. garage. Stor. closets thru-out. Priced to sell. She lves in cellar. Open House Sun 11–5. 117 Battersea. Dorrie Allsop, Heritage Estates, 555-9697.

Aside from the fact that the dumbwaiter was stuck fast, he didn't see too much to get worked up about. Except for one thing. "She lives in cellar?" Jack asked. "Who?"

Dorrie's face was red with frustration. She shook her head so fast, a strand of hair caught in her mouth. She brushed it away. "No! That's just what it shouldn't say. It should read '*shelves* in cellar' not '*she lives* in cellar.' My instructors said this would happen. They said things will happen that you cannot control. They said it over and over again." She stomped her foot with the words *over and over*. "But I always thought they meant things like market fluctuations and clients with really bad taste. Not that one of my ads, my very first ad, would make me out to be a liar."

Thinking it might not be a good time to bring up the dumbwaiter's refusal to budge, he reached out and patted her shoulder. "Don't worry. Nobody is going to think someone's living in the cellar. I've always had trick vision. The ad looks terrific. You'll get loads of people, seriously."

Her eyes met his. "Seriously? You think so?"

He nodded, rattling the tinfoil. "I almost want to go see it myself."

"Do you really think you should be here during the open house?" asked Snowden from his favorite perch beside the fireplace. Today, however, Jack could relax. The doctor's trousers were sufficiently soaked from the icy rain outside as to render them soothingly flame-retardant.

Jack poked at the logs and sat back in his chair, chuckling into his shirt collar. "As it turns out, I've very few alternatives."

"And how does that make you feel?"

"Like shit."

"Can you expound upon 'like shit'?"

"Like total shit."

Snowden glowered at him. "Could you manage sitting at a neighbor's for a couple of hours?"

Jack laughed harder and sighed out loud. "No."

"Well, then. Perhaps you should double your meds and have your son escort you to a library or to your ex-wife's place."

"And sit on the sofa, glassy-eyed and drooling, beside Flourishing Yale?" Jack shook his head. "I don't think so."

"Why does her new husband's health concern you so much?"

"Boyfriend. They're not married yet."

"Answer my question."

"Who says it concerns me? It's nice that he has the time to take pride in himself. Very nice. Maybe if I'd spent less time glassy-eyed and drooling and more time researching which mineral would make my hair shinier, things would have turned out differently."

"Ah. Passive aggressiveness." Snowden flipped a page in his little pad and clicked his pen open. "What would our time together be, if not for our dear old standby?"

Jack grunted and leaned closer to the heat of the fire. "Predictable?"

"I was thinking more along the lines of productive." Snowden looked down at his pad and began scribbling as Jack checked his watch and sighed. Thirty-three minutes to go.

Chapter 12

Real Woodsmen Use
Chamomile Night Cream

Upstairs, Harlan stuffed a sea-foam-green turtleneck into his duffel bag, right on top of his Playboy mansion robe. At one end, the duffel was filled with his sleeping bag and My Little Pony pillow. Outer gear lined the bottom; and the other end held various other things Harlan deemed essential snow-cave supplies: a bobble-head spaniel wrapped in towels, a Magic 8-Ball for life-or-death decision making (like which snowdrift is best for relieving oneself without encountering a polar bear), and a miniature battery-operated strobe light to ensure that all other snow-cave dwellers' icy grottoes weren't nearly as "uncool" and happening as Harlan and Yale's—the effectiveness of this resting, of course, on the tiny strobes' ability to penetrate a wall of ice two-feet thick.

"But if you aren't going camping until next weekend, why are you bringing all this gear to your mother's place today?" Jack asked, from the foot of Harlan's bed.

"I told you, Yale wants us to Heli-ski to our campsite. He's got some alpine guys to take our gear to the site before we arrive. You can't drop from a 'copter with a duffel bag on your back," Harlan said like a weather-beaten woodsman as he searched for a safe spot for his chamomile night cream.

"No. I suppose your pore-minimizing mud-mask container might crack and leak blue clay all over your robe."

"Hilarious." Harlan wrapped his night cream in a towel and slid it into the folds of his sleeping bag. He glanced up at Jack a few times before saying, "Just remember to give me a list. You know, of stuff you need me to get for you before I leave. Wouldn't want to come home to find you eating out of the cat tin or anything."

Jack grunted. "I'd eat the cat first."

"Seriously, Dad. Don't do anything crazy. Write down everything you'll need and I'll get it this week."

"Thanks. For a mountaineer, you're a good guy." Jack ruffled Harlan's hair, drawing a scowl from his son, whose hands flew to his head to rearrange his bowl cut. "You know, the other night, in front of the girls . . ."

Harlan's face practically disappeared into the duffel.

"And the time with Melissa. I know how important that was to you. I just wish I could—"

"Whatever," Harlan interrupted from inside the bag. "I don't want to talk about it."

"I know your life would be easier if I were more—"

"Forget it. I know, I know. You would if you could. I don't want to talk about it. Mom and Yale are normal enough, so I'm not getting all damaged or anything."

Yes. Thank God for Penelope and Yale. Jack's failings made them look spectacular. He was thankful he could be of service to them both.

Jack was already kicking himself for agreeing that Penelope could have Harlan two weekends in a row. First of all, Harlan couldn't even throw a football, so how he was going to just plunge right into this he-man weekend was utterly beyond Jack. The boy packed a loofah, for crying out loud. He was tender. He bruised easily. He was a man of mockery, not rockery.

This Yale character clearly didn't know Harlan. Wanted to stepfather him without respecting who he really was. You couldn't just step into a boy's world and inflict your savage lifestyle on him just because you're marrying his mother. Bedding his mother. Only a self-important lout would be so presumptuous as to try to outfather the boy's father.

That's what he's trying to do, Jack thought, narrowing his eyes. Out-father me.

"Just remember to speak up if you're at all uncomfortable," Jack said. "Just because Yale sees himself as invincible doesn't mean you have to go tempting any avalanches or anything. This guy thinks sleeping in the ice makes him a man? He should try living one day in my shoes." Jack snorted. "It takes a real man to live with my problems, let me tell you." He watched as Mrs. Brady's bonnet floated past the doorway in the hall. "Surely, if I was completely without anxiety and had heaps of cash and a vitamin-enriched body, surely then I'd sleep in any cave on any mountainside the helicopter left me. Any idiot could."

"Dad."

"Sorry, Harlan. I didn't mean you, of course. It's very manly of you to rough it like this. Impossibly manly." Jack nodded his head. "Not too many other guys will be out there who have ever given themselves a pore-minimizing mask, I can assure you."

With a roll of his eyes, Harlan zipped up his lumbering sack of adventure and pushed his great brown goggles farther up his nose.

Chapter 13

She Lives in Cellar

Jack squeezed past two or three couples in the dining-room entryway on his way to the kitchen. At Dorrie's insistence, he'd brewed a full pot of coffee for the open-house guests, or potential buyers, as she preferred to call them. Potential buyers *my ass*, thought Jack, who recognized at least half of them as neighbors looking for a good excuse to ogle the old hermit place down the street.

Anyway, the smell of the coffee was getting to him. Screw the potential buyers, real or fake, he was going to plunk himself down at the kitchen table with a nice cupful and read the Sunday paper. Dorrie had shown up with particularly rich, freshly ground beans from Rose's favorite coffee house. The ill-fated Rose, it would seem, couldn't catch a break. Her beloved ten-year-old parakeet dropped dead that very morning, and in an effort to cheer up her best friend, Dorrie had convinced Rose to stop by the open house for a cup of coffee and a quick tour. Apparently, Rose's louse of an ex-husband had even refused to drop off their son to cheer up his mother.

It wasn't her scheduled weekend.

The upside, Dorrie was quick to point out to Jack, was that the little bird's demise brought Rose's yearly quota of unfortunate happenings to a solid five, and the woman was now certain to enjoy a few months of peace and stability.

Settling himself with a nice view of the sunny but snow-covered backyard—his best vantage point if he was going to try to ignore the houseful of strangers—he sucked in a deep, slow breath and let it out, drinking in the feeling of calm that his perfect white walls exuded. If he could only bottle this color and drink it in whenever he left the house, without the groggy side effects of the Nervy Durvies, well, he'd be not only a very calm man but a rich one as well.

An older couple, very possibly the late-night dachshund walkers, strolled into the kitchen in their socks—Dorrie's idea; anything to inconvenience the snoopers and ensure the icy floors chill them to the bone—and headed straight for the cupboard doors, yanking them open and banging them shut again. Jack glanced over, incredulous at their gall. What could they possibly need to see inside the cupboards? Which flavor of soups he preferred? Whether he was dangerously low on paper towels, which he was?

They could see that there were plenty of cupboards. And it didn't take a rocket scientist to imagine there being shelves inside the cabinets. They didn't need to rattle open his junk drawer and inspect his jumble of string and his complete and utter lack of stamps!

The woman smiled at Jack before turning to her husband. "I've always liked a white kitchen. This white looks a bit tired, though. Just picture it in a nice fresh coat of pure white. Like snow."

Jack grunted out loud. Shows what she knows, he thought. Snow isn't as white as everyone thinks. It's got a very distinct undertone of blue.

She continued. "Oh, Edward. Our pink curtains would fit perfectly over the window. That's something to consider." Her husband turned to face the window and nodded, clearly considering the practicality of reusing kitchen curtains. Almost made the four-and-a-half-million-dollar price tag seem reasonable.

"I do like those pink curtains of ours," he said, as if in a dream.

Pink? Jack wanted to shout. Pink at the window would make your whole fucking kitchen glow pink. Then, all the bother of repainting the perfectly tinted walls in a pure white would be redundant. Are people blind? Do they not see that adding a tinge of red to a south-facing room will make it positively stifling in the summer months? Not only that, but it could very likely drive Edward into such a fit of newfound passion as to shatter the comfortably sexless pattern that may have naturally evolved over the past few decades.

"You know what I'm thinking," Mrs. Dachshund said, crossing her arms. "If we laid down linoleum on top of the marble floor, it would be *so* much warmer on the feet."

Edward nodded with a wiggle of his toes. "Softer, too, for when I'm making my oatmeal."

Jack couldn't take it anymore. Some people just asked for it. He coughed to get their attention and said, "My wife, may she rest in peace, wanted to put in linoleum." Leaning forward, with his elbows resting on his knees, he buried his face in his hands, then looked up. "But I said no. I argued that it's wrong to cover up original marble tiles."

The couple looked at each other before Mrs. Dachshund offered Jack a cautious smile. "Your wife, she's no longer living?"

He shook his head in grief. "The very day of our argument, she tripped over the phone cord and hit her head on the marble floor." With his voice cracking in all the right places, he added, "Fell on the very spot you're standing."

"Oh!" They both stepped away and stared at the lethal black tile.

"But that wasn't what killed her," Jack added. "Sadly, no one was home but the cat."

Mrs. Dachshund gasped. "She died waiting for help?"

"Well, the cat helped as best he could. The smoke was getting quite thick."

"There was a fire?" Edward asked.

Jack blinked back dry tears. "Sorry. It's still painful for me. Her cigarette ignited the laundry basket she'd just set down. Whole main floor went up in flames."

Edward glanced quickly around the room. "Was the structure affected?"

His wife poked him with her elbow before saying to Jack, "So she was trapped? She died trapped in the fire, alone?"

"No. The cat, bless his little soul, dragged her from the house and into the blinding snow."

The Dachshunds immediately looked toward Mrs. Brady, who was pawing at his bonnet. Mrs. Dachshund tried to work out the physical probability, while her husband scoffed, "*That* cat dragged an adult woman from the house?"

Jack sniffed. "They say he had the power of ten cats that day."

Edward squinted. "So you're saying your wife survived hitting her head on the marble and being dragged out of a burning house by a cat, only to die outside of exposure?"

"No. She survived the blizzard. When I got home and saw she hadn't folded the laundry, well—" Jack shrugged. "I did what any husband would do."

Stunned, they said nothing at first. Then they sneered and shook their heads at him in disgust. Edward immediately led his wife away from Jack and out of the kitchen.

After a self-congratulatory stretch, Jack reached for his coffee and slipped into the butler's pantry, whereupon he made like the old butler himself and topped up his coffee with a couple of splashes from a dusty bottle of cognac. If he was going to survive this day, he'd need a bit of help. Mind-numbing help.

Recapping the bottle, he heard Dorrie stomping into the kitchen like a spooked mare. "Jack," she whispered so loudly she was probably heard clear up to the third floor. *"Jack, help!"*

"In here," he called, licking the cognac from his finger, which he'd used as a stir stick.

She burst into the tiny room, one side of her hair pulled completely out of her ponytail. "I'm so glad you stayed today. If you'd listened to me and left for the day, well, I don't know what I would have done. I always learned homeowners should never, ever be in residence during an open house. You never want the potential buyers to picture anyone but themselves living in the—"

"Dorrie," he interrupted, if only to let her pause and catch her breath. "I'm here. It's okay. What do you need?"

Her eyes welled up. "There's a . . . a dead sparrow. It's horrible, really. Dead as a barn mouse, claws up to the wind. I think it might actually be"—she paused here to collect herself—"frozen solid."

"The one out front? Beside the porch?" Jack said, loving the burning sensation in his throat as he swallowed a mouthful of butler's coffee. "Don't worry about it. No one's going to notice it."

"Rose is going to notice it . . . under the circumstances."

"Ahh." He considered the implications of Rose confronting this terrible visual reminder of her beloved pet's sudden expiration.

"I'm expecting her any minute. She was taking the eleven-thirty bus. I need you to remove it. Quickly."

Jack stared into his mug, drinking hungrily now. This was going to be a problem. "You say it's on the sidewalk?"

Her eyes, as blue as any Jack had ever seen, bugged open as she nodded furiously. "Please." She looked so helpless, Jack really did want to come to the rescue.

As he was setting his coffee down with a bang, an idea struck him. He stood up a bit taller. "You head upstairs and chat up your potential buyers. I'll take care of the bird so Rose doesn't see it."

She threw herself forward and wrapped herself around Jack, who could not have been more surprised if she'd announced giving up real estate altogether. She squeezed him tight and immediately stepped backward, adjusting her Heritage Estates blazer. Her face burned red and she disappeared, her giant pumps clattering in the hallway like loose horseshoes.

Grinning to himself, Jack walked to the front door with a swagger in his step, the Groper in his hand, and a paper bag in his pocket. Jack to the rescue. It felt good to be generous today, he thought, as he heard Dorrie chatting with a young couple, talking up the holes in the walls as if they were designed by Rodin himself. It felt good to be a man.

What was more, he didn't even care if anyone saw him with his crazy-looking tool today. Who on earth wanted to handle a disease-infested dead bird? He swung the front door open wide. It wasn't often that Jack Madigan was able to come to the rescue. Peering over the porch railing, he could see little Tweety's lifeless toes, just as Dorrie had described them, claws up to the wind and frozen stiff.

The Groper should ju-ust reach.

Buoyed by his success with the Dachshunds and partially anesthetized by his butler-powered coffee, he looked down at the stoop and set one stockinged foot into the center. Lowering the Groper, he poked at the bird and shuddered when it fell over, claws landing on the ice with a click. Revolting. He tried to flick it with his hook but missed. He needed to get closer. Stepping out with his other foot, he was now standing outside his house, perfectly calm and without drugs. Not in pill form, anyway.

The bird was so small and the hook so narrow it was difficult to swing down and actually make contact. Realizing he wouldn't be able to scoop it up and drop it into his grocery bag, he decided to knock it into the bushes on Lucinda's property. Maggots be damned. Then he could replace his tool and proudly inform Dorrie that he'd taken care of things. It would feel good.

Ignoring his mildly pounding heart, he swung clumsily at the bird again, clanging the tool on the iron railing instead. Once more he swung and missed. He inched closer to the edge of the stoop and pulled his arm back for another swing, this one well aimed.

Too perfectly timed to be coincidence, Mrs. Brady darted out of the house and—pausing only to shoot Jack a disgusted look, as if he was embarrassed to live with such a poor excuse for a man—snatched up the rigid bird in his mouth and raced down Battersea Road. The only part of the bird not hidden by the cat's little-girl bonnet were the tail feathers and one crooked claw.

"Damn it," Jack muttered, leaping back to the threshold.

Can't a man be a man, just once in his life, without being outmanned by a cat in a polka-dotted bonnet?

THROUGHOUT THE AFTERNOON, people gasped at the holey walls, fanned themselves as they toured the cellar, and tried to escape Dorrie's endless prattle—not difficult to do, as the size of her shoes tended to slow her down.

By four o'clock, there were no more neighborhood spies or potential buyers in the house other than a museum director from Chicago shopping for an East Coast investment. A man with closely cropped hair, probably in his late forties, with a dangerous-looking goatee and tiny wire glasses perched on the end of his nose, he was originally from England and, most important, was a huge Baz Madigan fan.

Jack followed Maxwell Ridpath through the house. "This is where Baz wrote all his music," Jack said, stepping onto the fourth floor. "His biggest single, 'Crash,' was written up here; see the dent in the door over there? That was a rare moment of frustration." As soon as the words left his mouth, he regretted them. This guy loved Baz. Loved the dents and holes. Would maybe kill to get his hands on Baz's home. The home where he died, even. The home with the famous dumbwaiter.

As much as he was enjoying Maxwell's interest, Jack needed to redirect it.

"Rare?" Maxwell laughed. "From what I hear, moments of frustration were the norm for Baz Madigan. I've remodeled my Chicago loft after Baz. They call it the Million-dollar Pauper look."

Jack grunted. So, Penelope did the guy's loft. He debated mentioning her having given birth to Baz Madigan's only grandchild but decided against it. It could only heighten Maxwell's interest in the house.

"Cool," Jack said, leaning against the dumbwaiter door. "Not many people truly understand that Baz was a very . . . dull guy. Boring, even. Just a bit—"

"Artistically frustrated," Maxwell finished for him. "I know, I know. I've got his unauthorized biography." He paused to pick something out of his teeth. "By the way, what's the real deal with the shell?"

The shell. Every fan of Baz's eventually got around to the shell. "The famous shell." Jack ran his finger along the frame of the dumbwaiter. "I wish I knew. I wouldn't be selling this house if I did, that's for certain."

"Money can make us do terrible things," said Maxwell, glancing around the room. "Smashing," he whispered. 'Must have brilliant acoustics in here."

"Not really," Jack lied. "The rafters muffle most of the good stuff. It's really more for an old poseur like me."

"That stage," Maxwell said, pointing. "Did your dad have it installed?"

Which was better? That he did or that he didn't? "No," Jack lied again. "The whole place was converted into a geriatric-care facility in the forties. The old folks used to get up there and, you know, dance, make out . . ." Jack shuddered very realistically and turned toward the stairs. "Sickening, if you think about it."

"Madness," Maxwell said, with eyes shining. "Pure madness."

Jack shrugged. "Want to buy a used guitar? Take a little piece of Baz Madigan home to Chicago?"

"Baz's?"

"Of course Baz's." Jack stood up straighter. If he could sell this guy a guitar, today, he could call off this whole stinking open house. This whole fucking nightmare would disappear. "It's a rare bit of memorabilia."

"Sorry, mate. Bit of a minimalist, I'm afraid."

Of course. The one Baz Madigan fan he'd come face-to-face with in years, and he's a minimalist.

Back downstairs, Jack helped himself to another cup of now-stale coffee, while Maxwell wandered through the butler's pantry from the dining room and stopped in the middle of the kitchen. Arms folded across his chest, he grunted.

"Nice white you've got in this room. Mind if I ask the name?"

Looking up from his cup, Jack was too shocked to speak for a moment. He looked at his beloved walls. "You like it?"

"It's fabulous. Old and new at the same time. Cool enough to go with the floors, yet warm enough to not feel chilly. It's brilliant."

Jack just smiled.

"Is it from Farrow and Ball? Have they expanded their line of colors?"

"It's called French Linen."

Maxwell nodded. "Perfect. It actually feels European. Natural. Simple."

"Sounds like you know your way around a paint deck. Are you an artist as well as a museum director?"

Maxwell motioned toward a kitchen chair and looked at Jack for permission to settle himself at the table. Receiving a nod from Jack, he slid into a seat and crossed his legs. "We're building a new art museum in Chicago. I'm heading back there tomorrow. Very exciting project. Photographic art only. I've been hired as the director there, based on my years of curating at the Museum of Contemporary Art. I suppose one develops an eye for this sort of thing, after years of looking for that perfect white to showcase the works."

As he slid into the chair across from Maxwell, Jack's eyes were gleaming. "She's a mysterious beauty, that perfect white."

Maxwell nodded. "And with the simplicity of black-and-white photography in particular, the background needs to sing. But whisper-soft. The lack of complication in the art itself must rise above its surroundings, all the while seeming a part of them." He sighed and crossed his legs. "It's a very complex marriage."

"Of course," Jack said, leaning forward onto the table. "And any hues showing through in the paint could potentially taint the artists' vision—aesthetically and emotionally altering the viewer's connection with the work."

"Christ. That's precisely what I've been telling the architects. They've suggested using this Cloud White, this CC-130, from Benjamin Moore.

They say it's a hit with designers and is used everywhere as a clean, neutral white. But to me, that's not good enough. I want to go further. I want a white tailored specifically for our light conditions, our art, and our massive scale. We'll be displaying some of the most important works of modern photography in the world. I feel these pieces deserve the best home we can offer."

"It's nice to know someone out there shares my appreciation for white, in all its sophistication."

Maxwell was staring at Jack now. "Right. You never told me, which company makes this French Linen?"

"Jack Madigan, Inc."

"You own a paint company?"

"I am the paint company. All my equipment is right down in the basement. I've been developing the right white for this kitchen for years now."

Maxwell extended his hand. "Well, congratulations, mate. You've achieved that and more. Who do you do work for?"

Anyone who comes through my front door, he almost said. "A couple of designers. I've had a few private homeowners. Last spring I got a call from a frantic interior designer, some woman named Gordon, if you can imagine, who'd had a custom steel handrail done for some ritzy client. But when it arrived, the steel looked too new, too industrial for their French Country home. So they hired me to make it match a two-hundred-year-old fireplace grille. Another time, a designer wanted to match a bookshelf made of primered fiberboard to the original oak trim in their historic house, so I mixed the three colors I saw in the baseboard sample they brought me and handed the mixtures over to a decorative artist who did the wood graining. The designer swears you can't tell the difference."

"Incredible. You've obviously got loads of talent."

Jack shrugged. "Just passionate. It's a shame you're all the way over in Chicago. I'd have loved to have gotten involved."

"Chicago's not so far. We could probably work something out."

Dorrie came clomping downstairs and stopped to fiddle with papers in the foyer before disappearing into the main-floor powder room. "Excuse me?" Jack asked him, willing Dorrie to stay out of the room.

Maxwell smiled. "I said we could probably overcome the distance—"

Jack could barely comprehend his luck. Imagine a job of this caliber landing smack in the middle of his kitchen. Quickly he tried to calculate how much he could charge per gallon of custom-tinted paint.

"You mean, you'd work with me from Chicago?" Jack asked.

"Why not?"

"Why not indeed." Jack smiled.

"The thing is, we won't be able to give you much lead time. We're going to be finishing the interior very soon."

Jack nodded, staring at the ceiling as if consulting his bursting Day-Timer. "Let me just think a moment. Yeah. Yeah, I think I could probably squeeze you in."

Just then, Dorrie came out of the powder room and into the hallway, shooing away the cat. She called out to Maxwell, "So, has Jack sold you the house, Mr. Ridpath? Shall I bring my forms in there so you can start signing the paperwork?" As she passed by the kitchen door, Jack saw that her Heritage Estates blazer was stuffed down the back of her skirt along with a long, twisted strand of toilet paper, obviously still attached to the roll and unraveling fast as she made her way down the hall. From the kitchen, Jack could hear the little paper roll spinning madly in an attempt to keep up.

"Kee-rist," Maxwell leaned closer to Jack, nodding his head toward Dorrie. "Is she the one that lives in the cellar?"

THE KITCHEN CLOCK ticked loudly, amplifying the silence. Sitting across from each other, staring into Aquinnah and Dex's wilting flowers, neither Jack nor Dorrie spoke. Both sides of Dorrie's ponytail had now fallen free, and tousled blond strands rested against her cheeks. She shifted in her chair, picking leaves off the stolen centerpiece, crushing them one by one into teensy balls, and lining them up in front of herself on the Formica table.

Jack himself was still intoxicated with excitement about working for Maxwell. It was the single biggest job he'd ever taken on. Maxwell had taken Jack's number, along with three quickly painted Bristol boards in Jack's favorite whites, dried with a hair dryer in the cellar, to try them out in the new space. He promised to call Jack to set up the next step.

Dorrie, who had had a terrifically miserable day pointing out the house's never-ending flaws, was exhausted. She'd frightened off both snoopers and potential buyers. When she finally spoke, her voice was shaky. "At least Rose had some good news."

Rose arrived buoyed by the discovery that her bird hadn't died after all. Just prior to her departure, the little thing had let out a loud squawk and flapped right back up to his perch as if nothing had happened. Certainly, she'd be stopping by the veterinarian's office on Monday morning with the tiny fellow, but for now, all was well.

"Yes. Terrific news," Jack agreed.

"Yes. Terrific."

"Yes."

"Of course, this brings her back to four." Dorrie pushed a piece of hair behind her ear, only to have it fall into her face again.

"Excuse me?"

"Four bad things. You have to wonder now what the fifth will be."

"That's silly superstitious talk. There won't be a fifth."

"I hope not." She didn't sound convinced.

"For sure not."

They returned to silence, and Jack felt his stomach grumbling. He really hadn't eaten since before his morning coffee. Mentally rummaging through his refrigerator, he wondered if he had anything suitable to toss on a plate and place on the table. Was peanut butter on celery sticks too tacky? Actually, that wouldn't work. The peanut butter was all gone. There was that unopened container of vanilla frosting though . . .

"The thing is," Dorrie blurted out suddenly, "they're all counting on me to fail. Crossing their fingers."

"Who?" Jack asked. She could obviously fail pretty spectacularly on her own; she didn't need anybody's help.

"The other agents. Back at the office. They all wanted this listing, every last one of them. But my uncle Dave insisted that it go to me. See, I never got into Harvard like my cousins. I only got into Northeastern Real Estate Academy"—she dropped the leaf she was crumpling and looked up at Jack—"I know it sounds kind of prestigious, but truthfully, it wasn't.

"I was always the problem cousin. Jeffrey had his football scholarship, Becky had her science awards and eventually med school, and Stevie, well, Stevie had his ballet. Still does. When he got accepted into the New York City Ballet, it was an even bigger deal than the others going to Harvard and Yale combined.

"Anyway, Gabby married into the Capitol Trust Dynasty, and then there was me. I wasn't good at anything except playing with my doll-house"—she coughed a high-pitched, squeaky cough—"a real estate agent among doctors, lawyers, ballet dancers, and equestrians.

"This house is my way to make myself, I don't know, important somehow. At least I could be the Beacon Hill agent. The Girl from Battersea Road, you know?"

Jack nodded. He did know. He wanted to be the Boy from Battersea Road. Or continue to be, anyway.

"Did you hear what happened to your neighbors? The young architect couple down the street?"

He wasn't going to admit he had no idea a young couple lived down the street. "Those sweet kids? What happened?"

"I heard it during the open house. From another neighbor of yours who came by. Said she's considering buying a second property on the street, a rental property."

Like hell she is. Another snooper. "You heard what?"

"Frankly I'm surprised Doug and Janice didn't tell you themselves. They only live two doors down."

"Tell me what?"

"About the break-in. They were robbed last week. Someone broke in their kitchen door while they were upstairs working in the attic. Ever since they installed the skylight, she says, they much prefer the light up there. Moved their third-floor offices all the way up to the top floor. Of course, *they've* installed a proper elevator." Dorrie paused for breath here and blinked at Jack.

It didn't appear that he was going to get the rest of the story without a nudge. "And?"

"And now Doug's knee doesn't act up nearly as much."

He sighed. "What about the break-in?"

"Ah, yes. The burglars barely made a sound. Moved out a TV, some valuable art and camera equipment from the small bedroom on the fourth floor—right beside the office."

"And this couple, Doug and . . . Judy?"

"Janice," Dorrie scolded.

"Janice, they didn't hear?"

"They were working with the door closed. She thought she heard a bump once but figured it was the dog. It was only after the fact that she realized the dog was under Doug's desk. Doug keeps a heater at knee level and the dog loves to lie beneath—"

"Were they caught? The burglars?"

She shook her head. "That's why they warned all the neighbors last week. You couldn't make it to their get-together? They had everyone over for coffee and cake."

Jack flicked lint from his shoulder. "I had a prior engagement."

"Too bad. I hear the cake was delicious." She let out a long sigh and looked toward the darkened window. "I'm terrible at this, aren't I?"

"At what?" Following Dorrie's train of thought was making his head hurt.

"Selling real estate."

"No. Not terrible," Jack insisted, patting her hand, then pulling his hand away quickly when he felt the softness of her skin. "But since you're asking. There might be a *couple* of things, small things really, that you might want to consider." How could he not help? As much as her hopeless bungling of every showing suited him, she looked so . . . lost. "You might, if you really wanted to improve your prospects of selling houses, you might think about pointing out the actual good points of your listings. The positives."

Her eyebrows shot up and got lost in hair. "I'm pretty sure I *have* been—"

Nodding, Jack held his hand up to stop her. "Yes, I can see where it might seem that way. But let's say a house had a spectacular view and rather nasty plumbing. Which should you focus on?"

She had to stop herself from raising her hand. "The plumbing, of course." Smiling, sure of herself, she leaned back in her chair and crossed her arms.

"No! Not the plumbing." Jack squinted at her. "Why the plumbing?"

"Because the view will sell itself. But the plumbing needs help. I focus all my energy there and try to turn a negative into a positive. See?"

"No. I don't see." Actually, he did see, sort of. Her logic wasn't bad; it just failed miserably in the execution. "You should take those clients, who probably stare out their kitchen window and into a brick wall or a gas station, and *romance* them on the terrace."

Her face turned cloudy.

Jack ran his hand through his hair. "You sell them on the romance of waking up Sunday mornings to coffee and the crossword puzzle on their beautiful terrace overlooking the water. See?"

"I do." She was nodding now. "So you're saying I shouldn't point out the plumbing at all. Even to give them advice about how to remedy the problem?"

"Right. That way you're selling the sizzle. Not spending all your time sawing away at the fat."

"Jack, you're so good at this. Maybe you should be helping me here." She motioned around the room.

"No. I can't help with this house." Jack tore off a leaf, crumpled it, and lined it up with Dorrie's leaf balls. "Any other house, though."

"Anything else?" she asked, her eyes shining, intoxicated.

"Well, you might consider . . ."

"What? Consider what?"

He looked at her and hesitated. "You might consider silence as a selling tool."

"How so?" She leaned so far forward she nearly crushed the lineup.

"When you enter a room, resist the urge to fill the silence with chatter. Close your mouth and maybe let the client say a thing or two. You might find they sell themselves on the place." Quickly he added, "Not *this* place. Other places."

She squeezed her lips together, hopefully considering the virtues of silence. After blinking a few times, she said, "My mother would agree with you. She'd say, 'Less telling and more selling.' At least that's what she'd say if she knew real estate jargon. She spends most of her time knitting the tiniest caps for premature infants. She and her friends get together and just knit and talk and smoke. Knit and talk and smoke. Imagine the parents taking their newborn baby out of an incubator that smells like a truck stop . . ."

Jack got up to pour them both a glass of wine. This was going to take a bit of work.

Chapter 14

Toes on the Porch

Pulling back the bath curtain, Jack rolled up the sleeve of his robe and dipped his fingers into the steaming bathwater. Just a couple of degrees shy of blistering the flesh. Perfect. With a high-profile tinting job like the Chicago gallery practically stuffed into his back pocket, he could afford to splurge on a tubful of scalding-hot water.

As he draped his robe over the splintered wicker lid of the laundry hamper and perched his wineglass on the tub's edge, he remembered an old bottle of lavender-scented bath oil Penelope used to keep under the sink, and peered inside the cupboard to see if, by chance, she had left it behind.

Ah. There it was, tucked behind the empty Kleenex box and covered by a fuzzy film of oily grime.

It was a good sign. A sign that things were about to turn around for him.

With great flourish, he poured nearly a quarter of the bottle into the still-running bathwater and watched purple billows roll and tumble across the tub in great, bubbling lilac clouds. When it had evenly tinted the rest of the water a spirit-soothing mauve, he stepped into the water, winced at the heat, and slipped under the bubbles.

Sipping from his now-steamed-up glass, he smiled. This Maxwell knew what he wanted. Understood color. Jack loved working with knowledgeable clients. Clients who understood the intricacies and refinement of white. Such people were rarities in Jack's experience.

As he sipped again, a loud thump came from somewhere inside the house. The empty house. He sat up, bubbles running down his chest.

Harlan had left for the mall with Melissa an hour ago. He wouldn't be back until ten, at the earliest, because Gwendolyn had driven them and was taking them to dinner.

Thump. There it was again. Had to be the cat. He peeked past the gap in the bath curtain and through the fog to see Mrs. Brady cleaning his tail atop Jack's robe.

It wasn't the cat.

It would be silly—nonsensical even—to think anyone would break into this place. What would they leave with? A half-bottle of stale bath oil, which really didn't smell like lavender in the slightest, and a sack of kitty litter? A fifteen-year-old television?

If they'd broken in hoping to leave with a pricey electric guitar, good luck to them. Anyone smart enough to get the dumbwaiter working was a better person than Jack, and was welcome to the guitar.

The next thump sounded closer. Jack closed the curtain tighter and lay perfectly still in the rancid bathwater. Certainly, they couldn't have gone to all the trouble of breaking in just to murder an aging recluse, could they? Where was the challenge in that?

He held his breath as the bathroom door squeaked. Mrs. Brady meowed softly.

There was no sense in hiding. If he was going to die, he wasn't going to do it covered in purple bubbles. He was going to step out and cower naked in the corner, like a man.

He yanked back the curtain.

"What the hell?" Harlan spun around to face the tub. The mirrored medicine cabinet door struck the wall. "You scared the crap out of me!"

"*I* scared *you*?" Jack said, yanking his robe from under the cat. "I thought I was about to be bludgeoned to death. What are you doing creeping around in here?"

"Who's creeping?" Harlan made a face. "And why's it so foggy in here? How hot is your water?"

"You were supposed to be staying at the mall for dinner. Meeting Gwendolyn."

"How come I can't have baths this hot?"

"What happened?"

"I always get reamed when my water's the tiniest bit warm. And where'd you get the purple bubbles?"

"Harlan! Why didn't you stay with Melissa and her mother?"

"I bailed. So what?"

"Why?"

Harlan put something back in the cabinet and shuddered. "Bra shopping."

"Ah. You should have gone over to that new music store. The one with the Shaun Cassidy compilation."

Harlan shrugged before reaching over to pick up the cat and pass Jack a towel. "Didn't think of it."

As Harlan turned back to rummage through the medicine cabinet, Jack said, "What are you looking for?"

"What?"

"In the medicine cabinet. What do you need?"

"Tylenol."

"We're out." Jack dropped the towel on his head and scrubbed his wet hair. Harlan said something he couldn't quite hear. Jack pushed his hair back with the towel and wrapped the towel around his shoulders. Harlan had a small bottle of pills in his hand. "What'd you say?"

"I said, how do these Nervy Durvies make you feel anyway?"

AFTER BREAKFAST THE following morning, Harlan thundered out the door either in desperation to get to calculus class or in retaliation against his father's nosy questions about when, exactly, he had fallen out of allegiance to Shaun Cassidy. Jack followed him to the front door and stepped onto the threshold to check for mail.

No mail yet. But just as he was removing his hand, his knuckles grazed a small slip of paper. He pulled out the folded note. It smelled of an improbable mix of dusty attic, vanilla wafers, and summer beach house.

> *Jack,*
>
> *Just stopped by to drop off some sales flyers I had printed up to display in the foyer. That way, potential buyers can take something with them when they leave. They're in the bag on the porch.*

Jack looked down. Sure enough, a blue bag, tied into about eighteen knots to prevent it from blowing open, sat beneath the mailbox. He returned to the note.

Feel free to set them out on the hall table where that cat won't get at them. They cost almost 17¢ each. 19¢ if you factor in the copies that fell under my car into the slush.

Dorrie

Bringing the bag and the note inside, Jack closed the door, the corners of his lips twitching in amusement.

"YOU'RE UNUSUALLY COOPERATIVE this afternoon, Jack." Dr. Snowden sat comfortably on a kitchen chair he'd dragged out onto the front porch, his knees and tender hips wrapped in a thick quilt, insulation against the cold, gray afternoon.

Jack squatted on the threshold, his toes resting uncomfortably on the doormat. The doctor had stooped to guerrilla therapy now, forcing Jack to endure their entire forty-five-minute session half inside and half outside his safe zone—in some sort of Never Never Land designed to lull Jack into a level-three frame of mind.

"I'm no different."

"You're smiling."

"I'm not smiling. I'm just losing feeling in my feet." Jack shifted closer to the door frame and leaned against it for balance.

"Have you made any progress in redeeming yourself with the bank?"

"Can we move inside now?"

"Answer the question please."

"Not really."

"Then what's got you so accommodating? Have you scared off your real estate agent? Or worse, stashed her body parts in a freezer?"

"Dorrie? God, no. I'd never hurt Dorrie. It would be like stomping on a puppy."

"Interesting. Tell me more about her."

Jack looked up. He wasn't going to be led in this direction. Oh no. One word about not actually despising another woman and old Snowden had cartoon hearts flapping all around his head. "She's nothing special."

"Interesting. And how do you feel when you're around her?"

"Tall." Jack rested back on his bottom just inside the threshold.

"Toes on the porch, Jack."

Rolling his eyes, Jack crossed his legs and tucked his feet underneath him, making Snowden scribble angrily on his pad. "Actually, I'd like to discuss Harlan," said Jack.

Snowden's pen continued moving. "Mm-hm?"

"I offered him a few dollars to buy Shaun Cassidy CDs the other day and he couldn't have cared less."

"Well—" Snowden chuckled. "Shaun Cassidy isn't for everyone."

"Not just that, he's mopey. And he's been asking questions about my meds. How they make me feel."

"He's a teenager. Teenagers mope. Not only that but they have an unhealthy fascination with thrill-seeking. Anything that can be inhaled, injected, or swallowed for less than a couple of dollars that will transport them far away from the tiresome world inhabited by their parents has immediate appeal. He sounds perfectly normal to me. In fact, when you consider the unstable example he's got to follow, I'd say he's doing better than the average."

Jack wondered what the old doctor would do if he just swung the door shut right now, bolted it, and went upstairs to bed. "Very flattering."

Snowden ignored the reproach. "So long as he isn't growing overly fearful or exhibiting any of your own symptoms—dizziness or, more specifically, feeling he could die from the dizziness—there's nothing to worry about."

THAT NIGHT, AFTER drying and putting away the dinner dishes, Jack wiped his hands and spread the dish towel across the cool marble of the counter to dry. Yawning, he reached his arms over his head and stretched before tying up the overstuffed garbage bag on the floor and lifting it up to toss into the garbage bin on the back porch.

With Snowden safely out of the way, Jack was free to think about Dorrie's flyers. She had actually pointed out several of the house's more positive features, like the marble floors and kitchen counters and the high ceilings. Certainly, he was pleased to see she was learning so quickly, but she wasn't supposed to sample her burgeoning skills on *his* house. Not this quickly. He made a mental note to work on developing skills that might help one in securing multiple listings. Give her some-where else to focus her efforts.

As he was reaching for the doorknob, Jack's left foot caught itself on a strap, sending him sailing into the door and sending the trash bag hurtling toward the floor, where it split open, spilling coffee grounds and eggshells onto the floor.

"Damn it," Jack swore, kicking Harlan's backpack out of the way. They went through this almost every night. Jack would tell him to pick it up off the floor. Put it on the kitchen table. Harlan would say, "Yeah, I'll get to it in a sec." Which he never did.

"Harlan!" Jack called, stomping into the hallway. "What did I tell you about leaving your schoolbag on the kitchen floor? Harlan? I damned near killed mys—"

Passing the dining room, Jack noticed Harlan's legs lying toes-down on the floor, the rest of his son hidden behind the table and chairs. There was a gaping hole in the heel of one of his striped toe socks, and his heels were knocking together.

"What are you doing?" Jack asked, crossing the room.

Harlan's head poked up, and he held a finger up in front of his mouth. "Shh. She'll hear you," he whispered. He had pulled the rags from the lowest part of the hole and stuck his goggled face into it. Jack knelt down beside him and peered through the legs of Samantha Ballard's dining-room hutch to see her slender ankles topping dangerously high heels.

"You're spying?"

"Shh." Harlan's face was creased into a big, goofy grin. "She's about to take off her shoes."

Sure enough, one foot disappeared, and a stiletto shoe dropped to the floor. "I didn't think we'd have to walk that far," Samantha complained to someone in the room. "My feet are *killing* me." The other shoe dropped, and the first foot disappeared again. "Mmmm," she moaned. "I need a foot massage."

From the heated-up look on Harlan's face, Jack thought his son just might slither through the wall and get to work on it himself. Utterly reprehensible behavior on Harlan's part. Rude. Invasive. Overtly sexualized. Jack smiled to himself and breathed a silent sigh of relief.

Perfectly normal conduct for a seventeen-year-old boy.

He forced a stern look onto his face and whispered, "All right. That's quite enough of this peep show. Get up to bed . . . *after* you clean up the garbage in the kitchen, please."

"Aww," Harlan groaned, pulling his eyes away and stomping through the butler's pantry. "You should have known my bag was there. It's *always* there."

"Precisely the reason *you're* cleaning up the mess." Just as Jack turned away to stand, Lucie's voice came chattering into the other room.

"Mom," she said, rattling what sounded like a sheet of paper. "Look, the Ice Starlets are coming to town. In three weeks! Could we go? Please? Carolina Yamaha is in it. Do you think we could go?"

Both Samantha and Rick made tired sounds. "That's the weekend of the Tillmans' party," said Samantha. "Rick, isn't the Tillmans' party the weekend of the twenty-third?"

Rick confirmed: "The twenty-third."

"The Tillmans' party is the twenty-third," Samantha repeated uselessly. "Maybe next year." She paused. "I feel a draft. Does anybody else feel a draft?"

Quickly, Jack stuffed a few more rags into the hole, leaving it just big enough to peek through with one eye.

"But there's a Saturday performance," Lucinda said. "There's Sunday. There's even matinees. Couldn't we go to a matinee?"

"I'll be at Rico's for my hair all day Saturday, and Sunday morning there's a brunch. It's a very important party, Lucinda. Your father's boss will be there."

"Dad?"

"No can do. I've got a squash game."

"Then I can go alone. Send me in a cab, I'll go."

"No." Samantha sounded weary. Children could be such an impediment to one's social schedule.

"Please. I'll take a cell phone."

"Think of how it would look, Lucinda," Rick said. The television was turned on. "It would seem like we were careless parents."

"There'll be another show next year," Samantha added.

Lucinda's bare feet came into view. Fuzzy, blue pajama bottoms were cuffed around her ankles. "And what if there's another party next year?"

Her mother yawned. She'd had enough. "Lucinda, go to bed. It's almost ten o'clock."

With that, Lucinda dropped to her knees and into full view. The fuzzy, blue PJs went all the way up to her neck, one piece and also cuffed at the wrists. A low grumble churned from deep inside her chest. And then, like a junkyard dog behind a rusty chain-link fence, desperate to get at the bullies who'd been poking sticks through the fence all summer, she lunged forward, sinking her disproportionate teeth into Samantha's creamy ankle.

Jack hooted so loudly, he had to grab the rest of the rags and stuff them into the hole as fast as he could, before falling on his back and silently cheering her on.

Chapter 15

The Ice Storm

All night, the storm raged, ice tapping against the window relentlessly. The big house seemed to shiver and groan in outrage, and Jack's sleep was continually interrupted by visions of potential buyers looking in on him, knocking on the window and trying to slide the house off its very foundation to get it out of his grasp. He'd wake with a jolt, and toss and turn for another hour or two before beginning the whole cycle all over again. Sometimes it would be Yale tapping on the glass.

Pillows over his head didn't help, the house's complaints being too cavernous and yawning to allow him to relax for fear of being swallowed whole. Sometime during the night, Harlan appeared at Jack's door with his pillow, the one he hadn't packed for his ice cave on the weekend. He hadn't said anything, just crawled into Penelope's side of the bed, yanked the covers over to his side, and fell asleep.

It wasn't until well past five o'clock that Jack finally fell into a deep slumber. He opened his eyes to dazzling brightness and a pillow with Harlan's drool stains all over it. Jack looked at the clock. 9:08. Throwing back the edge of the scant covers that Harlan had allowed him, he padded across the cold floor to the window.

It was nearly too bright to look at. The trees, the buildings, even the festive twosome of twig reindeer across the street, everything was coated in shimmering ice. It was as if the world had been candy-coated like a Macintosh apple, only diamond-clear. With great difficulty and much jerking and bashing, Jack slid the window up and reached out to touch the ice. He cracked it with his knuckles and peeled a shard away from the sill. Just like candy. He licked it, then tossed it out onto the street.

Within an hour, the house, otherwise empty—Harlan having left for his last day of classes before winter break—smelled gloriously of coffee, and Jack's fire roared, crackled, and danced in defiance of the chill outside. It was the sort of day everyone, not just agoraphobics, wanted to spend hiding away inside, trying to purge their minds of the relentless holiday tunes that wouldn't ease up until the new year. The sort of day Jack could spend entirely guilt-free. One was, after all, *supposed* to sit by the fire all day when faced with such treacherous atmospheric conditions.

More important, potential buyers couldn't very well view a house if they couldn't get up the front steps, could they?

He settled himself next to the blissful heat, balanced his coffee on the arm of his chair, and he flipped open the morning paper.

"Housing Market Shatters Early Winter Blahs," read one headline. Scanning the body copy, Jack frowned upon learning the Boston market was, despite being in the midst of what was typically the slowest season, Christmas, flourishing with all the vigor of spring tulips punching through freshly thawed flower beds. He laid the paper on his lap and stared into the fire. That wasn't good. Definitely not good.

Hearing a clatter of commotion on the front porch, Jack rushed to the door to find not a potential buyer but Lucinda dropping a shovel and two different sizes of brooms into a pile.

She looked up at Jack and held out a mitten. "Lucinda Ballard. Future Olympic team member."

"Honored," Jack said, taking her bulky mitt and giving it a reverential shake. "Isn't today a school day? The last school day before winter break?"

She made a face. "Private school. You get twice as long off, but the teachers are twice as mean, so it pretty much evens out." Looking up at the sky, she began to twirl around the tip of one skate. "Plus you have to wear a scratchy uniform and have not one single solitary scuff on your shoes," Lucinda announced as she spun on the icy porch. Faster and faster she went, staring at the mailbox as she turned, snapping her head around and back to the doorway as she began the next spin. Her head whirled around so quickly, Jack worried not only that she'd damage her neck but that he'd vomit on the mat from watching.

"Okay, Lucinda. Not so close to the house."

"You should try it. Just pick a spot on the wall and you can spin as many times as you want; you won't get dizzy. Try."

"I don't think so." He smiled. "I try to keep the spinning to a minimum before noon."

Finally, she stopped, her little body heaving up and down as she caught her breath. She stared at him, clearly seeing through his attempt at humor. "At least you got the frozen bird off my rink. That's something. Something pretty big, if you ask me."

"All right." Frankly, he didn't like to discuss any incident where he had been shown up by his cat. "Enough ogling the Astonishing Talents of Jack Madigan."

"You should just keep coming out here," Lucie said with a shrug of her small shoulders. "That's all."

Jack said nothing to this. He waved his thanks for the unwanted advice and closed the door, returning to the living room and settling himself back into his chair by the fire, with his newspaper and his now-lukewarm coffee.

"Well, *I'm* going to try out my ice," Lucie called through the old mail slot in the front door. "It definitely won't get my blades all chunked up with gravel now."

THE PHONE RANG, but the ringing came from far away. Jack flew out of his chair, hoping against hope that it was Maxwell Ridpath calling to say he needed Jack's color expertise next week and did Jack mind receiving such large payment via one-day courier?

Where was that cordless phone? Following the distant ringing, he padded out of the room and through the foyer, once again pulling open the front door. He stared out onto the porch. There lay his ringing cordless phone, three steps down on the icy staircase with Lucinda beside it, removing her skate guards.

"How did you get my phone?"

She smiled a sweet schoolgirl smile and walked on her toe picks toward her little rink, which glistened and sparkled under its fresh new coating of ice.

"*Lucinda!* It might be a very important call. Please pass it to me."

"Remember what I said?" She removed her mitten and bent down to touch the ice with her bare hand. "You don't want to stop going out. You don't want to go backward."

"Lucinda, I demand that you hand me that phone. This isn't funny. I'll cement over the hole in the wall."

She scrunched up her nose. "You wouldn't do that," she said, stepping onto her rink's bumpy surface. "You need the heat." And with that, she cupped her big mitts over her ears and started to spin.

Damn it. His heart banging a level-eight or -nine warning, Jack stepped out onto the icy porch and, holding on to the railing for dear life, down the steps. As he descended, very slowly—he couldn't afford to break his neck on top of everything else or they'd snatch up his house while he was laid up in traction—the cat slithered past, knocking the phone clear across the sidewalk.

Faster now (the phone had already rung some five or six times), he slipped and skidded across the ice in his socks and grabbed the ringing phone. "Hello?" he shouted as he stumbled back inside and slammed the front door on Lucinda's giggling.

"Jack? Dave here. From Boston National."

Dave. He'd risked paralysis and death by agoraphobic spinning for a call from the enemy. "Yeah. What more can I do for you? You need a kidney?"

"That's my man. Never lose your sense of humor, I always say." He paused here; then, when Jack said nothing, continued. "Listen, I know you're having a hard time with everything and I just wanted to pass on a little tip. My older sister is moving out of her apartment over by Wellington's Bistro, a three-bedroom with a view of the Commons. Thought of you immediately."

"Thanks, Dave, but I'd rather not discuss this right now. With you."

"Suit yourself. Just thought I'd lend a hand."

"If you really want to lend a hand, you'll give me more time. A few more months . . ."

Dave exhaled into the phone. "We've been through this. I've done nothing *but* give you more time. If I do it any more, I'll be fired. Even branch managers have their managerial limits. Oh, and Jack?"

"What?"

"In case you change your mind, I checked with my sister. The building allows cats."

Terrific. Jack hung up and tossed the phone on top of Dorrie's flyers. He pushed his hands into his pockets and walked over to the living-room window. Lucinda's rink stretched the five or six feet between his porch and the Ballards' porch and was about the same distance deep, but there she was, skating as if she was going for 2010 gold in Vancouver.

Gliding in a circle, she crossed her right leg over her left as she tightened the circle toward the center and pushed it back out wide again. Then she went straight back to the middle, gathering speed in the two short steps it took her to arrive there, and spun, her body pitched forward, arms straight out from her sides, and one leg pointed back, as straight as a ruler. Still spinning, she straightened and tucked her arms in close, spinning impossibly fast for a girl in the fourth grade, even one who lingers over a few cups of coffee on Saturdays. When the spinning slowed, she hopped into a plucky finish, playfully cocking her hip and throwing her arms into the air. On a final, imaginary musical beat, she brought one hand down to her hip and pointed straight out with the other, presumably at the invisible French judge, who might be most easily swayed by the coquettish attention suddenly cast his way.

It was shameful that her talent was going to waste, rotting away while her mother made every attempt to pretend she didn't exist.

He looked again. Clearly, the ice was bumpy. Not the ideal surface. Probably not even safe, but she didn't appear to care. The look on Lucinda's face was pure joy, what little of her face was visible under her hat.

Sighing, he turned away from the window, picked up his stack of mail, and sauntered into the kitchen to consider what, if anything, could be done.

Chapter 16

Muriel Danby's
Figure Eights Skating School

It was the problem before the problem. Not only did Penelope's wedding demand Jack leave his home for three to five surely terrifying hours on a bitter evening in deepest, darkest January, but now he needed to go out into the world to buy himself a tux. A very inexpensive tux. Thankfully, Harlan, with his intimate knowledge of Boston's second-hand retail underbelly, had insisted that pre-Christmas was the perfect time to snap up formal wear. He said that most well-heeled and well-suited partygoers upgrade their tuxedos and frocks just prior to the holidays, and that the thrift shops typically round up countless trash bags full of castoffs to display them for the party season of the underbelly itself. Underbelly or "tier two" parties, according to Harlan, were far preferable to ritzier affairs, and generally displayed Christmas balloons instead of live garland and white fairy lights, offered warm Budweiser instead of iced Cristal, and served much tinier shrimp, the kind that came in shrink-wrapped plastic bags in the freezer section of the A&P, shrimp that was probably wise to avoid entirely. In Harlan's opinion, these parties had much more to offer a Man of Cheese like himself.

While not fully certain that dressing like the underbelly, while attending an affair where the shrimp would likely be the size of Mrs. Brady's head before the great snowplow made its way along the menacing drifts of Battersea Road, was such a good idea, Jack did as his son wished. Having neither the funds nor the desire to doll up for Penelope and Yale's betrothal, he realized he had very little choice in the matter, popped a couple of his chalky little friends, and strapped himself into the passenger seat of the old Buick.

Before pulling out of the garage, Harlan swiped his lips with cherry ChapStick and slipped on a pair of gigantic mirrored aviators. Thrift-shop Ray-Bans. He flipped up his vinyl collar and muttered, "Clear for takeoff," before peeling out into the alley in a shower of flying gravel and blue smoke.

Traffic on Battersea was slow, which forced Harlan to curb his flight, and instead drum annoyingly on the steering wheel and crane his head to the left, then right, then left again to plan his escape. Finally, at the main intersection, traffic opened up, and he threw everything he had into his left-hand turn.

"Slow down, Harlan," called Jack. "You'll get us both killed!"

"Hang on to your Nervy Durvies, Dad. I'm going to beat the old bird in the Altima." The car lurched forward.

"My pills are going to wear off too early," Jack said. "I've only got one left and it's for the ride home. It's all *very* well timed."

"I'll get you there so fast you won't need it." With a jerk of the wheel, Harlan pitched the car into the left lane and passed a red Toyota with a driver's training sign on the roof. A teenage girl clung to the steering wheel as if she were clinging to the edge of a cliff. "That's how it's done, sweetheart," Harlan called.

Jack closed his eyes and shook his head. "I'm going into a coma now. Wake me when we get there."

The big rusted car rocketed to a stop in front of a shabby storefront covered in huge painted cabbage roses. Jack didn't need to look up at the peeling sign to know what it said. SECONDHAND ROSE. The home of the giant-sized pumps. In Heritage Estates red.

"Isn't there someplace else we could try?" asked Jack, clutching the door handle. Stepping out of the car was much like stepping off a sail-boat in troubled waters: the ground continued to heave and pitch for a good ten minutes. He clung to the door, waiting for the seasickness to subside. "I'm not sure I'm up to chatting with Rose about her latest ca-tastrophe."

"Dorrie's friend Rose?"

Jack nodded carefully, as the horizon continued to throb and swell.

"*She's* Secondhand Rose?"

Again, Jack nodded.

"Whoa. It's like knowing a celebrity. This place is the best. And they're having a tuxedo sale. Come on, I'll take you in." Harlan slammed the door behind him, pitching the car back into turbulent water again, and galumphed into the store.

A bell tinkled as Jack entered. The floor, walls, and ceiling were painted white, an ailing, fleshy white Jack would have to call Soft-tissue White, with huge, fluffy roses—not quite as big as the monsters painted outside but big enough to swallow a man whole, should they so desire. The effect was rather sickening; or maybe Jack hadn't fully recovered from Harlan's driving.

"Jack!" Rose called out from behind a rose-encrusted counter. "How nice of you to come check out my little store."

"Hey, Rose."

"Are we looking for something special? Can I give you the grand tour?" Mercifully, the phone rang. Jack was still far too nauseated to stand and toss around polite banter, which, with Rose, might very easily digress into ghastly tales of post-op stitches being removed. Or, worse, staples. She held up a finger to assure him she'd be right back.

He slipped past and, holding on to passing racks of pilly and stretched-out sweaters for support, headed toward the back of the shop, where Harlan was whooping aloud over a rack of assorted sherbet-inspired formal wear. Jack's plan was to grab anything cheap and not too hideous, and get the hell out of this nightmarish depot. As he walked, roses appeared to follow him, and by the time he reached Harlan, his armpits were damp with sweat and worry.

Harlan held up a light blue tuxedo with a matching ruffled shirt. Only the blue of the shirt had picked up a sickly cast of green from careless sorting in the laundry. He held it up against Jack, who looked in the mirror and thought he'd pass.

Reaching for a black tux, a surprisingly elegant-looking one, with a crisp, white pleated shirt, Jack held it up in front of the blue tuxedo. Other than the pant legs and sleeves being a little long, it looked fantastic.

"Did you see this?" Jack asked as he reached inside the jacket to read the tag. "Jesus. This is an Armani. For . . ." He fumbled with the sleeve, looking for the price tag. "Only seventeen dollars and fifty cents. It doesn't look like it's ever been worn! You weren't kidding about this place."

Harlan took one look and crinkled his nose. "Ech. Don't be fooled by fancy designer labels, Dad. You haven't even looked at the rest. There's a green one, a brown one with a matching beige ascot—extremely decent—and, oh look, another blue one with Liberace ruffles." He handed it to Jack. "You've got to try this one on. Come on, *Liberace*."

But Jack was already stepping into the dressing room and latching the flower-coated door. "You try that one. It'll go great with your white dress shoes. I'm good with this."

Harlan made a hard-done-by grunt. "Mom wants me to wear a rich-boy, fancy-ass tux. She's buying it for me. I could puke every time I think about it."

Of course, Jack thought. Yale's new stepson could never be seen in powder-blue ruffled rags from the South End. "Wonderful," Jack said, pulling off his jeans and unclipping the sleek tuxedo pants. "You'll look every bit the son of the Million-dollar Pauper's creator. I'll make sure to bring the camera."

"Don't threaten me!"

Under the change-room door, Jack could see Harlan slide down onto the floor in a sulk. The boy had been particularly moody ever since he'd gotten back from his long weekend with Yale. The snow-cave weekend. It hadn't materialized, apparently because of an ill-timed stomachache of Harlan's. So, not only had Harlan been forced to spend the entire weekend in bed but Yale had been unable to stop the advance journey of his suitcase and Harlan's duffel bag, which were currently lying inside a tent in Northern Quebec. Harlan wouldn't be seeing his Hef robe or his grandfather slippers for days yet.

Jack buttoned the white shirt all the way up and tucked it into the pants, all thoughts of ravenous flowers long gone. Admiring himself in the mirror, he came to a realization. He'd never seen himself in something quite so . . . respectable. He looked wealthy, dashing. Like the kind of man who drops by his girlfriend's workplace to take her for a surprise lunch. Not a sandwiches-in-the-park, either. A real lunch in a restaurant where the waiters call him sir.

The bell jingled from the front of the store. As Jack slipped into the Armani jacket, sharp footsteps echoed through the shop.

"Excuse me," said a distinguished-sounding man. "I'm looking for a bag of clothes my housekeeper may have dropped off the other day by accident." He chuckled. "Or maybe it was my personal assistant, I'm not sure. Neither one is 'fessing up to it."

Jack heard Rose laugh and say, "Well, we've had quite a few bags dropped off this week. Do you remember what sort of bag it was and what, exactly, was inside, Mr. . . . ?"

"Chambers. Walt Chambers. The bag was large. Stiff white paper with corded handles. One of the things inside was a black scarf, a Michael Kors. Thick and long. The sort of thing you'd wrap around your neck when you take your kids out to the stables. You know how barns can be. Damp and drafty."

Rose didn't answer right away. Probably because she, like Jack, was plotting how quickly she could get her own Michael Kors scarf—in black—for the next such equestrian occasion. "Right," she said. "This is our belt-and-scarf rack. We've got a couple of black ones, as you can see."

"Hm. These appear to be made of some sort of man-made fiber . . ."

Jack couldn't resist. He stepped up onto the change-room stool and peered over the door to see a well-dressed man, fiftyish and tanned, with a sprinkling of gray in his otherwise pale brown hair, fumbling awkwardly through the scarves.

Harlan, too, was spying, hooting silently over his good fortune. Being able to witness this privileged creature strutting around inside of the holy land—the hallowed floral walls of the uncoolest place on earth.

Finally, Walt held up a scarf. "Ah. Found it." He turned it over and over, inspecting every thread. "Thank God. Now, there was also a DKNY charcoal V-neck."

"We have a whole lot of sweaters. A hundred maybe . . ." said Rose. "It's gray, you say?"

"Yes. Simple with a slim fit. The type of thing you could layer under a suit if you think the boardroom might be chilly, or casually toss on with a pair of jeans for window-shopping on Newbury Street. You know, lightweight but with tooth."

"D, K . . . how did you spell it?" Rose asked.

"DKNY. Donna Karan New York?"

Rose nodded and led the man in the direction of the change room, so

Jack leaped down and resumed his position in front of the mirror. Just to be sure he had enough cash, he pulled his wallet out of his jeans' pocket and counted the bills with shaky fingers. Twenty dollars. Wait. It was all too possible to miscount when you wanted something really badly. He didn't want to get to the cash and come up short while paying for a thrift-store tuxedo. He counted again.

Unable to bring himself to take off the tux and go back to being just Jack, he opened the change-room door. Perhaps a quick twirl for Harlan.

"Yes, that's my sweater," Walt was saying. "Now, how about my dark utility wash straight-leg Calvins and my cashmere boxers?"

Jack stepped out and stood in front of his son, who was rolling not only his eyes but his entire body.

"Cashmere boxers," Harlan whispered. "Oy! Kill me now."

"Shush!" Jack motioned for Harlan to stop spying. Then he reached down and dropped his wallet into Harlan's lap. "Count my bills, would you? Just make sure I have enough." He spun around with what he imagined to be something of a James Bond squint. "So, what do you think of your man-about-town father now?"

"Not much. I told you to try the blue."

Rose and Walt moved closer. She explained that all undergarments are disposed of immediately upon donation. Store policy.

"Disposed of? But they were in a package. They'd never been worn."

Rose shrugged. "Store policy."

"Are you absolutely sure they're gone? They were *extremely* difficult to find. Most companies intentionally mislabel regular wool boxers, double the price, and sell them as cashmere."

"I'm sorry, Mr. Chambers. But our policy extends to all undergarments."

Walt Chambers let out a slow, angry breath and clenched his chiseled jaw. "All right. If they're gone, they're gone. I just need my tuxedo and I'll be on my way."

Tuxedo.

Of course. Immediately, Jack looked down at the dress suit that accomplished the impossible. Transformed a penniless hermit into someone nearly upstanding. Someone worthy of protecting his neck in breezy stables, and brazened enough to show up both sweatered *and* suited to the annual meeting. Someone deserving of the title Son of a Rock Star.

Someone able to leave the house without meds.

Walt continued, "Obviously it's black. A three-button Giorgio Armani with notched grosgrain lapels. And classic wing-collar evening shirt."

Jack's heart sank. It would have been too good to be true, for Jack to be able to stride into his ex-wife's wedding looking like a million bucks. Or, if not quite a million, a hell of a lot more than the $17.50 on the price tag.

"My tuxedo!" Walt's face went chalky and sunless with horror. "Someone's inside it. It's a two-thousand-dollar Armani and you have people trying it on?" He turned his back to Jack and Harlan so they wouldn't hear. But they did. "Would you ask that . . . that customer to kindly step out of my Armani?"

From his designer-name dropping to his clothing descriptions, Walt had clearly unglued Rose. She approached Jack, wringing her hands. "Jack? I believe the tuxedo belongs to Mr. Chambers."

But Jack wasn't parting with his rakish new 007 persona so fast. Nor did he like being called "people." He cleared his throat and looked at Chambers. "You think this is your tux?"

"I know it's my tux."

"Mm. But can we be totally sure? Perhaps yours has been sold. Surely it would never do to have you wear someone else's castoffs?"

"Forget it, Dad," whispered Harlan. "Get the blue one."

"It's mine. The jacket size is forty-two regular."

Jack chuckled, shaking his head. "A very popular size. Some might say the most popular size of all."

Walt shifted his repossessed items to one arm and pointed at Jack's chest. "There's a business card in the breast pocket. Cynthia Summers."

Jack pulled the jacket open and, raising his eyebrows, nodded toward the pocket.

Clearly tiring of the whole charade, Walt sighed and nodded back.

If this was someone else's life, there would be no card. Jack would rummage around in the empty pocket and offer an I-told-you-so shrug. Then he would laugh, shake his head at Walt's pathetic attempt to snatch the tux off another man's back, slap twenty dollars on Rose's cash counter, and saunter back to the old Buick with his son.

Jack slid his hand into the pocket. The lining was impossibly cool and silky. Impeccably made. As his hand went deeper, his fingertips brushed against . . . what else? A business card.

He pulled out Cynthia's card and handed it to Walt. "It'll just take me a minute to change," he said, stepping back into the change room.

Clearly, this was not someone else's life.

By the time he came out dressed in his just-Jack clothes, Walt was gone. "Come on," he said to Harlan. "Let's go."

"But you still need a tux."

Rose said, "There's a nice one over here. It's made by Starlight Toggery."

Jack just smiled and moved toward the door.

"Made in Detroit," she added, as if it was a real sale-clencher. "This one's only seven fifty."

"Dad. Mom will kill you if you don't buy one."

Jack stopped, rubbed his stubbly chin, then grinned at Rose. "All right. I'll take the Starlight. But only if you swear it really is made in Detroit. I don't want to support any of these mislabeling scam outfits."

Rose crossed her heart. Harlan smirked.

At $7.50, he didn't really care how it fit. It was black and cheap. Nothing was going to come close to the Armani. He turned to head over to walk to the cash desk, also covered in man-eating roses, and walked straight into a woman holding a pair of red shoes.

Dorrie Allsop.

This day was just getting better and better.

"Dorrie." He felt his cheeks burning at being found here. In her special shop, buying a shabby tuxedo. Though, he supposed, he should be thankful she hadn't been here to witness his public-undressing moments earlier. "This is a surprise. What are you doing here?"

She smiled, holding up her shoes, which Jack was fairly sure were smaller than the other pair. "Picking up another pair of work shoes. They're a bit tight, but the color is perfect." She paused a moment, chewing on her lower lip and staring at Jack. She cleared her throat. "I don't buy *all* my work clothes here, you know."

"No. I'm sure you don't."

"Mostly I get them at Filene's Basement." She sniffed. "They have excellent prices. Nice selection."

He nodded, feeling his pulse race. Wondering what about him made her think he was so narrow-minded when it came to the origins of her work wardrobe; he tugged at his coat, pulling it wide open. The heat seemed to be pouring straight down on him from a vented yellow rose directly above his head. He nodded toward his tux. "Fancy wedding," he explained.

Her mouth dropped. "You know I didn't even know you were engaged? Such a man of mystery."

As much as he liked the title, he smiled and said, "No, no. My ex-wife is getting married."

"Oh dear. I'm sorry."

A moment of silence followed, during which the heat from above burned hotter.

Jack scratched at his turtleneck. "Do you find it warm in here?"

She shook her head, and something on the next aisle caught her eye. "Ooh, excuse me a second," she said. "I've been looking all over . . ." Her voice trailed off as she bent over and examined the sleeve of a blouse.

Checking his watch, Jack realized prickly heat wasn't his only problem. His Nervy Durvies were about to expire. He whispered to Harlan, who was hiding behind him, "*Quick*, give me my wallet."

Harlan handed it over and rolled his eyes as Jack unzipped the pill compartment. There was nothing in it. The pill he'd placed in the pocket that morning was gone.

He looked at Harlan. "Where's my pill?"

"I dunno." Harlan slunk out of the store with his hands deep in his pockets.

Searching through the other pockets of his wallet, Jack started to panic. The Armani, the heat, the mammoth roses, and now Dorrie, were all taking their toll on him. He had to get home. He'd pick up the tux later. Send Harlan for it.

As long as he could escape this—

"Are you sure it'll fit?" Dorrie was back, pointing at the black tux.

"Hm? Yes. But I might leave it for now . . ." He looked toward the door to see if Harlan was in the car, warming it up.

"Let's see." She took it from his hand and held the sleeves up to his arm, shaking her head. "No, definitely too long."

"It's just as well," he said, stepping away. "I'll have to keep looking."

"Nonsense. I'll take it up for you. A well-cut tux like this is a real treasure. You won't find a nice black one, a tux by Starlight Toggery, in any other secondhand shop in Boston. It's from Detroit, you know." She handed it back to him and started walking toward the cash register. "You've struck oil here, Jack. Come. You'd better pay for it before someone else comes in here and snatches it right out of your hands."

Hm. Yes. That would be terrible. "No, really—"

She turned around. "Rose will ring you up. And I'll get you my ten-percent frequent buyer discount."

It was too late. Rose was already reaching for his tux and whispering to Dorrie. He sidled up to the counter very slowly, since Rose seemed to be speaking about him, repeatedly peeking over at him and then disappearing behind Dorrie to mumble excitedly. Dorrie swatted Rose's murmurings away as if they were flies on a rose petal.

As Jack got within earshot, he cleared his throat with a mighty grunt to announce his proximity. The stares and whispers were piling right on top of the flowered walls into one gigantic, suffocating pile of hot, sticky fear. And not only that, he was pretty sure he smelled natural gas.

"So, I hear you're going to a wedding?" Rose's grinning eyes darted from Jack to Dorrie and back again. "That'll be nice." She drew out the word nice far too long, then accentuated it with a sharp snap of her gum.

"Mmm. Do you smell gas?"

Dorrie sniffed the air, shaking her head, but Rose just went on smiling and chewing. "If there were a leak, I'd smell it," Rose said, still fondling the tux. "I've got a nose for gas."

"I'm pretty sure that's what I'm smelling . . ."

Rose pointed toward a small metal spray can on the desk. "You're smelling my aromatherapy atomizer. English Rose, it's called."

What else? "Mm." Jack was forced to wait, gripping the counter for support, throughout the lengthy process of folding, wrapping, bagging, discounting, paying, and waiting for the temperamental register to spit out a receipt; all the while wishing another exasperated used-tux shopper would walk in the door with a shotgun and shoot him dead.

As Secondhand Rose handed him a blossom-covered bag with a wink and a snap, Dorrie took his elbow and guided him across every ravenous floor rose she could, as she led him out of the store. "I was thinking, Jack, and you can say no if it bothers you, I was thinking maybe we could paint your front-hall area. Maybe even the living room. We wouldn't have to even patch the walls. We could leave that for the new owners, but I just think a nice solid color instead of that tired wallpaper would . . ."

"Sure," Jack said, bursting through the tinkling door and into the air. He aimed himself toward the car and marched forward. Where the hell had that pill gotten to? Could he possibly have forgotten it?

"How about tomorrow? I was thinking we could start early and I could bring my wallpaper steamer . . ."

"Right. Bye then, Dorrie." He jumped into the car and sped off, watching Dorrie's confused expression in his mirror.

"HOLD THTILL, DACK," Dorrie said with pins between her teeth. "There. That's the latht one." She got up off the floor, where she'd been pinning his trouser legs, and twirled her arm, instructing him to spin around.

Stiffly, he held his arms out from his sides and turned in a slow circle. "I really do appreciate this," he said as she adjusted a pin on one arm. "I'd have shown up at the wedding looking like an ape."

She smiled, spitting pins into a small plastic container. "Your date wouldn't have appreciated that, I don't suppose. Dancing with an ape. You can change now."

Terrified to move lest he die a thousand deaths by pinpricks, he shuffled from the living room. Going up the stairs was a problem, however. He managed to step up by spreading his legs wide and waddling up straight-legged. He called back, "I'm not bringing one."

"One what?"

"A date. I'm going with Harlan."

There was a pause, then she called, "That'll be nice."

Up in his room, Jack stepped out of the tuxedo as though its pockets were packed with bombs, and pulled on a ratty gray sweat suit. One he'd had since Harlan was a toddler, as evidenced by the stains of children's grape-flavored cough syrup spattered across one shoulder. It made for a perfect painting outfit.

Trusting his highly developed sense of color, Dorrie had left the paint decision to Jack. He smiled, thinking of the three cans sitting in the front hall at that very moment; paint cans with complicated formulas scrawled across the lids. What he hadn't written on the lids, as he normally would have, was the name of his latest color. Dorrie might have caught on and argued for a more uplifting shade, like the French Linen in the kitchen.

He was almost certain she wasn't expecting his latest creation.

He trotted down the stairs, whistling. Dorrie waited patiently beside the paint cans; she'd wanted to make the moment a true unveiling, just like the TV decorating shows, and be right beside the buckets when the lids came off. She looked so excited Jack felt a pang of guilt as he swung down onto the checkered floor.

"So." He clapped his hands. "Are we ready to see our new color?"

"Ready? I could barely sleep last night. With your eye for color . . . oh, I can't wait." She squeezed her hands together and tapped her feet, which were shod in white sneakers. She, too, was wearing painting clothes—an oversized man's dress shirt and old jeans. No sign of real estate agent, Jack thought. Not today.

Jack reached for a screwdriver and pried open one side of the first can. Before lifting it off, he glanced up at Dorrie, who was covering her eyes. She peeked through her fingers at him. "You're going to torture me, is that it?"

Smiling, Jack pried open the other side. "Are you ready?" he asked before removing the lid.

She swatted him with a clean rag. "Yes! Open it."

With great flourish, he swung the lid off the can to reveal his creation in all its murky, swamp-monster glory.

He called it Bile.

She didn't move. Then she kneeled closer and peered into the can. "I thought it would be white," she said, looking up at Jack. "It's more of a . . ." She glanced back at the Bile. "Green, is it?"

"Very complex formula, too." Jack nodded. "Green, as you probably know, represents life and harmony; it lowers tension; it's harmonious with nature. Renewal. That's what it's all about." But not when mixed with yellow and brown, he didn't say. Never when mixed with yellow and brown. That only calls to mind puppy vomit. Even cat sick is a better color.

She blinked. "Renewal. I like it. We'll call it Renewal." Trying to smile, she dipped a stir stick into the polluted bog water and stirred, clearly hoping to improve it. "If you like it, I know it's good," she said. "I know how much you love these walls."

Jack passed her a brush. "Shall we begin?"

BY EVENING, BOTH the main-floor hallway and the living room were complete, Dorrie was exhausted, and Jack was ecstatic. The front part of the house glowed with weeping, oozing, gangrenous light. It made him sick to look at it and, with any luck, would only fester in the curing process.

From her spot on the living-room floor, Dorrie gulped her wine, a celebratory indulgence Jack had insisted upon in a moment of guilt. She trusted him so completely, he felt as if he was lying to an innocent toddler. He was hoping alcohol would wipe the look of pride from her eyes, and the feeling of being a filthy liar from his conscience. "Would you say it's a khaki, of sorts?" she asked, her voice rising into a squeak.

"Of sorts," he said, rolling his protective tarps into a ball. "A mossy khaki."

"I hope people can recognize the sophistication of such a color. People can be very narrow-minded. Do you think it would go well with red?"

She was probably thinking of Heritage Estates red. "As well as with any other color, sure."

"Maybe you'll come in and pick colors for all my listings." She looked up at him. "When I list a few more, that is. And when I'm really well known, I'll bring you into every home and have you work your magic. I'll convince the homeowners you're worth every cent." She folded up a smaller tarp and handed it to him with a smile.

That would mean he'd have to leave the house lucid enough to make a proper decision. "I'm really best with whites."

Carrying a stack of tarps through the hall to the cellar, he heard sounds coming from Lucinda's side of the wall. Muffled shrieks and barking. Slowing his step but not stopping, he moved closer to the wall and bent over. Lucinda crawled in quick, nimble circles around her mother's feet, yapping and snarling, while Samantha swatted at her with a rolled-up newspaper, screeching something about not retching on the new rug. Catching Jack's eye, Lucie crinkled her nose into a lopsided grin and scooted out of sight, her mother calling, "Get back here, young lady, or I'll rub your nose in it!"

Chuckling to himself, he tossed the sheets down the cellar steps, and before heading back into the living room to see Dorrie out, he stopped to pick up some fallen mail beneath the phone table. He stacked the envelopes and papers into an orderly pile and froze. The top flyer, powder-pink with a terrible drawing of something resembling a figure skater in the center, read at the top:

MURIEL DANBY'S
FIGURE EIGHTS SKATING SCHOOL
(617) 555-4134

Staring at the flyer, he pursed his lips and grunted. A skating school, right down at Frog Pond, in the park.

Close by.

Reasonable rates.

Individual attention.

He picked up the phone and dialed. "Yes." Pausing, he glanced toward the dining room. "You teach kids to skate?"

SAMANTHA BALLARD'S YOGA shoes moved in time with her every thought. Jack yanked hard on the phone cord, which stretched all the way from the kitchen to a spot just across from the hole in the dining-room wall where he and Lucie sat cross-legged, spying on her mother's feet from across the room—close enough to see Samantha's laces were untied but far enough to ensure Jack's voice, muffled by his free hand, wouldn't be heard. An unnecessary precaution, most likely, as her blaring New Age music would surely block out any errant noises from Jack's side of the wall.

The figure-skating flyer rested between Jack and Lucinda but was slowly being inched closer and closer to Lucinda, who held her breath as she waited for her mother's answer.

"Lucinda once begged me, down on all fours—which is not in itself so unusual, really—to enroll her in ballet lessons," Samantha finally said. "She loved ballet, she said. So, I took her." The shoes stood still. "Know what happened?" As she announced what happened, she paced again. "She quit after three classes."

"Yes, well—"

"I realize you're trying to help, Mr. Madigan, but we've been down this road with Lucinda before. It's a phase. She'll grow out of it." One foot tapped the ground as if waiting for a bus. Not, of course, that this particular foot, or shoe, had likely *ever* set foot on any form of public transportation.

"Certainly it's worth a try. She might surprise you this time."

"You know where she is right now? At her friend's house learning to knit. It'll last a week, I promise you. "

Lucinda rolled her eyes and giggled, holding up a pair of knitting needles caught up in a huge tangle of yellow wool.

"Surely *someone* could take her," said Jack. "Another family member who doesn't have as many pressing demands on her time. The lessons are held every Thursday, six o'clock."

"It's not like I don't want to. It's that I'm training to be a yoga instructor myself and I have to log a certain number of hours—"

"Right. I understand. It's just that Lucinda's so talented. Doesn't she have an aunt—what about that tall, thin woman you brought over here for one of Baz's autographed photos?"

"That was Rick's sister, Karen, and she's since moved to Australia." Samantha paused. "I've been meaning to ask you, Mr. Madigan, do you have any more of those signed photos? Mine's somehow gone missing and you know I'm your dad's biggest fan."

Damn. He could have used a photo as collateral. "No, that was the last one, actually."

"Oh. Do you have anything else with his signature? I'd be willing to pay you for it."

"Unfortunately, no. About these skating lessons . . . ?"

Lucie's head shook side to side. Her tiny shoulders drooped a bit as she stared down at the floor.

"I appreciate your help, Mr. Madigan, but it's just a hectic year for us. And Thursdays are our busiest days."

Seeing an opening, Jack said, "Muriel Danby has one space open on Saturday mornings as well. Nine-thirty, I believe, but we'd have to book soon or it'll go—"

"Saturdays are definitely out. Rick goes into the office and I have a class."

"I *told* you," Lucinda said under her breath as she picked at her sock.

"But certainly something can be done. I'd take her myself, but I don't have the . . ." mental fortitude to step out my front door, Jack didn't say. The floor on the other side of the hole grew quiet as Samantha's foot stopped tapping.

"Seriously?" Samantha perked up. "Baz Madigan's son taking my own daughter to skating class? Wow. You wouldn't mind?"

"No! No." He started to object. Glancing at Lucie, he could see her cheeks burning red as she tried to make herself smaller. "No . . ."

"Are you sure? It's awfully kind of you. I mean we'll pay for the lessons and everything. And pay for your gas and—"

"No! Wait," Jack said.

"Forget it," mouthed Lucinda silently, shaking her head. She shut her eyes and turned away.

"We really appreciate this, Mr. Madigan. Wait'll I call Karen in Australia and tell her. She'll die."

Lucie stood up and started toward the back door, her face hidden.

"Wait!" Jack whispered loudly enough to stop the little girl in her tracks. Into the phone, he said, "It's no problem, Samantha. I don't mind a bit."

Lucinda walked back toward him as he dropped the phone into his lap and tried to figure out how he was going to accomplish the impossible. "What are you doing?" she asked. "You can't take me. You *know* you can't."

"We're going to get you there." He patted her head on his way back to the kitchen where he hung up the receiver. "Leave the details to Jack."

Chapter 17

Every Thursday at Six

For the second time in two days, Jack was told to keep still. This time by Harlan, who was trimming Jack's hair straight across the back to give it time to settle before the wedding.

"What do you mean, every Thursday at six and make sure her laces are tightened?" Harlan asked with a whine. "I'm a very busy person. A *senior* in high school."

"Sometimes we do things that inconvenience us just because it's good for someone else. Like me going to your mother's wedding." Jack's arms were growing tired from leaning over the porcelain sink in his bathroom with a big towel wrapped around his shoulders.

"I have a life," Harlan pointed out with a snort, snipping rather erratically. "*You* take the kid."

"That's not funny."

"Well it's not so easy being your son, you know." The scissors flailed wildly behind Jack's head as Harlan spoke. "It's a lot of extra work."

"Don't get fancy with those blades, kiddo. It's one hour, once a week. Consider it your opportunity to give back to the community. Besides, of course, the obvious gift we all get from viewing your hairy ankles in flood pants." Looking in the mirror, Jack turned his head slightly to assess the damage.

"They're called floods." Harlan sighed, heavily inconvenienced, and resumed snipping. "Sometimes I don't know why I bother educating you . . ."

"I assume your tuxedo won't have 'floods.'"

"My tuxedo is a complete joke."

"Well, we should look like quite the pair when we walk into the reception all dolled up." Jack laughed to himself. "We can only hope the
ladies manage to contain themselves."

Harlan stopped snipping and stared at the back of Jack's head. "Uh,
Dad? I'm not going with you. I have to be there early for photos and
shit. I'm sleeping at Mom's the night before." Looking uncomfortable,
he started cutting again. "But I'll see you there lots. Melissa and I will
come by your table . . ."

Jack spun around. "Your mother didn't even put us at the same
table?"

"There's some kind of head table. I asked her if you could sit there,
too, but she said it wouldn't be appropriate or something."

"Well, who am I sitting with?"

Harlan shrugged, turning Jack's head toward the mirror again so he
could get on with the job. "Yale's family from Santa Barbara. His grandparents, I think. And a great-uncle and a few great-aunts whose hus-
bands already dropped dead." Harlan looked at Jack. "You might want
to consider bringing a date, Dad. The grandparents are in pretty rough
shape. He's gone all freaky-like, and she can't see. Could be a rough
table. And those creaky widows might even start looking at *you*."

The Table of Broken People, Jack thought, furious. Wasn't that just
like Penelope, to gather the phobic, the decaying, and the infirm together at one table to protect the regular guests?

This was what it had come to. He hadn't been a convenient husband,
and now he wasn't even a convenient guest.

He calculated how long the blessed night would be. No more than
one hour for the ceremony. About a half hour of milling around drinking and nibbling crudités before being seated for dinner, which wouldn't
start for another hour at least, not until after a few dance numbers and
what would probably be a nauseating amount of speeches—the longest
of all surely being Yale's, as eager as he would be to capture his vitamin-
enriched vitality on film.

Add in the two-hour dinner, peppered with dancing and carousing,
and you had yourself a conservative four and a half hours of revelry and
fun. Or, for Jack Madigan, spinning and sucking back pills.

A date. Of course, it would help having someone to talk to. Especially
someone who still had her teeth.

But who? Mrs. O'Sullivan, his neighbor on the other side, was at least fifteen years his senior. The girl at the grocery store, the one Harlan had accused him of flirting with when he commented on her hairstyle, was a possibility—or would have been a possibility if she hadn't opened her mouth to expose what better resembled Stonehenge than a proper set of adult teeth.

Certainly, there was Dorrie.

As if reading his mind, Harlan stopped cutting. "Why don't you ask the broad with the big red shoes? Dorrie."

Jack leaned closer to the mirror, tilting his head left, then right. "Nice job. Very nice." He turned around and shook the towel from his shoulders, wadded it into a ball, and reached for the broom to sweep up the hair scattered across the white honeycomb-tiled floor. "How much do I owe you, sir?"

Harlan didn't move. "Didn't you hear me? Dorrie. Ask *her*. At least she still has bladder control."

Jack stared at the hair he was sweeping into a small pile.

Dorrie.

He could see how spending a night in her company could be entertaining. He now knew for sure that she owned clothing other than her gawky work uniform. He might actually enjoy himself—sufficiently anesthetized, of course.

He stopped sweeping.

There lay the real problem. He couldn't count on himself to hold it together, especially if Harlan wasn't by his side. Anything could set him off and render the Nervy Durvies useless. And if he had a dizzy attack, did he really want Dorrie to witness it? She didn't know about his . . . problem.

"No," he said to Harlan as he swept the hair into a dented metal dustpan. "It wouldn't be professional. Now, would you pass over that plastic bag behind you, please?"

FAIRLY CERTAIN IT was another telemarketing call from overseas, Jack didn't rush to answer the ringing phone. He stuffed the remainder of his sandwich into his mouth and placed his plate into the sink.

"Yeah?"

"Jack Madigan? Maxwell Ridpath here."

Jack chewed and swallowed in a hurry. "Maxwell. Nice to hear from you. How goes the project?"

"Just came out of a planning meeting actually. I've got a question for you and hope you've got the answer we're looking for." He laughed but sounded dead serious.

"Shoot."

"I think I mentioned before that this project is going to be very important to the art world here in Chicago. That we're representing the most important works of photography in the world—"

"You sure did."

"You see, the design is truly unique. We've assembled an exceptionally forward-thinking team of architects, who've given us exactly what we wanted . . . a space that is progressive in every way. Unique to us alone. Inimitable, really."

Not sure how to respond to this, Jack just waited.

"*Architectural Digest* is doing a cover feature on the project next season."

"Wow. Good stuff."

"Yes. We're all terribly excited."

"I'm hoping I can play a small role in it," Jack said, attempting to spin the conversation around to the part where he can bring his mortgage back into good standing.

"That's why I rang. We're all fairly certain we'd like to bring you on as color engineer."

"Fantastic." Jack grinned so wide it hurt. "I won't argue with your choice."

"Yes. And we'd like our colors not only to be customized to our space but to be exclusive. The planning committee would like a commitment from you that we could buy absolute rights to your formulas. We may keep the colors to ourselves, or who knows? We could reproduce them and sell them one day to patrons. So long as we maintain full rights. I know it's a lot to ask—"

"No, no. Not too much to ask. I've got no problem with selling the rights to my magic potions," Jack said with a laugh.

"Of course, your remuneration would be rather handsome. Not

unlike buying a piece of art. One of our longtime patrons is just as fussy as I am about getting the right white for the project and is willing to fund your fees. I've told him that you're an old master with color."

"Well. *Old*. I wouldn't quite say—"

"Would one hundred fifty thousand dollars cover us for fifteen separate formulas? One for every area of the gallery . . . ?"

Maxwell was still speaking. But Jack had stopped listening. Forget redeeming his mortgage. That kind of money could save his house. Just like that. No more real estate showings, no more sign out front, no more Dorrie. Every problem solved.

"Jack? If you're concerned it's not enough . . ."

"What? No. No, it's just fine. More than fine."

"Excellent. And if this goes well, we'd like to refer you over to the sister gallery we're building in Phoenix. Very similar in scale and global importance, this next project will feature largely landscape photography . . ."

Another project—similar in scale? Another one-fifty? That would be the end of any mortgage whatsoever. He'd own the house outright. Once again. Just like in the carefree, mortgage-free days before The Rotted Core's Great North American Tour. Or the Great North American Mistake, as Penelope called it.

"I assume, Jack, you'd be willing to help on future projects?"

Too relieved to stand any longer, Jack slid down the wall and dropped his head into his hand. "I'm your guy, Maxwell."

"Brilliant," Maxwell said. "Ring you in a fortnight then with hotel and flight arrangements."

Hotel and flight arrangements? Jack hung up the phone. Why ever should he need to know Maxwell's hotel details? As long as he showed up with a nice fat check, Maxwell Ridpath could fly the plane into Boston himself for all he cared.

LUCINDA DANCED AROUND the kitchen, clutching the Muriel Danby's Figure Eights Skating School flyer to her chest. "I couldn't even sleep all night!" she said, her thin hair flying out in all directions as she moved. "I know just what I'm going to wear for my first lesson. My black skating skirt with blue snowman tights. And on top, I'll wear my red wool sweater with the white dots. 'Cause it matches my red mittens and hat."

From the top of his stepladder, Jack reached into the cupboard he was cleaning out and scrubbed it with a rag before loading the cans of creamed corn and boxes of Hamburger Helper back onto the shelf. The house had been particularly chilly, and he'd wrapped his ratty bathrobe over jeans and a sweater. "I've always meant to ask: Did your mother actually knit you the mitts and hat?"

Lucinda rolled her eyes dramatically and made a clucking sound with her little tongue. "As if. She got them at some fancy place. Only Rosalind got the blue set. She always gets the blue clothes and I'm the one with the blue eyes!"

Jack smiled and pulled the soup cans off the next shelf. "Seems to me, you've got more of a red personality. Seems like they suit you just fine."

"They're okay. I'd just have liked to choose. Just for once."

He nodded. He wouldn't have minded a little choice in his life, himself. "Keep in mind, the lessons are in the park. You're going to need a jacket. And a scarf."

"But a jacket will ruin *everything*. I'll be all puffed up. Besides, once I'm warmed up it would get too hot."

She actually had a point there. He attacked a gummy spot on the middle shelf. "Maybe just for the journey there and back, then."

"You got your hair cut," she said, ignoring his suggestion.

He grumbled, "Ex-wife's getting married soon. I wanted to give it time to lose that 'just-cut' look."

"Hm. Smart." She opened a package of marshmallow cookies on the counter and helped herself to two. "I don't need Harlan to take me. I could walk there myself. One time, before my mom signed me up for the bus program at school, she forgot to pick me up from first grade and I walked the whole way home."

"The whole way home? How far?"

"I counted six stoplights."

"At what age?"

"Seven. *And* it was raining. A guy in a van stopped and said he'd take me, but I said no." She shrugged. "You know, because of molestation and murder."

Jack turned around, unsure as to which was more disturbing, a seven-year-old crossing six major intersections in the rain, *alone*, or her flat acknowledgment of the degradation of society. "Harlan is looking forward to taking you. Said he'd be honored to escort the next Olympic champion to her first lesson." He lied, smiling.

"Oh. But what about the second and the third and the . . ."

"The fourth and the fifth and so on."

This pleased her. Grinning again, she looked at the flyer. "Muriel Danby. Sounds like a good coach, don't you think?"

"Perfect."

"When I win my first gold medal, I'll thank her. It's all because of Muriel Danby's Figure Eights Skating School, I'll say. And Jack Madigan, of course."

Jack smiled from inside the shelf.

"Is she nice?" asked Lucinda.

"Very nice."

"Is she a mother?"

"I didn't ask."

"Do you think she teaches her own kids? *Lucky*. They probably get to go to every single lesson. Do you think she takes them to every single lesson?"

Jack smiled a sad smile. "They might not like to skate."

"Is she pretty?"

"What difference does that make?" Climbing down from the stool, Jack rinsed the cloth in the sink, wrung out the excess water, and climbed back up to tackle the bottom shelf.

"If she's really ugly, like if she has a big old crooked witch nose or something, I might not be able to look at her. It could mess up my training, that's all."

"I can almost guarantee that she does not have a big old crooked witch nose. Or green skin, or warts, or a broom."

"Good." Lucie sighed happily. "I hope she's as pretty as Dorrie Allsop."

Jack's foot slipped off the edge of the stool, damn near knocking it over and toppling him onto the marble floor. "What do *you* know about Dorrie Allsop?"

"I hear things." Lucie grinned. "I *see* things."

"You mean, you spy on us?"

"I think she's beautiful. She needs No-More-Tangles shampoo, but she's very pretty."

Jack didn't say anything and, unwilling to let Lucie see his burning cheeks, pushed his face farther inside the cupboard.

"Is she coming with you to Harlan's mother's wedding?" she asked with her mouth full of marshmallow.

"Dorrie is the real estate agent trying to sell my house out from underneath my feet. She is *not* coming with me to my ex-wife's wedding."

"Whatever. Don't blow a tire over it."

"I'm not *blowing a tire* over it!"

Her feet padded along the floor in what he knew, without looking, was some sort of spiral spin under an imagined blue spotlight. "I hope it doesn't snow," she said.

Jack cracked his head on the middle shelf. This child was infuriating. "What?" He looked out from the cupboard now to see her spinning with her arms straight above her head. "Must we spin in the kitchen, Lucinda?"

"On Thursday," she explained, twirling faster and causing a pit of hollowness to form in Jack's stomach. "I don't want it to snow during my lesson. Or I hope the ice doesn't melt. It would be terrible if the ice melted the day before my first lesson."

"The weather should be fine. Didn't your mother teach you not to spin with cookies in your mouth?"

"Swallowed already," she said, leaping into a grand finale on her knees. She sauntered back to the cookie bag and pulled out another, carefully chewing the chocolate shell off the marshmallow center. After licking the white goo clean of all chocolate traces, she looked up at Jack with chocolate between her teeth and tilted her head. "You could get her number from the sign."

"What?"

"Dorrie Allsop's phone number." She pointed toward the front of the house. "It's right there on the sign."

Jack shook his head. Everybody's a matchmaker. He sighed to himself.

• • •

HE STARED AT the phone. Pick it up, he told himself. Just pick it up and dial. People ask other people out on dates all the time.

He picked up the receiver, staring into his French Linen wall for confidence. At the very least, Dorrie admired his color sense. And she might enjoy going to a fancy wedding. Women loved that sort of thing, didn't they? It gave them an excuse to get gussied up and dance. Satisfied their princess fantasies, or something, he'd read.

Of course, she'd have to pick him up; he'd never drive under the influence of the number of pills it was going to take to get him out the door without Harlan. Before he could change his mind, he dialed the number printed on her Heritage Estates business card. Once the ringing started, he imagined her lunging at the phone, so excited to hear it jangling she'd nearly yank it off the desk. It rang for a second time, then a third. A fourth. Maybe she was off buying another pair of red shoes. It rang again; that made five rings. Jack had just started to hang up when she picked up.

"Doreen Allsop. Heritage Estates."

"Dorrie." He made his voice sound jaunty, casual. "It's Jack here."

"Jack." Was it his imagination, or did she sound disappointed? "Is something wrong?"

He laughed. "No. Everything's fine. I, I was just sitting here wondering. I was wondering if, well, you know I've got this wedding coming up in a couple of weeks . . ."

"Oh yes. Your ex-wife's wedding." She clucked her tongue in disapproval. Very encouraging, Jack thought.

"Yes. That's the one. You see—"

"Oops. Hang on; I've got another call coming through." She put him on hold. Of course, it was possible that her phone was jangling with more frequency now. She picked up again. "Sorry, Jack, you were saying?"

"Yes, I was saying that I'm going to this wedding and—"

"Hang on again." Someone in the background asked her something about a courier package. "Thanks, Colleen," she said, before returning to Jack. "Sorry again. Busy day."

"I was wondering if you'd like to come to the wedding with me."

The pause that followed almost killed him. Dead. "As your date?"

He laughed. "Yes, I suppose you'd be my date."

Another pause. "But I'm your real estate agent."

"Sure, I've thought about all that. I know you're trying to sell my house, and I'm trying to hold on to it. But it's your job. It's not like you showed up on my doorstep out of the blue and tried to wrestle my house away from me now, is it?"

"I meant that you're my client. I have a very strict policy regarding dating clients. I don't do it."

Jack hadn't considered this. "But how can you have a policy yet? I'm your only listing. Your only client."

"Still. Rules are rules. I'm sorry, Jack. It could lead to any number of terrible things. You could fall for me, making any future showings rough and prickly; or I could fall for you and allow my feelings to disrupt any future offer. Or we could both wind up despising each other, with me telling half of Boston that you've got rusted pipes and you telling the other half that I'm a sorry excuse for an agent."

She left out the one remaining possibility: of their both having a decent time and nobody actually sinking to the tempestuous slandering of anyone else. "I truly was just thinking of a date. I wasn't attaching any long-term emotional obligations to it. Just the one evening."

"It would still break the rule."

"We could consider this a business meeting; we could talk about my house during the speeches. Lord knows we won't want to hear the speeches."

"I'm so sorry, Jack," she said. "It just wouldn't be right. You understand, don't you?"

"Sure. I understand. Have a nice day, Dorrie."

Click.

He stared at the floor now. So, that was that. She refused to go out with him. He was a client and nothing would tempt her into the dodgy territory of mixing business with pleasure. Well, maybe not pleasure exactly, in this case. He wasn't sure how pleasurable it would have been for Dorrie to babysit her heavily anesthetized date at the geriatric table anyway.

Of course, not dating clients could be a ruse. A tactical contrivance to get her out of sticky invitations from repugnant clients. Women did that sort of thing, didn't they?

He picked up the phone again and punched out a quick speed-dial code.

"Dr. Myron Snowden."

"Snowden. Jack Madigan. Your favorite agoraphobe."

"Yes, Jack. How are you today?"

"I've got an emergency."

"Oh dear. Did the house sell?"

"What? No. I've got a question about women."

The doctor sighed loudly. "Don't we all?"

"If a woman tells you she can't date you because you're a client and that it's a rule she lives by, is there any chance she's telling the truth? Or is it a broad screen to cover for the fact that she thinks you're a lunatic?"

"Jack, you're hardly a lunatic. Your problems may interfere with ordinary living, but you're surprisingly composed for a boy who lived in a crate. I mean, not many people suffered through a traveling childhood the way you—" Snowden paused. "Did you just say you asked a woman out? On a date?" He sounded shocked. Pleased. "May I take this as a sign that you're ready to break down your walls and make a little progress?"

"Don't get your trousers in a twist, Snowden. I was thrown before getting out of the starting gate."

Chapter 18

The Groper's Day Off

At first sight, Jack was nearly sure he was Yale Strasser. Tall, lightly tanned, and heavy on handsome, Dirk Van Dervan took Jack's hand into his own beefy paw, giving it a vigorous shake that nearly pulled Jack off his feet. "Good to meet you, Jack. I hope you don't mind my interrupting you like this on a Saturday. But during the week, I can never get away from the office. You know how it is." He patted Jack on the shoulder like one of the old boys from the golf club. "Luckily, Dorrie here offered to give up her Saturday for me." He winked in her direction, a move that threw her into action, straightening the pile of 117 Battersea Road flyers and handing him the top sheet while staring at his shoes.

His hair was at least as mussed up as Dorrie's, but it was obvious he'd spent hours in the bathroom with sculpting waxes and pomades, whereas Dorrie's usually, and today was no exception, looked as if she'd just been rescued from eight months on mountaintop with nothing more than a three-pronged stick to use for grooming.

Still, Jack thought, it somehow suited her.

"This," Dorrie began with a sweeping wave of her arm, working hard at avoiding Jack's eye, "is the spacious foyer, freshly painted. The ceilings are twelve feet and, yes, the black and white tiles *are* marble and original to the house."

A very impressive beginning. So impressive, Jack thought, that had he not had the answer to his problems tucked neatly in his pocket—the answer to his financial problems, anyway—he might have felt a bit panicky.

"I like to start every client out in the living room, so if you'll follow me . . ."

As Jack watched her lead Dirk the Client toward the front window, he had a thought. Jack Madigan wasn't her client. He wasn't buying a house from her, nor had he hired Heritage Estates to swoop down and take away his house. Dave Strom was a client; or, rather, Boston National Bank. The *bank* was the client.

His name wasn't on any paperwork. He was nothing more than a spectator in this whole thing. A spectator with a hell of a lot to lose, but definitely not a client.

"If you'll pay careful attention to the paint color, you should find yourself overwhelmed with feelings of peace, harmony, and nature," she added.

Dirk appeared to be considering the color, nodding his head and squinting. "It's a bit depressing, is it not?"

"Not when paired with red," Dorrie assured him, resting her jacket sleeve against the wall. "It really pops, don't you think?"

"Yes. Yes." He stepped back and reconsidered. "I see it now. God, it's fantastic. It *does* pop."

Something was obviously popping. Jack watched Dirk's eyes travel along Dorrie's outstretched arm and up to her light blue eyes.

"Why don't you start in the cellar, Dirk?" Jack said, louder than he'd intended. "Always best to look at things bottom to top," he added. "I need to have a word with Dorrie. It'll just take a sec."

After watching Dirk disappear downstairs, Jack was left with Dorrie blinking at him in the murky hallway.

"See?" she asked. "It's gotten uncomfortable already . . ."

"The thing is, Dorrie, you've got it all wrong."

"Jack." She sounded tired. "You're a wonderful man, really. I'm sure that there are ladies lined up to go out with you—"

He sucked in a deep breath. "*I'm* not your client. Boston National hired you. Not me. Now, if you still don't want to go, I understand and promise to never bring it up again. But I had to point it out. It's Dirk and Dave Strom and anyone at Boston National you can't date. Not me. I'm in the clear."

She appeared to be mulling this over.

"I realize I'm putting you on the spot, so I'm going to head straight upstairs to my office and let you think about it. No pressure, okay?"

Before she could answer, he bounded up the stairs. Harlan was in the office talking on the phone, his romantically magnetic Wallabies spread across Jack's desk. This was not good. The office needed to be empty when Dorrie came back upstairs with her answer. Jack poked his head inside and whispered to Harlan, "Off the phone, please. I've got an important meeting."

Harlan held up one finger and said into the receiver, "No. I won't do the history project with you unless you agree we start and finish it *this* weekend." He paused. "So? I finish all my assignments weeks early. No procrastinating, Missy. Ever. I have rules about these things."

Everyone had rules, Jack thought with a wry smirk.

"Whatever. Team up with Rachel and I'll do mine myself. It's cool." Harlan rolled his eyes at Jack. "I'll call you back. My dad is hovering."

"Sorry, Harlan. I've got something to attend to." Before Harlan loped out, Jack asked, "Why don't you bend your rules just this once?"

Harlan groaned. "When I could have the whole thing turned in two weeks early and get a possible bonus mark? As if."

"Oh, come on. You'd be working with Melissa. Surely the two of you would have a few laughs?"

He shook his head and stormed toward the door. "Rules are rules, Dad."

Jack was left to wait. Pacing across the office floor, he rubbed his chin hard. This was no good. He needed to get away from the office, at least until she came up from the cellar. Do something else, before the silence of her shoes not climbing the stairs drove him insane. Jack made his way into the bathroom to pop a Nervy Durvy before the waiting killed him. He opened the mirrored medicine cabinet and flipped the cap off his bottle.

There were only four left. Replacing the tiny bottle, he decided he could not afford to waste a whole pill on dating-related stress. Every pill in the bottle needed to be saved for the wedding, since he couldn't guarantee he'd be seeing Dr. Snowden between now and then for a refill. He couldn't even guarantee Snowden would live that long.

He needed to ration.

Footsteps rang out from the first floor. Slamming the medicine cabinet shut, Jack flew down the hallway to the office. Out of breath, heart pumping, he fell into his chair and picked up a leaky pen, pretending to doodle on a black pad.

The footsteps came closer now, partway up the stairs.

He scribbled harder. A dark, menacing tornado that grew increasingly larger at the top of the page, threatening to spill over onto the desk.

Sounded as if they'd reached the second-floor landing now. Dorrie said, "You just have a look at the main restroom down the hall, Dirk. I'll be right with you."

And there she was. Standing in the doorway, with a completely blank face.

Jack dropped his pen.

"Sorry it took so long," she whispered. "Dirk wanted to look inside the furnace. Then he showed me photos of his new baby niece. She was a bit tiny at birth and had to stay in an incubator for a week. Thankfully, Mom and tot are doing fine."

"Great," breathed Jack. "That's great."

Her fingers tapped against the door frame. "So, I've been thinking about what you said. About you not being my actual client."

"Yes?"

She grinned. "And, well, the thing is, I'd love to accompany you to the wedding."

HE SAT PERFECTLY still until all footsteps were safely on the fourth floor. Then, leaping out of the office and up onto the banister, Jack let go and slid down to the main floor, actually enjoying the feeling of wind in his hair for the first time he could remember. He whooped silently and hopped off the end and onto the tile floor. But he didn't stop there.

Jogging right past the Groper propped against the wall, he pulled open the front door and eyed the newspaper, which had been kicked by careless pedestrians nearly halfway across the sidewalk. As if it was the most natural thing in the world, something he did every morning, he trotted out of the house and down the five steps, three paces across the sidewalk, to scoop up the paper and skip back inside. He leaned on the door and whooped again, this time out loud.

• • •

JACK LOOKED OUT the back window into the dark backyard. It was nearly seven thirty. Harlan should be pulling up any moment with Lucinda, who had been so anxious about her first lesson with Muriel Danby's Figure Eights Skating School she could barely lace up her skates. Seeing the Buick's widely spaced headlights turn in from the alley and wink at him through the splintered slats of the garage, Jack yanked open the back door and stuck his head out. He hoped Lucinda hadn't thrown up on the ice.

She shot into the yard, still wearing her skates, and thundered up the back steps and into the kitchen.

"Muriel Danby is the nicest lady on earth!" she said. "When I first saw how chubby she was, I thought, she's definitely no Dorrie Allsop, but at least her hair's all brushed nice, then she gave me my first drill and I knew she was perfect. PERFECT. Smokes a lot, though. She showed me how to do crossovers and how to stop using my toe picks so much. Then I had to ask her to put out her cigarette. She didn't like that too much."

"What?" Jack interrupted. "You told her to butt out?"

She nodded, pulling off her hat. Statically charged blond hair stood straight up toward the ceiling, and her cheeks burned red from the crisp night air. "I told her athletes shouldn't breathe in secondhand smoke, and Jessica Bueller, who has seriously weak ankles, has a bad cough. After that, she blew her smoke in the other direction."

"You mean there were other girls in your class?"

"Two girls and a boy." She smiled and tucked her chin into her coat, before sitting on a chair to unlace her skates. "Michael Michaelson. He's got brown eyes and can do a backflip on ice. There's this space between his front teeth, but it's okay. He's getting braces on when he turns twelve this summer. Don't you think Michael Michaelson is a good name?"

Jack grinned, pulling the skates off her feet and setting them on the floor. He pulled off a few paper towels and handed some to Lucinda, so they could both wipe the snow from her blades. "Michael Michaelson," Jack teased. "Sounds like he's brutishly handsome."

She jutted out her chin and frowned. "I don't like him or anything."

"Absolutely not," Jack assured her. "An Olympian-in-training doesn't have time for thoughts of romance. Poor Michael Michaelson will just have to wait."

She looked at him as if trying to assess whether he was poking fun at her or not.

Harlan stomped his boots on the doormat and stepped inside, kicking them off in a shower of snow. "*Man*, it's cold out."

"Harlan bought me hot chocolate after," Lucie said, gathering her skates.

"Actually, Michael Michaelson bought you the hot chocolate. I just carried it for him so he wouldn't dump it on his skates," Harlan said with a wink. "Those were *some* fancy skates he had. Sparkles and everything."

Lucie, clearly still processing the fact that she'd consumed hot chocolate paid for by the shimmering Michael Michaelson, was quiet for a moment, then shot back with, "His skates weren't sparkly—that was stretchy material that wrapped right over them. It was attached to his pants."

Harlan looked impressed. *"Cool,"* he said, probably wondering if sparkle-footed pants came in his size.

She stood up, grabbing her skates. "Gotta go. Thanks, guys." She hugged Harlan, then Jack, and scampered out the back door.

"Michael Michaelson," Jack said with flourish. "Sounds like quite the ladies' man."

Harlan laughed. "All the girls are in love with him. Even Muriel Danby herself. She lets him choose what exercise the class works on and when it's time for a break. He's definitely a cheese boy in the making. Girls love that flashy stuff." He sniffed, pulling his coat off and wiping lint from his rainbow sweater.

Chapter 19

A Shimmering Mermaid and a Kindly Troll

Secretly, Jack thought his tuxedo's pant legs were too short but didn't mention a word to Dorrie, who'd been kind enough to bring the altered suit with her when she picked him up. The cuffs barely skimmed the tops of his shoes and rudely exposed his leg hairs when he sat, a look Harlan would cheer, but it made Jack feel just plain oafish.

They had fairly good seats, on the bride's side of the room, five rows back. Jack found that if he leaned toward Dorrie, he could see around the wide-rimmed black hat in front of him and should be able to view the ceremony quite well. The organ music had gone from an innocuous tune of general Godliness to the wedding march, but no one had opened the door in the back to march down the aisle, which forced the organist, a giddy woman with owlish eyes and a kelly green suit, to launch into it a second time, only this time with more gusto, probably to goad any hesitant parties into a marrying kind of mood.

He was almost looking forward to seeing Yale kiss the bride, now that he'd finally had a good look at him. Yale was definitely not what Jack had expected. No dazzling teeth, no hard body, and no south-of-France tan. Not even close. When he'd bumped into Harlan and Yale in the men's room, he'd thought the short, rounded man with a whispering of hair clinging around his ears was maybe a distant uncle on Penelope's side—a fusty old guy no one ever bothered with except when the time came for celebratory checks to be doled out.

Then Harlan had introduced them. Not only was Yale shorter than Jack, but his shoulders were lined with a dusting of gluey-looking gray dandruff.

"You must be Jack," Yale had squeaked in a high, girlish voice, extending his tiny hand and inspiring Jack to immediately check the guy's feet for size. Upon seeing patent leather shoes so small they'd pinch Dorrie's feet, Jack thrust out his hand and gave a mighty shake. Penelope hadn't traded up. She hadn't even traded sideways!

Suddenly, Jack felt manly. Virile.

He'd swaggered back to Dorrie in the lobby area and poked her playfully in the side. With any luck, she'd notice the change.

Obviously feeling his eyes on her, she looked away from the best man, who'd just taken his position next to Yale at the podium, and smiled at Jack. He felt good, as if he'd already downed a couple of glasses of champagne. Yale was a kindly troll, Jack was out on a date, and the pills were working just fine. Not only that, but he felt reasonably secure that the backup pill in his breast pocket was safe from harm, standing brave and ready to pick up the slack when the first two began to fade.

Dorrie looked beautiful in a strapless gown in shimmering yellow satin, flaring out where it hit the floor. Like a mermaid, Jack thought. Even her hair seemed to be behaving tonight, demurely tucked behind her ears as if terrified to call attention away from the bride. Her slender shoulders were covered by a gold wrap, something Jack very much hoped she'd discard after the service.

Finally, the rear doors opened and the ceremony kicked into motion. An usher, a nephew of Yale's, led an older woman who could only be Yale's mother to the front row on the groom's side of the room. Then came a red-faced Harlan, loping along in his "rich-boy, fancy-ass" tuxedo. Penelope's mother struggled to match Harlan's gigantic gait, practically jogging to keep up. Harlan dumped her off on the bride's side and went to mope beside Yale's nephew.

Next came two bridesmaids, whom Jack recognized very well as his ex-wife's friends from high school and the bridesmaids at his own wedding to Penelope. There was something inherently creepy about seeing Rhonda and Suzie all dolled up again in their second attempt to usher their friend into a good marriage. It made his pulse race, so he averted his eyes and tried to focus on the maid of honor behind them—mercifully, a new friend of Penelope's, someone wholly unconnected to Jack and his failed marriage.

The grinning flower girl was clearly at the apex of her young life, preening and fluffing her pink princess dress while her royal subjects offered up the appropriate oohs and aahs, whereas the ring bearer held it together by staring directly into his velvet pillow and counting his steps in a loud whisper.

The music changed, and every guest twisted around backward to get a glimpse of the bride on her father's arm. Although, under the circumstances, shouldn't she have been on Jack's arm? Wasn't he the one truly giving Penelope away? She looked beautiful, as expected. She wore a knee-length wedding dress, very modern, even for his ex, Jack thought. White lace boots came up to her knees, and a simple veil covered her face.

As she approached, Jack was struck by an uneasy feeling. Something wasn't quite right. He stared at Penelope in her dress until it hit him. She was wearing the same wedding dress she wore when she married him—her mother's dress! Certainly, she'd had it remade; she hadn't been willing to expose quite so much leg when she married Jack, and he was pretty sure the dress had sleeves back then. But there was no mistaking the pattern of that fabric—Jack had once joked that it looked like white germs multiplying in a Petri dish. If he looked carefully enough, he might still find the bruise on his arm where she'd swatted him.

He'd recognize those microbes anywhere.

This was not good. His heart thumped wildly, and he somehow forgot how to breathe. How could the effect of the pills wear off so suddenly? The room became claustrophobically warm, and his skin grew clammy. He tried to slow his breathing before he lost feeling in his fingertips, and the fact that escape was nearly impossible from his seat in the middle of the third row was not helping.

How could Penelope do it? Did she think he wouldn't notice?

He could barely feel his feet. Quickly he reached into his pocket for his backup pill, but the pocket was empty. It wasn't possible; he'd placed it in there not two hours ago. Trying to steady his trembling fingers, he felt around more carefully until he found . . . a hole.

A fucking hole! His pill, his one lifeline to sanity, was lost in the Detroit-made liner. He gulped down some air while the room whirled around him. If he'd arrived at Rose's thrift shop thirty minutes earlier, he'd have never laid eyes on that Walt Chambers. He'd have walked out in the Armani, which, he happened to know, had impeccably well-made pockets.

The priest was talking now, and Harlan stood watching the ceremony with his hands clasped in front of his groin. Harlan! He might have thought to bring a pill. Certainly the boy knew his father well enough to expect the worst.

Jack coughed, eyes boring into what he could see of Harlan's head behind the other usher, willing the boy to look his way. He didn't. Jack coughed again, louder this time. Still nothing.

He had no choice. It was either get Harlan's attention or pass out at Dorrie's feet. He had to fake a good coughing spasm. He began slowly, with a few quick hacks, before launching into a full-blown choking fit. A few heads turned, including Harlan's.

"Pill!" Jack mouthed.

Harlan mouthed back, "What?"

"Pill!"

Harlan shrugged.

By this time, Penelope had caught on. She shot a murderous look at Jack before whispering "Pill!" to Harlan, who bulged his eyes in horror and shook his head, miming empty pockets.

Oh, God.

"Are you okay?" whispered Dorrie. Jack smiled and waved that he was fine, before standing up and forcing the entire row to slide their knees out of the way or stand up as he scrabbled his way to, if not freedom, at least a more private place to decompose.

Bursting through the rear doors and into the lobby, Jack stumbled to a window ledge beside the cloakroom and dropped his head between his knees, to at least slow the spinning. A counting exercise of Snowden's popped into his mind . . . counting odd numbers up to thirty-one and back again.

Over and over and over.

Waiters were preparing the lobby for the cocktail hour. Bars were set up, as well as different food stations. Champagne was being poured into flutes, and to Jack's delight, a waiter set a tray of bubbling glasses on a table nearby and left to speak to someone behind the bar.

Fuck this counting. He'd been up and down the odd numbers three times, and his hands still felt like pincushions. Why struggle when there was a whole tray of spirit-numbing relief calling to him, not ten feet away—free?

Quickly he leaped to his feet and grabbed two glasses. He tossed one back, then the other, and reached for two more. Already he felt relief. At that moment, the doors to the main room flew open, and Penelope and Yale fell into the lobby, laughing, kissing, chattering. As the rest of the wedding party filed out after them, Yale wrapped his arms around his new wife and spun her around. She kissed his waxy little cheek before looking up and spotting Jack downing a third glass of champagne, with the next one ready and waiting in his other hand.

She narrowed her eyes at him and shook her head. A moment later, she was swallowed up by a crowd of well-wishers and, mercifully, disappeared from Jack's sight.

BY THE TIME Dorrie found him, Jack's panic had subsided, and he was languishing in a near–117 Battersea Road state of composure. Had his bank account been better endowed, he'd very possibly consider installing some sort of champagne cellar in his basement. If he felt this good all the time, leaving the house for AA meetings would be a breeze.

"How's your cough?" asked Dorrie.

"Turned out all I needed was a little drink. Speaking of which." He passed a glass to Dorrie.

"Harlan was worried. He's with his mother in the receiving line, so I told him I'd check on you."

Jack held his glass up. "As you can see, I'm doing fine. How about a toast? To rats and cats and crumbling pilasters."

She touched her glass to his with a twinkle in her eye. "To my first sale."

"To your first sale being any other than my place."

"Hey," she scolded.

"To other listings, then." Jack chinked his glass against Dorrie's and drank. She didn't need to know about the tinting job in Chicago. Why muddy things up before he'd strolled into Boston National with check in hand? With any luck, she'd have a few more listings by then anyway.

"I've an idea; let's vow not to mention houses, real estate, selling, buying or listing for the rest of the night. How does that sound?"

She smiled, slipping her wrap from her shoulders and hanging it over her forearm. "Sounds perfect." She placed her empty glass in his hand. "Now, Mr. Madigan, while I'm off to find the ladies' room, do you think you can find me another glass of this fabulous champagne?"

He watched her go, marveling at what a proper-fitting pair of shoes can do to a woman's walk.

"Excuse me."

Jack looked up to see none other than Walt Chambers. Wearing the beautiful Armani tux. On either side of him stood what Jack assumed to be his elegant wife and equestrian daughter.

Walt squinted and wagged an index finger at Jack. "I've been trying to figure out where I've met you. You're Jonathon Galt from the Cypress Group!"

Not about to answer, "No, I'm the penniless bargain hunter from Sec-ondhand Rose who crawled around in your tux and refused to give it back." Jack looked around to make sure Dorrie or Harlan or, worse, Pe-nelope wasn't around. "Yes. Good to see you, Walt. I'm actually looking for my girlfriend. You'll have to excuse me . . ."

"I knew it." He turned to his wife. "Didn't I tell you it was Jona-thon?" Pulling a card from his well-stitched pocket, he added, "Give my secretary a call, we'll do lunch at the club."

Jack slipped the card into his chest pocket and lost himself in the crowd.

"AND, WELL." PENELOPE giggled under the spotlights, standing at the head table, with Harlan sulking on one side and Yale beaming on the other. She had removed her floor-length veil before being seated, and dark hair fell in front of her face. "The moment I saw him on the tennis court, I pretty much knew." The guests half-giggled, half-sighed in ro-mantic rapture. "He's everything I could ever want in a man, and much, much more."

The elderly ladies at Jack and Dorrie's table nearly collapsed with emotion. Esther, wearing lavender sequins that came clear up to her ears, tapped a spoon against her coffee cup until the whole room filled with the sound of chinking china. Yale grinned and feigned weariness before saying, "Well, if you insist!"

The geriatric table had turned out to be much livelier than he'd anticipated. Esther had forced Harlan to slow-dance with her a few times, and Yale's grandparents had been particularly entertaining. Mr. Strasser was anxious to get to his Saturday-night poker game back at the retirement home and was caught leaving the reception heading for a bus stop on Dartmoor Street, and Mrs. Strasser was reprimanded by the staff for smoking in the cloakroom.

As a tuxedoed waitress filled their coffee cups, Dorrie leaned closer to Jack and whispered, "I'm having a ball, Jack." Her hair tickled his face.

Momentarily, he moved away while his plate was cleared, then leaned back toward her until his cheek touched her hair again. "Most women do, when they're out with Jack Madigan." He shrugged, pouring cream into his coffee. "Entertaining beautiful women. It's what I do best."

Swatting him with her napkin, she laughed. "Stop it, or you'll have Esther all over you."

Dorrie was fabulous. Not only was she the most gorgeous woman in the room, Jack thought, but she devoured her food and entertained the aged with stories of her own parents' many, many cruise vacations: her father being assaulted by monkeys in Costa Rica and her mother having accidentally swallowed a laxative prior to a jungle tour of Paraguay. Had the whole table in hysterics.

He watched as she reached over to Mr. Strasser and wiped a few crumbs from his shoulder. It was definitely time to tell her. She deserved to know.

"Dorrie?"

She turned to face him, her face glowing. "Yes?"

"There's something you need to know. About me."

Moving closer, she nudged his elbow with her own. "Sounds intriguing."

He laughed and pressed his hand into his knee to stop it from shaking. "Not intriguing exactly. More quirky. Unique."

"Sounds good so far."

"Yes, well, don't get your hopes up." He sucked in a deep breath. "I'm not the person you think I am. And maybe I should have said something sooner, but it's not so easy to work something like this into conversation. I'm, well, I'm, uh . . ."

"Go on."

"I'm agoraphobic, actually. Have been for most of my adult life."

"That's great." She placed her hand over his arm. "I am too. I hate spiders."

"No. Not arachnophobic. Agoraphobic. I can't leave the house."

"But that's ridiculous. You're out of the house right now. And looking very brave."

"I'm highly medicated right now, so, technically, only my body's being brave. My mind's comfortingly coated in a thick, murky soup designed to weigh down the hysteria. Slow its ability to strike. But as soon as the soup thins, believe me, the hysteria will rise up strong again and try to kill me."

"But you don't seem drugged at all."

"That's your champagne. It's making me look good."

She tucked her arm under his and laid her head on his shoulder. "That's where you're wrong, Jack Madigan. You looked just as enticing before I took a single sip."

He didn't know what to do. He'd told her, and instead of faking a headache and calling a cab, here she was, snuggling close and patting his hand.

This couldn't be happening to him. It had to be the meds.

At any rate, imagined or real, he wasn't going to waste this moment. He lowered his cheek into her hair and lost himself in the smell of fresh apples.

With the worst possible timing, Harlan slumped into the empty chair beside Jack. "This is *so* lame," he groaned. "Can you guys take me home now? Mom says it'll go on past midnight."

"Where's your date?" Dorrie asked, sitting up straight and officially ending the moment. "The two of you should be dancing."

"Melissa went home pissed."

"Drunk?" Jack asked, astonished.

"Mad. Said I was bringing her down."

Jack picked up his water glass and twirled the ice cubes. "Can't imagine that."

"Cut it out, Dad, all right? I want to go home."

Placing his hand between Harlan's shoulders, Jack massaged his back. "Come on now. This is your mother's big night. She's married her prince. You need to be here to share it with her."

Shrugging off his father's hand, Harlan stood up. "It's not *my* night. Just look at me." He motioned toward his elegant tuxedo, which fit him beautifully. "I'm big poseur man."

Dorrie stood up. "I think you look just *perfect*, Harlan. Like you've just won an Academy Award. And I, for one, think Melissa was crazy to leave a handsome devil like you unattended." She held out her arm and smiled. "Would you do an old lady a favor and dance?"

Blushing and trying to conceal his smile, Harlan took her arm and slunk toward the dance floor.

Dorrie was very perceptive. Knew just what to do. He glanced up to see her sashaying between the tables to the dance floor, where the band was playing the Jackson Five's "ABC." Great song. And just cheesy enough for Harlan to approve of.

Smiling to himself, the scent of green apples still in the air, Jack signaled to a waiter to top up their wineglasses and glanced again toward the dance floor.

Right away, he could see there was a problem. Harlan looked back at Jack with a pleading expression on his face, nodding toward Dorrie. Directly across from Harlan, Dorrie was dancing. Jerky, frenetic arm movements threatened to box anyone who came within a three-foot radius. One after another, she raised her knees to the side and heaved her torso toward them. Her head flailed side to side in a way that seemed downright insensitive to the delicate structure of the upper vertebrae.

She was a terrible dancer.

Other dancers on the floor had noticed. They were beginning to clear some space, either for a better view or simply to stay out of range of thrashing limbs. Several couples at tables near the dance floor pointed, nudging their neighbors.

Jumping to his feet, Jack marched between the tables and past waiters carrying huge dessert platters. He stepped onto the dance floor and motioned for Harlan to make his escape. Looking into Dorrie's eyes, he moved closer to her and wrapped his own arms around hers, pulling them down to her sides and forcing her body to sway softly with him from side to side as they moved in a gentle, dreamy circle.

By some divine chance, or maybe a well-timed suggestion from Harlan, the music changed. Slowed. In the first three beats, Jack recognized the tune as one of the softer Bazmanics' songs, a seldom played track called "Sleeping." Jack's grandmother had told him that "Sleeping" was written for him, when he was a newborn, napping in his mother's arms. Baz had had, apparently, at least a passing interest in fatherhood. At least for an hour or two.

It was Jack's favorite song.

From across the dance floor, Walt Chambers caught his eye, nodded toward Dorrie, and winked his approval. Then he spun his wife around and mouthed to Jack, "Call me."

However undeservedly, and with a tuxedo from Detroit, Jack Madigan was having a Cinderella moment.

People lost interest in Dorrie and, one by one, resumed dancing or eating or talking. Her body began to relax as she leaned into him, eventually closing her eyes and smiling, her head resting on his shoulder. Continuing to sway, she lifted her head. Their faces nearly touching, she said sleepily, "This has always been my favorite song."

For the first time in his life, Jack Madigan didn't stop to think.

Didn't analyze, or second-guess himself, or check the rhythm of his heartbeats.

Didn't stop breathing or sway with dizziness.

Didn't wonder where his pills were or how much time it would take to get home.

He just kissed her.

Chapter 20

The Pill Between the Floorboards

Squinting into the dazzling morning sunlight, Jack reached for his rumpled tuxedo dropped to the floor the night prior in his state of exhaustion. He shook out the pants, before folding them carefully and laying them on the bed. Then, while brushing off the jacket, he heard something tiny fall to the floor. Laying the jacket over a hanger, he peered down at the floorboards, looking for what sounded like a button. He gasped out loud when he saw it.

A small, white pill lying in a crack between the floorboards.

He'd forgotten all about it. The last tranquilizer. It meant that after the champagne wore off, he'd been out, drug-free.

Without a single thought about tearing apart his jacket to find the little pill trapped in the lining.

He'd enjoyed himself so much that he'd forgotten all about it. Danced, talked, joked, *kissed,* all on his own and miles from home. He leaned over to pick it up and carried it into the bathroom to lock it safely in the pill jar. Closing the medicine cabinet above the sink, he stared in the mirror.

A smile crept across his face.

"Jack! Maxwell Ridpath here. How's our favorite color genius?"

"Particularly well, as a matter of fact," Jack said with a grin. This day just kept getting better and better. He winked at Dorrie, who was thumbing through a magazine and trying not to look at the cat sunning himself on the kitchen table.

"Brilliant. I'm calling to report that we're finally ready for you and that expert eye of yours."

"Super. My eye is ready and waiting."

"When do you think we could get together?"

Jack paused to think about his upcoming week. Other than hustling Harlan home in time for Lucinda's Thursday-night skating class, he was fairly wide open. Although he might ask Dorrie to come over for his famous spaghetti dinner on Tuesday, so he'd best see Maxwell after that. "How about Wednesday afternoon? On the early side?"

"Smashing. We'll book your flight. All expenses paid by the committee, of course."

Jack stopped breathing. "*My* flight? I thought you were coming here? I've got all my tints here and my workshop . . ." Dorrie looked up at him.

Maxwell laughed. "You can't very well assess our space from your kitchen window, can you? That wouldn't be worth much to us."

"But certainly you have access to some good photographs, and as long as I know from which direction any natural light is coming and the precise color of the floor and whether you're using halogen lighting or fluorescent . . ."

Dorrie closed her magazine.

"Jack, Jack. My team is anxious to meet you. Don't worry; we'll take care of everything. You'll be booked into the Four Seasons with a view of the water, if you'd like. Consider it a working vacation."

Jack's head spun fast. "It's just that—"

"You know I even got a call from that Carlston over at the MoMA the other day? He'd heard about you from one of our architects. But I told him he couldn't have you until we skimmed off the best of your talents first." Maxwell laughed and sipped from a tinkly cup. "The fella's got this bet going that we can't reach their numbers of visitors from last year in three years! I told him to sod right off . . . Jack? You still there?"

Barely. "Yeah. Yeah, I'm here." Jack breathed deeply as a cloud passed over the dazzling sun outside the window. "I'm thinking I could develop many, many sample boards and ship them over to you, so you can hold them up in each room and get back to me—"

"'Fraid not, mate. The committee members won't settle for anything short of your khakis on that plane. Are we set for Wednesday, then?"

Wednesday. Could he rise above his terror of stepping onto his front porch and drag himself down to the airport on Wednesday, strap himself onto a lumbering plane, soar thirty thousand feet above four or five states to land in a city he'd only been in as a sleepy child in a splintered crate, and impress a gallery full of architects and curators with his cool-headed proficiency with white paint without cracking into a million tiny, jagged emotional pieces that spiral and spin and fling themselves out into the endless open space to never be whole again?

Up until last night, never. But, in some small way, he felt he was a new man. Or, at the very least, on his way to becoming one. Becoming a new man, the sort of man who functions in multiple cities, could take a bit of time.

"Jack? Have we got a fiddly phone connection?"

He'd need to work with Snowden, really work with him. Drop the passive-aggressive see-if-you-can-try-to-fix-me attitude and actually try the old guy's suggestions.

"Jack?"

"I, uh, I can't make Wednesday." A lump rose up in Jack's throat, lodging the rest of the words there and preventing them from coming out.

Pause. "'S all right. We'll do it next week, then. The team'll be slightly miffed, but they'll get over it, won't they?"

"I'd need a bit more time. A couple of months' notice."

"Excuse me?"

"I can't travel to Chicago just now." Jack swallowed over and over to push the lump back down.

"Can't travel?" Maxwell laughed. "Carrying twins, are you, old boy?"

"No. I just can't, that's all."

"Well, take the bleeding train if you don't fly. Just get yourself here as soon as you can."

"Three months. I can be there in three months. Maybe two."

The silence on the phone line was roaring loud. Jack watched as a robin, the first of the season, landed on the roof of his garage, looked around, unimpressed, and took flight again. Dorrie's worried eyes never left Jack's face.

Maxwell clicked his tongue. "Well. We've got ourselves quite a problem then, haven't we?"

"Not really, not if you can agree—"

"Sorry, Jack. Quite frankly, we'd love to use your services, but it's got to be done our way. You see our conundrum?"

"Well . . ."

"We'll just have to use that Sutherland chap from London. His eye's not quite as sharp as yours, but he'll have to do. Should you change your mind, you give us a ring."

The line went dead. Along with any hope Jack had for saving his home.

"Everything all right?" asked Dorrie.

The lump rose up until he could barely swallow. All he could do was nod.

Chapter 21

Dorrie Does Some Thinking

She tried her best to appear unconcerned. Pushing her hat from her eyes, Lucinda glanced up at the kitchen clock and swung her skated feet from the vinyl chair. One of the skate guards kept rapping against the metal table leg. She scratched her shoulder and checked the clock again.

"He'll be here any minute," Jack assured her.

"And besides, the way he drives, we'd still probably be early."

"Exactly."

"Anyway, if you get there too early, your muscles will get chilled. It's why I wear two pairs of tights. So my leg muscles don't get chilled. You don't think he forgot, do you?"

It was exactly what Jack thought.

Jack couldn't bear to tell Lucinda. "He's probably roaring along Battersea right this minute, frightening old ladies up onto the hoods of parked cars."

She brightened. "Hope so."

Jack wiped the tops of the salt and pepper shakers and pushed them up against the wall. "I'm certain so."

Clunk, clunk, went the skates on the table leg.

They both went back to silent worrying and clock-watching. Another ten minutes went by with no sign of either Harlan or the big rumbling Buick.

Finally, a rattling sound came from the front hall. Jack sprang up from his chair, clapping his hands. "What did I tell you? There he is now. And too smart to waste time pulling around the back. Up, up, let's move it." He waved his arms to hurry her along, not that he needed to; she was already halfway across the kitchen.

They rushed into the hallway to find Dorrie, frosty and shivering, kicking the snow from her boots. "You won't believe the parking space I've just found. Right smack in front of the house. Can you get over that?"

"Shocking," Jack said, telling her about Harlan's nonappearance and Lucinda's skating lesson—now in great peril. "You wouldn't, by chance, be interested in taking a little girl skating?"

Dorrie smiled at Lucinda. "Would you like to go with me, honey? Shall we go down to the ice pond together?"

Lucie looked unsure. "Rink."

"Mm?" Dorrie looked up at Jack and winked.

"It's a rink. Pond is when it's not all frozen up," said Lucie.

"How about it?" Jack asked, patting Lucinda on the back. "Dorrie'll zip you over there no problem."

Dorrie shuffled back toward the door, waving for Lucie to follow, but the child stood still, her little mouth pinched into a surly ball.

"What's wrong, Lucie?"

She shrugged and kicked at the floor with her guards.

"You don't want to go with Dorrie?"

She glanced sideways at Dorrie and moved closer to Jack, shaking her head no.

"She's really nice," Jack said. Then he whispered into her ear, "And really pretty. You said so yourself. Won't you go with her?"

Lucinda pointed at Jack and then at Dorrie.

"What? What's with all the pointing?" Jack asked. "What happened to that voice of yours? The one that never stops?"

"Only if you go, I'll go with her."

"Come on. She's a really nice lady . . ."

Finally, Lucinda looked up at him. "It's not because of molestation and murder, if that's what you're thinking. I just want you to come is all."

Dorrie spoke up. "Jack, you need to come. She'll be more comfortable. Take your pill and I'll drive."

"Please," Lucinda said. "We'll help you through it. I can't miss this class. I've finally perfected my back crossovers. Please, Jack." Her pleading face was nearly lost in the knit cap. Her legs were so skinny they looked as if the weight of the skates would snap them in half. But her eyes were huge. *"Please."*

How could he refuse this poor child whose only friend was a nutcase with no one but a half-headed cat and a wet paintbrush to keep him company most days? She lived for these lessons. She counted on Harlan and Jack—well, truthfully, Harlan—to get her there and back safely. Was it too much for a little girl to ask? One hour of attention, once a week?

Jack headed upstairs to pop a pill. "Get your coat on, Lucinda."

Tramping through the snowy path beside the rink, Dorrie passed Jack a steaming hot chocolate. "Did you know they charge a dollar seventy-five each for these?" she asked, giving Jack what appeared to be way too much change. "I told him I didn't think they were worth much more than about fifty cents."

Jack's hands shook with either cold or fear; he was too numb to tell, and the pill he'd dry-swallowed had made him drunk with sleepiness. "You're paying for the atmosphere."

Overhead lights shone down on the frozen Frog Pond, surrounded by darkened trees and city buildings lit up like jeweled boxes. The ice was mostly full of recreational skaters: young couples holding hands, parents straining their backs by bending over toddlers on bob skates for the first time. Snow fell lightly, just enough to add a dusting of powder over the entire setting. All around was the clear, metallic sound of laboring blades hitting thick, heavy-duty ice.

"I've been doing some thinking, Jack."

He looked up to find Dorrie watching him with great intensity.

"A lot of things have happened recently, you know, between you and me, and priorities tend to change sometimes when certain relationships evolve. I mean, you can't always predict how you'll feel about things—"

"Dorrie. What are you trying to say?"

"I've decided to back out of the house listing. Yours. I'm handing it over to Caroline Weinberger at the office."

"But you've worked so hard. And it's your only listing . . ."

"I'll be signing another property next week."

Jack felt sick. "So, you and I interfered with your career after all. Client or no client, it messed things up for you."

"No, Jack. Nothing's messed up. Everything's clearer now. Since we've been, you know . . ."

"Together," Jack finished for her.

"Yes. Together, I've been, well, happier than I've ever been."

Jack grinned. "Me too."

"And I realized I could never be the one to take your house away from you. You'd always remember that and I, well, quite frankly, I couldn't do it to you. Not since we've been . . ."

"Together?"

"No. Kissing and everything."

He took the hot chocolate from her gloved hand and set it in the snowbank before wrapping her in his arms and kissing her as she deserved to be kissed just then, surrounded by parents, skaters, spotlights, and softly falling snow, all the while wondering if he'd ever get to kiss her in private.

Still holding hands, still glowing, they turned and watched Lucinda demonstrate a jump for the teacher while the class looked on. A boy with blow-dried hair and fuzzy earmuffs—Michael Michaelson, no doubt—looked most interested, kicking the ice with his toe picks—possibly the ice skater's equivalent to the snorting and pawing of an amorous bull—whenever Lucie looked his way, which was all too often. Jack supposed that subtlety in flirtation came at a much more advanced age than nine.

Her face set with determination, Lucie gathered speed at one end of the rink, pumping her little legs as fast as she could toward the center, where she tucked in her arms close to her body and spun around in the air, landing on one foot. Clapping his hands and whistling, Jack lost half a cup of hot chocolate into the snow beneath him.

Another man, wearing a thick tan coat and a plaid scarf, shouted, "Nice one," as she landed. A cloud of steamy breath hung in the cold air for a second in front of his face, then vanished. He glanced at Jack and smiled. "You her father?"

How he'd have loved to say yes. Instead, he smiled and shook his head. "No. I'm just a neighbor. I'm just hoping she'll remember me when she's on the Olympic team one day." Jack laughed.

"From the looks of it, she shouldn't have much trouble being chosen."

"You think?"

The man held out his gloved hand. "Zeke Ellery. I'm a figure-skating coach over in New York State." He nodded toward Lucinda. "I've been watching your little neighbor. She's got exactly what we look for. Small frame with big might. Smooth, fluid motion. The ability to finish every move. Nice jumps for her age. Incredible extensions. You need to tell her parents to get her some real training. She should be trained to compete statewide, with an eye toward the nationals. But tell them they've got to move now. She's what, about eight or nine?"

"Nine."

"It's a bit late, but she's got the talent. I saw her last week, too. She's got the determination to advance quickly. If she was my student, I'd set my hopes very high for her."

"Wow," said Dorrie. "You should tell her parents, Jack."

The man handed Jack a business card with a skating-association logo in one corner. ZEKE ELLERY. HEAD COACH, it said, under the acronym of his skating club, AFSC. The phone number printed across the bottom had a 518 area code. "Give her parents my card. I can recommend a better local coach." Zeke looked up at Muriel Danby, who was hunched over the ice, choking on either a mouthful of nicotine or one of her big plastic earrings.

Jack thanked him and slipped the card into his pocket. The hour was almost up, and his sleepy pill was losing much of its strength. His head was starting to clear. And a clear head half a mile from home wasn't a good thing for Jack Madigan.

"Call Lucinda over, okay?" Jack whispered to Dorrie. "We're going to need to move fast."

Chapter 22

Manhattan Transfer

When he opened the back door, he wasn't entirely sure who she was. Glossy brown hair so expensively cut the edges looked as if they could slice bread, and teeth so perfectly even, she clearly felt obliged to reveal not only the top set when smiling but also the rarely exposed lower set, forcing her face into an unconvincing half-grin, half-snarl.

It was then that Jack recognized her. Samantha Ballard, Lucinda's mother. Over the last year, he'd seen very little of her north of the ankles.

"Hi," she said, extending the tips of her fingers for shaking. "I've got a bit of a problem."

Jack panicked for a moment. Was she going to put a stop to Lucinda's lessons? He said nothing.

"You seem to be home a fair bit," she said. "I'm expecting a package this afternoon, and I wonder if I stuck a note on my front door, directing the package to your house, if you'd mind holding it for me? I have to go out."

Pretending to mentally check his day planner, Jack stared up at the sky and twisted his mouth to one side. "Let's see now. I've got a very busy day. What time are you expecting it?"

"Oh. I don't know. Sometime this afternoon, the real estate agent said—"

"Real estate agent? You're moving?"

She rolled her eyes. "Rick's being transferred. He's with Atlantic Life, as you probably know . . ." Jack nodded as she spoke, for who in the greater Boston area had not followed Rick Ballard's every career step?

Samantha continued, "And with the opening of the new branches in Albany and Manhattan, they had to put really top people in place to head them up. Rick was a natural choice after his overwhelming success at the Back Bay location."

"You're moving to Manhattan?" With Lucinda?

Her face tightened, and she laughed testily. "Why does everyone think he wants the Manhattan transfer?"

"No, I just assumed . . ."

"You know, Albany is a much bigger responsibility."

"Absolutely."

"His expertise would just be diluted in Manhattan, spread about across a couple of hundred people."

Jack clucked his tongue in understanding.

"This way, in Albany, he'll have much greater impact, greater autonomy, and will stand out, being from a larger city." She shook her head. "I almost feel sorry for anyone taking the Manhattan assignment."

"Well, congratulations to the both of you. I suppose it's very exciting."

"Exciting for Rick. Not so for me. I hate to leave loved ones . . ."

"You have relatives here in Boston?" Jack asked.

"No, my trainers. There's Pietro from Pilates. Then Barcone, he's yoga. Sounds silly, but they've become like family."

"Right. But does your *whole* family know about this move?" Specifically, Lucinda, he wanted to ask.

"My mother knows. Which is the only bright spot in this whole move. She lives in Albany; it's where I grew up. And, we're hoping, with her being a retired teacher and all, that she'll help out with the girls."

Lucinda had never mentioned a grandmother in Albany. "I suppose, living so far from you all, it's difficult for a grandparent to connect," he said.

She snorted. "Let's just say she hasn't seen her grandchildren in seven years. But now, with us living so close, she'll have no excuse for ignoring my problems with Lucinda any longer."

Yes, it really was tragic how problematic Lucinda was. What with all the pesky growing and walking and talking and expressing her own desires. Needing food and clothing, not to mention encouragement and support. Delinquent in her very existence.

And now this woman was taking her away. Just like that.

That the hole would be discovered and sealed over by new owners barely mattered. The chill that would settle over his life would have very little to do with a simple lack of heat.

"You know," Jack said, determined to keep Lucinda close, "if you're truly sorry to move, I mean, if you'd like to stay put and close to your . . . loved ones, all you really need is one dreadful real estate agent. Truly terrible. One that'll talk her way out of any sale. Focus on the very worst your home has to offer."

She moved closer, cocking her head to one side. "Interesting. But where on earth would I find one so bad?"

"Closer than you might think."

"You know of one? One so bad my house won't sell? Really?"

He smiled, nodding back toward his house. "Mine."

Samantha's eyes bulged.

Jack laughed. "Sign on with Dorrie and you'll still be on Battersea when you're ninety."

Something crashed on the floor behind him. He spun around just in time to see Dorrie's face, blank with disbelief, before she disappeared into the darkened hallway.

The front door slammed.

Chapter 23

While You Were Sleeping

She wouldn't take his calls. He'd left some thirteen messages on her Heritage Estates voice mail and had even attempted to ring through to the receptionist, who told him Dorrie was in the middle of serious negotiations and had specifically requested not to be disturbed. Under any circumstances.

Of course, he wasn't buying that story. She simply wanted to avoid the cruel wretch who had publicly confirmed what her family had suspected all her adult life. That she was faulty. Hopeless. A disappointment.

He wound the phone cord around his finger as he waited for her to pick up. Again, her message came on. "This is Dorrie Allsop of Heritage Estates. I can't come to the phone right now . . ." He hung up and immediately pressed redial, listening while the phone dialed her number for the fifteenth time. Mrs. Brady, having long lost his bonnet, leaped onto Jack's lap from out of nowhere and began kneading his sharpened claws in Jack's lap. With a swat, he shooed the cat out of the kitchen and rubbed at the needle pricks in his pant legs.

"Doreen Allsop. Heritage Estates."

Jack straightened. "Dorrie, it's me. Jack. We need to talk."

Her pause was too long. Excruciatingly long. "Jack." She sounded tired. "This isn't a good time."

"I didn't mean what I said. You know I respect you, but she said she was moving Lucinda away and I thought—"

She sighed into the phone. In the background, he could hear phones ringing, people talking excitedly. "I've been up all night, I can't do this . . ."

Switching tactics, he laughed. "Ah. I told you I had that effect on the ladies. Don't say you weren't forewarned."

She covered the phone and spoke to someone in the background, and then another voice, a man's voice, shouted, "Congratulations, Dorrie." It sounded like a party. And he couldn't be sure, but he thought he might have heard the pop of a champagne cork.

"Jack. I was up all night working."

"At night?"

"That's real estate. The hours suck."

"Well, then. You should take the rest of the day off. Swing on over here and let me make it up to you with a Spanish omelet and some fresh-squeezed juice."

"Jack. I need to tell you before Dave does." She paused and sighed into the receiver. "Your house just sold."

Words began to form, but nothing came out of his mouth.

"Did you hear me, Jack? I said I've sold your house."

Chapter 24

The House That Lived and Breathed

He needed to stop the shaking. Stop hyperventilating. The closing was just weeks away, and Jack couldn't have been in worse shape. And Penelope's efforts weren't helping. Her daily phone calls from her honeymoon in California, always on some flimsy pretext, drove him mad. Do you need help packing, Jack? Do you want Yale to find you a new place, Jack? He won't mind. Do you know how much money you'll clear, Jack? You're much better off, Jack.

Of course, he'd clear a nice sum of money. But that wasn't the fucking point. What good was any number of millions if they had to lock you up in a padded room? Or, worse, if you had to spend the rest of your days so drugged up you couldn't even write a lousy check without drooling all over it? If you were so damned hysterical no woman would ever want you?

How much fun would that be?

Once he was out of the house, he'd have very little to remember Baz by. The photo above the television, of Baz playing at being a dad. A few instruments and some song sheets. Baz's house, his legacy, was all Jack really had. The dark, soaring oak walls, the creaking floors, the crumbled brick, the butler's pantry, the dumbwaiter, and, most of all, the holes, were all he had left. To Jack Madigan, the towering town house lived and breathed his father; watching over him as Baz never had. And, like a father, the house became the strong arms that wrapped around him whenever he'd been scared, lonely, as a boy. The trousered legs he'd always been able to hide behind.

Sitting in his fireside chair, Jack shook his head. What a pathetic half-wit he'd become. So hard up for parental approval, he'd transferred his attachment to a brick building. It might be what Dr. Snowden would say later that afternoon when he arrived for their session, if he stayed awake long enough to listen.

It had gotten to the point where he didn't even pick up the phone when it rang. There really wasn't any point. When the new buyers wanted to come in and measure, they could knock on the door until their knuckles bled, for fuck's sake. Wait for Dorrie to let them in with her key.

Harlan loped into the kitchen to find Jack where he'd been sitting for hours, with his hands wrapped around an empty coffee cup. Placing the cordless phone on the table, Harlan slid into the chair across from his father and grunted.

"That was Mom."

Of course. Another sympathy call. "Surprise, surprise. Was she calling to make sure I haven't thrown myself from the fourth-floor windows? Overdosed on Nervy Durvies?"

"Not really."

"Hm. Bragging about her success?" During her last call, she'd dropped a bomb on Jack. She and Yale were now house-hunting in La Jolla, making plans to keep the Boston condo as an East Coast crash pad, while living full-time on the West Coast. Apparently, the Hollywood crowd couldn't get enough of the Million-dollar Pauper look, and she'd been approached by a movie studio to consult on set-design for an upcoming film starring Beatty and Bening.

The only upside, he supposed, was that after Penelope's move, Harlan and Melissa would be free for dinner on Wednesday nights.

"No. She wasn't bragging."

"Mm. What then? She's leaving Yale and wants me to move into her new beach house?"

Harlan laughed quietly. "I don't think so."

"Then?"

"She's sending me a ticket. She wants me to come down for two weeks."

Jack looked up sharply. She wanted Harlan in California? Now? The timing couldn't possibly be worse.

• • •

So THAT WAS that. Whether Jack survived it or not, Harlan would fly to LAX the following day to join his mother and his lumpy new stepfather on their extended honeymoon.

Love and Adoration, Part Two.

Why they needed to haul Harlan around from open house to open house was beyond Jack. Harlan would hate all the sunshine and money and the whole poseur-breeding lifestyle. But according to Penelope, Yale had plans to take him camping on a beach without a tent. They'd sleep under the stars and wake at dawn, hopeful to find a whole mess of seals waddling across the sand to inspect their sleeping bags.

Harlan, of course, was dying to go.

It was the only reason Jack had agreed. Besides, it might not be terrible for the boy to escape his father's sulks for a while. The atmosphere around the house had grown increasingly morose. Perhaps by the time Harlan returned, Jack would have found some way to tweak his gravelly attitude. Perhaps not.

Tweaks or no tweaks, however, when Harlan got back, Jack planned to enlist him in his own house-hunting and encourage him to get out of his figurative Den of Cheese and live a little. Not with Jack, of course, who'd almost certainly spend the rest of his days under his bed . . . wherever that bed might be.

"I've BEEN DISCUSSING your case with a colleague," Snowden said later, taking the little brown pad out from his breast pocket. Jack didn't know if it was the unusually warm February weather or a satisfying nap back at the office, but the old doctor looked especially chipper that afternoon. Snowden flipped his pad open and stopped, looking up at Jack. "I do this periodically when faced with a plateau in a patient's progress. Of course, in your case, we've still not risen from the valley. You don't mind, do you?"

Jack grunted. "As long as he's not recommending electroshock therapy, what do I care?"

"Hm. I didn't think to ask him." Snowden settled himself in his chair. "Anyway, I've come up with a few ideas that just might nudge you toward progress."

"Let's not get all excited about progress. Right now, I'm just hoping to survive."

"As luck would have it, survival is exactly what I'd like to discuss. Human survival."

"Oh Christ. I'm not up for a lesson—"

"You see, a baby's survival is fully dependent on a strong parental connection. It is through this connection the baby receives the food and care he or she needs to stay alive. Mother Nature is a brilliant planner. And in certain cases, where little or no parental connection exists, the baby's very survival is threatened . . . not only physically but emotionally. This broken connection manifests itself in anxieties and depression later in life. For the infant."

"Mm-hm."

"Don't you see?"

"What?"

"Your emotional survival needs weren't met when you were a baby; hence, you're afraid to leave the house."

Jack blinked several times in confusion and held up his empty hands. "That's it?"

"In abbreviated form."

"Your big conclusion is that I'm afraid to leave the house? Have we not established this already? Isn't the larger issue that I'm about to be forced from my house and might not survive it? Isn't that the *real* survival issue here?"

"On the surface."

"On the surface? The fucking surface is going to kill me! How I came to be this way is really not top of the list for me right now."

"Ah, but it should be. My colleague suggested I take you through a therapeutic rebirth."

Jack stared at him. "I don't like the sound of this."

Snowden leaned forward and leaned on his knees, clasping his hands together with enthusiasm. "Ever heard of it?"

"No."

"It's typically done with children, but I thought, since we cannot seem to get past this wall you've put up, it might be worth trying. It's where the therapist, me, takes the patient, you, through the major stages of life, starting with birth, and reparents you as you ought to have been parented from the start. We'd start with the day you were born."

Too shocked to laugh, Jack squinted and rubbed the stubble on his chin. "You've got to be kidding me. You want to be my mother now?"

"Or father."

"I don't need a fucking parent today!" Jack stood up and backed away from Snowden. He turned and stomped toward the hall stairs, not caring how red the doctor's face was growing. "I don't need to be born again, I don't need to progress . . . I might need that shock treatment, though, if you'd like to arrange for that! I don't need anyone's goddamned concern or peer-approved strategies for survival. I just need a fucking roof over my head, for my son to stay home with me, and for everyone else to leave me the hell alone!"

Chapter 25

A Crumpled-Up Bag
at the Back of the Drawer

The phone rang. If it hadn't been right there beside his foot, on the floor of the dining room where he'd sat slumped against the wall for nearly four hours after the airport limousine picked up Harlan, he'd have let it ring.

"Yeah?"

"Oh, Jack." It was Dorrie's pushy coworker, Caroline. "I'm so glad you picked up. I just couldn't let this one slip us by. I've just seen a place by the park—a rental that might be perfect for you. Give you time to adjust. And the owners might be willing to consider selling in the next year or two. It's a terraced flat with parking. Three bedrooms and two fireplaces, and it's definitely affordable for you. It's sweet and charming and, most important, it's available immediately . . ."

"No."

"Have you already found yourself a place to live?"

"I just can't deal with it today."

"Then when? When the moving van is loaded and the driver asks you for directions? I know how hard this must be, but you've only got a few weeks . . ."

Jack was quiet. He reached for an iron poker and nudged the logs, watching sparks dance about onto the floorboards and stamping them out with his socked foot. Exhaling hard, he said, "Okay. I'll consider the place."

Heaving himself out of his chair, he shuffled into the kitchen, picked up the newspaper, and opened a cupboard. He supposed he'd pack the electrical appliances first, the ones he rarely used. Reaching for one of the cardboard cartons in the middle of the floor, he dragged it over to the open cupboard and began to pack.

LATER THAT WEEK, having boxed up most of the kitchen and smaller items on the main floor, Jack had shifted his attention to the bedrooms on the second level, starting with Baz's room. Ironically, the methodical sameness of wrapping objects in newspaper, placing them into boxes, then taping the cartons shut, first one way, then the other, and labeling them with a fat black marker soothed Jack, who had yet to hear back from Snowden's office regarding his recent request for a refill. Seemed once you left the old doctor to see himself out, midsession, a return phone call became the height of inconvenience.

He laid out several cartons in front of each of the three bedrooms, the office, and the bathroom, before opening the door to his father's room. Pausing with one hand on the doorknob, Jack sucked in a slow breath.

The door creaked in umbrage, having rarely been opened the past few decades. Jack had left the heavy curtains drawn, just as they had been on the day of Baz's death. Anything of value had long since been seized, but all of Baz's other possessions remained just as they always had been: his cologne; the beloved brush used to tame those long, crazy locks; his faded leather wallet, so worn that his canceled credit cards poked right through in spots; and his motorcycle boots, complete with "venting," as Baz called the gaps between leather and sole.

Walking across to the huge bay window, Jack finally pulled back the curtains, thick with dust, and looked down at the street below. Baz would have hated the prudish neighbors across the street, with their ceramic figurines lining windows framed by scalloped lace. He'd have opened up the fourth-floor windows when the band practiced, amps jacked up to full power, just to "fawk with their brains."

Exhausted suddenly, Jack climbed onto Baz's enormous bed and rested his head on the pillow, where Baz's head had lain every day during those terrible last weeks. He wasn't sure if he imagined it. The pillow still smelled faintly of Baz's cologne. Inhaling deeply, Jack felt he could reach out and touch him, so strong was the image the woody-musk scent brought to life.

But it had been almost thirty years. No scent could possibly last three decades. His mind was screwing with him.

Nothing new about that.

Baz had been so sick at the end that, really, he should have been in the hospital, but Baz, being who he was until the end, flatly refused. How many times had Jack wished he'd stayed home that night? He might have been playing in the hallway when his father came out, staggering, most likely.

He breathed deeply again and smiled. The scent was pure Baz.

Running his finger along the edge of Baz's bedside table created a rut in the thick grayish-white dust. He sat up. The dresser contents should really be packed up first. Yanking open the top drawer, he kicked a box underneath it and, one by one, began dropping rolled-up socks and folded underwear into the open carton, not quite sure why he was saving his father's undergarments. Pausing for a moment, he determined that these items he could part with. There really wasn't anything sacred about underwear.

He closed one flap of the box and scrawled CHARITY across the top. Surely there were people out there who needed free underwear?

At the back of the drawer, behind the last pair of tube socks, was a crumpled-up plastic bag. Pulling it open, Jack peered inside. Empty. Without giving it another thought, he tossed it into the trash bag in the doorway.

"Jack?" Lucie called from downstairs. "Jack? You up there?"

Christ. He'd forgotten about her lesson. And Harlan was away. He sighed, dropping back onto the bed and resting his head in his hands. He couldn't do it. Couldn't bring himself to take her all the way to the park and stand around, dying from dizziness, until she was done. Not now. His pill bottle was empty.

So was his spirit.

If he had to weigh the significance of a little girl's skating lesson against his home being ripped out from underneath him, his own troubles won out.

Her blond head poked through the doorway. "Hi, Jack. It's past five-thirty. Where's Harlan?"

He shook his head. "I'm sorry, Lucie. I forgot to tell you he's with his mother in California. My mind's just been so . . ."

"That's okay. You and me, we'll go together. Get your coat."

His head throbbed. "It's just that, well, it's not a good time for me to go out. I can't do it today."

"But I *have* to go today. It's my second-to-last class before we move. If I don't go today, I'll miss it. And I won't be able to get Michael Michaelson's phone number because he's going to Florida the next week. So I'll never, ever be able to call him." She blinked at Jack. "I have to go today."

Jack's head felt as if it might implode. His eyes watered from the pain. "I need a Tylenol. Sorry, Luce. Can't do it."

"Jack, please! I need to go."

"*Not* today."

She exploded, stamping her little foot on the floor. "You can't just not take me! Why doesn't anyone care about me? No other kid's grown-up just says, 'No, I'm not taking you today! I don't feel like it!'" She paced to the window and spun around, her skates swinging from her shoulder. "You're just like my mom."

"I'm nothing like your mother. I'm just not up to it today. And you were going to have to stop anyway. It's just slightly sooner."

"That doesn't help." Tears threatened to spill onto her cheeks.

"Adults have responsibilities, Lucinda. I have responsibilities in this house, here, now. You're not my responsibility, don't you see? I'm not your father . . ."

It was as if he'd slapped her face. She raced out of the room and down the stairs, skates crashing against the walls, and out the front door, which slammed so hard the overhead light in Baz's room swayed. He ran to the window to see her stomping down the sidewalk, her chin stuck way up in the air.

She was going without him.

Goddamn it! It was lunacy. A young girl tramping through the city streets after dark? There was molestation and murder to think about; she'd said it herself. Any sicko could pull his car to the side of the road and scoop her up. He struggled to unlock the window and pull it open.

But after nearly thirty years of inactivity, the wooden frame stuck solidly in place. Uselessly, he banged against the glass. She kept walking and turned the corner, disappearing from sight.

Obstinate little creature! Risking her life over a stupid lesson with a chain-smoking alcoholic. Or, at least, someone who looked like an alcoholic, swaying on the ice while her students tried desperately to win her approval.

He stormed along the worn runner in the hall to his office and dialed the Ballard house. These parents of hers were going to have to just step the hell up and go after their daughter. Christ. She could lose her way and end up at the waterfront, be murdered by some parolee recently released from jail, or simply be beaten up by a gang of wild teenage girls—God knows, there were a lot of teenage girls roaming the neighborhood in packs.

The phone rang and rang, eventually going to message. Of course they weren't home. Why ever should they interrupt their lives to be there for their youngest child? His head throbbed harder now.

He should go after her. He should *fucking well* get up and go! What kind of person stays inside in a situation like this, hoping for the best? Already, he could feel his hands shaking. Tingling. Slumping forward onto the desk, he dropped his head into his folded arms, tears stinging his eyes.

AT QUARTER AFTER seven, there was still no sign of her. But then, if the lesson ended at seven and she changed into her boots, it would likely be a good half hour before she appeared. Forty minutes, if she stopped to flirt with Mr. Michaelson and get his phone number.

Still. Jack had a bad feeling.

Sprinting downstairs, he reached for his coat and dashed out the front door, pulling his coat on as he tore down the icy sidewalk.

He raced along the main road, dodging shoppers and couples out for a leisurely stroll after dinner, past canopied restaurants with people inside drinking, talking, laughing, without a care in the world. He burst into the park, past the dog walkers and joggers, and toward the overhead spotlights illuminating Frog Pond.

It was a clear night but very cold—the frosty air made his lungs ache. As he got closer, he saw the only skaters on the ice were adults. He

jogged into Pond Cottage, hoping to find Lucie lined up for hot chocolate, but not only was she not there, her classmates weren't, either. Back
outside, Muriel Danby walked toward Tremont Street.

"Hey!" he called, racing after her. She stopped, turned around, and
sucked on her freshly lit cigarette. By the time he reached her, he could
barely speak. "Hey." He paused to catch his breath. "Have you seen Lucinda?"

She took another drag and pointed her cigarette in the direction Jack
had come. "She left ages ago. Went home. I told her I'd call her a cab,
but she . . ."

Jack was already gone, running back the way he'd come. Why hadn't
he passed her? He'd taken the shortest route. The route he and Dorrie
took her the other week. Where the hell was she?

When he hit Charles Street, he jogged slower, looking into shops and
restaurants in case she'd stopped off somewhere to get warm, but didn't
see the familiar red knitted hat pulled down to her nose. He'd give anything to see that hat right this moment. He cut down toward Battersea
from another street, a similarly narrow, heavily treed street, counting on
her having mistaken the streetscape for her own.

About a half block along the quiet sidewalk, he saw it. The red hat.
The rest of her was hidden by the bench's backrest.

"Lucie!" he called.

She turned, pushing her hat up from over her nose and tilting her
head back so she could see him. A big smile crossed her face. "Jack!" She
stood up and, leaving her skates lying in the snow, ran to him, jumping
into his arms as he lifted her up to his chest and held her close. Her tiny
body heaved with sobs. "I knew you'd come. I knew it," she whispered.

Standing beneath the flickering glow of the gaslight, patting Lucinda's back, Jack was suddenly conscious of the vastness around him. The
wide street and the long sidewalk. The size of the bare trees. The infi-
niteness of the black sky.

The absence of Nervy Durvies.

His heart thumped a warning.

More and more, Jack thought, life was forcing him outside. It had
stood by patiently all these years, watching, waiting. Hoping he'd do
something about his ridiculous situation. But eventually it became clear

that Jack Madigan was hopeless, so life took off the gloves and came stomping after him.

Jack looked down at Lucinda's tear-streaked face. "I should have taken you."

"No. You couldn't."

"I could've. I'm sorry, Luce."

"I thought I was on Battersea . . ."

"Shh." He placed his hand on the back of her head. "You're safe now."

Her sobbing slowed, eventually stopping. He set her down gently and slung her skates over his shoulder before they turned to walk toward what was still, for both of them, home. As they picked their way along the frozen sidewalk, she took his hand with her mittens and squeezed it tight.

Chapter 26

The Only Man on the Sidewalk

Jack taped up a box full of pots and pans, slumped down on top of it, and pushed his hands through his hair, surely yanking out what remained of his once-lush pelt. As he stared at his beloved kitchen walls, the door buzzer rang out.

Snowden. At least he could finally get some pills.

A few moments later, the two of them were sitting across from each other at the dining-room table. Maybe the old guy was trying to minimize the enormity of what was happening, but his lack of concern for Jack was astonishing. He'd limped inside, sat himself down, handed Jack a card with anxiety-relieving tips (which included such surefire panic-busters as keeping a journal of the move and avoiding caffeine and sugar), and ordered himself a coffee with, naturally, extra sugar.

Worse than Snowden's useless advice card, however, was his total lack of interest in where Jack might be relocating.

"My new address is on the table there, on the back of that envelope," Jack said when he returned from the kitchen with two coffee cups. "So you'll know where to come get your sugar fix."

Snowden flipped over the envelope and stared at the address, saying nothing.

Jack added, "It's not far. Just past the park on the other side."

"The other side of the park?" the doctor asked.

"Yeah." Jack swallowed hot coffee and felt holes burning through his esophagus. "Pretty much the other side of the world for me though, huh?"

Snowden furrowed his brow and stared upward. "But isn't that road a one-way street?"

"I guess so. Aren't they all?"

The doctor pulled a Boston road guide from his satchel and flipped through it for what seemed to be about eight hours before slipping it back into his bag and shaking his head. "I'm sorry to tell you this, Jack, but you're no longer on my way home."

"What?"

"My house calls are strictly limited to houses on my evening commute." He folded his hands on his stomach and stared at Jack. "This new place is out of the way. The connecting street runs counter to my evening commute."

Jack laughed, disbelieving. "For a couple of blocks."

"Seemingly, but with the city's tangle of one-way streets, it would take me too long."

The coffee burned so badly now that Jack could nearly feel it seeping through his abdomen and onto his clothes. "But I'm your patient."

"To be truthful with you, I've been thinking you'd benefit from a change in therapists. There's very little I haven't tried, and nothing seems to have helped. It appears I've reached the end of my usefulness to you."

Snowden was dropping him? "That's ridiculous. You've been very useful—"

"We've achieved virtually no progress in the last few years. You might do better with someone younger. Fresher."

"That's not true."

"You're telling me you *have* made progress?"

"No. Definitely not. But it's my fault. It's all me. I've been closed off to your attempts. But I can change that now. I can start . . ."

Shaking his head firmly, Snowden pulled out a pen, scratched out a name and telephone number on his pad, and tore off the sheet, handing it to Jack. It read DR. JACOB FAULKNER, with an illegible phone number.

Jack looked up at him and blinked. "But you've been seeing me for fifteen years. You're my psychiatrist. Just like that, it's over?"

"It's time, Jack. And don't worry; Faulkner's rates are similar to mine. And you're definitely on his way home. He works just around the corner from your new place."

Jack could barely breathe.

Snowden coughed and leaned back with pen and pad in hand. "Shall we begin our final session?"

The matter was, apparently, closed for discussion. It was over. All fifteen years of it. Jack had been cast off. He'd never been more than a patient file with a handy address and a sorry attitude. A way to pick up a few extra bucks on the old man's way home.

"MR. MADIGAN," MRS. Buxley said. Jack wasn't sure if there was a Mr. Buxley, and he didn't really care. "I hope you'll have cleared the cellar of those dented paint cans before you . . . move on with your life."

Of course, Mrs. Buxley knew the whole situation. That the bank had sold his house to her from underneath his pallid feet. She was just being delicate in an elderly sort of way. Well, fuck delicacy. Delicacy made Jack want to puke.

He looked up to see her speaking again but didn't answer. Instead, he looked away and swiped at an imaginary flaw on the banister. Dorrie hadn't said two words, just stood beside Mrs. Buxley in the doorway— not an easy feat, as the woman was particularly heavyset and tottered and swayed with the brittle precariousness of old age. Her spine had long since eroded and buckled over around shoulder level, so much so that he could practically hear the upper vertebrae splintering like dead twigs as she tried to look up at his face. And when she finally let go of the door frame and began to steer herself through the main floor, the going was painfully slow and perilous.

Dorrie remained by her side, as much to act as an emergency support as to be ready to step between Jack and her buyer, should Jack lose control and lunge at the old girl with his Groper. As they hobbled toward the living room, Jack caught Dorrie's eye. She quickly looked away.

"I'll just get out of your way," he mumbled, turning away to head upstairs. "Got more packing to do."

He had signed the lease on the "charming flat by the park" that Caroline had recommended. Hadn't even gone to see it. Caroline had shown him some photos, and he signed some papers. Simple as that. What did he care? As long as his son, his furniture, and, regrettably, his cat fit inside, what the hell did it matter where he was going?

"Mr. Madigan," Mrs. Buxley called out in a voice worn thin with years. "Our contractor is meeting us here tomorrow morning to measure for carpeting. You can be ready for us at nine-thirty. Sharp."

Jack had an idea. "You folks think you might be repairing the dumb-waiter before you move in? I've got a few things stuck inside. I'd rather not leave them behind." If he could arrange for them to get it moving before he left, he could make one last-ditch attempt to sell the guitar lodged inside. Slap the cash on Dave's desk and stop the deal before it closed. Underhanded, but hey, this whole lousy transaction was under-handed.

Mrs. Buxley's whole body swayed as she looked up, her chin wob-bling from side to side with the strain. "Oh yes," she said. "That'll be last on our list. After the pipes are replaced, the house is rewired, and the furnace put into proper working order. But we don't have much use for a dumbwaiter, so it'll be ripped out and a proper elevator installed." She turned to Dorrie, who was closer to her height and not so difficult to get a good look at. "My husband doesn't move around so well. Bad back, I'm afraid."

"It's helpful when you're doing repairs," Jack said, unwilling to give up. "Sending tools up and down. Those four flights can tire out your workers' legs mighty quickly."

"I'm sure our contractor is fit. Some sort of Ironman athlete, he says."

Of course he was.

Mrs. Buxley called out again. "You'll pick up your things that are stuck in there, though, your dishes and your little guitar, once we get the shaft cleared out. I don't want your belongings hanging all about for my Harold to trip over. He doesn't move around as well as I do."

Behind him, Dorrie whispered something to Mrs. Buxley, something that had her fussing and murmuring, "All right, then. If you must." Dorrie climbed the stairs after him, catching up on the second-floor landing.

"You're being wonderful, Jack. I want you to know that. You didn't even have to let her in today." Her eyes were wide. Sincere. "I know how hard this is for you."

"Yeah. Well, what good would it do me to stop her?"

"Still. Thanks." To his surprise, she leaned toward him and hugged him tight. "You're all right, Jack Madigan."

Embarrassed, he pulled away and looked down at his feet. "I should get on with my packing, I guess . . ."

Dorrie moved toward Baz's room and looked inside. "This was his room, wasn't it?"

He nodded.

"He died here?"

Moving closer, Jack pointed toward the dumbwaiter. "There, actually. Though no one really knows why he was up. He could barely lift his head at the end, let alone take a walk."

She looked from his door to the dumbwaiter and down the hall. "Where was your old room? Your childhood room?"

He pointed toward Harlan's room. "Before Baz died, this was my room. After, well, after, I sort of avoided the second floor for a while. Moved upstairs."

She looked at the distance between the two doorways and back at Jack. "He was coming to see you. That much is very obvious. He got out of bed to see you. What else would get him off his deathbed but his own child?"

He laughed sadly, shrugging. Baz wasn't your typical parent, he wanted to say. When he looked up at her, her eyes were shimmering. "I'm so sorry," he said. "What I said before, it was so ridiculous. You must know I didn't mean it. I believe in you. I do."

She smiled as he moved closer, wrapping her in his arms. "I know . . ." she said.

"I'd do anything for you. Anything."

Shuffling sounds echoed from the front hall. Mrs. Buxley was on the move. "Dorrie Allsop?" she called out. "Dorrie Allsop? Are you up there? Dorrie Allsop?"

"Yes." She pulled away and hurried downstairs with a backward smile at Jack. "Coming, Mrs. Buxley . . ."

FROM THE SOUNDS of it, Dorrie wasn't having an easy time of getting Mrs. Buxley out the front door. Something about her boots not fitting all of a sudden, and her thinking Dorrie was somehow responsible, had gotten her worked into a state.

"But I just don't see how they fit coming in, and now they don't fit. Maybe you're wearing mine," said Mrs. Buxley.

"No, Mrs. Buxley. Mine are brown. Yours are black. And mine have heels."

"Lord in heaven, don't be telling me now that my boots don't even have heels. What kind of boot-maker makes boots without heels?"

Jack jogged down the stairs to find Mrs. Buxley slumped on the bottom step with Dorrie struggling to fit a small black boot onto an old cramped foot. "Need some help, ladies?"

Behind her blowsy blond hair, Dorrie looked red-faced and exasperated as she bashed the boot farther up Mrs. Buxley's foot. "We're okay, aren't we, Mrs. Buxley? Just a slight problem with swelling."

"Swelling? I tell you, someone's been messing around with my boots. Nothing like this has ever happened to me. Don't give me 'swelling.'"

Jack stepped in to save the day. With a wink at Dorrie, he took the knotty foot between his knees and used both hands to wiggle the boot farther up her ankle until he could tie it nice and snug with the salt-encrusted laces. Giving the foot a fatherly slap, he stood up. "There we are. You're ready for action."

Mrs. Buxley wasn't so sure. She struggled to stand, holding her arms out to Dorrie and Jack for assistance. Once they finally got her upright, she tapped her foot against the floor. "I don't know. It feels a bit strange. Like something's inside it."

"I put my hand clear inside. It's empty." Jack laughed. "Or at least it was. Once you start walking, it'll sort itself out." He slipped his arm through hers. "May I help you to the door?"

The three of them shuffled toward the door, which Jack opened and helped steer her through. "We'll be seeing you tomorrow morning then." He winked at Dorrie and ducked back inside to resume packing. The third floor was going to be a big job. There was his bedroom, which would take a half-day at least. Then there was the linen closet, overflowing with towels and sheets in various states of fraying shabbiness. Not halfway up the stairs, he heard Dorrie calling his name from out front.

"Wha—" he started to say as he pulled the door open. Mrs. Buxley was lying on the sidewalk on her left side, with Dorrie yanking on her arm to set her upright again.

"Jack," Dorrie said as she tugged in vain. "Please. Help me."

"Did she fall?" he asked.

"Of course she fell," Dorrie snapped. "That boot wasn't on all the way." She nodded toward a boot lying about two feet away. "Come down here and give me a hand, please."

Instinctively, he patted his pockets for pills. Shit. Empty, of course. With the shock of being dumped by his psychiatrist, Jack had forgotten about his refill until after the doctor had left. At which time, Jack was no longer officially Snowden's patient, but that hadn't stopped him from stalking Snowden's secretary by phone for that one last refill for the road. The old guy owed Jack that much.

Eyeing the distance from the front stoop to where Mrs. Buxley lay complaining, Jack placed one foot on the porch. He did it last night, didn't he? When Lucinda was lost. Of course, Lucinda had been in great danger. A tiny waif of a girl, a nine-year-old, alone in the darkened city. Just waiting for some madman to scoop her up. It was a dire emergency. Not like this. His heart pounded, and he stepped back in. "Try getting her feet beneath her. Mrs. Buxley, tuck your feet beneath you."

"If I could move my feet, do you think I'd be lying here like a dead dog?" she said into her buttoned-up bosom. "You need to lift me from behind. That's the way the paramedics do it."

"Paramedics?" Dorrie nearly cried. "You need paramedics to get up?"

"Not if your boyfriend would help. And fast. I can't move my neck."

"Jack, please. It'll only take a minute." Dorrie's red blazer had fallen off one shoulder in the struggle. "Less than a minute."

He stepped out onto the porch with both feet this time, willing life to step in and take the reins again. But it didn't. He grabbed hold of the handrail with both hands.

Do it, he shouted silently. Dire emergency or not, do it! Dorrie needs help! For God's sake, *be a man*. Glancing back into the house was a mistake. It made the panic rise up, writhing and hissing around his neck.

"What kind of real estate agent lets her client lie on the ground? Like a bum?"

"Jack!"

Leaning on the railing now, he set a foot on the first step. He could do this for Dorrie. He could! He could progress. Sweat rolled down his face, and he looked back at the door. God, he longed to go back inside. Had to get back in. "Maybe I better call 911," Jack called. "She might have broken something. It would be terrible to move her if something's broken."

"The ground's so cold."

"Jack, she's *cold*!"

Just as he lowered his foot down toward the next step, almost touching solid concrete, a piercing feline yowl sounded from under the porch, and the cat blasted out from beneath the bushes, through Jack's legs and inside the house. Jack's heart went wild, and the world outside seemed to rise, hurling the street up and down like a blanket flapping in the wind, flaunting life itself before his eyes.

Life was too fickle.

He was going to be sick.

"Jack!"

Behind Dorrie and her fallen client, a cab pulled to the curb and honked twice, without a glance at the skirmish on the sidewalk. The driver reached toward the meter, then sat back again to flip through a magazine, without a worry in the world.

Stepping back toward the doorway, Jack swallowed hard and blinked back the sparks that were dancing in front of his eyes. The taste of bile burned his tongue like acid.

"Jack, please. That's her cab. Let's get her into it."

"I'm going to give this Heritage Estates a piece of my mind. What's the name of your superior?"

"Jack!" Dorrie wailed.

Hunched over, he stepped down the step and back up again, swallowing the rush of saliva filling his mouth. "I want to, but . . ." He shook his head, clutching his stomach. "I just, I can't."

It was at that moment Dorrie's face changed. No longer pleading and persuasive, her eyes grew cold. As if a steel door had slammed shut, severing their connection. He watched as Dorrie waved to the cab driver, who tossed aside his magazine and rushed out to help.

In about fifteen seconds, the cabbie had her on her feet. Guiding her delicately toward the car, he shot Jack a look. Not so much a look of absolute disgust as one of moral supremacy, of being not only the bigger man but the *only* man on the sidewalk.

Dorrie didn't look back at all.

Chapter 27

Laurel Canyon White

Dad?" Harlan always sounded so much younger on the phone.

Sinking onto the kitchen floor, Jack smiled. He hadn't heard from his son in days. "Harlan! How's the sand and surf treating you? Are you missing the snow yet?"

"Yeah, right! I can't wait to freeze my ass off waiting for the Buick to warm up. That'll be supreme. The weather is so incredible here. It never, ever rains. Not ever."

"So the song says."

"I went surfing this morning. With Yale. He's, like, this awesome surfer."

The same Yale who married Penelope? "I hope he put sunscreen on his head. He might burn something fierce out there."

"*Dad,*" Harlan said. "He's a nice guy."

"I know. I'm just kidding with you. Did you manage to stand on your board?"

"For about three seconds. But Yale got into the green room."

"Green room?"

"It's the tube inside the wave."

"Yes. Ridiculous for a Bostonian not to know that."

"How's Mrs. Brady?"

"Oh you know. Delightful as always. Yesterday he chucked up a hairball right in front of the new owner."

"Nice."

"I thought so."

"Yesterday I saw Paris Hilton at a Pogo stand. She actually smiled at me. How righteous is that? Then she wolfed down two Pogos and, like, a bucket of lemonade. I should have asked her out."

Jack grinned. "She might be a bit old for you. And a bit too experienced." Not a trace of the reclusive, snappish Harlan remained. Well, a bit of snappishness, but, after all, he was seventeen. Snapping at your parents was obligatory at that age.

"Whatever. I don't care."

"Have you kept up on the work your teachers sent with you?"

Harlan snorted. "Yeah. I've got to apply to college soon."

"Well, you're home in a couple of days; we'll get busy on your applications. There are plenty of excellent schools on the East Coast. And, I suppose, the one good thing is that I can now afford to send you anywhere. You won't need to apply for scholarships."

"Yale says I should apply to UCLA."

Jack laughed again, nervously this time. "UCLA? What, you're, you're going to live there year-round? In all that heat and smog? You wouldn't even get to wear your polyester leisure suits in the heat. And just imagine how your feet would roast in your vinyl loafers."

Harlan didn't answer.

"And besides," Jack continued, "the very best schools are in the East. Without all the distractions of Paris at a Pogo stand. *Melissa* is here. Certainly you don't want to leave Melissa behind, do you?"

"Melissa is kind of looking into UCLA as well."

"Harlan, listen to me. You don't hinge your entire future on one sunny day, do you hear me? You could go to *Harvard* with your grades. Haven't you always said you wanted to go to Harvard?"

"That was before, Dad. You know that Laurel Canyon house Mom just bought?"

"Yes."

"She's giving me the pool house. It's down a little valley from the main house, with all these weird jungle trees dripping down all around it. Like some kind of Tarzan house, like it just grew there. It has its own kitchen and a loft with a huge window facing the pool. All the walls inside are wood but painted white, and there's a stone fireplace right in the middle of the living-room floor. And the best part—the hills are filled with coyotes. The old owners had three little dogs eaten up last year alone. But I wouldn't let Mrs. Brady out of the pool house, so don't worry."

"Comforting." How could he compete with a pool house surrounded by jungle trees and coyotes? A house with a fireplace in the middle of the floor and all the walls painted in Laurel Canyon White? Or should he say, Full-custody White?

"So, Dad? Can I stay? Can I?"

"Put your mother on the phone, son."

LIKE HELL PENELOPE didn't encourage Harlan to stay. Jack slammed down the phone and climbed up to the third floor to find his Magic Marker. Offering him the pool house? He never should have allowed Harlan to fly down to see her in the middle of the school year. Should have waited until spring break, when Harlan's application to Harvard was safely in the mail.

Penelope obviously didn't feel she had enough going for her. A wildly successful career, a new marriage, houses on both coasts—she had to take Harlan as well.

Where was that fucking marker?

So, it would be just Jack moving into the charming cottage. Not even the goddamned cat to keep him company.

Ah. The marker had rolled down in between two boxes in the hall. Jack picked it up and trotted back downstairs. At least he'd convinced her to let Harlan come back as scheduled, to wrap things up at his old school and arrange for his transcripts to be sent to the high school in the canyon, and to visit with his pathetic old father—in that order.

Something was banging around in the dumbwaiter shaft. Sure enough, Mrs. Brady had crept in through the open door and was squatting on the dumbwaiter, sharpening his claws against the bricks and pulling out chunks of mortar, which were sprinkled all over the top of the metal car.

"Get out of there." Jack swatted at the cat, who completely ignored him and continued to paw and scratch. "That's enough now." Reaching inside, he picked up the cat and deposited him onto the carpeted runner. Immediately, the animal spun around and dove back inside. This time, Jack pulled him out and closed the heavy wooden door.

Shooting Jack a look of utter contempt, the cat spread his back legs and began cleaning his privates with a mocking grin, anything to avenge the killjoy who dared interrupt his elevator-shaft merriment.

"Revolting." Jack reached into Harlan's room and flicked on the great mirror ball, wondering if his son would now consider it too dorky for the pool house. Dropping down on his knees in front of the sealed cartons, he crossed out the words HARLAN'S ROOM, and scrawled furiously, in block letters, LAUREL CANYON.

Chapter 28

Lucie, Come Home

Jack watched the mailman disappear around the corner. He'd barely stopped as he tossed Jack's bills into his hands. Just nodded and kept walking without even mustering up the energy to say good morning. Seemed it had become a pattern in Jack's life. People walking away. Like he was invisible. Before turning back inside, Jack noticed an elderly woman wearing a tweed hat and carrying a slip of paper. Pausing in front of his house, she looked confused.

"Can I help you?" Jack called.

"Yes. I'm looking for 117 Battersea Road."

"This is 117."

She took hold of the railing and stepped slowly up the steps in her thick, wrinkled hose and sensible shoes, and set a carpetbag neatly on the porch. When she reached the top, she peered into Jack's face and squinted. "My eyes aren't so good anymore. Are you Rick?"

"No, Rick's next door at 119. You're talking about Rick Ballard?"

She nodded, tight curls bobbing alongside powdery cheeks. "He's my son-in-law. But I haven't seen him in years. I'm Samantha's mother, Ruth."

"Oh yes. They're right next door." He reached out to shake her hand. "I'm Jack Madigan."

The evil, uncaring grandma who spawned Lucinda's mother. In the flesh. Only she looked so squishy and harmless and kindly, Jack almost wished she was his long-lost granny. Clutching her handbag, she smiled and batted her eyes at him. "Oh my. I must have written the number down wrong. So silly. Terribly sorry to disturb you."

"It's no disturbance at all. Samantha and Rick aren't home right now; I saw them leave about two hours ago. Were they expecting you?"

"Oh dear. I'm a day early, I'm afraid. You see, my neighbor was driving this way and I thought, rather than taking the train, oh my. I really should have called . . ."

"Never mind." Jack picked up her bag and motioned her inside. "You can wait in my place. We'll hear them pull up. Rick's Hummer doesn't exactly sneak into its parking place out front."

"Very kind," she said, stepping inside.

FEET AND KNEES pressed together primly, Ruth sipped her tea by the fire and complimented Jack on everything from his lovely view to the beautiful shot of him and his father over the television. There was little resemblance between Ruth and her daughter. Where Samantha was hard, Ruth was soft. Where Samantha was brusque, Ruth was soothing.

"It's so lovely to see a parent and child so loving and close," she said, looking at Baz. "I only wish . . . oh, never mind."

One thing was perfectly clear. Any feud existing between Ruth and Samantha was all on Samantha's side. Ruth had spent the last seven years pining for Lucinda and Rosalind, though Jack was pretty sure he detected a soft spot for Lucinda. It seemed that Ruth hadn't agreed with Samantha's having handed over her youngest child to a nanny to raise while she spent her mornings at the club, lunches in tearooms, and afternoons shopping; and had told her daughter precisely how she felt. Samantha's reaction was simple. Cast off any inconvenient advice by hacking off the source. Cut Grandma off from any contact with her grandchildren and see if that doesn't teach Granny a thing or two about keeping her mouth shut.

Ruth's heart had broken all over again when, every Christmastime, her carefully chosen gifts for the girls were returned, unopened. Delicately, Jack dropped hints—not exactly calling Samantha the cold-hearted, lying bitch that she was—that, perhaps, the girls didn't know how very much their grandma cared for them; and that, particularly in Lucie's case, having Ruth back in their lives was not only desirable, it was imperative.

With teary eyes, Ruth looked up at Jack. "You think the girls will re-member me?"

"Oh yes," Jack said. "I can't speak for Rosalind, but Lucinda often speaks of her grandma in Albany. She's going to be pleasantly surprised when she meets you though."

"I suppose Samantha's been creating images of green skin and a warty nose. And a steaming cauldron of boiled children in Grandma's living room."

Jack laughed. "Well. Not quite that bad. Will they be moving close to you in Albany?" Desperately, he wanted this woman to swoop into Lu-cinda's life and fill it with hugs and kisses.

"You could say that. They're buying an estate on five acres with a guest cottage. I'm moving into the cottage. My building's full of nosy old ladies and cockroaches anyway. And it'll be nice to be able to garden again." She hesitated and shot a shy look at Jack. "Maybe Lucinda would take an interest in growing roses with me. Does she like roses?"

Living with Lucie! Right on a five-acre property. Just imagine the ice rink Lucie could build herself on five acres. Jack wanted to whoop for joy. "I'm sure she'd love planting roses. One thing's for sure. She'll make you the best coffee you've ever tasted."

Laughing, Ruth wiped away a tear. "She always used to have a special spark in her eye, that one. Like a little pixie. I've missed her so much. Ah, there I go again. Telling people all my thoughts. My neighbors have been so kind. Every day for years, they've been listening to me go on and on about my two little girls. Though, I suppose they're not so little any-more."

"Nine and eleven. Still pretty young."

"Does Lucinda still love dogs? She always used to love dogs."

Jack had to turn his head he smiled so wide, thinking of the time she chased Samantha's girlfriends through the dining room, with a mouth foaming with rabid, foamy toothpaste. "She still appreciates dogs. But what she really loves, *adores* actually, is figure skating. She's been taking lessons."

"You don't say. Did she tell you that I was state champion back in my day?"

"You were a figure-skating champion?"

She smiled, lifting up her feet and looking at her toes, swinging them from side to side. "Number one in New York State."

Of course, Samantha had hidden that from Lucinda. It wouldn't have helped her cause at all to have Lucie knowing she was genetically programmed to skate. Jack was beginning to think he might die from excitement if Lucinda didn't get home from school soon. He couldn't imagine a better scenario for the child. "Lucie is going to flip when she hears this. She gets her talent from you." He leaned closer, crossing his legs. "You know, more than anything, she'd like to continue her lessons after she moves. And she's got some serious potential. Are there any decent training facilities in your area?"

"Ooh, yes. The best facility is run by a fellow named Zeke Ellery over at the Albany Figure-Skating Club. Nice man. He's coached several youngsters right to the Olympics; why, he trained Paula Reesen and that redheaded fellow, what was his name? Lincoln something . . . ?"

"Lincoln Cole Zanner? Lucinda always talks about having his poster on the wall in her room."

"That's the one. He trains at the AFSC with Zeke."

Why did the name Zeke Ellery sound so familiar? Jack stood up, trying to think where he'd heard that name. "I'll bring in the teapot," he mumbled, heading toward the kitchen, lost in his thoughts.

"Such a nice man you are, Jack," Ruth called.

Zeke Ellery. He walked straight to the desk beneath the phone. It was a terrible jumble of mail, flyers, and other papers Jack still had to sort before packing them. He picked through the mess and stopped dead when he saw the business card with the skating-association logo.

ZEKE ELLERY, HEAD COACH, it said.

The figure-skating coach from Frog Pond. The one who thought Lucie had talent and extensions and nice jumps for her age. Dropping letters and papers all over the desk and floor, Jack jogged back into the front room.

"Zeke Ellery?" He flashed the business card. "You know *this* Zeke Ellery?"

She took it from his hands, tried to read it. "Oh dear. Where are my glasses?" She reached into her purse and fumbled with an embroidered case. With shaky hands, she pulled out the glasses, unfolded the arms, and set the glasses on her nose. She looked down at the card and smiled. "Zeke! However did you get a hold of Zeke's business card?"

"He saw her. He saw Lucie skating at the park. Said she's exactly what he looks for in his skaters. Said she should be training seriously."

"Well. Isn't that a coincidence?" she said. "May I keep this card? I'll call him on Monday."

Jack couldn't contain himself. "Yes. Yes. Call him on Monday. Tell him she's the one with the red hat and mittens. The one from Frog Pond in Boston. I told him I was her neighbor; he'll remember talking with me. Red hat and mittens, remember."

"Slow down." She laughed. "If I tell Zeke my granddaughter wants lessons, he'll give her lessons. I changed his diapers when he was a baby. His mother trained with me for fifteen years. Zeke's more like family than, well, you know."

Jack reached down and hugged her so hard he nearly knocked her teacup onto the floor. He squeezed her thin shoulders and stepped back. "I'm sorry. I'm just so amazed . . ." He stopped. "Did you hear that?"

"My hearing's not quite as good as it used to be, I'm afraid."

He checked his watch. Nearly three thirty. "The front door. I think Lucie's home next door. Wait here, I'll get her." He marched out of the room. Before he turned into the hall, Ruth called, "Jack?"

He looked back.

She patted her flowered dress with nervous hands. "Do you think I look all right? To meet her?"

Smiling, he said, "You couldn't be more perfect," before dashing to the hole in the dining room and whistling for Lucinda.

Chapter 29

The Minute After

Jack had woken with a terrible headache that had only grown worse throughout the day. The weather wasn't helping. Temperatures had risen slightly in recent days and today, of all days, the skies had burst open with icy rain. The roof was leaking onto the stage, and the depressing drip-dripping could be heard echoing throughout the house. Not the way he wanted to remember the place on his last day.

Every hallway was covered in thick, green paper runners taped to the floor so the movers wouldn't soak the floorboards on their many trips in and out, up and down—moving some thirty-odd years' worth of belongings into the huge yellow van parked out front. A long metal ramp ran from front door to sidewalk so the dolly could roll furniture smoothly out of the house.

He had to be out of the house no later than four o'clock, when the deal officially closed, and the Buxleys became the new owners of 117 Battersea Road.

As he stared out the front door, watching the movers load the dining-room table onto the van, a small black car pulled up and parked crookedly in front of Lucinda's house. A few seconds later, Dorrie stepped out, pulled a hood over her head, and unlocked her trunk.

She trotted over to her Heritage Estates sign, now covered with huge SOLD stickers on both sides, and began to pull it out of the ground.

"Dorrie," Jack called. As she looked up, the freezing rain fell harder, and she ran toward the house. As she burst across the threshold, Jack tried to think of something intelligent and witty to say. "It's really coming down out there." It was all he had.

"Yes," she said, barely glancing his way. She pulled off her hood to reveal neatly combed hair. Her cheeks were pink and wet from rain. She looked so healthy, so alive.

"If you just wait a few minutes, it'll probably slow down," said Jack.

"I hope so."

They stood in the doorway watching the rain. A moving man came through with a box on one shoulder. "Excuse me."

"Sorry," Jack and Dorrie said at the same time as they stepped aside.

"Jinx," Jack said, smiling.

Dorrie looked confused. "Pardon?"

"I said jinx. Remember the old children's game? If two people say something at the same time, one says jinx and the other can't speak until she hears her name."

She reached up to tuck her hair behind her ears. Her earrings looked new—tiny gold cubes glittering above her black turtleneck. "I never played that game."

"Ah! I didn't say your name yet!"

"Jack." She shook her head and stared outside again. "I'm really not in the mood for kids' games."

"Right." Stupid thing to suggest! Jack noticed the rain slowing outside. "How about Rose? Is she well?"

"She's fine, thank you."

"Good, good." Jack teetered back and forth from his heels to the balls of his feet. "And you? You've been well?"

"Very well."

"Good." The rain had all but stopped. "Listen, Dorrie, I was wondering if, maybe if you're not doing anything on Saturday, if you'd like to come by my new place and help me decorate." Jack laughed and waved his arm toward the living room. "You know firsthand how little talent I've got."

She turned her face away from the street to look at him. "I have plans on Saturday. Sorry."

"Sunday, then? I could build a nice fire—"

"I don't think so, Jack. I'm sorry. I've got to get going now." She pulled up her hood and stepped outside. "Good luck with the new place and . . . and everything else." At the bottom of the steps, she looked back at him. "You'll be fine, you'll see."

And in about five seconds, she'd pulled up her sign, dropped it in the trunk, and sped away.

Behind him, someone cleared his throat. Jack turned around to see another moving man, an older guy, puffing on a cigar, with an uncovered box of paint cans in his arms.

"Right." Jack stepped away from the door and back inside. "Sorry."

IT WAS JUST past three. With nothing left to do but wait until the movers finished up and then climb into the truck with them, spinning and shaking and vomiting all the way around the park to the new place—he didn't trust himself to drive the Buick in his state, especially without so much as a half-pill for sustenance—he wandered the rooms on the second floor, stopping at Baz's.

Leaning against the wooden door frame, he drank in every detail of the narrow room, committing it to memory: the leaded-glass bay window, the massive oak cornice moldings and baseboards, the thickness of the walls, the dark gloom that filled this space—even on the brightest day.

He loved it all.

The floorboards were a paler shade where Baz's furniture had been, protected from all the years of dirt and grime. He walked across the room and opened the closet door for one final check. A few hangers clanged together, but it was otherwise empty.

Nothing was left.

It was all so delicate, so temporary, this thing called life. One minute this was your world; the next minute it was gone.

The minute after that . . . who knew?

Just like Baz. One minute he was wild, glorious onstage. The next minute . . .

Maybe Snowden was right. In his own twisted way, Baz did try. Created what existence he could for himself and his son—however flawed that existence may have been. Maybe it was true . . . he'd done the very best he could. Then vanished.

How could Jack expect more than that? He'd been so hard on Baz all these years. But was he himself really any different? Had he not done the best he could? And failed, just like Baz?

Baz. He listened to the sound of movers thumping down the stairs, nodded his head, and smiled sadly. Maybe he'd failed worse than Baz. He looked around the room. One minute this was his world. He was about to live the next . . .

Maybe it all came down to believing in the minute after. Trusting that everything will right itself the minute after.

Maybe not.

From the other side of the closet wall, Jack could make out a faint, clunking sound, which grew louder as he backed out and headed back into the hall. The cat was in the dumbwaiter again. Strange, he thought. He'd kept the second-floor door closed since the last time he'd found the cat in there.

Pulling upward on the tarnished brass handles, he yanked the door open to see Mrs. Brady's sightless, soundless side facing him, while the other side was pressed against the bricks at the back of the chute. One paw was pushed deep into a dark crevice where a brick had long gone missing.

In his desperation, the cat must have leaped down into the crumbling shaft from the third-floor door, which had been left open. At least a twelve-foot drop.

"Ssst," Jack hissed, swatting at the cat, who ignored him. Some things never change, Jack thought, his head still pounding. "Get *out* of there." He reached for the cat's tail, giving it a tug. Mrs. Brady swiped at him with a front paw, raking his claws across the back of Jack's hand.

"Shit!" He watched as three slender slash marks filled with blood. Walking into the bathroom, he wrapped his hand in toilet tissue and returned to the cat, who didn't seem to care that he might be left behind to face a life with the Buxleys. He took hold of the cat and pulled him out. Again, the cat shot back inside and thrust a paw back into the darkened fissure.

What the hell was in there? Curious now, Jack jogged downstairs to the open box he'd left on the kitchen counter. The box filled with things he'd need right away at the new place: things like hammer, nails, screwdriver, tape, flashlight, a couple of cans of soup, and a can opener. Necessities.

Trotting back upstairs with flashlight in hand, he swatted again at the cat, who attempted another slashing but missed, prompting Jack to stomp his boot on the floor to scare the cat into the now-empty Den of Cheese. He flicked on the flashlight and shone it into the hole.

There was definitely something large in there—but too rough-looking to be a dead rat. He couldn't quite get a good look; the hole was fairly high up in the shaft and was quite deep.

Climbing up onto the ledge of the dumbwaiter shaft, he teetered for a moment, then paused and steadied himself, balancing on his knees. He braced one arm against the thick door frame and aimed the flashlight closer to the hole.

It was filthy, filled with dust and rubble, but toward the back was something whitish and round, covered in rubble and paw prints. It was too far back to reach without risking falling onto the roof of the dumb-waiter and plunging to his death.

He needed something long and thin. A pole.

Trotting downstairs and into the cellar, he found the Groper leaning against the wall behind the furnace. Moving into a new place, being sur-rounded by new neighbors—it hadn't seemed like a good way to start out, as the guy who picks up his paper with a hockey stick each morn-ing. He'd been planning to leave his tool behind.

Back up on the second floor, he climbed up onto the frame and once again steadied himself, this time bracing one leg against the back wall of the chute for support. He needed his arms: one for the flashlight and the other to maneuver the Groper.

Once the beam of light was properly positioned, he pushed his Groper—correctly angled so the puck-shooting end could slide straight into the crack—inside and knocked it sideways with the hook. Slowly he moved the hook around to the back of the lumpy object and nudged it toward the mouth of the hole, careful not to knock it down onto the elevator rooftop, where it could smash to smithereens, or, at the very least, make a deafening crash and send Jack reeling backward onto the floor.

When the filthy object was poised at the edge of the brown bricks, he cautiously pulled the end of the Groper out of the hole and out of the chute, letting it clatter onto the hall floor behind him. He braced an arm now against the back wall and picked it up, blowing away years of sandy grit and dust.

He gasped; his whole body tingled with recognition, tears pricking the corners of his eyes. It wasn't possible. After all these years, after all the searches . . .

The turtle shell.

Dropping to the floor, he felt every hair on his body stand on end. He turned it over and over, stopping when he saw black markings on the underside. He wiped it with his shirt.

BAZ MADIGAN. It said BAZ MADIGAN.

The jaggedy black letters swam, as his eyes filled with tears. No longer able to see, he pressed it to his chest, rolled onto his side, and wept like a child. Lying on the floor where his father was found dead so many years ago, he was struck dumb by what it meant.

Baz died leaving his son the most valuable thing he had. The very item the whole world of Bazmanics fans had searched for. But the dumbwaiter must not have been there, waiting, on the second floor when he collapsed. Maybe it landed on the roof of the dumbwaiter as it climbed up the chute, and skittered to the back when Baz collapsed. Or it could have landed on the floor of the little backless car and been thrust back toward the wall.

None of that mattered. Jack Madigan finally had what he'd wanted his whole life long. Hard, bumpy, physical proof that Baz had actually cared.

The cat, who had crept back onto the second floor, approached silently and sniffed the shell, licking dirt from the edge until the shell underneath gleamed brown. Jack had to smile. Mrs. Brady, his very own broken cat, saved his home.

Wait a minute. Jack checked his watch. Quarter to four. He sat bolt upright. The house sale closed in fifteen minutes. He could stop it. With the shell, he could stop the whole fucking nightmare. He pulled off his sweater, wrapped it around the shell and bolted down the stairs, grabbing a coat and tearing out the front door into the sleet.

"Mr. Jack," called one of the movers, closing the big doors of the van. "Wait! We don't know where we're going!"

The crowded sidewalk was too slow. He tucked the covered shell into his coat and shimmied between two parked cars and onto the street, running alongside the cars, oblivious to their honking. Rain streaming down his face and neck, cold slush seeping through his shoes, he wrapped the shell tighter and, looking for cars on Boylston, turned and ran headlong into oncoming traffic.

Boston National. He could see the sign down the block, across the street. Faster he ran, imagining Baz cheering from above. Praying it wasn't too late, he looked again at his watch, but the face had clouded up in the rain.

He dodged the cars on Boylston now, ignored the honking and swearing, tearing up onto the slippery sidewalk and into the bank. Bank customers lined up for the teller parted to let him pass, probably more from fear of being robbed than any great civility.

Dave was in his office. In his chair. He looked up, shocked to see Jack panting and dripping on his olefin carpeting. "Jack? What are you doing here? The sale's closing in a few minutes."

"No," Jack gasped, unwrapping his treasure. "No sale. You said I had until closing to make good." He laid out the shell on Dave's desk, belly-up. "I have the shell."

Dave crinkled up his face in confusion. "A turtle shell?"

"*The* turtle shell."

Dave's jaw dropped. "The shell? The one that disappeared? This is it?"

Jack beamed. "It's signed. And if you look close, you'll see his teeth marks in the right armpit."

Dave reached for his phone and pressed a button. "Marianne, I need to verify a signature. Baz Madigan. Should be scanned in the computer under Archives."

For what seemed like years, they waited, staring from each other to the shell and back again. Finally, Marianne burst through the door with a piece of paper, which Dave snatched from her hands and held next to the shell.

His hand started to shake.

"Get security," he said.

Marianne was staring at the shell. "Is that . . . ?"

"*Get security!*"

Red-faced and beaded with sweat, Dave turned to Jack. "Christ. Does anyone else know you've got it? The press? Because I want to get this sucker in the vault as quickly as we can . . ."

"Dave?"

"Yeah?"

"It's almost four and you've got a phone call to make."

Dave looked at Jack and shook his head. "Jesus Christ, Madigan. You're one hell of an exciting client."

Chapter 30

Spin Doctor

For late afternoon, an awful lot of light poured through the fourth-floor dormer windows. Spring was less than a month away, and while winter hadn't loosened its icy grip on the city, the days no longer felt weighted down by the blanket of premature darkness. Jack stared up at the heavy wooden rafters of the ceiling and spread out his arms and legs. The floor of the stage felt hard and sturdy beneath his back.

But it was no longer cold.

Slowly, the town house was being lovingly restored. The heat was back on. The roof had been retiled, cracked windowpanes replaced. The dumbwaiter parts were on their way to Boston from England; and just as Dominick the Sneezer had promised, the repairs were going to cost a fortune. But Jack didn't care. The dumbwaiter, for all it signified to Baz Madigan's son, would never be replaced or torn out.

The note inside the shell had been a surprise. Luckily Dave spotted it before the guards locked it away in the bank vault; it was so carefully lodged inside the shell. Jack had slipped it into his pocket and devoured it once the Buxleys' purchase was called off and he finally returned home, for good.

To Jack, it made up for all the years of neglect and indifference. Knowing that Baz loved Jack more than life itself and regretted every minute he didn't appreciate his boy gave Jack the peace he'd been seeking all these years. It offered a sense of closure, resolution. Confirmation that the world wasn't such a terribly shaky place, after all. His father had loved him; and at the very end, he died trying to protect Jack's future and provide the security Baz himself had never offered.

Jack shut his eyes and breathed deeply.

He must have fallen asleep because when he opened his eyes, Lucie was kneeling over him, flicking his cheek with her finger.

"Jack? Are you dead?"

He chuckled, swatting her fingers away and stretching. "No. I'm afraid not."

"You changed your hair. It's all pushed back now."

"Yeah." He sat up, rubbed his eyes. "It was time for a change."

"Whoa. You have nice eyebrows." She leaned closer to his face. "You might want to think about plucking those hairs in between, though."

"No," he said, too loudly. "I don't pluck. Ever."

"Whatever. Don't split a zipper over it."

Standing up, Jack brushed off his pants and checked his watch. "Is it time?"

She nodded. Her hair was brushed neatly, pulled back in a wide black-velvet hair band. A blue wool coat was done up to the fuzzy black collar. She looked like a little lady. "I had to say good-bye. And thank you for everything."

She fell into his arms, squeezing his neck tightly as he patted her back. Pulling away, she sat back on her heels. "Promise you'll keep going out. Just pretend I got lost in the dark again." She giggled.

"I'll try. I promise."

She looked around the room, sighing happily. Standing up, she said, "I love this room. Whenever I'm in town for skating competitions, I'm going to bring my sleeping bag and stay up here."

"Fine with me." Jack watched her turn in circles, staring at the ceiling. "Who knows, maybe the 2014 Winter Olympics will be held in Boston. On Frog Pond. You could stay here while you compete," he teased.

Stopping, she rolled her eyes. "Jack. The athletes stay at the Olympic Village. Don't you watch sports?"

He stood up. "Clearly not enough. But I'll follow figure skating now. Watching out for you in your red mittens."

Lucinda began to spin, slowly at first, then turning faster and faster, her shiny black boots tapping the stage floor. "One last spin on Battersea Road, Jack. Come on. Spin with me."

He laughed, looking down and kicking at an imaginary clump of dirt on the floor. "No thanks. I'll just watch."

Her feet moved faster now, her shoes thumping louder. "Spin, Jack. Do it with me. *Spin*."

"No . . ."

"Jack. Spin! Do it for *me*, then!"

"But the dizziness . . ."

"That's all it is. Only dizziness. It can't kill you. Say it over and over, it's only dizziness. It's just dizzy. Spread your arms out and spin, Jack, *now*!"

Slowly, he turned his feet, moving in a circle. "This doesn't feel good . . ."

"Just do it. Turn faster. It's just dizzy, Jack. Say it." Her scarf was flying straight out as she twirled.

He moved his feet faster, arms reaching out wide. "I'm getting dizzy. It's starting . . ."

"Good!" she shouted. "Go faster!"

The centrifugal force felt like Harlan's spinning the old Buick out of the alley. His hands were forced outward, while his body propelled itself firmly into the center as he twirled.

"Good," Lucy shouted. "*Say* it."

"Dizzy," he whispered. "It's just dizzy."

"Louder. FASTER."

He spun faster now, as fast as he could. The dormer windows flew by so quickly, strobes of light flashed in his eyes. "It's just dizzy. JUST DIZZY."

"Nothing else."

"Nothing else," he shouted.

"Now, close your eyes," she said, still spinning. "*Now*."

"I'll fall . . ."

"Then fall!"

Squeezing his eyes shut, he moved faster, stumbling a bit, gaining his balance and stumbling sideways again. "It's just dizzy."

"Nothing else!" Lucinda had stopped now.

He felt her watching him as he went round and round, finally tripping over his feet and collapsing on the ground in a tangle of arms and legs. He lay on his side, the house heaving, twisting, and pitching like Dorothy's in the twister. "Oh God, it's spinning worse now . . ."

"It's just a *feeling*, Jack. A great feeling. It'll go away." She knelt down beside him and put her small hand on his forehead. "You okay?"

He thought about this, shifting his arms and legs, moving his head, and watching the room whiz by him. "I think I'm going to puke."

"Good. Dead people don't puke. See?" she said, shaking her little head. "It didn't kill you."

Breathing deeply, he patted the floor beneath his hands. The same gritty floor he'd been sleeping on before she woke him. Nothing had changed. "No. It didn't kill me." He sat up and rubbed his stomach. "It's slowing now. I still might puke, but it's stopping."

Laughing, she kissed his forehead. "You're going to be okay." She stood up and walked toward the stairs. "You're going to live to be ninety."

"Hey. Don't be miserly. Give me a hundred, at least."

At the staircase, she looked back and grinned. "One spin and he's getting greedy." Her feet clomped down the stairs. "Bye, Jack."

"Good-bye, Lucinda."

"JUST DROVE RIGHT past your front door," Dave Strom boomed into his cell phone, though their connection sounded perfectly clear to Jack. "Wanted to drop off some papers but couldn't find a place to park. Too many damned reporters out front."

Holding the phone away from his ear, Jack peered out the front window at the collection of news trucks, cameras, and impeccably groomed journalists. "They're just packing up. I've given them their story . . . the words and feelings behind my discovery, you know. They needed a photo to go along with the headlines. A couple of quotes to toss around in big bold letters, that sort of thing."

"They got their hard story at the auction, I guess. They needed some soft stuff."

"You got it. A cameraman just told me that as soon as the price went past three million, all the reporters started drooling, calling their papers, and begging for the front page."

"I remember the excitement. Auctioneer nearly stopped the bidding.

Banned cell phones from the room. I hear the British fellow, the buyer, knows you?"

"Yeah. Maxwell Ridpath. Came to see the house a while back. And the best part is, he's agreed to put the turtle shell on display at the Rock and Roll Hall of Fame in Cleveland. He's not taking it out of the country."

"I hadn't heard that. Very good of him. And nice to see interest in Baz is picking up. My own wife's been begging me to get your autograph. Next best thing, she says. I told her I couldn't be bothering my number-one client with nonsense like that."

Jack smiled. How things had changed. "Tell her I'd be honored to sign." He paused before adding, "For my dad."

WEARING LEATHER GLOVES and armed with a bucket of freshly mixed cement, a piece of thick mesh, and a trowel, Jack stared at the hole into Lucinda's darkened house. The new neighbors on the other side could do whatever they liked, but Jack wanted his side to remain an opening in the bricks, filled over with rough cement. He jammed the mesh up into the hole and secured it all the way around, stopping at the Dombrowsky Brothers' faded sticker on the back of the dining-room hutch—too big to ship to Albany—and smiling.

PHILADELPHIA, 1888. THE CABINET MAKERS WHO . . .

Now he knew. The Dombrowsky Brothers, the cabinet makers who changed his world, allowing for a brave little girl to slip in and out of his life without detection, forever changing life on his side of the wall.

He scooped up a trowel full of cement and quietly covered over the hole.

The other holes in the house would remain untouched. Baz would have wanted it that way. Would have laughed. The other holes were nobody's business but his own. Of course, that didn't mean the walls themselves would remain untouched. Oh, no. Jack had been hard at work in the cellar, creating a wardrobe of whites to suit the light conditions of every unpaneled room. All plaster walls could now be treated to the same rich variances and subtleties in tone as the glorious walls of the kitchen, bringing a freshness and buoyancy to the old town house that had been sorely lacking.

Bile, the vomitous green in the hallway, would be the first to go. Paint cans, tarps, and brushes waited, lined up and ready to spring into action after lunch. The paint color of choice, the white specially developed to counter the cold bluish light reflected from the gray-painted facade of the place across the road, contained a spot each of black and raw umber for age, a spot of yellow for warmth, and a dollop of orange to neutralize the blue. He'd already tested it out on a small square of plaster in the foyer and examined it until absolutely certain not a trace of peach surfaced. Once he'd assured himself that it was just right, he scrawled the name across the lids of the cans. The Minute After, he called it.

Chapter 31

Baby Rattlesnakes

Another car full of teenagers had stopped in front of the house, their pimply faces fogging up the car windows as they ogled number 117, smiling and pointing, nodding their shaggy heads in awe. The story of the turtle shell disappearing from the concert stage, going missing for longer than they'd been alive, and being found in an elevator shaft by a one-eyed cat was too much for them to resist. All necessary ingredients for the making of a modern-day miracle were there—and then some: sex, drugs, rock and roll, with a lavish sprinkling of mutilation, mystery, and utter depravity. It seduced them. Students of all ages, from near and far, had been making the pilgrimage to Battersea Road with cultlike reverence and devotion for their new long-deceased idol.

How ironic that only two months ago, they'd have dismissed the Bazmanics as part of their parents' scene, not having lived through the whole lead-singer-being-murdered-by-a-missing-turtle commotion in the latter part of the seventies. These kids wouldn't be born for another whole decade.

Not that only the kids were drawn in. It seemed that every Baz fan, or at least the ones without any kind of permanent employment, also came to shiver and share in the worship, some even setting up blankets on the still frigid sidewalk and blasting Bazmanics' tunes from tiny boom boxes. Jack didn't mind, as long as everyone respected his rule— they could stare and chant all they want, but *no one* used the house for any kind of bodily relief. No necking, leaning, spitting, purging, or urinating. Not even for posterity.

No exceptions.

So it came to be that Battersea Road became the Mecca for truant teens and middle-aged no-hopers. The odd child or senior citizen passed by but not often; they tended to cross the road one block back to avoid the cloud of sweet-smelling smoke hanging over the sidewalk. One biker had gone so far as to pass out black T-shirts with a white outline of a snapping turtle on the front. On the back, they read, BAZ-MANSLAUGHTER. Navy blue T-shirts, for women, had an outline of the town house on the front and read I GOT BAZ-MANHANDLED IN BOSTON.

Mrs. Brady, having become the real celebrity, had had his picture—bonnet-free—splashed across every newspaper in the country, especially the tabloids. Out of kindness, Jack burned these papers. Mrs. Brady blog sites were popping up in every country, peddling sexual ambiguity as an alternative lifestyle.

And he hoped that the rumors weren't true, but Jack had already heard gossip about a company in Nebraska putting Mrs. Brady Halloween masks into production, anticipating an early September rush of sales.

That the old cat was going to be shipped to Laurel Canyon to live in a pool house surrounded by wild dogs was probably a good thing. It would force the cat to stay inside, living a life free from hungry coyotes and overzealous asexuals.

With a wave to the teenagers, who pulled out video cameras and started filming, Jack, still in his bathrobe, bent over his doormat to collect the morning paper. Two girls jogged by, waved, smiled, and shouted, "Hey, Jack!" as the boys in the car made asses of themselves, honking and whoo-hooing to get the girls' attention.

How his status had changed. From "Hermit Man" to just plain "Jack." Laughing to himself, he slipped his hand hopefully into the mailbox. No mail. He did, however, feel a small card and pulled it out.

It was a note from the young couple who'd moved into Lucinda's house. Evidently, they loved the fresh white paint he'd developed the week prior for their new home. The perfect white, they called it, saying even their designer was amazed, having opened the cans and thinking for sure the color would appear too cold.

Too cold, laughed Jack. The raw umber in the formula, with its ever so slightly green-tinted brown, was balanced by just the right amount of red. The ultimate effect being a dead neutral, old white. Neutrality, he'd called it, a name they apparently loved. It would never appear cold.

Carrying note and paper into the kitchen where his coffee awaited, he waved Mrs. Brady away from the back door. "Sorry, old boy. We can't take the risk." With an indignant flick of his tail, the cat spat at him and trotted down the hall to the full-length mirror, where he'd been spending a lot of time now that the turtle shell was no longer around to entertain him.

Jack sat down and sipped his coffee, staring at the note. He'd enjoyed creating his latest shade of white. They were sweet kids. Being admired was a relatively new experience for Jack Madigan. He'd really only been admired for his father's accomplishments. Even his own son, who was due home for a quick visit later that afternoon, hadn't ever admired his dad. Loved him, but likely didn't admire him.

A HEAVY THUMP came from the front door. Half expecting to find pilgrims in the foyer, diving for Mrs. Brady, he was shocked to find Harlan dragging two huge suitcases into the hall.

"Harlan! You're hours early." He pulled his son into his arms and held him tight. The boy seemed taller and smelled like coconut oil. Pulling back to have a good look, Jack said, "You've even got yourself a tan! I'd never have believed it . . ."

"I didn't mean to. I accidentally used Mom's sunscreen. SPF 2 or something."

Jack grinned. "I warned you about all that sunshine."

"You should have warned me about the whole place." Harlan's face was screwed up in one big pout. "I hate California. I'm never going back. Mom doesn't know it yet, but I'm staying here."

Trying to hide his joy, Jack bit the inside of his lips, then said, "Really? You want to stay?" Everything was falling into place. For the first time in his life. The turtle shell, the note from Baz, the house, and now his son. He beamed wide now. Harlan was home for good. "You're sure?"

Harlan snorted, dropping his coat to the floor. "Yeah. It's so totally hot there all the time. I hate having a tan, and none of the girls there can appreciate that I wear these glasses to be ironic, *not* because I think I look good in them. This one girl on the beach actually asked me if I was from the Netherlands. As if no one in her country could possibly dress like me. How completely shallow can a person be? They don't even come close to getting it. Freaking plasticized sun zombies."

"Well, there might be an unusually high number of superficial types in L.A."

"And the sand! It gets in your pockets, in your shoes; it even gets inside your gotchies, *way* inside, if you know what I mean. Scratches your racquetballs."

Jack could only imagine the prickliness, squirming uncomfortably. "Yes, beaches can be terribly sandy places."

"Melissa's going to be totally pissed at me. Both our UCLA applications are in."

"We can't worry at this stage of life what every girl thinks, now, can we?" Jack picked up a suitcase and started hauling it upstairs. "The important thing is that you've made a big decision and that we fill out the Harvard paperwork as soon as possible. And after that, I think we might get ourselves a sturdier car. You can't be seen roaring into the parking lot at college in an old relic like that Buick. We'll call your mother as soon as we get you unpacked."

"And Mom and Yale know all these obnoxious movie people. They keep dragging me to all these movie premieres and private screenings. They didn't even care that I didn't want to go. I wanted to stay at the hotel, in my room. Movies make me totally sick."

Jack had stopped midway up the staircase. "Certainly there must be some kind of movie you enjoy. If you give films a chance, you might find—"

"I don't, okay, Dad? *God*. You're just like Mom. That's the exact same crap she feeds me. 'Come with us Harlan. Give it a chance, Harlan.'"

"Did you watch any of their movies?"

"*Yes.*" He looked away. "And then Yale took me mountain-biking!" Harlan's face was getting red now. He pulled the other suitcase up a few steps and set it down. "Of all the stupid sports. He actually expects me to risk my life speeding along a three-inch-wide path full of divots and rocks. This guy should be locked up for child endangerment, Dad. It just wasn't safe."

"You would have rather stayed in the hotel? In your room?"

"Yeah. *Duh*."

"Where it's safe?"

Harlan rolled his eyes again and slapped his suitcase. "I'm not like you, Dad, if that's what you're thinking. I'm not agoraphobic."

"I didn't say you were. It's just that, at first, you were enjoying it so much. You loved it. Couldn't wait to move into the pool house. I'm just wondering what happened." He looked at Harlan. "Did something happen?"

"No, okay? Nothing happened, except I started hating it, all right? You don't have to analyze every little thing I say. Stuntman Yale thinks I should be surfing every weekend. And there are sharks in the Pacific! I once felt something touch my leg."

"Seaweed, maybe?" Jack asked.

"Not seaweed! Something big and rubbery. So I got out and waited for him on the shore. He saw me waiting and pretended not to notice. Just paddled out, looking for another wave. He thinks he's so *freaking* cool."

"Okay, Harlan. That's enough. He's only trying to help you."

"Help me? How does it help me to leave me standing on the shore-line, which stretches out so far in both directions that it's actually sicken-ing. Yeah, sickening. I got so dizzy I thought I was going to die, right then and there. Either that or puke up my—" He stopped, feeling Jack's stare. "No." He shook his head from side to side. "I didn't mean dizzy, Dad."

Dizzy. He said dizzy. Jack felt a brick hit him in the stomach. *He thought he'd die from being dizzy*. Harlan was becoming his father. Carry-ing his father's demons like a tombstone strung around his neck. Now that it was out there, Jack realized he'd seen it coming. Now it was so clear. The questions about Jack's pills, the refusal to go to the movies with friends. And now, now the dizziness.

The dizziness that thinks it can kill you.

"Harlan."

"Dad, I didn't mean it. I just said that because it's what you say. I'm not stupid. I know it won't kill me—"

"It won't. It's just dizziness. Nothing more. Don't you ever think it's anything more."

Harlan's eyes flooded. "I don't. I swear it. I'm just better off with you. Taking care of you. You need me. Mom doesn't."

Jack climbed down to the step Harlan had collapsed onto and wrapped his arms around his only son. His next question was very important. "Har, did you go into any of the movie theaters with your mother and stepfather? Actually right inside and sit down."

He nodded, blinking hard and sniffing.

"Did it make you dizzy? Harlan, did you get dizzy inside the theater?"

Harlan's face crumpled. He pressed it into his father's chest, his body heaving with sobs. "Yes. It was horrible. I left and waited in the bathroom. Told them I had cramps. One time I waited in there the whole two hours. I don't want to go back, Dad. It's bad for me there."

Jack stroked Harlan's head, knowing full well what he had to do. The only reason it was better for Harlan here, on Battersea Road, was that he could hide behind Jack's restrictive lifestyle, a lifestyle even Jack wanted desperately to shed. And of all people, Jack knew the consequences. The deeper you hide yourself away the harder it becomes to come out. The hiding takes over your life, becomes what you live for.

Like a baby rattlesnake, the fear has no control valve, no stopper. Floods you with all its venom, all at once, without so much as a rattle of warning. If only he'd faced his own fears at an earlier age; if he'd had a support system or the courage to talk about it, it might never have taken him so far inside his terror. So far inside that he'd fight it in degrees for the rest of his life. Hopefully more manageable degrees.

He didn't want the same for his son. It was no way to live.

Certainly, there were psychiatrists, younger ones who could stay awake throughout an hour-long session on the couch; but the determination and courage to overcome fear—that came from the patient. And watching a parent struggle through his own fears on a daily basis could never help.

He held Harlan tighter, closing his eyes and drinking in the sweet smell of his son, who wanted nothing more than to stay home with his dad. Hot tears filled Jack's eyes. He wrapped his very soul around the boy he wanted so badly to protect, to never let go of. He clenched his mouth and swallowed. The only thing he might die from now would be the words he had no choice but to say.

"Harlan. Son. I love you more than life. You know that. I'd give you my life if I thought it would help."

Harlan looked up, his eyes scared. He knew what was coming. "No, Dad. Don't . . ."

Jack pressed his face into his son's hair. His voice was barely more than a whisper. "You've got to go back."

Chapter 32

A Pair of Red Mittens

Jack watched the roller coat the living-room walls in thick white paint. Very little gave him more satisfaction than reviving dull, scuffed wall surfaces, or walls covered in especially bilious tones, and watching, astounded, as they came to life again. Became pristine. Flawless. Vacuuming cat hair off his bedroom carpet came close, but, of course, cat hair was no longer an issue. Harlan had taken the sorry old feline onto the plane.

If only such a cream existed for people. Two quick coats, with a suitable dry time between, and voilà. Skin as fresh as the day you were born. Maybe even fresher, Jack thought. When Harlan had been born, he'd been all red-faced and puffy. Spitting mad, the boy looked around the delivery room and found nobody to blame for the debacle but his parents. Much like the way he looked back at Jack when he boarded the plane back to California the other day.

Jack dipped the roller into the tray and rolled off the excess, pausing to sip from his beer bottle before resuming his painting, closer to the front window now. An angry teenager is never one for reason, especially when fear is involved. But Jack had had a long discussion with Penelope and Yale, who had increasingly suspected that Harlan's fear was hereditary in origin. No surprise. All three agreed that Laurel Canyon was best, with all its movie premieres, endless shorelines, and rough terrain, and Yale had volunteered to introduce Harlan to a child psychologist working out of UCLA. Jack, of course, was welcome to fly down any time and stay with his son in the pool house, and Harlan would return to Boston during school breaks, once his fury subsided.

As Jack moved closer to the windowsill, which framed the heavily falling evening snow outside—one final blast of winter flexing its might before shoving off for another six months—he slowed his movements to avoid splattering the old wood. Once he'd rolled the white about two inches from the trim, he'd take a sharp-edged brush and carefully cut around the window. He preferred to cut and roll simultaneously as he moved around the room, convinced that wet edge meeting wet edge made for a much smoother finish.

Already, he liked the room better. The browns in the furniture, floor, trim, and new curtains contrasted handsomely with the rich cream. Very masculine. He smiled to himself. Very simple.

He reached down to shift the scattered sheets of the days-old newspaper along the floor to catch any drips as he moved around the room, stopping as he noticed a large, bold headline on page four: "Thrift Shop Fire Claims Owner's Life."

His brush clattered onto the floor as he snatched up the paper. "Believed caused by a massive gas leak, raging fire tore through popular flower-covered South End thrift shop, causing over $300,000 damage to that and neighboring stores. Body of longtime owner known to many as Secondhand Rose was found in the basement, the area firefighters believe to be the source of the blaze. Funeral arrangements . . ."

Holy shit. Rose was dead. Bad things did come in fives for Rose. Just as Dorrie said.

Dorrie.

He glanced at the date on the paper. Rose died on Tuesday.

Three days ago.

Dorrie was no longer taking his calls. She'd given up on him. Jack glanced at his watch. 8:45. Friday night. She'd still be at work; Friday evenings she liked to stay late, catch up. But she didn't want to see him. She'd made that very clear.

He picked up his brush and stood up to cut around the window. Very slowly, he dragged the edge of the brush along the crack where trim met plaster. His hand shook, smearing paint up onto the dark wood. Swearing, he pulled a rag from his pocket, spat on it, and wiped the paint away. He breathed deeply and started again. Once more, his hand wobbled.

"Damn."

He looked out at the snow. It was a bad night to go out. Especially for him.

Pacing the floor, he remembered Dorrie's excited chatter as she planned Rose's surprise party. How she whispered happily with her friend at the rose-covered cash desk.

She would be devastated.

Dropping the brush again, he marched into the hall and fumbled around in his jacket pockets for his new bottle of pills. Empty. They must be upstairs. He looked from the staircase to the front door and back again. No, he thought. She could leave the office at any minute.

He burst out the front door, down the steps, and through the deep drifts on the sidewalk, blinking into the blowing snow as he half-ran, half-climbed down the block. Traversing the sidewalk was tough work, snow filling his boots as he tripped through it. Walking would take too long. Spotting a cab moving toward him, he leaped over a snowbank and scrambled onto the road, waving his arms as the cab passed without slowing.

"Shit!" He trotted backward along the road until he spotted another cab. Running straight toward it, he waved his arms and shouted, "Taxi!"

With no choice but to pull over or run Jack down, the cab pulled to the side of the road. "Crazy man," the driver roared. "You get yourself killed on road."

"Gloucester Street" was all that Jack said.

INSIDE THE BUILDING, having rushed past the empty reception desk, Jack followed the narrow hallway to the back, poking his head into darkened offices as he passed.

TREVOR JONES, said one nameplate. KARA WHITLEY, read another.

Just past the coffee room he saw her . . . seated at her desk, facing a middle-aged couple. As he approached her doorway, she caught sight of him marching toward her office and flushed red, her eyes dropping down again. He marched straight in.

"Excuse me," Jack said to the couple. "I just need Ms. Allsop for a moment."

Dorrie stood up. "This isn't a good time . . . Mr. Madigan, I'm busy with the Woodhills—"

"She'll be right back, I promise." Jack winked at the couple as he slipped his arm into hers and led her, protesting, into the hallway.

Partially closing her door behind them, she yanked back her arm away and faced him. "How dare you barge in here and interrupt—"

"I know. You've got every right to despise me."

"I'll say!"

"I just heard. I wanted to see you. I know how much you cared—"

"So *now* it's convenient to be there for me? Here on a Friday, after nine o'clock? This time slot is acceptable for you to comfort me on my friend's death, is it? Well, forget it. I don't need your three-days-too-late concern."

The soon-to-be-signed Woodhills, still in their chairs, craned their necks to get a good look through the crack in the door. Dorrie smiled at them, saying, "Won't be a minute," before pulling the door shut.

"That's the thing, Dorrie. I want to be there for you. Always."

"Ha!" She laughed so sharply that the agent in the next office lifted his head and shushed her. "Do you know Mrs. Buxley reported me? Told my broker I put her safety in jeopardy? Do you realize I've been on probation ever since?"

Jack closed his eyes. "Oh God. I'm sorry. But this time I came out. Came all the way here. Don't you see? Things are going to be different now . . ."

"That's the problem, Jack. With you things are always different!" She opened the door and backed into her office. Her voice sweetened artificially. "Good evening, Mr. Madigan."

"Dorrie, I love you . . ."

But the door was already shut.

OUTSIDE, THE SNOW was still falling steadily, though much lighter than before. A lineup of snow-covered cabs waited just outside the building. Dropping into the first one, Jack gave the driver his address and slumped down in his seat, knocking snow from his jacket.

Swaying and bumping along with the driver's jerky maneuvers, Jack felt a familiar seasickness wash through his stomach. Harlan and the cabbie just might have attended the same driving school. Lurch forward and hang back. Pitch to the right, then change your mind and veer back again with all your might. Add slippery roads to the mix, and you had yourself an infallible recipe for passengers vomiting out the back window.

Jack's mouth went dry as he concentrated hard on calming his stomach and his nerves. The beer he'd had while painting was bubbling up his esophagus, forcing him to belch into his coat collar. Not long now, he assured himself. A few more blocks, and we'll be at the park. Almost home.

His head began to reel, and tiny lights sparked before his eyes. He couldn't make it. Had to get out. With the snow-covered trees of Boston Commons in sight, Jack instructed the driver to pull over and dropped a few bills into the front seat. He stumbled out the back door and gulped the night air with greed, hoping the wet, sloppy snowflakes would slap him into calmness.

The ground rippled and pulsated, just as it did after a Harlan voyage, seeming to rise up and hit him in the knees, making his head spin faster. "It's just dizzy," he told himself out loud. "Just dizzy. Doesn't hurt. Doesn't kill."

Slipping and skidding, he jogged across Boylston Street and into the park toward the lights of Frog Pond. His beer threatened to rise up, land him choking and retching over the snowy path. Swallowing hard, he remembered Lucie's words.

Dead people don't puke.

He asked the girl at the rental counter for men's skates.

"It's nearly ten," she told him, without charging him. "Just bring them back when the rink lights go out."

He nodded and sat on a snowy bench to lace them up. It's just dizzy. Breathe deeply. Just dizzy.

Unsteadily, he stepped toward the frozen pond and onto the ice. Taking tiny steps, he aimed toward the far end of the rink, first walking, then gliding in short, sporadic movements. His legs were rusty; he hadn't skated since Harlan was very young. Snow hit his face harder as he increased speed, fell into his collar and down his neck, but he ignored it, pumping his legs harder and feeling the nausea subside. He fell into a steadyish rhythm; so long as no one cut him off and forced him to stop, he might be okay. Very few people had braved the weather anyway; only three or four other people were crazy enough to pull themselves away from their cozy fireplaces to play in the storm.

He moved closer to the center now and let himself glide. Once he reached the middle, he spread his legs apart, toes pointed outward as if on a big ring. Pushing with one foot, he let himself turn around in a wide, slow circle.

"It's just dizzy," he whispered. "Just dizzy. Nothing else."

The trees and apartment buildings whirled past him; the spotlights passed faster and faster as he pushed harder with his left foot. Snow swirled into his eyes as he tilted his head back and stared up into the on-rushing flurry.

The dizziness continued, but Jack began to settle. It wasn't killing him. Wasn't hurting him. In fact, it was rather beautiful being here, watching the illuminated snowflakes rushing down from the blackened sky. Freeing. Turning slower now, he smiled and closed his eyes, letting the spinning sensation release him.

The ice under his feet grew rough, and he lost his footing. Arms flailing, he felt his weight pitch backward as he scrambled to get his feet under him. A flash of red passed in front of his face as someone caught him from behind, wrapped their arms around him, and held his flailing arms close to the side of his body, stopping him from crashing onto the ice. A pair of red mittens pressed into his chest. Regaining his balance, he stood up and turned around.

Dorrie, in a puffy black jacket and red mittens, smiled back at him, her hair gleaming almost white under the lights. Snow clung to her eyelashes.

Scrunching up her nose, she shook her head. "I guess I never really liked things to be the same all the time anyway."

He smiled and reached toward her, taking her mittens in his hands. Her hands felt tiny inside the wooly mitts. The snow fell heavier as the other skaters made their way off the rink and disappeared into Pond Cottage. One by one, the bright spotlights went dark. Their faces lit only by the buildings watching over them from the street, Dorrie and Jack began to twirl.

Acknowledgments

Great thanks go to those who put up with me along the way . . .

Dear cousin Taryn Cohen, who believed in me solely on the basis of my impeccable dental hygiene. Jane Sarah Staffier of Beacon Hill Realty Partners for giving me a peek into the exquisite enclave that is Jack's neighborhood. John Lindsay for staying up until the wee hours with my first draft and cursing me in the moonlight when he ran out of pages. Dr. Karen Sharf, because psychology sounds better with the sirens of New York in the background. Barbara Fogler for showing me that therapy can come with four hooves and a mane. Donny for supplying them. Doreen Resnick, who loves whatever I do before I do it. Jennifer Lindsay-Kolari, M.S.W., for sharing her knowledge of cognitive behavioral therapy, for enthusiastic reads and making first-draft house calls with chocolate. But most of all for letting me be Princess Leia instead of Chewbacca that *one* time.

VERY SPECIAL THANKS go out to different parts of the world:

At HarperCollins, my wonderfully enthusiastic editor, Alison Callahan, who truly "gets" this book, and her tireless assistant, Jeanette Perez. Also, my publisher, Carrie Kania. At HarperCollinsCanada, my lovely editor, Iris Tupholme, Rob Firing, Kate Cassaday, et al. At btb/Luchterhand, my German editor, Susann Rehlein. At Thomas Schlueck, my German agent, Bastian Schlueck.

At Brillstein-Grey, my film agent, Kassie Evashevski, and her assistant, Adam Blankheimer. At Scott Free Productions, Michael Costigan. At Fox 2000, Maria Faillace and a huge thank you to Drew Reed, who played no small part in getting it all started!

My seriously brilliant literary agent at Writers House, Daniel Lazar. Oy, where do I start? For taking a chance on a Canadian girl, for having the sharpest eye around, for unexpected fashion advice (at no extra cost), for not giving up and for never letting me get away with a thing. All this without a cape. Also at Writers House, my foreign rights agent, Maja Nikolic.

Most of all, I thank my family. My mother for her caustic humor that always kept us laughing. My father for always having a book in his hand and for telling me I could do anything I wanted. My husband, Steve, for being the best first reader and never asking "What's for dinner?" And for my best, my boys, Max and Lucas, for laughing at all the right parts, for constant inspiration and for letting me share in their lives. You never know what you might accomplish sitting on the bench at a skate park.

About the author

About the book

Read (and listen) on

Insights,
Interviews
& More . . .

A Conversation with Tish Cohen

Let's start simple—Where were you born and raised?

I was born in Toronto but moved almost immediately to Montreal, just down the street from a basset hound named Tish. This, combined with my mother's insistence that a barber could cut a girl's hair "just fine," did very little for my social life. So when my parents divorced, I was more than happy to move to Toronto with my dad and brother. Halfway through junior high, just when I'd gotten myself a Dorothy Hamill haircut and—shockingly—landed a boyfriend, my father announced we were moving to California, which was much more exciting than the boyfriend. We stepped off the plane at LAX and drove straight to my aunt's Laurel Canyon house—a funky hillside home completely covered in what looked like prehistoric undergrowth. Barely thirteen, freshly shorn and still pasty from the Canadian winter, I headed out to the pool to find six or seven naked actors floating in the water, too stoned to swim. Life in California turned into Gene Kelly making me screwdrivers when I was underage, Rosanna Arquette hanging out in our kitchen, the boys from Toto washing my dishes, and me hiding behind a sofa watching Kevin Costner and Cindy Silva make out after school. Eventually, I reached a point where it all seemed normal.

When did you start writing?

I remember sitting in my sister's closet when I was about six or seven and staring at

66 Barely thirteen, freshly shorn and still pasty from the Canadian winter, I headed out to the pool to find six or seven naked actors floating in the water, too stoned to swim. 99

a particularly good likeness of Snoopy I'd done, and knowing I was meant to not only quit ripping off other artists' work or one day face litigation, but to develop characters of my own and write a book. I knew it right down to my toes. But then my mother called us downstairs for chicken noodle soup, so I went. I really like chicken soup.

Do you remember the first book you fell in love with and why it affected you so strongly?

I fell in love with books and started reading pretty early, so I'd have to say the first one was Maurice Sendak's *Pierre,* which my sister and I got for Christmas when I was three. It came in a set of four teeny tiny hardcovers, all beautifully illustrated. *Pierre* was a bold little story about a boy so determined not to care about anything, he let himself be swallowed whole by a lion. You've got to admire that kind of spunk. The writing was lyrical and addicting and I read it over and over. Somehow the other three books got lost, but my sister wound up with *Pierre* and keeps it in her basement. Harsh. She swears she loves it, but I think I can safely say that I loved it more.

It's rumored that you wrote Town House in under a month— Is that true? What is your writing regimen like?

I wrote *Town House* in three and a half weeks, but I'd already developed a detailed outline, so I knew where I was headed with each scene. I wrote ten to twelve hours a day, then thought out the next day's scenes each evening, scribbling down tiny details or scraps of dialogue. I'm compulsive once I begin a draft. I just have this neurotic need to get it ▶

Meet Tish Cohen

Greg Dean

TISH COHEN is the author of a series of children's books forthcoming in Summer 2007. She has edited an online women's magazine and contributed articles to some of Canada's largest newspapers, including *The Globe and Mail* and *The National Post.* She lives in Toronto. *Town House* is her first novel. Visit her Web site at www.tishcohen.com.

❝I wrote *Town House* in three and a half weeks.❞

3

A Conversation with Tish Cohen (continued)

all down. My life is completely on hold until I finish. Someday, I plan to achieve balance.

I understand that you also write for young adults. Do you find the process of writing an adult novel to be a much different experience than writing for a younger audience?

I love kids and am incredibly immature, so writing middle grade is quite a lot of fun. All the big stuff still has to be there—the pacing, the story arc, the character development, etc.—so it's not as if writing for kids is any easier, but the books are certainly shorter. So is the audience.

A film adaptation of Town House *is in the works. How has the experience of knowing your words will be translated to the big screen been for you? Are there any actors you would love to see in the main roles? Have you been involved in the screenwriting process at all?*

Doug Wright is writing the screenplay, so that's both exciting and intimidating. The moment I heard he'd been hired, I rushed out to pick up *Quills,* which I watched with my mouth hanging open. His writing talent is staggering, no exaggeration. All I could think was, "I'm not worthy." So far, he hasn't involved me and I'm cool with that. But I never leave the phone, just in case.

For the main roles . . .

Jeremy Piven as Jack, definitely. He'd show Jack's anxiety with compassion and humor, without resorting to condescension or slapstick comedy.

Reese Witherspoon would be a great

Dorrie. If no one can afford Reese anymore, the ethereal Kate Hudson, who might play off Piven's edge better anyway.

Dakota Fanning's little sister, Elle, not only looks like Lucinda, but is just the right age. Elle would be a dream Lucinda.

Harlan is a tough call. Someone sarcastic, with an unhealthy dose of woe. And it wouldn't hurt if he had legs as long and shapeless as elm saplings and looked good in man blouses.

Who are some of your writing influences? Are there any authors or books you consider personal favorites?

No one has influenced me like Jane Austen. I've read *Emma, Pride and Prejudice, Northanger Abbey, Mansfield Park,* and *Sense and Sensibility* so many times I should be investigated. Her wit, delicacy, and social observations are every bit as fresh today and I find that astonishing.

John Irving's *The World According to Garp* and *A Prayer for Owen Meany* hooked me in terms of eccentric characters and emotional scenes that crackle with soul. I probably shouldn't admit how many times I've read these, both as a reader and as a writer, because it shows an extreme dearth of resourcefulness on my part.

More recently, I fell in love with Alan Hollinghurst's novel *The Line of Beauty*. While the story is subtle, his humor and attention to social nuance is intoxicating. He's the type of writer who makes other writers flat out give up. I'm working this one into my already busy rereading schedule. ▶

> **Reese Witherspoon would be a great Dorrie. If no one can afford Reese anymore, the ethereal Kate Hudson.**

A Conversation with Tish Cohen (continued)

Other authors I reread: Rex Pickett, David Sedaris, Daphne du Maurier, John Blumenthal, Tom Perrotta, Nick Hornby, Jonathon Tropper, Anne Tyler, Edith Wharton, Simone de Beauvoir, Arthur Golden, Mark Haddon, Elizabeth Flock, Josh Kilmer-Purcell, and Ayelet Waldman.

Your novel takes place in Boston, yet you live in Toronto. Do you have a personal connection to Boston or a love for the city?

I first visited Boston for a conference and was so charmed by the city that I blew off most of the seminars and poked around the streets. Beacon Hill, with its narrow laneways, lacy trees, gaslights, and stunning architecture, particularly enchanted me. You can't help but wonder about the lives of people lucky enough to live in one of those town houses.

I recently returned from another trip to Boston, during which I headed straight for Frog Pond, where Jack makes his first honest move toward curing himself and spins on the ice in the final scene of the book. Of course, Jack was on ice skates and I visited during the summer, so I took off my shoes and stepped into the water. While children splashed—and likely urinated—at my feet, I waded to the center and twirled like Jack. That spot, right in the center of the pond, with buildings peering over the treetops, is magical.

There are a lot of references to music of the seventies and eighties in Town House. *Are you a big music fan? What music or bands do you love?*

> I first visited Boston for a conference and was so charmed by the city that I blew off most of the seminars and poked around the streets.

6

Much of Jack's playlist is what I like, though my taste is somewhat more schizophrenic. I'll listen to the Ramones, followed by Bach, followed by Elvis Costello, followed by a soundtrack from a Woody Allen film, followed by Siouxsie & the Banshees. I'm sure this says dreadful things about my mental stability.

What are you working on now?

I'm finishing up a novel called *Inside Out Boy* centered on a learning-disabled boy obsessed with rodentia—the rodent world—and how he brings the adults around him together in surprising ways.

I'm also beginning the second book in my middle-grade series, about a seventh-grade go-to girl nicknamed the Zoë Lama. This one is titled *Will the Real Zoë Lama Please Stand Up?* When Zoë goes away and misses a few weeks of school, she returns certain that her friends and teachers will have fallen apart in her absence. But another girl has stepped into Zoë's place and her friends' lives are running smoother than ever. They barely noticed Zoë was gone. Zoë needs to put a stop to all this pleasantness . . . and fast. ❧

A Girl Named Bowser and a Beloved Old House

FROM THE MOMENT I understood what wishes were, and that they'd only come true if you wished on a star, drove under a moving train or blew out birthday candles, I made the same wish over and over again. I wished I would turn into a dog, Lady from *Lady and the Tramp,* specifically, because I thought she was the most beautiful being imaginable. I wished harder and harder with each opportunity, convinced that if my conviction was stronger, it would happen for me. It never did.

Eventually, I grew old enough to understand I wasn't going to turn into any kind of dog, whether cartoon or real-life. So I saved my wishes for more material things and channeled my canine energy into pretending I was a dog. I crawled around the house on all fours and spent way too much time finding the sunniest spot on the living room carpet to circle several times, before curling in a ball and pretending to nap. When I awoke from these pretend naps, I would pant a little, lick my chops, then stand up and stretch before padding into the kitchen in search of a snack. Probably too frightened to seek out a child psychologist, my family humored me, calling me Bowser and barely complaining when I made off with their shoes.

While I gradually played Bowser less and less, that passion for dogs stayed with me, eventually working itself into a blond, waif-like character named Lucinda. I knew she'd pretend to be a dog, I knew she'd look like me, and I knew she'd eventually fall through her

> ❝ I wished I would turn into a dog. . . . I wished harder and harder with each opportunity, convinced that if my conviction was stronger, it would happen for me. ❞

bedroom window while gazing at her pretend ponies, also like me. But this Lucinda would be much bolder than I ever was. She'd be bold enough to bite people in the leg and sneak into someone else's house, something I only did once, when my best friend wanted to steal a real baby diaper for her new doll, and the guilt and terror nearly crushed me.

So here I was with a character, but no book. Another, far less embarrassing, obsession I have is with old houses and architecture. I was watching a show on HGTV in which a dilapidated town house was being renovated in preparation for sale. Only the exterior was shown, but it was four stories with original windows and trim. The homeowner wistfully mentioned that the entire fourth floor was a stage and that she'd raised her children there through many rough times, times when they had no heat and no furniture. 117 Battersea Road was born.

I had my setting. I had my girl. All I needed now was a hole in the wall and someone on the other side with a really big problem. Someone who had put up their own invisible walls that Lucinda could not only break through but ultimately break down. Someone like Jack. ᔕ

❝ I had my setting. I had my girl. All I needed now was a hole in the wall and someone on the other side with a really big problem. ❞

Jack Madigan's Perfect White, French Linen

AS THOSE WHO KNOW ME CAN ATTEST, I've been on a longtime quest of my own for the perfect shade of white for my home. I worked as a decorative painter for a few years and never quite found what I wanted—a neutral white with history. Eventually, I invented it myself, and Jack's French Linen was born.

Using Benjamin Moore tints:

OY—13
OG—1
BK—2¼
GY—7½

My Favorite Agoraphobe, or Why Woody Allen Is the Perfect Spokesperson for the Groper Once Some Farsighted MBA Puts It into Production

I COULD TALK ABOUT Barbra Streisand or Kim Basinger or even the sequestered and much-feared Boo Radley. But I have very little in common with any of them. I can't sing, Kim is so good-looking it depresses me, and Boo, well, you gotta love a guy like Boo, but he's too reclusive, even for me.

Which brings us to Woody. It won't surprise many to hear Woody Allen is not only claustrophobic but agoraphobic. Many of his films featured Woody playing the role of a neurotic pessimist, obsessed with death and forever whining to his therapist. (I can't be the only one who finds that sexy. Can I?) He gave phobias panache. Suddenly everyone wanted one. Or at least that's what I told myself the first time I lowered myself onto "the couch."

For Woody and me, it's the phobias that bind. Besides the fact that we share the same birthday, December 1, we share a love for black glasses, an addiction to analysis, a fear of certain doom, and my love for nearly everything he's ever written. If I had the energy, I'd be his stalker. On my wedding day, I had Woody Allen pre-approved as my celebrity exception to fidelity. That he doesn't know or care only makes me want him more.

In a 2005 *Vanity Fair* article, there's a rare photo of the man himself, sitting at his messy wooden desk in his office at the Manhattan ▶

> **❝** If I had the energy, I'd be [Woody Allen's] stalker. On my wedding day, I had [him] pre-approved as my celebrity exception to fidelity. **❞**

11

My Favorite Agoraphobe *(continued)*

Film Center. Seeing his workspace with its not-quite-black walls, antique filing cabinet, and bulletin board full of photos and notes, filled me with awe. Particularly exciting was what he kept on his desk. Amongst the rolled-up posters and CDs and courier packages, tucked between a stack of papers and a roll of Scotch tape, stood one plucky little bottle of Purell hand sanitizer. The very thing I keep on my desk. And in my purse. And my car. It was almost too much to bear. I could barely tell where he ended and I began.

It's not that I admire Woody for his phobias. It's just that I get it. I'm an agoraphobe waiting-to-happen, two empty Purell bottles away from holing up inside myself.

P.S. The font on the cover is a hand-drawn rendering of Windsor, Woody Allen's favorite typeface. Call it thievery if you like, but after two decades of worship I needed something concrete. Stealing his font seemed infinitely less troublesome than going through his trash. ❧

Tish Cohen's Favorite Male Characters in Literature

TICKNOR by Sheila Heti

George Ticknor, a resentful little fusspot of a failed writer is on his way—pie in hand—to his successful historian friend's house for a party. With every rain-soaked step forward, he becomes more and more convinced that Prescott's invitation is steeped with ulterior motives. He works himself up into such a lather, he ultimately turns around and goes home.

SIDEWAYS by Rex Pickett

Miles Raymond is a rejected writer, recently divorced and broke, with a propensity toward panic attacks. Nothing goes his way, no matter how badly you want it to. I read this book shortly after submitting *Town House* to my agent and thought that if the world could love Miles, a total underdog, there might be hope for my Jack.

A PRAYER FOR OWEN MEANY by John Irving

It's not easy to encapsulate Owen Meany in any way other than his size. He's loud and brash; he's manipulating and overly opinionated. Besides that, his ears are transparent and he's covered in granite dust. He's a marvel.

WHAT'S WRONG WITH DORFMAN? by John Blumenthal

Martin Dorfman is near militant in his hypochondria. He's a failed screenwriter

> " I read [*Sideways*] shortly after submitting *Town House* to my agent and thought that if the world could love Miles, a total underdog, there might be hope for my Jack. "

Tish Cohen's Favorite Male Characters in Literature *(continued)*

convinced he's battling a deadly disease. Another neurotic underdog. Is anyone else sensing a pattern here?

PRIDE AND PREJUDICE by Jane Austen

Mr. Darcy. Sigh.

THE ACCIDENTAL TOURIST by Anne Tyler

Macon Leary is depressed and withdrawn and his life is being controlled by his late son's snapping corgi. He washes his clothes by stomping on them in the shower and pretends to read a book called *Miss MacIntosh* on the plane so his seatmates won't speak to him. That's good enough for me.

THE TALE OF TWO BAD MICE by Beatrix Potter

While Tom Thumb clearly has rage issues, he does have the decency to fess up and pay for the damage to Lucinda and Jane's dollhouse. And I don't think Hunca Munca would put up with any less.

117 Battersea Road Playlist

Jack

Barenaked Ladies' "Pinch Me"
The Ramones' "I Wanna Be Sedated"
Everclear's "Wonderful"
Dead or Alive's "You Spin Me Round
    (Like a Record)"
The Clash's "Should I Stay or Should I Go"
Elvis Costello's "Beyond Belief"
The Beat's "Sole Salvation"
Joe Jackson's "Steppin' Out"
The Beat's "Save It for Later"
Oingo Boingo's "Only a Lad"

What Jack listens to when Harlan's out:
Ashlee Simpson's "Pieces of Me."

Harlan

The Kids from the Brady Bunch's
    "Sunshine Day"
Captain and Tenille's "Muskrat Love"
Tracy Byrd's "Wildfire"
The Partridge Family's "I Think I Love You"
The Brady Bunch's "Time to Change"
Donny Osmond's "Puppy Love"
Paper Lace's "Billy Don't Be a Hero"
The Go-Go's version of Todd Rundgren's
    "Cool Jerk"

What Harlan listens to with the windows shut,
and even then, only when Jack's in the
basement with his paint mixers on: Michelle
Branch's version of David Bowie's "Life on

Mars," as recorded for GAP stores nationwide.
(Free with Melissa's dark rinse straight legs.)

Baz

Eric Clapton's "Cocaine"
Alice Cooper's "Welcome to My Nightmare"
Led Zeppelin's "Black Dog"
Black Sabbath's "Paranoid"
AC/DC's "Hells Bells"
Van Halen's "Running with the Devil"
Rush's "The Temples of Syrinx"

What Baz sang in the shower (on those rare
occasions he was showering alone): the radio
broadcaster's lyrics from Meat Loaf's
"Paradise by the Dashboard Light."